I absolutely loved *A Boundless Place* from the start and was captivated by each of the characters. As the characters changed and grew, I fell in love with them even more . . . I finished reading it in about three days, then mourned that it was over.

—Beth Whipple, Middle School Teacher

Especially in these challenging times, it is nice to finish a book that leaves you, as this one does, feeling hopeful about people and that reminds you of what it's like when we hold each other up.

—Mark Brzostowski, Active member of Princeton Writers Group since 2016

A heartwarming, delightful debut. You can't help loving Pamela Stockwell's grumpy, quirky characters, and you'll wish you were their neighbor on Magnolia Avenue too.

—Linda Rosen, author of *Sisters of the Vine*

Stockwell's writing is heartfelt and touching . . . The characters will stay with me for a long time.

—Virginia McCullough, author of *Island Healing*

Ms. Stockwell's attention to detail takes the reader back to the summer of 1969, evoking the anticipation and patriotic pride felt by Americans of the decade. The novel delivers delightful dialogue and brassy banter that easily glides the reader from chapter to chapter.

—Claudia Moose, Public School History Teacher

Pamela's style of writing is wonderfully descriptive, and the characters that she develops win over your heart. The seamless weaving of the characters and the events throughout the story tell a wonderful story of how neighbors with seemingly little things in common eventually become friends. This is a story that will enchant you and stay with you for quite some time.

—Wanda España, Publishing Professional

The characters are well thought out and people you really want to get to know.

—Mary Trautner, Retired Federal Executive

This was a heartwarming and heart-tugging story that we need in these days where it seems like every day we lose connections. How many of us go about our days not knowing or not caring about our neighbors? When you are done reading this book, you will think twice about your anonymity. At its heart, it is an epic love story. I couldn't put it down.

—Linda O'Connor

Pamela Stockwell reminds us that doors are meant to be opened, conversations are to be started, and communities are formed by coming together. This more than ever is what we need, and *A Boundless Place* shows us that it is possible.

—Jennifer España, An Avid Reader

The relationships between each of the characters were so inspiring and detailed that a spinoff of any of the backstories would be just as captivating as the book itself. The humorous tone paired with the comforting and heartwarming stories told made this an excellent read.

—Sara Baron, Recent College Graduate

A great feel-good story of love and friendships that form between quirky, damaged, yet lovable characters that I thoroughly enjoy spending time with. Stockwell's poetic voice transported me to the Carolinas with such ease. I laughed and cried with Violet, Arabella, Nick, and all as they stay with me long after I have kept the book down.

—Priya Gill, Author and Engineering-Management Professor

A Boundless Place is one of those books that makes you feel good. I think we all find ourselves at one time or another in our lives wanting to be left alone to deal with life's cruelties. But this story does a great job at showing the reader that connections are important and that we can find ways to connect with those around us in the smallest of ways with a big impact. If you're looking for a book that takes you away from all of the awfulness in the world today, and even gives you a little hope for mankind, then this is one you should read. You will not be disappointed!

—Denise Blevins

A Boundless Place

Pamela Stockwell

Best wishes!

Pamela Stockwell

Ten|16
PRESS

www.ten16press.com - Waukesha, WI

For information, please contact:

www.ten16press.com
Waukesha, WI

Cover design by Faith Smith
Art Director: Kaeley Dunteman

This book is dedicated to my husband, Rich, and children, Kiana, Connor, and Kyra, with my deep gratitude for their unending love and support.

And to my father, who is still with us, and my mother and sister, who aren't. You are in these pages, hidden like gems, and in my heart like a neon banner.

PART

1

May-July 1969

1
Violet

May 1969

Violet set the milk crate full of shampoos and soaps on the counter of her new master bathroom. She turned to fetch another box but stopped as her reflection caught her eye. As always, the face looking back at her surprised her. The woman in the mirror still looked twenty-four, still looked reasonably attractive with shining dark hair and large brown eyes, still looked like the whole world lay at her feet. But the woman on this side of the glass felt one hundred and twenty-four and like five miles of bad road that led to a dead end.

She turned her back on her mirrored self and returned to the living room as Jerry placed a cardboard box on the carpeted floor. He mopped his forehead with a handkerchief. "That's the last box," he said, studying her. Did he think she would change her mind? Dissolve into tears? Neither seemed that far-fetched.

"Thanks, Jerry. You were always my favorite brother," she said, hoping her attempt at humor would reassure him.

"I was always your only brother. But I am still the best brother you could hope for." He grinned at her.

"I know. You want me to make some tea? I could dig out the pitcher and glasses . . ."

"I better get back to Shirley. She'll be pulling her hair out with the kids." But he didn't turn.

Violet hesitated as well, wanting him to stay, wanting him to go.

"Are you sure you are doing the right thing?" he asked.

"Yes, I am sure." Violet stiffened her spine.

"I worry about you, Vi. We all do."

"I know," she said. *And that's the problem. Too many people hovering over me, wrapping me in soft cotton, making sure I don't break. Except I am already broken.* "I'll be fine," she added. "And I am just a couple of hours away."

She hugged him, resting her head on his shoulder and breathing in his cigarette-smoke-and-aftershave scent.

"All right," he said, giving her a little squeeze. "You know where to find me if you need me."

He stepped off the porch into the South Carolina sunshine, already hot for May. As he drove away, he waved out of his open window. She stayed where she was and watched Jerry's truck trundle away from her, rocking back and forth on the dirt road, his dusty wake drawing a curtain between her old life and her new one.

Was she doing the right thing?

She had thought so when she decided to finally move out of her parents' house. It had been eighteen months since . . . everything had gone so horribly wrong. Wasn't it time she started over? Began to live her life again? She had thought so then, but doubt was bumping at her, lapping at her ankles, tiny waves of a rising tide.

She entered her new house and scanned the boxes. Her

panic inched up, the tide surging, breaking now at her knees. She closed her eyes and breathed deep. *I'll start with music. That will cheer me up.*

She pulled an album out of a milk crate—skipping over Simon & Garfunkel and Joni Mitchell and choosing the more upbeat 5th Dimension. She placed it on the turntable and set the needle in the groove. The strains of "Aquarius/Let the Sunshine In" filled the little trailer. She headed to the kitchen, but the haphazard stacks of boxes stopped her, an insurmountable wall of work she was too tired to climb. She massaged her forehead with the tips of her fingers. What had her father said? "Just put one foot in front of the other, Vi, and the next thing you know, you won't be standing in the same place anymore."

Fine. She could do that. She spotted a carton marked "Books," thinking that would be an easy start. She picked it up to relocate it to the living room, and, as she straightened, the bottom fell out and books tumbled onto the floor and her feet. She swore softly and hurled the useless box against a wall, feeling childish and not remotely satisfied with the action.

I will not cry over spilled books, she thought, but the little joke fell flat. She blew a strand of hair out of her eyes and bent to pick the books up. As she did, she spotted a bit of blue plaid on the other side of the table. Jerry's shirt. He had taken it off and draped it over the back of a chair, finishing the move in his short-sleeved undershirt. The garment now lay on the rounded chair back as if on a thin, slope-shouldered man. She lifted the shirt and fought off a ripple of longing to go back home. Determined, she folded the garment over her arm, and Jerry's silver lighter and pack of cigarettes clattered to the floor. She pursed her lips. He must have been really worried about her to have forgotten his smokes.

Sighing, she picked up the Marlboros and lighter, and as she rose up, she whacked her head—hard—on the metal edge of the table. She yelped, rubbed her head, and sank down on the cool linoleum floor in defeat. The tears she had been fighting spilled out.

This was not the future she planned. Life had taken her far from the road she had started down five years earlier. It had dumped her here, with no signposts and no map to make her journey clear. She knew where she was. She knew where she had been. But she had no idea where she was going. She thought that by moving into this rented mobile home, she might get a reprieve from the guilt and grief that had become her constant companions. She had tried to pack them away like her dishes or books, but the mental box she had packed them in was the first thing to spring open. She had thought she would feel a little lighter, a little more buoyant with hope. But the same loneliness, the same sadness, the same anguish she had felt in her hometown still weighed her down here. The only difference was now she would cry in different rooms and stare through her tears at different views. She was like a sapling, bowed down by a violent storm. She needed time and tending to stand up straight again.

Violet wiped her eyes and wondered how long she had been crying. Her album still played, so it hadn't been too long. She sighed and got up, rubbing the top of her head where a small, tender lump had formed. She turned on the tap and splashed water on her face, and groped in a box for a roll of paper towels, leaving dark, damp splotches on the cardboard. As she blotted her burning eyes, a knock at her door made her jump. *That must be Jerry, returning for his things.* She sent up a prayer of thanks that he had not caught her in an emotional heap on the floor. Straightening her shoulders, she smoothed her hair and headscarf, throwing the paper towel on the counter.

Instead of her brother, a little girl stood on the porch, her face framed with two blonde, uneven pigtails. A constellation of freckles marched across her nose. Her legs already bore the badges of summer play even though it was still spring. Her bright, expectant smile reminded Violet of a flower seeking the sun.

"Oh! I thought you were my brother," Violet said.

"No, ma'am," the little girl said earnestly. "My name is Arabella Constance Fitzgerald."

"Well, that is quite a big name. What can I do for you?" Violet suppressed the urge to wipe at her gritty eyes, and instead blinked them several times, hoping they weren't too red from her little crying episode.

"I wanted to say hi. I'm your neighbor. I live over there." She pointed to the double-wide mobile home across the street.

"Alrighty then. Hi."

Arabella peered around Violet and said, "You have a lot of boxes. I could help you unpack."

Violet turned and scanned her living room. "You know, I didn't think I had much stuff until I had to fit it all in boxes. But unpacking all this is a lot to ask someone." She said it as nicely as she could manage. She was in no mood for company.

"It's OK. I don't mind."

Violet groped for another excuse. "Well, your parents probably wouldn't appreciate me putting you to work."

"My mama would be happy because my baby brother is asleep and this way I won't wake him up. And my dad says we should always try to make the world a better place, and one way to do that is to help each other." She held up one finger and puffed out her chest.

"Your dad sounds like a wise man."

"He is. So if you want to make the world a better place, you have to let me help you. Plus, I'm a really good helper."

Violet blinked. She tried again. "I am sure you have other things you'd rather do. Ride your bike? Play with friends?"

Arabella shook her head so vigorously her ponytails whipped around her face. "I ride my bike aaallll the time." She drew the word out as she spread her hands to encompass an ocean of time. "And nobody lives on this street but grown-ups and some teenagers. So you'd also be helping me out, too. I help you, you help me." She nodded emphatically.

Violet could not think of how else to say no in a way that wouldn't erase the happy, eager smile that brightened the girl's face. And that would not, to use the girl's words, make the world a better place. Violet might be miserable, but she didn't have to spread that around. "I guess you might as well come in."

She lifted the hook on the screen door and let Arabella in. She turned down the sound on her stereo so that "Those Were the Days" strummed in the background instead of blaring through the house.

"So, you're the welcome wagon for this little neighborhood, hmm?"

Arabella's eyebrows drew together like delicate blonde wings of a tiny bird. "What's a welcome wagon?"

Violet couldn't help but smile. "Just what they call people who welcome new neighbors," she said.

"Oh. Should I have a wagon?"

"I think that's just an expression. Or maybe it comes from back before there were cars. So, Arabella Constance Fitzgerald. I am Violet Wentworth. Would you like a soda? I'd offer tea or lemonade, but I don't have any made because I don't know where anything is."

"I am not allowed to have soda. Except sometimes my mom or dad asks me to get theirs, and I take a little sip." She stopped, worry erasing her smile. "But don't tell them that, OK?"

Violet winked at her. "Your secret is safe with me."

"Just so you know, we've moved a lot, so I am good at unpacking."

Violet considered this. She might as well give her something useful to do. "Well, let's put your expertise to work. You can help me in the kitchen."

Violet led the way and hesitated in the doorway, staring at the mounds of boxes, and exhaled heavily. "I don't even know where to start. I thought I was so organized."

"My grandmother says when you don't know where to start, you just jump in with both feet and quit thinking so dang much about it. Except she didn't say dang, but I can't say the other word."

Violet laughed. "What excellent advice! Sounds like something my father would say." She pried open the nearest box and plucked out an object wrapped in newspaper.

"There ya go. Glasses. Maybe I will be able to make you something besides soda after all. Tell you what. You unwrap these, and I will wipe out the cabinets. Think you can be careful with these?"

"Yes, ma'am." Arabella crossed her chest with an index finger. "Cross my heart and hope to die." She set to work, slowly freeing the glasses from their newspaper cocoons, tongue sticking out of the corner of her mouth in concentration. Violet hid a smile as she dug out a sponge and wiped the shelves. As she arranged the glasses in neat rows on one of the shelves, it occurred to her that having someone with her kept her moving. She didn't stop and wallow.

They worked steadily. Violet occasionally asked Arabella where things should go, and the little girl grinned, seemingly pleased to be consulted.

As they worked, Arabella talked. "Do you have any kids?"

Violet's heart clenched, and her hands froze. "No, no kids. Not married, either." She hoped her tone sounded as light as she was trying to make it. She reached into a box and held up a plastic pitcher with far more enthusiasm than the find merited. "Ta-da! Found it!" She placed the pitcher beside the sink and crumpled the newsprint wrapping, tossing it in the recently emptied glasses box.

"So you live all by yourself?" Arabella asked. "Is it scary or fun? Do you like it? Do you worry about being alone?"

Violet raised an eyebrow, trying to decide which question to answer. "It has its ups and downs. Have you thought about growing up to be a reporter?"

"I am going to be a paleontologist."

"That would certainly go well with your name."

"How does it go with my name?"

"It's long like . . . Oh, never mind. My poor attempt at humor. Why don't you tell me about your family?"

Arabella balled up her newspaper, mimicking Violet, and tossed it into the empty box. "Score!" She raised her arms in victory as it went in. "So, it was just me for the longest time, but now I have a little brother. He is really new. He's kind of cute, but he's also a lot of trouble. I haven't made up my mind if I like him or not."

Violet's mouth twitched up for a minute, but, keeping her face serious, she said, "Little brothers can be like that."

"Do you have one?"

"I do not. I have an older one. And an older sister. But I've heard stories from friends about their little brothers. And it seems like they stay that way for a long time. Kind of cute and kind of a lot of trouble. But you can have fun with them, too. I take it he's still pretty little."

"Yeah. He was just born in April."

"He is very little." Violet opened another box, this one filled with pots and pans of varying age and wear.

"Yeah. I thought he would do more. All he does is kick his feet and look around like he is not sure where he is. And he poops. A lot. And spits up. I mean, how can you have fun with that?"

Violet laughed. "I guess when I was born, my brother and sister felt the same about me. But he'll be walking before you know it, and then he'll be more fun. I bet he will adore you."

"That's what my mama says. But I'll believe that when I see it."

Arabella cocked her head, holding up her hand. "Speaking of my mama, I hear her calling. Guess it's lunchtime."

"Goodness. What big ears you have."

"That's from Red Riding Hood!"

"It is, indeed."

"Can I come back later?"

"I guess," Violet said. "I'll be here. Thanks for the help."

"You're welcome." Arabella started out the door but stopped and turned. "You look like Jackie Onassis, by the way."

Violet gave a tiny laugh. "If you are going to say things like that, you can come over anytime!"

"Bye, Missus Wentworth."

"You can call me Violet."

"Oh, no I can't. My mama would send me to my room for a month."

"How about a compromise? You can call me Miss Violet."

"OK. That might work. I think. I have to go home now and eat and look up the word compromise." Arabella slipped out the door.

Violet had just washed her plate from her own lunch—a casserole her mother had sent along—when a rhythmic knock sounded at the door. She dried her hands as she headed towards it. "I see my favorite assistant is here."

"You like the knock? My dad taught me. He said it means shave and a haircut, two bits. But I have no idea what that means. But I like the knock. Don't you?"

"Absolutely," Violet said when Arabella took a breath. "It's a very nice knock."

"I'm going to use it from now on and then you'll always know it's me. Do you need more help?"

Violet gave her a tight smile and wondered how she could politely urge the little girl to find friends her own age. It had helped to have her here, but once she was settled in, she wouldn't want her dropping in at every opportunity. The whole point of moving here was to have time alone. She'd have to think on that, but for now, she might as well accept her help. "Sure," she said. "I'm working in the bedroom right now."

"You bet!" Arabella hopped over the threshold, legs together, swinging her arms to give herself momentum.

"Ah, the energy of the young," Violet said.

"I'm not that young," Arabella protested. "I turned seven two weeks ago."

"Seven? That is quite an accomplishment. And quite old. Happy belated birthday. Did you have a party?"

"Not really. We don't know too many people here as we just moved here right before Christmas. We lived in the Philippines."

"Wow. That must have been interesting."

"We had house boys who cleaned our house. My dad says labor there is very cheap. Here, we have to clean our own house. Mama says it's good for me."

"I kind of agree with your mother that it's important to learn how to do these things for yourself. Though I must say, having someone to help out with cleaning seems quite appealing."

"They used to tie rags on their feet and skate on the floor. They made housecleaning seem fun."

"Maybe I will try that."

Arabella giggled. "I think that would be funny."

Violet nodded. "It would be, wouldn't it?"

The two went to work tucking away Violet's folded shirts and shorts in the chest of drawers. When they turned to the closet, Violet stood, hands on hips, staring at the hodgepodge of clothes dangling haphazardly on the rod. She looked down at Arabella, who gazed up at her, waiting patiently.

"I guess the hanging clothes are a little over your head." She chuckled as Arabella drew her brows together. "Pun intended."

"What's a pun?"

"Oh, boy. How to explain. It's when you say one thing that can be meant two different ways. And one of them is usually funny. Like doing things over your head means it's hard for you. But in this case, it's literally over your head."

"Oh. I think I get it."

"So how about you do the shoes? Let me find the shoe box." Violet surveyed the room. "Aha! Shoes!" She nudged a large square box to the closet and opened it. "They've gotten all jumbled up in here, so if you can match the shoes up and place them under the clothes, that would be a help."

"I can do that!" Arabella dug into the shoes and began pulling out shiny, colorful pumps and strappy flats and one pair of high, white boots. She lined them up precisely as Violet sorted the hanging clothes, untangling crossed hooks and sorting them by category until the closet was as neat as a clothing ad.

They stopped for a snack. Violet had unpacked more kitchen items in Arabella's absence and had found some crackers, which she now set on the table along with a pitcher of tea she had made. She apologized for not having better snacks, but as Arabella sat down at the table, she said she was perfectly happy eating saltines and drinking sweet tea. Violet retrieved an ice cube tray out from the freezer and pulled the frosted metal arm, popping the cubes out of their molds, placing some in two glasses. She topped them off with the tea and handed Arabella a glass, clinked hers to it, and said, "Cheers! To my little helper!"

"Cheers to my new neighbor!" Arabella said, kicking her legs back and forth.

Violet smiled. The girl had been surprisingly helpful. But once the unpacking was done, Violet would find a way to extricate herself. Having a little girl pop over every day was not part of her plan.

Later that evening, Violet closed the blinds on her new views. Not that they offered much. Violet's new home sat on Magnolia Avenue, a grand name that conjured visions of stately houses with white picket fences. Or perhaps an antebellum mansion, with a long boulevard lined by the namesake flowering trees. But instead, flat-topped mobile homes of varying ages and conditions marched along the little dirt road. Some had their V-shaped hitches in place as if ready to make a quick getaway, while others had added skirting, lending them an air of permanence. Some dripped rust down their side, while others shone like new pennies. And while the little street boasted many trees, only one or two were magnolias. Most were loblolly pines that shot up, straight as matchsticks, and provided only small patches of shade. The best one could say about all those trees—even the tall pines with their ungenerous canopies—was that they provided the yards with an abundant shelter from the harsh Southern sun.

Violet had sensed the rental agent's reluctance to show her the house. The street, even in the glorious, bright rays of May sunshine, appeared as buttoned-up as a Baptist minister on a Sunday morning. While a couple of houses looked lived in—a bike in the yard across the way, and a football at the house next door to that—several looked to be empty. The street seemed to be a place where people kept to themselves. Where friendships were not cultivated, where one might come and go and not be noticed. Violet decided this was what she needed. And the price was right. The realtor could not hide her surprise when Violet said she'd take it.

Violet turned her back on the closed blinds. The place was starting to come together. Her furniture sat in a pleasing array in the living room. The kitchen was orderly and settled, with cutlery and crockery and cooking utensils neatly put away. She had made a run to the grocery store to have food on hand. Here, in her bedroom, the bed lay ready with clean, crisp sheets and plumped pillows. Everything was in its proper place. Except her. She buried her face in her hands and sank down on the bed and cried. Again. Thanks to her newfound little friend, she had held it together all day. When she opened the door, her heart had sunk when she saw not Jerry, but a small child. She had wanted to tell her to go away, but she didn't have the heart. But the little girl had saved her from sobbing into every box she unpacked. She would have drowned in tears and soggy cardboard without her.

As she faced the night ahead, miles from anyone she knew, she wondered if she had made a mistake. She longed for her parents and the familiar roads and rivers and marshes of her low-country childhood. She longed for her old life. The one *before*. Her new life stretched out before her, long and empty and joyless. She simply existed, putting one foot in front of the other, one day after another . . . and for what? She had a job at a restaurant where she would put on her happy smile until her cheeks ached and her soul cracked. Then she would come home to her barren house and her barren life. It was empty here in this new place, and it had been empty in the old one. It made no difference at all.

2
Violet

May 1969

Violet stepped onto her front porch, the morning sun already hot on her arms and face. She added an empty box to the growing stack to the right of the door, and, as she turned to go back inside, she caught a glimpse of a slight, elderly woman with a white nimbus of hair shuffling up the unpaved driveway from her mailbox. As Violet watched, some envelopes slipped from the woman's hand and fell to the ground, and she struggled to bend down far enough to retrieve them. A breeze lifted several, skimming them along the dirt and flipping one over, putting them just out of reach of the woman's hand. Violet hesitated, torn between wanting to help her and wanting to stay in her little bubble. A flash of color caught her eye. Arabella was skipping across the street. She stopped, taking in the scene, then ran to the old woman and picked up the stray letters. She brushed the sand off and handed them to the woman. A stab of guilt pierced Violet. What was wrong with her that a little girl was behaving better than she was?

The woman clutched her mail against her chest as if afraid Arabella would try to snatch them back. "I suppose you expect something in return for this." She brandished the letters.

Arabella frowned. "No, ma'am. I just wanted to help you."

"Fine. You've helped. Now go on about your business."

Arabella cocked her head. "I don't really have any business."

"It's a figure of speech."

"Oh." Arabella stood there for a minute longer.

"Are you afraid I am going to keel over?"

"No, ma'am. But I did want to make sure you're all right."

"I'm old, but not decrepit. You may go."

"Yes, ma'am," Arabella said, and turned, waving wildly when she spotted Violet.

Arabella joined her on the porch, rocking back and forth on her feet, breaking into her infectious grin.

"Little Miss Arabella," Violet said. "Would you like to come in?"

Arabella glanced back at the old woman's house as she slowly mounted her steps and disappeared into her house.

"I would love to come in. What does 'decrepit' mean?"

"It means old and feeble. Kind of weak." Violet waited for Arabella to say something about what had happened, but she didn't.

"You sure like music," Arabella said instead as they stepped into Violet's living room.

Violet turned down Tommy Roe singing about being dizzy. "Do your parents listen to music?" she asked.

"Sure. Sometimes. Not a lot. Right now, we can't wake the baby, who sleeps an awful lot."

Violet chuckled. "What kind of music do your parents like?"

Arabella squinted up at the ceiling, tapping her finger on her chin. "Let me see. The Beatles. Glen Campbell. Johnny Cash. The Beach Boys."

"Which is your favorite?"

"'Puff, the Magic Dragon.'"

"Ah, you're a rebel!"

Arabella furrowed her brow, puzzled.

"Sorry," Violet said. "I'm not used to talking to seven-year-olds. If you ever want to know what I mean, just ask. I don't mind. What I meant now was you didn't pick the music you said was your parents' music. So you have your own likes and dislikes."

"Oh. Yes, I do. I like the Beatles OK, but the rest is boring. Your music is not boring. It's fun."

"Thanks for the compliment." Violet tucked a strand of hair back into her kerchief. "If there's an album in there you'd like to hear, let me know."

"OK, I will. I came to see if you needed more help."

"As a matter of fact, we can start with the albums. I am tired of looking through the boxes for them. If you could put them here, like this." She took an album and placed it upright, like a book, on the empty shelf below the record player. "I will warn you, they are in alphabetical order. You can do that, right?"

Arabella nodded enthusiastically. "Oh yes! I am very good with the alphabet!"

"Let's get started," Violet said.

As Arabella worked on the records, Violet unwrapped some knickknacks, placing them on the stereo cabinet, the coffee table, a bookcase. Arabella made quick work of the albums, and, after she had finished, she peeked into the next carton.

"You like to read?" she asked Violet.

"I do, indeed. I find books and music are loyal friends. Always there for me when I need them."

"I never thought of it like that, but it's true."

"You like to read, too? In addition to listening to 'Puff, the Magic Dragon'?"

"I do. My mama said I was born with a book in my hand, though now that I've seen Baby Allen, I'm pretty sure that's not true."

"That's what's called a 'figure of speech.'"

"Mrs. McCabe next door said those exact words to me today. What is a figure of speech?" Arabella asked.

"It's when someone describes something to get an idea across, but they don't mean it literally. Like your mother, I guess, was trying to say what a wonderful reader you are, even for one so young."

"Ohhhh. Like when my dad says my mama's more nervous than a long-tailed cat in a room full of rockers."

Violet laughed. "Yes, exactly!"

"I always picture the poor cat, though, with this long tail and all these rocking chairs going back and forth. If it was a smart cat, it would jump up on one, then jump to another until it got out of that room."

"That would, indeed, be very smart of that cat."

"Do you have any pets?"

"I do not."

"Do you like animals?"

"Yes, but it's hard to have pets until you are settled. I have been kind of unsettled the last few years. What about you? You have pets?"

Arabella bobbed her head. "We have a cat. It's my job to

feed her. Her name is Tabitha, like on *Bewitched*. I got her for Christmas. I couldn't have a pet before because we were unsettled."

"That is a charming name for a cat. I take it she's not actually magical?"

"No, but I keep hoping."

Arabella moved about the room, examining the mementos Violet had placed here and there. Most were seaside souvenirs: a plaster lighthouse; an owl made with miniature shells; a Myrtle Beach snow globe with an underwater scene of coral, shells, a sunken ship, and glitter.

"You like the beach?" Arabella said, turning the globe upside down and back again, watching the sparkling bits drift lazily through the water to land on the minuscule branches of coral and the tiny deck of the ship.

"I do. My family lives not far from one in Beaufort County. My grandmother gave me that when I was young. Maybe about your age. One summer, we all went to the beach and stayed for a long weekend. We usually only went for the day, so it was a special trip. Being able to sleep and wake up there was heaven. My grandmother gave me the snow globe to commemorate that weekend." Violet fell silent, remembering.

"I don't think I would have moved away from the beach! I would have moved closer."

"A lot of things haven't gone the way I thought they would. Or the way I would prefer."

"Like what?"

"You don't miss a trick, do you? Let's save that story for another day. Since you've found my books, would you like to put those on the shelves right here?"

"Yes! Are they in alphabetical order?"

Violet nodded and laughed. "You're starting to figure me out. Yes, they are. Alphabetical by the last name of the author, unless it is an oversized book. Does that make sense?"

Arabella nodded firmly. "What do I do with the oversized ones?"

"You can put them on the ends of the shelves, or lay them on their sides and stack them largest to smallest. Whatever you want to do. So while you do that, I am going to take care of these linens I didn't put away last night."

Arabella went home for the midday meal, and Violet had her lunch as well—peanut butter and crackers. She didn't want to bother with anything else. She ate mechanically over her kitchen sink, oblivious to the food's taste and texture. She studied her backyard and thought how once, she would have been delighted with the azaleas, wisteria, and two dogwood trees that graced the property. Although their blossoms had come and gone now, they had been bursting with blooms when she first saw the house, but she hadn't cared. She wished she could talk herself into some kind of enthusiasm over that or anything else, but she had tried and failed. Several times. Multiple times. Everyone had told her it would take time, but she couldn't imagine ever feeling better. She pushed the thoughts away. *Just concentrate on what you need to do right now.*

Arabella's knock made her jump. She quickly rinsed her hands of any food residue and hurried to the door.

When Violet opened it, she found Arabella was not alone but accompanied by a woman who had to be her mother. Arabella looked exactly like her down to the freckles on her nose. The woman carried a baby, and Violet stiffened her spine. *I can do this.*

"You must be Arabella's mother." Violet's smile felt strained, but it was the best she could do.

The other woman reached out and shook hands with Violet.

"How do you do? I hope you don't mind my popping over, but I—" She paused, glancing down at Arabella. "I wanted to make sure you were OK with her coming over. I know she's enjoying your company. And I wanted to welcome you to the neighborhood, of course."

"Arabella has been a huge help. Come in, come in. It's too hot to stand here chatting. It feels like summer already, doesn't it. Can I get you an iced tea?" Violet made her usual detour to the stereo and turned down the sound.

"Oh, no, I'm fine. Thank you. We just had lunch."

Arabella thrust a cookie tin towards her. "We brought cookies. Pecan sandies."

"I love those." Violet opened the tin and inhaled. "Oh my! They smell like heaven! I will definitely have some later." She turned to Arabella. "And this must be the baby brother you've told me so much about."

Arabella's mother chuckled. "I bet she has. I am afraid it's been kind of hard on Arabella, having a little brother and putting up with all the changes a baby brings."

"No, it hasn't, Mama. I like being a big sister."

Her mother smiled down at her fondly. "And you are very good at it." She looked up at Violet. "I am Caroline Fitzgerald, by the way."

"Glad to meet you. I'm Violet Wentworth. Please. Sit down." She gestured them farther into the room. Caroline and Arabella settled themselves on the square cushions of a brown couch that did not come close to matching the blue armchair Violet perched on. But the furniture came with the trailer, and it was the best she could do right now. As she sat, Violet placed the cookie tin on the coffee table. Arabella beamed, looking from her mother to Violet and back again.

Caroline arranged the baby in the crook of her left arm, and he opened his rosebud mouth in a miniature yawn, tiny fists curled against his chest. "So what brings you to our little neighborhood?" she asked as she gently bounced Allen and absently patted him with her right hand.

Violet took her time brushing away imaginary lint from her light-blue pedal pushers before answering. "My family lives in Beaufort County, and I love them to pieces, but sometimes you want to make your own way. Having them give me advice all day and night was starting to wear on me. I know they mean well, but I thought a little distance might make the heart grow fonder." *None of that is even a lie. Just not the whole truth.*

Caroline smiled. "You're close enough to visit, so that should be a plus. But I have to ask—how on earth did you find Ashford Estates? It's kind of out of the way unless you're with the Air Force."

"I had a realtor help me. She showed me some places around Edenton and some other towns around here. Found this place, then looked for a job. Luckily, I found one at Turner's T-Bones. So it all kind of fell into place."

"Your job will make you quite popular with my husband. He loves that place. What is it with men and giant slabs of beef?"

Violet grinned. "Excellent question. I see it every day. Men look at our menu like it's Raquel Welch."

"It's not the highest class place," Caroline said apologetically. "I mean Ashford, not Turner's T-Bones. But it's not bad. We moved here last year. My husband is in the Air Force, and I am not crazy about living on base. They tell you when to cut your grass and how low to cut it. Plus, you have to apply. And moving out? The cleaning is ridiculous. This seemed easier. I've had to live on base sometimes, but I will avoid it if I can. Here, the neighbors do seem to mind their own business, and that suits me just fine."

"That suits me just fine as well."

"Mrs. McCabe lives next door to you. She's an elderly widow, a bit cranky."

"We saw her this morning, didn't we?" Violet said, and Arabella nodded.

Caroline continued. "The Taylors live next door to us. They have been there a long time, from what Mrs. Taylor told me. Nice people, but they are busy and not home much. They have two teenagers. The teenage boy sometimes has friends over, and they can get kind of rowdy. But he hasn't broken my windows or trampled my flower beds. Which may be because I haven't planted any."

Violet laughed. "Probably a little hard with a new baby."

Caroline laughed as well. "Yes, I may have been occupied with other things. I should also warn you about the man on the corner. Mr. Pritchard. He is known to be . . . well, kind of grumpy, I guess. He gets quite bent out of shape when kids cut across his yard. He threatens to sic his dog on them. At least that's what Mrs. McCabe and Mrs. Taylor told me."

Violet raised her eyebrows. "I'll definitely be careful about crossing his yard, though I don't know why I would want to."

Caroline chuckled, and Allen started thrusting his fists and fidgeting and making mewling noises. Arabella leaned over, tickled him, and made cooing sounds. Allen raised his tiny, nearly invisible eyebrows, little wrinkles appearing on his forehead and disappearing again.

"Arabella, it seems you have the magic touch," Violet said.

Arabella straightened and smiled. Caroline stroked her hair. "I tell her that all the time. She is a very big help to me."

Allen gave a little cry and turned his head, looking around.

Caroline rocked him and smoothed his bib. "I think that is my cue to leave before he starts wailing. One thing I can say about him is he has a powerful set of lungs."

"You're welcome to drop by anytime," Violet said, surprising herself when she realized she meant it.

"And likewise. It was nice meeting you." She turned to Arabella. "Arabella, don't wear out your welcome."

"Yes, ma'am." After the door closed, Arabella glanced around. "You look about moved in."

"Yes, it's coming along, isn't it?"

Arabella picked up the beach snow globe and turned it upside down, then righted it, mesmerized by the falling glitter.

"You really like that thing, don't you?"

"I do. It's so beautiful," Arabella said without taking her eyes off the glitter as it sank to the bottom. She placed the snow globe on its shelf. "So what are we working on today?"

"I was going to put up some curtains."

The trailer had come equipped with curtain rods, some of which were now leaning against the sofa. Violet picked one up and handed it to Arabella, then rummaged through a

box for the right curtains and came up with two long panels
of white cloth with sprays of yellow and orange flowers on
them. She handed them to Arabella. "Think you can slide this
rod through the top there? I am hoping the wrinkles fall out,
because I sure don't feel like ironing them."

"I can do that!" Arabella sat on the floor, the rod across
her knees, and stuck her tongue out of one side of her mouth
as she worked. It took a few tries before she got the hang of
bunching the fabric and then pulling it straight.

Arabella held up the first curtain for Violet's inspection.

"Well done! That looks great."

"Thanks!" Arabella said and moved on to the next one.
"So you told my mama you're a waitress. Do you like it?"

"It's OK. It pays the bills. But I have a long-term plan. I
had high hopes once of going to college when I first got out
of high school, but that didn't work out. So I plan to work
at the restaurant and save up. It's always busy, which means I
make good tips. After I save enough, I am going to enroll in
the community college."

"Why didn't you go to college before? Like when you
wanted to?"

"Sometimes, life takes us in a different direction." She
chose her next words with care. "For a while, I didn't have
time, but I had the money. Now I have all the time in the
world, but not enough money." She took a deep breath and
smiled at Arabella. "Never mind me. I get a little sentimental
at times. I think we need some upbeat music."

She pulled out an album and placed it on the turntable,
and a beat pulsed through the house. The Supremes started
singing "You Can't Hurry Love." Violet took Arabella's hands
and swung them back and forth, singing along with Diana

Ross and friends. Arabella started giggling, and a little flower of happiness bloomed in Violet's chest. The feeling took her by surprise, and, under other circumstances, she would have stopped to examine it, but Arabella was laughing and dancing with her, so she kept twirling the little girl around and decided to just enjoy the moment.

3
Violet

As she settled into her new house and neighborhood, Violet did not run into any other neighbors other than the Fitzgeralds. The blinds in the windows in the houses around her might have flicked aside at her comings and goings, but certainly no one stirred themselves to come and meet her, other than Arabella and her mother. She detected the usual rhythms of a neighborhood: the evening arrivals of men and some women coming home from work, the mowing of lawns on Saturdays. The men mowed early, suffering through the early morning blanket of humidity rather than the late afternoon pall of suffocating heat. It was a far cry from her parents' neighborhoods, where everyone enjoyed being outside in their yards on the weekends, calling greetings to one another, chatting on front porches as they fanned themselves, and puttering around in gardens until an afternoon thunderstorm chased them in. Quite frankly, this suited her. She needed time and space, and this little street, with its face turned away from the world, gave her just the refuge she sought.

Saturdays seemed a little busier. The elderly woman

next door—Mrs. McCabe, she remembered—made her way to her car about mid-morning. She heard the man on the corner hammering once. She saw the woman next door to the Fitzgeralds carrying in groceries. And, when she checked her mail, a teenage boy in a gray car raced by, going way too fast for this small street. She would have to warn Arabella to be careful crossing the road.

She liked her job well enough. The constant ebb and flow of customers kept her busy. Which kept her from thinking. Which kept her from crying. One would think that after all these months, the tears would have stopped, but they still came at random times: at night, when she turned out the light, or in the morning when she woke to face the day. Still, she knew she was better than she had been a year ago. The fact that she could find a place to live, land a job, pack and unpack, showed progress. And the moment when she danced with Arabella shone in her mind like a sunstruck crystal. She hadn't experienced such a spontaneous feeling—dare she call it joy?—in a long time. There had been a time when she moved through her life as though underwater, her movements slow and lethargic, her vision blurry and indistinct. She no longer felt like she was dragging herself through her own life. The problem with feeling better, however, was that it triggered her guilt. The seasons continued to change and the world rumbled on, and instead of eroding her grief, the passage of days reminded her she was still here when someone else wasn't.

As a week, then two, went by, Violet fell into a comfortable routine. Because she usually worked the dinner shift at the restaurant, she slept in. She spent her late mornings cleaning, doing laundry, grocery shopping, making progress on various projects. Keeping busy kept her from moping, which had a way of feeding on itself and making her mopier. Arabella often visited in the afternoons, and Violet found she looked forward to her visits. The next time she called home, she could honestly tell her parents she was trying her best to come back to the land of the living. Not that she would put it that way.

One late morning in early June, Violet worked on her latest hobby: crocheting a blanket. Its squares splashed vivid color across her lap and her sofa. It was her first attempt, and it was starting to shape up. She felt rather pleased with herself.

A knock sounded at the door, and it wasn't Arabella's usual code. Afraid to lose her place, Violet carried the blanket to the door. She peeked out the sidelight and was surprised to see it was Arabella after all. A breathless, red-faced Arabella.

"Arabella! Are you OK? Did you get hurt?"

"No, I'm fine," the little girl panted.

Violet stepped back. "Come on in, and I'll get you some water."

"No!" Arabella said. "I came to tell you about Mrs. McCabe!"

"Tell me what?"

"I think there's something wrong with her. She hasn't checked her mail in ages, and she always, always checks her mail."

"The woman who lives next door?" Violet's thoughts struggled to catch up with Arabella.

"Yes! Her mailbox is chock-full of mail, and she checks it every single day."

"Oh, dear. Did you tell your mother?"

"Well, I was going to, but she had her Allen Face on."

Violet raised her eyebrows.

"That's when she's fed up and wonders what she was thinking when she decided to have another baby." She tugged on Violet's arm. "Come on! We just need to go check on her."

"OK. Hang on. Let me put this down without tangling it up. Then I need to get my shoes." Violet disappeared down her hallway, leaving Arabella rocking back and forth on her heels, her body humming with impatience. Violet hobbled into the living room, trying to slip on a pair of yellow sandals as she walked.

"All right," Violet said. "Lead the way." She held out her hand, and Arabella tugged her out the door.

Violet hoped all was fine next door because she really did not want to get drawn into neighborhood drama. And she really, really did not want to discover—well, her mind refused to finish the thought. Hopefully, Mrs. McCabe was off visiting children or just didn't want to go out in the heat.

It was hotter than a skillet on an open fire. Violet eyed the old woman's yard. Long grass covered the lawn, and the hedges obscured most of the front of the old trailer. A few branches protruded above the rest, as though the shrubs were growing arms. The mobile home radiated the quiet air of abandonment. No sign of life betrayed its occupant, but then, it rarely did. Mrs. McCabe kept her windows closed, drapes pulled tight. But when Violet spotted the mailbox, her heart sank. Even without going down to the road, she was able to see the sheaf of mail protruding from the box and spilling onto the hanging door. That was not an encouraging sign.

They squeezed between the grasping arms of the boxwoods that all but swallowed the front porch. Arabella peered up expectantly at Violet, and Violet suppressed a sigh. She had accepted Arabella's daily visits a little grudgingly, but had ended up finding her a charming, chatty distraction. She asked a lot of questions, but Violet was able to answer them without much trouble. But she did not want to get tangled up with any more neighbors. She enjoyed Arabella's company, and she liked Caroline, too. But she also liked that Caroline was busy with her newborn. Still, she would do her neighborly duty and check on Mrs. McCabe, find out what was going on, and then be done.

She tapped on the door somewhat tentatively, but Arabella made a little motion with her head. *Harder*, the little nod implied. Violet widened her eyes at her but knocked more firmly. They waited, hearing nothing. Just as Violet raised her hand to knock again, they heard the small hint of a sound. Both of them craned their necks and tilted their ears to the door.

"Is that a cough?" Violet whispered.

"I think so," Arabella whispered back.

Violet knocked again and called, "Mrs. McCabe? It's your new next-door neighbor. Are you OK?" She leaned her ear toward the door and listened.

"I think—" Arabella started, but Violet waved at her to stop. She definitely heard something. Kind of a raspy cough? She took a deep breath and tried the door, but it was locked. "Crap." Arabella's eyes flew wide at the bad word. "Pardon my language. Let's try the back door."

They wriggled back through the encroaching shrubs and passed through a rusty gate to the backyard. That door was also locked. Violet thought for a minute, trying to ignore the perspiration trickling in places she couldn't mention.

"We need some help. Who lives there?"

Arabella's eyes widened even more than they had for the mild curse word.

"That's Mr. Pritchard's house. His dog will eat us."

"Oh, your mom told me about him. Desperate times call for desperate measures. Let's go back around front, and you wait by the door in case Mrs. McCabe opens it. Maybe she's just in the bathroom or something."

"Are you going over there?" Arabella squeaked.

"I don't know what else to do. He might be able to open the door. Is he home during the day?"

"Sometimes. He comes and goes a lot."

Violet nodded. "There's a pick-up truck there, so that's a good sign. I'll be right back."

Violet squared her shoulders and marched across Mrs. McCabe's lawn and into the forbidden territory of Mr. Pritchard's yard. She hesitated briefly as she contemplated his trailer, but she lifted her chin, walked up the three steps, and knocked loudly. A dog immediately began barking savagely, and Violet snatched her arm back as if the beast could reach through the door and grab her hand in a mouth she was sure was slobbery and fang-filled. The snarling moved closer. A man's voice cut through the growling, telling the dog to sit. Without opening the door, the man yelled, "Go away. I don't take kindly to door-to-door types. Sales or religion, I don't give a damn."

The dog had stopped barking, but Violet had not stopped picturing its menacing form. "I'm not selling or converting. I need help. Our next-door neighbor may be in danger."

"Call the goddamn police, why don't cha? Do I look like an emergency worker?"

Violet did not waste time pointing out she couldn't actually see what he looked like. "I don't have a phone yet. I just moved in a couple of weeks ago. Please. Can you help?"

There was some muttering, and then the door was yanked open with such force that Violet almost fell backward off the steps.

"What seems to be the problem?"

A tall, bearded man with wiry hair of no certain color (Was it brown? Blond? Gray?) and a fierce scowl on his face stood framed in the doorway. His age could be anywhere between forty and sixty.

"It's Mrs. McCabe, next door," Violet said, glancing at the dog who sat beyond the man. The brindle mutt with ears too big for his head sat obediently but quivered and growled, hostility pulsating from every hair. He was of some indeterminate breed: pit bull, bulldog, demon from hell. Who knew? Violet forced herself to focus on the purpose at hand. "She hasn't checked her mail. We knocked on her door, and she didn't come."

"That sounds like she's just out of town, not in danger." The dog growled his agreement.

Violet cleared her throat. "When we knocked, I thought I heard kind of a cough. She's old. If she's sick, she needs help."

"Who's we?"

"What?"

"You said 'we' knocked. Can't whoever's with you help?"

Violet's fear melted into exasperation. "The 'we' is me and a seven-year-old girl." She gestured to the trailer next door, and Mr. Pritchard peered around his door. Arabella gave a wobbly wave.

Mr. Pritchard rolled his eyes. "Fred, stay. I'll be right back." Before she could stop herself, Violet said, "Fred? Really?"

Mr. Pritchard narrowed his eyes. "And what's wrong with that?"

"He sounds more like a Killer. Or Satan. Or Devilspawn."

He did not dignify that with an answer, but instead stepped over the threshold and closed the door behind him, forcing Violet to back down the narrow set of steps.

"Before I call for help, let's go see what in seven hells is going on."

He trudged ahead of her, every step and gesture radiating his discontent like a radio beacon.

When they got to the door, Violet asked Arabella if she'd heard anything since she'd gone next door.

"Another cough," Arabella said, her voice small and tremulous as she stared wide-eyed at Mr. Pritchard, who ignored her. He shouldered past the overgrowth, making a long twig twang against the porch post. He knocked on the door. A sound clearly rang out from the interior of the trailer: an unmistakable rattling cough.

"Mrs. McCabe? It's your neighbors. We're checking to see if you're all right. If you are, you better come to the door, because if you don't, I'm going to break the glass in your window, and I sure as hell ain't paying for it. Do you hear me? Time's a-wasting. I'm going to count to ten." He began to count loudly and, Violet thought, altogether too slowly.

When he finished his count, he glanced around and snatched a garden gnome peeking out from under the hedge. He lifted it, hefted it in his hand, and turned to Violet and Arabella.

"You might want to stand back."

Violet hastened Arabella off the porch. Not that she needed much persuasion. They stood a few feet away in the yard, oblivious to the hot sun beating down on them. Mr. Pritchard pulled off his checked cotton shirt, revealing a sleeveless undershirt as well as a pair of broad shoulders and arms roped with muscles. He wrapped the shirt around his hand, took hold of the gnome, and smashed it into the sidelight. A bit of uncovered arm grazed the window frame. "Goddammit! Jesus H. Christ Almighty God in heaven!" Violet belatedly tried to shield Arabella's ears. Mr. Pritchard clutched his hand against his torso.

"Are you OK, Mr. Pritchard?"

"Hell, no, I am not OK. I will live, but I am not OK, not with any of this."

He used the gnome—which appeared unharmed and unfazed by its ordeal— to knock out the rest of the glass, then reached his shirt-covered hand in to flip the thumb lock. He opened the door and motioned for Violet to come up the steps and shrugged back into his shirt as he followed her.

They entered a living room that smelled sharply of moth balls. It brimmed over with bric-a-brac. If Mrs. McCabe wanted to open a thrift store, she could be in business for months before running low on inventory. The room bulged with knickknacks and lamps and pillows and doilies and tapestries and picture frames. So it was easy to forgive the trio for missing Mrs. McCabe herself at first.

She lay in an overstuffed recliner at the end of the room, near curtained windows that would have given her a view of Mr. Pritchard's property if she ever opened them. She moaned— which is what brought their attention to her reclined form— and they rushed over. Her skin was pale with a bluish tinge, and she appeared as thin as a matchstick lying beneath a brown-and-blue crocheted afghan. Her breath rasped.

"Mrs. McCabe, I'm your neighbor, Violet. We are going to call for some help."

"Don't. Need. Help. Will. Be. Fine." Mrs. McCabe's voice was barely audible between the pauses she took after each word to gasp a mouthful of air. "Just. Need. Water."

"Can you go in the kitchen and fill up a glass with water?" Violet asked Arabella. "Perhaps with ice, if there is any in the freezer." She felt Mrs. McCabe's forehead, and the old lady feebly attempted to swat Violet's hand away. "She's burning up with fever." She turned to Mr. Pritchard. "Would you call for an ambulance?"

"If this will get me out of here any sooner, damn straight I will."

He searched around, trying to identify a telephone among the many items crowding Mrs. McCabe's small living room. "Jesus Christ on a cracker."

"Will you please hurry up?" Violet said.

Mr. Pritchard turned to her with undisguised venom and seemed as if he were having a mighty internal struggle. With effort, he turned away from her and finally found the squatting, black kettle telephone on an end table along with some rabbits, chickens, and cats. All figurines, but quite a horde of them.

He picked up the handset and sighed. "Excuse me. Can you get off the damn line for a minute? I need to make an emergency call." His eyes met Violet's. "I hate goddamn party lines." He did not bother to cover the mouthpiece.

The high-pitched chatter from the phone did not sound happy.

"I don't really give a damn if my language offends you. I have an old lady here in need of some help, and if you don't get off the line, I will come over there and yank you off."

Violet decided this was not the time to throw the old adage "More flies with honey" at him. After a minute, he pressed the button down and released it, and the dial tone came through the line.

"Operator, we need an ambulance at 823 Magnolia Avenue. Yeah, in the Ashford neighborhood. Old lady, probably close to eighty or ninety, is coughing and feverish, conscious, but in distress." Violet's eyes widened. Not only had he delivered more than one sentence without a single cuss word, but he also sounded . . . almost professional.

He hung up the phone. "There. You happy?" As if he was doing her a favor. She glared at him.

Mrs. McCabe attempted to speak. Violet leaned forward, worried. "I'm"—gasp—"not even"—cough—"eighty."

Violet's eyes met Mr. Pritchard's. He rolled his heavenwards.

"We'll be sure to let them know," Violet said, patting her hand.

The ambulance seemed to take forever, but perhaps time stopped in rooms where three people had nothing better to do than grimace at each other. Arabella had fetched the glass of water and held it up so Mrs. McCabe could take a sip. Mrs. McCabe waved her hand, indicating she was finished. Arabella put the glass down on a table and held Mrs. McCabe's hand. For some reason—Violet thought delirium likely—the old lady allowed the little girl to do this. Finally, the distant strains of a siren pierced the day and grew steadily closer.

"I'm going to go make sure they find us," Mr. Pritchard said as he stalked out the door.

Violet watched him stride to the end of the driveway and wave the ambulance down. A minute later, Mr. Pritchard herded the EMTs into the house.

The EMTs asked a lot of questions Violet couldn't answer. But the question that stabbed her in the heart was about how long she had been in this condition. Violet had no answer, and a little flash of guilt flared up and burned bright.

The two technicians examined Mrs. McCabe, and one of them turned to Violet and Mr. Pritchard.

"We need to take her to the hospital. Sounds like pneumonia. She's also severely dehydrated." They retrieved a stretcher from the ambulance and lifted the old woman out of her recliner and onto it as if she weighed little more than the sheet they were placing her on. She fussed the entire time. She was breathless and sometimes had to stop and cough, and her voice was weak as rainwater, but she did not let this stop her from complaining about them lifting her, how they were lifting her, how they had probably tracked in dirt, how they should be careful with her knickknacks, and would they please shut the door as the air conditioner was running and she couldn't afford to cool the whole neighborhood. At the last minute, she asked for her purse, which Violet found and placed on the side of the stretcher. If complaints could keep her tethered to this earth, Mrs. McCabe had nothing to worry about.

Still, Violet was horrified. She stood back, hand over her mouth, seeing Mrs. McCabe's thin and papery skin, hearing her deep, ratcheting cough, remembering her feverish brow. She knew that in a woman of Mrs. McCabe's years, any one of those—dehydration, cough, fever—could be fatal.

As the ambulance pulled away, Violet sensed a warmth next to her and looked down. Arabella pressed lightly against her side, face tight with distress. Tenderness flooded Violet's heart, and she put her arm around her and gave her a squeeze. "The nice paramedics will take her to the hospital, and they will give her some fluids and some medicine and do everything they can to help her."

She caught Mr. Pritchard looking at her with an unreadable expression. But he did not say anything. He walked over to the door and said, "Guess I'll have to put some plastic over that."

"I'll find a broom and sweep up the glass."

Mr. Pritchard grunted and went out the door to his house. Violet found cleaning supplies in a small closet in the living room. She had swept up all the glass and dumped it in the trash can by the time Mr. Pritchard came back. He stretched a length of clear plastic over the gaping hole and attached it to the window frame with strips of duct tape he tore with his teeth. He paused mid-tear as he spotted Violet rummaging through a drawer in the end table.

"What in holy hell are you doing?" he said, the *rrriippp* of the tape punctuating his question.

"I am looking for a spare key because I may come back in here and check on the place. She has plants, and I'm betting she will hold you and me responsible if they die. And I wouldn't want the food in the refrigerator to spoil."

Another grunt. "Not sure she'll be happy about you snooping around."

"I'm not snooping, and I am not sure she'll be happy about anything."

Mr. Pritchard made a sound that Violet thought may

have been a chuckle. A rusty, unused noise that probably hadn't seen the light of day in years.

"I'm done here. If you need anything else, ask her dad." He pointed the duct tape at Arabella. "I'll be busy."

He took his duct tape and went home.

Violet found a key in a little wooden chest. She tried it in the door, and it worked. "Well, Arabella. This has been an interesting day. Perhaps I should walk you across the street and tell your mother about all the happenings."

4

Violet

June 1969

Caroline handed Violet a glass of iced tea.

"That was certainly eventful," Caroline said after Violet relayed the recent events.

"I'm afraid Arabella might have learned some, um, new words. Mr. Pritchard doesn't seem to be able to distinguish between how to talk in front of adults versus how to talk in front of children."

Caroline waved her hand. "It's nothing she hasn't heard when her father is playing handyman. I'm sure she knows not to repeat the things he said, right, Arabella?"

"Yes, ma'am," Arabella said and then cocked her head. "Does Jesus have a middle name?"

"Pardon?" her mother said.

"Does Jesus have a middle name? Because Mr. Pritchard said 'Jesus H. Christ.'"

Caroline flinched. "Oh, dear. No, that was Mr. Pritchard being, um, creative. Let's forget you heard that, shall we?"

Arabella nodded and went back to her peanut butter and jelly sandwich Caroline had made while Violet talked. In spite of her worry about Mrs. McCabe, Violet managed to make the story of Mr. Pritchard's surly demeanor and his ongoing struggle to deliver a curse-free sentence funny. Caroline had been struggling with a grumpy Baby Allen and completely missed hearing or seeing the ambulance.

"I can't believe all this happened right across the street and I didn't see or hear a thing. Although between being exhausted and dealing with Allen's fussiness lately, the ambulance could have driven right through the house and I might not have noticed."

"They did turn off the siren when they turned down our street if that makes you feel any better," Violet told her.

"It does. A little," Caroline said.

When Violet left a little while later, she pondered if she should visit Mrs. McCabe in the hospital. She didn't seem to have anyone to call. She decided she would stop by the next day, make sure she was OK, and then go back to her hideaway.

Late in the morning the next day, Violet drove to the hospital, stopping on the way to pick up a small bouquet of pink roses and white daisies in a clear glass vase. She strode up to the front desk and asked for Mrs. McCabe's room.

"Would that be Agnes McCabe?" said the woman behind the counter.

"Um, er, yes?" Violet said, although she had no idea what the old lady's first name was. *But how many Mrs. McCabes could there be in the hospital at any given time?*

When she found the room, she also found the right Mrs.

McCabe. She lay in the bed wearing an oxygen mask and a cross look. Her eyes were closed.

Violet perused the room and saw no other bouquets, no gifts, no signs that anyone but Mrs. McCabe and medical staff had been in the room. She tiptoed across the linoleum and gently placed the vase on a bedside table. As she turned to slip out the door, Mrs. McCabe's eyes opened and fastened on her.

"Oh, uh, hi. I brought you some flowers," Violet said. "And I wanted to see how you were doing."

"At," said Mrs. McCabe.

"I'm sorry, what? I didn't understand."

Mrs. McCabe lifted the mask slightly with a shaky hand. "I have a cat. Can you make sure he has food?"

Violet's heart dropped. She had seen no sign of a cat when she was in the house yesterday. Of course, with all the commotion, the cat had probably scurried under a bed. And now the cat had gone twenty-four hours without anyone checking on him.

"Oh, dear. Yes, I will go and check. How are you feeling?"

"Too weak to whip a gnat. But they tell me I'll be all right. Apparently, I have pneumonia. But I'll be fine now. They tell me I should be able to go home in a few days."

"That's good to hear. Hopefully, you will feel better soon."

"It would be hard to feel worse. And you can't get any sleep here. Nurses come in all times of the day and night and poke you and prick you and ask how you are feeling. I tell them not so peachy, and they say I should get some rest. And I say I would if they would just leave me be."

"They are here to make sure you get better, and I guess all the checks and pokes are all about that."

"Or they are all a bunch of sadists."

"Right. Or that." Violet straightened the front of her dress. "Well, I have to go to work now," she said.

"Well, go on with you, then. I didn't ask you to come anyhow."

Violet suppressed a strong urge to roll her eyes.

"Well, I'll be going." She headed for the door.

"Clyde."

Violet stopped. "Begging your pardon?"

"Cat's name is Clyde."

"Oh. Right. Clyde. I will check on him, I promise."

"See that you do."

Violet closed the door behind her. *Holy smokes, no wonder no one comes to visit her.* She squashed the unkind thought but shook her head as she walked down the hospital corridor.

Violet fetched Mrs. McCabe's key from her kitchen counter. She let herself into the house next door, and the sharp smell of cat poo and pee greeted her. *Uh oh,* she thought. *This is not going to be fun.*

She scanned the room but did not see a cat or any cat messes. She went through the rest of the house and found food dishes and a litter box in a tiny laundry room. The water dish held a trace of water, but the food dish was empty. Clay pellets lay scattered about the floor, and the box itself was obviously well used. Hopefully, Clyde was not too picky about a clean box and had continued to use it rather than go somewhere else. After cleaning the litter box, she rummaged around the cabinets and found a can of air freshener, which she sprayed liberally around the small room and in the hall.

She located the cat food in a kitchen cabinet. She also spotted a loaf of bread, which she inspected for mold and stuck in the freezer when she found none. She opened a can of food with an opener, piercing the metal with a click. A ball of fur flew into the kitchen and stopped a few feet from her. The cat crouched and stared at her with unwavering, narrowed green eyes.

"Well. I guess you decided a stranger with food is not such a stranger after all."

Clyde gave a low vibrato meow but did not come closer. He was sturdily built with a large head and tattered ears. Between his scarred face and squinty eyes, he resembled a grizzled, mistrustful old man. She reached down to pet him, but he cringed, so she pulled her hand back. "Understood. No touching."

"For a big guy, you aren't a very tough guy. Of course, I imagine living with Mrs. McCabe would wear anyone down. Come get your food." She carried the can to the laundry room and forked the food into his bowl, but Clyde didn't move. She stepped into the hallway, and he crept forward, scrutinizing her warily. Realizing he wasn't going to eat with her standing guard, she refilled his water bowl as he slunk back and crouched, waiting.

"Don't worry. I am almost done so you can have your dinner in peace." She spritzed a little more air freshener around the trailer. She turned to say goodbye to Clyde, but he had vanished, his dish licked clean. "Well, Clyde, wherever you went, thanks for not going outside the litter box. I'll see you later tonight."

Clyde declined to comment.

The next day, Violet decided she should visit Mrs. McCabe and let her know the cat was fine. Which is how she found herself standing in the hallway five feet or so from Mrs. McCabe's door, this time with a *Life* magazine and a chocolate bar, trying to will herself to go in and get it over with.

A nurse came up to her and said, "Are you a relative?" She cocked her head toward Mrs. McCabe's door.

"Oh, no, I'm just a neighbor."

"Oh." The nurse's smile faded. "We were hoping you were a relative or friend. You're the only visitor who's been here."

"I really don't know her well." Violet remembered the bare room, bereft of any evidence that someone cared.

"She told us she had no next of kin. No kids, or nieces or nephews. No husband. But we thought maybe she had somebody in her life."

"I couldn't say. I know she lives alone."

"It's nice of you to visit. Very kind." The nurse patted her arm. Was it? Was it kind? With her resentment bubbling over about having to do this, Violet did not feel kind at all.

The nurse returned to her duties, and Violet steeled herself for hers. She squared her shoulders, stepped forward, and pushed the door open.

Mrs. McCabe sat upright in the hospital bed. The oxygen mask was gone. Her skin still looked paper-thin, and the rest of her seemed as slender and breakable as a winter twig. But her color was a little better, a little rosier. She turned to the door.

"Oh. It's you."

"Nice to see you, too, Mrs. McCabe."

The old woman remained unfazed. "How is Clyde?"

"He is doing fine. I checked on him twice yesterday, and once today."

"He's eating?"

"Yes, he is."

"He's a bit timid, you know. He was a tomcat when I found him. Beat-up and skittish, he was. He looks like a brute, but personally, I don't think he had it in him to be a successful tom, up against all the other cats. So I took him in. He still takes off like a shot at loud or sudden noises."

"I've noticed that."

"He's a good cat though. Took him a couple of months before he let me pet him. Now he sits on my lap." Mrs. McCabe's voice softened as she spoke about the cat, and wait! Were her lips threatening to smile?

"Well, he's doing fine," Violet said. "Seems lonely, but not so much that I can pet him."

Oh, heavenly stars, Mrs. McCabe was chuckling. Violet stifled an urge to shake her head and rub her eyes.

"They say they are letting me out tomorrow. I've had IV antibiotics and IV liquids and IV this and IV that. Something must be working because I'm feeling better."

"I'm happy to hear that." A thought popped into Violet's head, and she wished with all her heart it hadn't. She took a deep breath. "Do you have a ride home?"

"Not unless they let me drive the ambulance they brought me in."

"If you get out in the morning or early afternoon, I can drive you."

"If they keep me any longer than that, they might as well just send me home in a pine box. The food here will either kill you or drive you straight to recovery so you can get away from it. I've about had my fill of cold, congealed mystery food and jello. I can't tell if I am eating mashed potatoes or a meat patty."

"That sounds awful."

"What have you got there?" Mrs. McCabe waved a bony hand at Violet.

"Oh! Um, here's a *Life* magazine. And a chocolate bar. I thought if you were feeling better, you might want a little treat."

"I hate chocolate. You can keep that. You want to make me happy, bring me a big, fluffy biscuit with butter. But I'll take the magazine."

With great self-control, she managed to not slap the magazine on the little rolling table that floated over Mrs. McCabe's lap. Instead, she placed it with exaggerated care on its laminate surface. And what kind of person hates chocolate?

"Was there anything else?"

"No. No, that's it. I guess I will be going."

"I need your number."

"Excuse me?"

"For tomorrow."

"Oh. Yes. Well. I don't have a phone yet. I will come by in the morning and see how things are going."

"What kind of young person are you? I thought all young people had phones and fancy stereos. I do hear your music blaring all day long. If you can call that music."

"I see there is nothing wrong with your hearing."

"I may be older than dirt to a little young thing like you, but that doesn't mean I don't have all my faculties."

"Duly noted."

Violet turned and stalked into the corridor, resisting the urge to slam the hospital door. Mainly because she thought it would probably bother the other patients more than it would Mrs. McCabe.

She walked to the nurses' station, grinding her teeth. The nurse she had spoken to earlier glanced up. Then grinned.

"I see you've spent some time with Mrs. McCrab."

Violet couldn't help but laugh and felt her ill will dissipate. A little, anyway.

"I shouldn't have said that, but we've all been on the receiving end of her lovely disposition. She's, um, forceful." She held her hand out to Violet. "I'm Frances."

"I'm Violet Wentworth. And I'm certainly not going to report you. I'm glad to hear it's not just me. And I apparently am not in my right mind because I volunteered to drive her home. I have a car, but no phone. Do you have any idea when she'll be discharged?"

"We usually do discharges before noon. There can be extenuating circumstances, but I don't foresee any in Mrs. McCabe's case. In fact, I think I can say that the staff will be happy to ensure her quick discharge. So let's say around ten, after morning rounds."

"Great. I will be here."

The nurse smiled at her. "Good luck. This should earn you a special place in heaven."

"Well, not if I end up strangling her. Probably would nullify that."

"That probably would, indeed."

In the afternoon, Arabella popped over. Violet asked her if she wanted to help her feed Clyde. Arabella's eyes lit up.

"I would love to! I am very good with animals."

Violet was doubtful. In her experience with her nephews and nieces, children of Arabella's age were rarely good with animals. They wanted to hold them and hug them like baby dolls. However, since she couldn't even touch Clyde, she suspected this wouldn't be a problem.

"Clyde is quite skittish."

"What is 'skittish'?"

"Shy. Kind of afraid. From what Mrs. McCabe told me, his life out on his own wasn't a happy one. So you might not be able to pet him. And certainly not hold him. That could end badly."

"OK," Arabella said absently. Violet hoped she was listening.

As they walked across the yards, Violet stopped short. Arabella looked up at her.

"What is it?"

Violet pointed. The bushes that had been threatening to take over Mrs. McCabe's trailer had been trimmed into neat rectangles.

"Well, I'll be d—" Violet cut her eyes at Arabella and cleared her throat. "Um, darned."

"Do you think Mr. Pritchard did this?"

Violet blinked. Several times. But the image in front of her did not change. "I don't know who else would have done it. Not your dad?"

Arabella shook her head.

"Well. Huh."

Inside, Violet brought the food dishes to the kitchen, hoping Clyde would eat in there while she cleaned the litter in the laundry room. As soon as she punctured the top of the can with the can opener, Clyde came running, once again nearly skidding to a halt when he saw strangers. Violet handed the can to Arabella.

"Here, kitty, kitty. It's OK. I am here to feed you and take care of you," Arabella said and scraped the food into the dish. The cat stared, and Arabella tapped the dish with the fork. "Come on, Clyde. Here's your dinner!"

"I will leave you two alone while I go clean the kitty litter. Remember, don't try to pick him up. Wouldn't want to come back and find you shredded."

"I'll be OK."

Violet went into the small laundry room and scooped the waste into a bag, trying to hold her breath. She sprayed air freshener, making a note that next time she should spray first and scoop second. She returned to the kitchen and found the cat crouched, eating contentedly and purring like a motorboat while Arabella stroked his back gently. As Violet approached, Arabella grinned at her, eyes shining. Just for that look, Violet would forgive Clyde's traitorous feline heart. But really. She'd fed him several meals and had yet to touch him. Rotten cat.

"See? He likes me."

"I do see that," Violet said dryly. Violet didn't bother to try to pet him. She didn't want to be humiliated in front of Arabella. As she watched, a knock on the door sent the cat flying down the hall.

Violet and Arabella exchanged looks, wondering who in the world would be knocking at Mrs. McCabe's door. Violet peered out through the plastic-covered sidelight. A hulking figure loomed on the other side.

She opened the door. "Mr. Pritchard. What can I do for you?"

He held a toolbox. "I'm here to fix the window."

Violet raised her eyebrows. "But I thought—"

"Had a free minute." His tone forbade any questions.

Violet stepped back to allow him entry.

Arabella hopped over to them, apparently deciding Clyde would not be coming back out with all the ruckus.

"You're not so bad," she said to Mr. Pritchard, watching as he put his toolbox on the floor and began to strip off the tape and plastic.

"What?"

"People say you're mean and scary. But you're not really."

"Yes, I am."

"No, you're not."

"I will be if you don't let me do my work."

"Come on, Arabella. It's time to go anyway," Violet said.

"I'll lock up here when I'm done," Mr. Pritchard said, unscrewing the plastic window frame.

"OK. I'll leave you to it."

They walked out and stood in the driveway for a minute. Violet turned back for a last glance at Mrs. McCabe's door and shook her head. "I'll be coming back one more time in the morning," she said. "After that, I'll be bringing Mrs. McCabe home. So if you want to help with Clyde tomorrow, be at my house at eight."

"Will do!" Arabella saluted smartly.

"Not too early for you?"

"Nope! Mama says I am an early bird."

"I'll see you tomorrow, Early Bird."

5

Violet

June 1969

The next morning, Violet awoke, filled with both dread and relief: dread that she would have to deal with the irascible Mrs. McCabe for a bit longer, and relief that by afternoon, she could, in good conscience, say goodbye and go back to being nodding neighbors. She had just sat down with a muffin and a mug of coffee when Arabella arrived at eight o'clock on the dot. Violet wondered if she had been at her house watching the second hand tick its way to the appointed time. Did she even know how to tell time? What age did you learn that? Well, it probably didn't matter with Arabella because Violet had found she knew a lot of things Violet didn't think other seven-year-olds knew.

Having turned down a muffin and a beverage, Arabella chatted as Violet ate and sipped her coffee. Violet made a mental note that if she ever invited Arabella over in the morning again to give herself fifteen minutes for her coffee before the little girl was due. Still groggy from working late and getting up early, Violet had trouble tracking Arabella's ramblings. She talked about Lassie and her grandmother and her cousin who worked in a bakery and dressing up for Easter, but Violet had no idea if any of the topics were related. Violet finished her muffin, cleaned her dishes, and walked with the little girl—who was still talking—to Mrs. McCabe's. Arabella fed Clyde and Violet took care of his litter. While he and Arabella exchanged confidences, Violet checked the fridge, poured out the milk, and decided she would pick up a few staples before she went to the hospital. *Milk and more bread,* she thought as she took the half loaf out of the freezer. *Maybe some pimento cheese or something else to make a sandwich with.*

She and Arabella parted ways, and, when Violet returned later, she brought with her eggs, a tub of pimento cheese, milk, bread, ham. Some bananas. Not too much, but enough to tide Mrs. McCabe over until she could get back on her feet and drive her old Chrysler to the store herself. As she put away her purchases, she boiled water for iced tea. Once she steeped the tea bags and added sugar and ice, it was time to go fetch the old woman herself. She told herself to not let Mrs. McCabe get under her skin. She should feel empathy for her, not resent her.

Frances greeted Violet as she exited the elevator.

"Good morning! She's discharged and ready to go." The nurse took hold of the handles of a wheelchair that had been parked next to the nurses' station and steered it into Mrs. McCabe's room.

"I had pneumonia, not broken legs," Mrs. McCabe said, eyes narrowing.

"I am well aware, Mrs. McCabe. But you might be a little weak, so we are here to help," Frances said with exaggerated patience.

"You've 'helped' me all day and all night until I am exhausted. I can't wait to get home to my own bed."

"We also can't wait, Mrs. McCabe."

Violet met Frances' eye over the old woman's head. Frances winked.

They got to Violet's car, and Mrs. McCabe climbed into the passenger seat, waving away any further assistance. Frances placed Mrs. McCabe's purse and a paper bag of medicine in the footwell behind her.

"She will need you to check on her and make sure she is taking her medications and not having a relapse," Frances said. "Older folks tend to be forgetful."

Violet had been walking around the car, and she stopped, turning to stare at the nurse over the roof.

"I beg your pardon, but what did you say?"

"If she forgets to take her medicine, she will end up back here in no time."

"But I hardly even know her." She realized she sounded petulant, but she had thought this was the conclusion of her involvement with Mrs. McCabe. She saw her plan of taking some time being away from other people evaporating like rain in a desert.

"I do hate to put this on you, but she has no one else. And it's only for a week."

Violet sighed. "I guess I can put on my armor and check on her. I am sure it will help build my character."

"That's the spirit." Frances started to go but stopped. "And Miss Wentworth? Good luck."

Violet opened the door.

"Hurry up, will you? It's hot as blazes in here. Are you trying to kill me?" came the querulous voice from inside the car.

"Thanks. I am sure I will need it," she said to Frances before sliding behind the wheel.

Violet drove with care, obeying the speed limit and taking turns slowly, worried that any deviation from the law would invite Mrs. McCabe's criticism. But Mrs. McCabe still offered her helpful advice.

"You drive any slower, you might as well swing by the funeral parlor and just drop me off. Save you a trip."

"Look out for that truck. I can tell he's an idiot just by looking at him."

"Good Lord, what are those girls wearing?"

The last comment came as Violet turned off the highway into their neighborhood and they passed three teenagers walking down the street. Mrs. McCabe turned her head to watch them in their miniskirts and shorts, long hair swinging in the sun.

"If those dresses get any shorter, they might as well not even wear them."

Violet hmmed and uh-huhed in answer to each comment. She pulled into Mrs. McCabe's driveway. When she got out, the heat pressed down on her like a hot iron. She rounded the car to help Mrs. McCabe, but she found the elderly lady staring, confounded. Violet followed her gaze.

"What happened to my hedges?"

"I can honestly say I don't know."

Mrs. McCabe turned to glare at her. "You don't know? Aren't you supposed to be watching out for my place?"

"Yes, but it's not like someone broke in and burgled it. Someone trimmed your hedges and didn't leave a note."

"Hmph." Mrs. McCabe started to swing her legs around, and Violet offered her arm to help her out of the car.

"Did the same burglar fix my window?" Mrs. McCabe said as they neared the porch.

"That I can say was Mr. Pritchard."

"Huh. You don't say. You think he did the hedges?"

"He didn't say, and I didn't ask."

"I don't blame you for that."

Violet helped Mrs. McCabe inside and settled her in her recliner with a glass of iced tea on the table beside her. Clyde came out, and Violet thought the old rascal seemed happy to see his owner. He walked instead of slunk, and he pointed his ears forward rather than flattened against his skull. He strutted over to Mrs. McCabe and rubbed his face against her legs, his tail flicking to and fro. Mrs. McCabe chuckled, reaching down to scratch his whiskers.

"There's a good boy," Mrs. McCabe cooed. She actually cooed. Violet felt she had fallen into some alternate universe.

"Can I do anything for you?"

Mrs. McCabe's face fell into its habitual scowl. "No. I'm fine. You don't need to check on me either. I may be old, but I have all my faculties."

"I am sure you do, but I promised the nurse I would check on you, so you can count on seeing me twice a day."

"Oh, yippee."

Violet closed her eyes and silently counted to ten.

"What in tarnation is that?"

Violet opened her eyes, and her gaze followed Mrs. McCabe's pointing finger.

"It's a bunch of bananas, Mrs. McCabe."

"I know that. But what's it doing here?"

"I bought them so you would have some food in the house. So you can rest and make a quick recovery."

"I didn't ask you to do that."

"No, you didn't."

"I'm not paying for them."

"No, you don't have to."

"OK, then."

"OK." Violet moved towards the door. "Would you like a sandwich before I go? You should probably eat something."

"What kind of sandwich?"

"Well, I didn't know what you liked, so I bought ham and pimento cheese. I can make you either one of those."

"You bought me ham and pimento cheese, huh? Well. I haven't had a pimento cheese sandwich in a month of Sundays. I think I'll have that."

Violet fixed the sandwich, set it on a plate, grabbed a paper napkin, and placed the whole shebang on the table next to Mrs. McCabe. "If that's all you need, I'll be going. I will see you later. A little before suppertime, as I have to go to work tonight."

"I'm tellin' ya, I can look after myself."

"I hear you, but I am not having you falling back sick on my conscience. So I will be back."

And without waiting for the sharp retort she suspected was coming, she let herself out the door. As she did, she heard the creak and thunk of the recliner footrest being released.

★

Violet decided she needed to see a friendly face, so she veered away from her house and headed to the Fitzgeralds. She knocked, and Arabella answered.

"Hi, Miss Violet!"

Violet's irritation eased a little. "Hi yourself, Miss Arabella."

Caroline appeared behind her daughter.

"Violet! Come on in!"

They drank iced tea and ate shortbread cookies while Violet related her morning with Mrs. McCabe. By the time she finished, she was laughing about it.

"The woman is completely incapable of saying thank you or please or anything gracious. Perhaps I will go way out of my way and be extra, extra nice and see how far I can go before she says thank you."

"Maybe if those words pass her lips, she will melt like the witch in *The Wizard of Oz*." The two women laughed. "I would offer to help . . ." Caroline continued as she poured more tea in her glass.

"No, no. I think having a newborn is a fine excuse. Take it and run!"

"I think I will, though I do feel bad for you."

"Oh, and I don't know if Arabella told you, but Mr. Pritchard came by and fixed the window he broke when we found her."

"Arabella did tell me. Do you think he's the one who trimmed her hedges?"

"I think so. I didn't before, but since he came and fixed the window, I think it might have been him. I take it you didn't see him doing it, did you?"

Caroline shook her head. "No, but then, remember, I am the one who missed the ambulance coming."

Violet shrugged and glanced at the clock. "It's about time for me to get ready for work. If you don't mind, I may pop over now and again for a dose of normal."

"Absolutely! And you can update me on your challenge of pushing Mrs. McCabe to the brink of gratitude."

"Will do!"

Violet pulled on her waitress uniform, and she gave herself a pep talk. *Only seven days,* she told herself, but she wondered how she was going to put up with the elderly woman for that long. In the abstract, she felt guilty for not spending more time with her. She must be lonely, living alone with no friends or family coming to see her. In actuality, Mrs. McCabe's string of complaints and sharp retorts made her grind her teeth. She wasn't looking forward to experiencing that on a daily basis. Twice daily. She checked her appearance in the mirror and fixed one of the buttons that marched up her pale pink dress, ending at the white collar. Sighed. Squared her shoulders. And headed out the door to Mrs. McCabe's.

She knocked.

"I guess that's you, whatever your name is, from next door," Mrs. McCabe called. Her voice certainly sounded stronger. "And guess you're going to come in, no matter what."

Violet opened the door to find Mrs. McCabe ensconced in her chair, the TV on and tuned to a soap opera. A blonde woman confronted a dark-haired man about his seeing another woman.

"My name is Violet. I introduced myself the day we found you sick, but I guess in the hustle and bustle, it was easy to miss." No response. "Yes. Well. I am going to clean Clyde's litter box so you don't have to."

"That's not necessary."

"As the nurse said, you might be a little weak."

"Fine."

Violet performed the task as quickly as possible and returned to the kitchen. "I am going to lay out your medicine. Is there anything else you need? Would you like for me to make you a sandwich?"

"I could do with a sandwich, but I could make it myself."

"I think you should take it easy until you get your strength back. I can make one for you. Ham, or pimento cheese?"

"Well, if you insist. I'll take ham. With mayonnaise. I like lots of mayonnaise."

"Coming right up." Violet went into the kitchen and washed her hands, and pulled out the things she needed to make the sandwich. An odd little warmth bloomed in her chest, and she paused in her sandwich making, considering it. Good Lord. Was that . . . could that be a prickle of enjoyment?

She took the sandwich to Mrs. McCabe. The woman regarded it skeptically, then looked up at Violet. "Did you wash your hands?"

And just like that, Mrs. McCabe squashed the little thrill. "Yes, Mrs. McCabe, I washed my hands."

"Good." Pause. "Are you going to stand there and watch me eat?"

"No, Mrs. McCabe. Is there anything else you need? I can bring you an iced tea."

"Yes, I would like that."

Violet filled a glass with ice and tea and brought it to the living room. "Anything else?"

"No."

"Well, all righty then. I am heading off to work now. Take your medicine at six. And don't forget, you are supposed to take it with food, so be sure to eat a little something or maybe drink a glass of milk."

"Yes. Fine." She sounded like a petulant child rather than a woman who was nearly eighty.

"Right. I'll be off," Violet said, but Mrs. McCabe was lost in her world of ham and mayonnaise and the cheating antics of the dark-haired man on TV.

Violet had the next day off. When she set out for Mrs. McCabe's, Arabella, who had been playing in her yard, jumped up and ran over. Violet remembered the speeding gray car she saw from time to time and shuddered.

"Do you look for cars when you cross the street?"

"I do. I promise."

"Just making sure. I wouldn't want you to get hurt."

"What are you doing?"

"I am getting ready to go check on our lovely friend Mrs. McCabe."

"Can I come?"

Violet hesitated. Would Mrs. McCabe scold her for bringing a child into her house or appreciate the company?

"Hmm. You know she's pretty grumpy, right? I wouldn't want her to hurt your feelings."

"I know. It's OK. Mama says I have thick skin, which means I don't let things bother me too much."

"Well, a thick skin might come in handy."

Violet knocked and heard the old woman call, "Come in." She opened the door in time to hear the old lady mumbling, "Only a little less fussy than those nurses at the hospital." Violet and Arabella exchanged looks, and Violet widened her eyes as though to say, "I told you so." Arabella covered her mouth, stifling a giggle. The humor pushed aside the irritation, and Violet sent up a silent prayer of thanks for Arabella's affable nature.

Mrs. McCabe stood in the kitchen, washing a plate.

"I brought our little neighbor from across the street. This is Arabella."

"What for? And I know her name."

"Actually, Mrs. McCabe, she is the one who told us you might need help. She noticed your mail piling up in your mailbox. Also, she's helped me feed Clyde."

"Did she now?"

"She did. It's good to see you up and about. You took your morning medicine?"

"I did, and I do not appreciate being treated like a child."

Arabella saved Violet from striking back with her own sharp response. "Me, either! It is very annoying when people think you can't do something when you can."

Mrs. McCabe dried her hands on a dish towel and turned to Arabella. "You are darn tootin'." She shuffled to the living room, holding on to the counters as she went. The house smelled of toast and coffee.

"So you had your breakfast?"

"I did."

"Would you like me to clean Clyde's litter box again?"

Mrs. McCabe paused, then nodded briefly.

Violet headed to the laundry room but listened carefully

in case she needed to rescue Arabella from Mrs. McCabe's biting tongue.

Arabella clapped her hands in delight. "I love Clyde! Where is he?"

"Well, he's certainly not going to come out if you're making such a ruckus."

"May I call him?"

"You can try."

She called his name, then, "Here, kitty, kitty." She turned to Mrs. McCabe. "That's how my mama calls our cat."

"Does it work?"

"Sometimes. My mama says cats are very finicky and will come when they want, not when you want."

"Well, I can't argue with that."

Just as Violet finished the litter, she spotted the big gray tabby sauntering by on his way into the living room. He brushed against Mrs. McCabe's legs. Arabella put out a hand, and he sniffed it tentatively, then rubbed the side of his face against it. She stroked him along his neck, and his rumbling purr filled the room.

"Why did you name him Clyde?"

"When I found him, he was all beat-up, scratched, and bleeding. I thought he looked like Bonnie and Clyde after they got shot up. You probably don't know about them, but they were bank robbers back in the day. Anyway, I caught him—he didn't really want to be caught, but he was weak as rainwater and couldn't object too much. I wrapped him in a towel and took him to the vet, who patched him up and kept him for a few days, then called me and said if I didn't take him back, they'd have to give him to the pound. And you know what that means."

"No, I don't," Arabella said. Violet winced, worrying about how Mrs. McCabe would explain that.

"Oh. Er, um, well, they can't keep all the animals they find, and they can't turn them loose." Mrs. McCabe stopped talking, and Violet thought she and the old woman might be on the same page about something for once.

"So what do they do?"

"Oh, dear. Well, they put them down."

"What does that mean?"

"Well, they put them to sleep. In a way where they don't wake up."

"You mean like dead?"

"Yes, I mean like dead. So let's get back to Clyde," Mrs. McCabe said, her words rushing out as if to run away from the topic at hand. "I didn't really want a cat, but I couldn't live with myself if I saved his old hide and then they just went and euthanized him. So I went and got him, and he's been here ever since."

"What does youth-anize mean?"

"It's a fancy way of saying put to sleep."

"Oh. It's a good thing you got him. How long ago was that?"

"Oh, about five years ago or so, now. Have no idea how old he is. But we get along pretty well, old Clyde and me. Neither one of us has much use for the world outside, so we just stay here."

"Aren't you lonely?"

Violet flinched at Arabella's direct question, but Mrs. McCabe did not bat an eye.

"No. I'm old and done with all that nonsense."

"But isn't it nice to have someone to talk to?"

"I have Clyde."

"I mean someone who can talk back. Ask you questions and stuff."

"Sounds like too much fuss and bother, if you ask me."

Arabella nodded, not at all put out by this answer. She sat on the sofa nearest the old woman and took in her surroundings. "You have a lot of neat things. Are they all special to you?"

Mrs. McCabe looked around as if she had forgotten all her knickknacks, and a ghost of a smile played around her lips. "Many of them are. Things I picked up here and there. Things people gave me."

Arabella held up a miniature globe on a pewter stand. "What about this? Was this something you bought? Or something someone gave you?"

Mrs. McCabe took the globe from her and gave the tiny planet a spin with one wrinkled, crooked finger. And she smiled.

"We bought that at the Chicago World's Fair. Oh, what a time that was." She stared at the wall of her little trailer in the middle of South Carolina, but she was seeing well beyond it, into a world she had left behind.

"I like that picture," Arabella said, bringing Mrs. McCabe back to the present. "Is that something you bought, or did someone give it to you?"

Arabella pointed to a framed print of Norman Rockwell's *Happy Birthday, Miss Jones*, which portrayed a prim teacher in a gray skirt and white blouse standing in front of a blackboard covered in birthday wishes drawn in childish scrawls. The picture hung on the wall next to Mrs. McCabe's chair.

Violet watched Mrs. McCabe's face change, a sad

tenderness crossing her wrinkled features. "That was neither bought nor given. At least not to me. My daughter was a school teacher, and her class gave her that the last year she taught."

Violet sensed that simple statement covered a large wound. She stepped forward to steer Arabella in another direction, but Arabella steered herself.

"Oh! I want to be a teacher when I grow up! I sometimes play teacher. I use my stuffed animals as students because no one else will sit and do what I tell them." Her stream of words filled the trailer. Mrs. McCabe's eyes met Violet's over the little girl's head. What did her expression say? Had she noticed Violet was going to intervene? She seemed . . . softer. Violet smiled at her. Mrs. McCabe gave her a tiny, inscrutable nod back.

As the week passed, Arabella continued to join Violet on her morning visits to Mrs. McCabe. She would call Clyde, and the cat would come out of hiding, and the old woman and the little girl would pet him. He rewarded their attention with a reverberating purr that all but rattled the windows. On the second such visit, Violet ventured to set out some milk, tea, and cookies, and they had a snack together. At Arabella's innocent questioning, Mrs. McCabe dropped more tidbits about her history. Violet wondered what had happened to the husband, son, and daughter who cropped up in her answers, but she didn't dare ask. She didn't insinuate herself at all in the conversations except to ease a plate of cookies towards the two on the little table next to Mrs. McCabe's chair. She found herself enjoying the stories Mrs. McCabe told of her life, and she tried hard to picture her as a young woman—a woman of the world, apparently, as she had not only traveled to Chicago, but to Europe as well.

If Violet had reservations about pressing Mrs. McCabe for details, Arabella did not.

"You've been to England? And France?" she asked, wide-eyed.

"Indeed, I have. And Switzerland. And Italy."

"I am always playing castle and knights and queens and stuff. I would love to see a real castle. Have you seen a real castle?"

"We did take a tour once. It was a lovely place, but I couldn't help but think how drafty and cold it must have been. All those stone walls and no heating. And England is quite cold and damp much of the time."

"What is your favorite thing you've seen?" Arabella asked.

"Oh, goodness. That is a very hard question for a woman who has lived almost eighty years. The Swiss mountains will take your breath away. They are simply majestic. And Venice is something to see. That is a city with canals in place of streets. People use boats to get around. Now Greece . . . Greece is like heaven on earth. There is nothing like the light and the sun and the water there. Every day and every view looked like a painting. But . . ." she said, leaning forward and lowering her voice a little. "But one of my favorite places is Stonehenge. Such an ancient, spooky place. I found it quite fascinating that ancient humans could build such a thing. There are these giant stones sitting on a vast plain, and you can feel the weight of history bearing down on you. I don't know quite how to describe it. It was quite, well, ethereal. I felt something there, a connection to all the hundreds and hundreds of years that had gone before."

"What is Stonehenge?" Arabella asked.

"Oh, goodness. It's time for a bit of a history lesson. Let me see." Mrs. McCabe scooted to the edge of her chair and used the arms to push herself to a standing position. She hobbled over to a bookcase. Violet thought that she looked a little stronger than she had the day before. A good sign. Mrs. McCabe pulled a brown photo album off a shelf and sat next to Arabella on the sofa.

"Here we go. This is our trip to England back in 1927. What a good year that was. We had left the First World War behind us, and the Depression had not yet reared its ugly head. Flynn, the kids, and I went to England. When Flynn could get away from work, we went sightseeing all over the countryside. One of those day trips was to Stonehenge." She settled back in her chair and opened the album, flipping a few pages. Violet leaned over to see a black-and-white photo of a young and pretty Mrs. McCabe with two children and a slightly older man with a cane. The family sat on one of the Stonehenge rocks, smiling at the camera. The girl leaned into Mrs. McCabe, who had her arm around her. The boy had his hands on his hips in a jaunty pose. All wore what would now be deemed formal clothes: Mr. McCabe in a hat and overcoat, and Mrs. McCabe in a cloche hat adorned with a wide, dark ribbon that appeared to match her knee-length coat. She carried a small cloth bag on a chain with her free hand.

Violet peeked over. "Mrs. McCabe! You were quite the stunner!"

Mrs. McCabe beamed. "I was a looker. Turned heads

everywhere we went, even here, when I was in my thirties. And to think I thought I was getting old then. Goodness."

"So you were going to tell me about Stonehenge," Arabella reminded her.

"Yes, that's right." Mrs. McCabe turned the page and pointed to a photo that showed the famous ring of stones from afar. "These stones were placed here by people living in 2,000 or 3,000 BC. That is over 4,000 years ago. And they didn't have big cranes to lift them, so it was quite a feat."

"What is it? Was it like a house or something? An old castle?" Arabella asked, peering at the photo.

"They think it was some sort of structure for astronomy or worship of their gods. It lines up with the sunset on the winter solstice—that's the shortest day and longest night of the year. And it also lines up with the sunrise on the summer solstice—the longest day and shortest night. But anyway, when we went, the sky was stormy and the wind was blowing and it felt . . . otherworldly. I am not explaining it very well, but it left such an impression on me. I can still picture that day like it was yesterday. Even my husband Flynn said he felt something there. And he was not a fanciful man. Very practical, Flynn was."

"So these are your children?"

Violet wondered if she should step in, but Mrs. McCabe nodded slowly.

"They are indeed. This is my son, Willis. And my daughter, Irina."

"He's handsome. And she is really pretty. I like her dress." Arabella held the album close to her face as she studied the photo.

"Why, thank you, Arabella. They were good children,

for the most part. Sometimes fought, sometimes got into mischief, but overall, good children."

"Where are your children now, Mrs. McCabe?" Arabella asked.

"Well, that is kind of a sad story. Are you sure you want to hear it?" Arabella nodded solemnly. "Both my children died."

Arabella appeared stricken. "Oh! That's terrible!"

"It is. They did live to be adults, so that's one consolation. Willis was forty-one, and Irina forty-five. Now that may sound old to a youngster like you, but when you're all grown up, it is way too young to die. But I am glad I had them for the years that I did."

"I am really sorry, Mrs. McCabe. My mama told me to say that when people lost someone they loved, but I don't understand why."

Mrs. McCabe smiled. "You say it to let the person know you feel bad for them and you sympathize."

Arabella brightened. "Oh! I get it! I kept thinking how I have to say I am sorry when I misbehave or don't do my chores, but that's got nothing to do with when people die. But it's like two meanings for the same word."

"Yes, but if you think about it, they are closely related. When you don't do your chores, you may be sorry you got in trouble, but your mother wants you to be sorry you didn't do the right thing. So it's about your feelings. Same thing when someone dies. You feel bad not because you did anything, but because someone else is feeling so bad. Does that make sense?"

Arabella nodded. "It does. You are really good at explaining things."

"Thank you, Arabella. Maybe you are just easy to talk to."

Violet had a feeling Mrs. McCabe had the right end of the stick on that one. She rose from her chair. "I think it's time we let Mrs. McCabe rest. She is supposed to be recuperating. Do you need something for dinner?"

Mrs. McCabe looked almost shy. "I would really like pizza."

"Pizza?" Violet said, the answer taking her by surprise.

"I love pizza!" Arabella said. "We get it as a treat sometimes."

"I love pizza, too," Mrs. McCabe said, leaning towards Arabella conspiratorially. "It's quite a marvelous invention."

"I'll bring you a pizza," Violet said. "What do you like on it?"

"Pepperoni and mushroom."

Arabella made a face. "Well, now you've just ruined it. Mushroom! You know that's a fungus, right? And something that is a fungus cannot be good for you."

Mrs. McCabe grinned at her. "Every once in a while, an old lady is allowed to have things that aren't good for her."

"Then you should choose cake or potato chips. Not mushrooms."

"I'll keep that in mind for next time."

6

Mrs. McCabe

June 1969

The wax and wane of the mail truck engine tugged Mrs. McCabe out of the pages of her *Reader's Digest*, where she was engrossed in an article about Russia and the Cold War. Earlier that morning, she had gone on her weekly outing to the beauty shop and grocery store. Two weeks had passed since she had come home from the hospital, and she was feeling almost like her old self. At the sound of the mail truck, she set the periodical aside and scooted to the end of her overstuffed recliner. As she stood, her joints creaked and popped—a symphony of old age. She slowly shuffled to the door, giving her knees and hips a chance to start working again. Everything always stiffened up when she sat too long. Like the Tin Man in *The Wizard of Oz*. If only an oilcan would work on her. She stepped out the door and into the late morning sunshine, glancing up at the broad arc of blue sky. The air vibrated with birdsong and was embroidered with the sweet scent of honeysuckle.

She shambled down the driveway, her gait smoothing as her joints loosened up. She remembered people back in her youth saying that getting old was better than the alternative, but Mrs. McCabe didn't always agree with that. For one thing, getting old hurt. No one had warned her that her body would protest so much about moving. And not moving made the aches and pains worse. You couldn't win. For another thing, she had lost too much in the past for her to enjoy the present. She drifted from one day to the next, getting mild satisfaction from her soaps, the catalogs that came in the mail, and Clyde. She enjoyed her weekly trip to the beauty parlor where she could sit quietly in the hair-spray-and-gossip-infused air and savor some undemanding attention. And she didn't really mind going to the grocery store. Her life was OK. Not the greatest, but she hadn't the energy anymore to work at making it better. She didn't see the point.

When she was halfway to the mailbox, the roar of an accelerating car reached her ears. Off to her right, that damn kid was flying down the road, although to what purpose, Mrs. McCabe could not fathom. He would just have to slow down at the sharp turn at the end. Plus, she was the only one around to see him, and she was completely unimpressed with his big engine and bigger noise. His gray car kicked up a cloud of reddish-brown dirt that hung in the still air like a shimmering curtain. Mrs. McCabe took a handkerchief out of her cardigan pocket and held it over the lower half of her face in preparation for the billowing dust she would encounter when she got to the mailbox. If she were younger, she might have retreated to the house, but dammit, she had made it this far, and she'd be damned if she wanted to do this all over again. She stood still, glaring as the car went past, unaware that her ferocity lost itself behind the little square of cloth. She followed the car's progress as it careened down the street, then screeched its brakes to make the turn. As it fishtailed around the corner, a brown blur caught her eye. She shouted—an involuntary cry that was part warning and part scream. But before her yell died down, Mr. Pritchard's brindle dog lay in the road. Mrs. McCabe did not hear Violet's screen door slam, nor did she hear her calling her until she felt her hand on her arm.

"Mrs. McCabe! Are you OK?"

"No! I mean, I am fine, but that poor dog." She pointed, and Violet gasped as she glimpsed the limp form lying prone on the far side of Mr. Pritchard's lawn. Mrs. McCabe tramped towards the body, crossing from her property to Mr. Pritchard's. Violet reached out a hand to stop her, but let it drop and, instead, walked with her.

It would be easy to think the dog was simply asleep, except that he lay in the road and had a small trail of blood trickling from his open mouth. Mrs. McCabe remembered his vicious barks from earlier encounters and watched as Violet approached him cautiously. She put a tentative hand to his chest, but her caution was unnecessary. She glanced up at Mrs. McCabe and shook her head.

"Oh dear, oh dear. Oh, you poor dog," Mrs. McCabe said. "We can't leave him here in the road." She looked up and down the street to make sure no cars were coming.

Violet nodded and lifted the dog. He was not large, but he was muscular and heavy and limp. She walked the few feet to Mr. Pritchard's stoop and laid him tenderly on the ground. Mrs. McCabe took off her pink cardigan and covered the dog with it. She straightened up and squared her shoulders and marched up Mr. Pritchard's three short steps and knocked.

"Don't want whatever the hell you're selling, so go away."

"Mr. Pritchard, it's Mrs. McCabe. Your neighbor. Please come to the door," Mrs. McCabe said as she stepped down and stood next to Violet.

He yanked the door open, anger darkening his features. "What in Sam Hill do you—" The rest of his sentence caught in his throat as he took in the women and the body at their feet.

"A car hit him, Mr. Pritchard," Violet said. "I am so sorry."

"Son of a bitch," Mr. Pritchard said, but his voice held no venom. Instead, Mrs. McCabe thought she heard it break.

He stood there for several minutes, staring as if he couldn't make sense of what he saw. He shook his head and looked up at the sky, then at the road, possibly expecting to see the car and driver, but it was empty in all directions.

"They drove away," Mrs. McCabe said. "I'm—I'm not sure they even knew they hit him."

"I don't know why he was outside. He was in the house."

He came down the steps and picked up the dog and took him, cardigan and all, into the house. Mrs. McCabe thought she saw a tear tracing its way down his rough, bearded cheek. Her heart—which she thought was permanently closed for business—broke a little for the gruff man and his loss. She would be devastated if something happened to Clyde.

Violet walked her back to her house. "Are you OK, Mrs. McCabe?"

"I'm OK, I think. That poor dog. That poor man."

"I know."

"There's a little blood on your shirt."

"Oh." Violet looked down. "Well, it's not the worst thing in the world."

"No, no, it isn't."

"You seem to have given away your cardigan."

"I have more."

"I am really glad Arabella didn't see that."

"Me, too."

They stood in the shattered summer morning, sharing a silent moment of grief, neither sure what to say. With a small nod, Mrs. McCabe shuffled to her small porch and pulled herself up her steps, slowly, heavily. Violet hesitated, and Mrs. McCabe looked back at her and waved her away. "I'll be fine. You go get cleaned up."

Mrs. McCabe puttered around her house, trying to put the morning's incident out of her mind, but it clung stubbornly. She ate her lunch mechanically, and as she washed her dishes, she realized she had never gotten the mail. She shambled down her driveway again and noted the day had grown more hot and humid. The air felt like wet cotton wrapping itself around her. At the mailbox, she retrieved a bill, a sweepstakes offer, and a Sears catalog. As she made her slow progress back to her house, she noted the dark clouds gathering in the west, bruising the horizon.

Inside her house, she flipped through the catalog, shaking her head at the clothing. The wool dresses were nice. Clean lines, solid colors. But the rest? Oh my. What were fashion designers thinking these days using these migraine-inducing hues and patterns? And if the women's clothes were bad, the men's were atrocious. What would her Flynn say to pea-green slacks and a matching striped sweater? The thought made her chuckle.

She heard a rumble of thunder as the storm drew closer. She put the catalog aside, sliding and heaving herself out of her chair to look out her back window. The clouds had bunched up behind her house, pushing the blue sky into retreat. The trees bent toward the east, flailed by the fronting winds. A piece of paper blew across her yard from Mr. Pritchard's. She pursed her lips as she thought about how she couldn't even complain to him about keeping his trash cleaned up. Not today, anyway.

Poor Mr. Pritchard. What a sad day for him. In the several years he had lived next door, she had never seen him have company. Much like her. Neither one seemed to have much use for people. She knew he worked, but she did not know where. She hoped for his sake it was a job that could keep him busy and occupied. But it was Saturday, so she guessed he would be alone all weekend. She found herself wondering about his family, then shook herself, surprised. It was not like her to go off into fancy flight about someone else's life. She hoed her own row and expected everyone else to hoe theirs.

The storm broke with jagged shards of lightning that pierced the black clouds, followed almost immediately by resounding cracks of thunder. Rain pounded her metal roof, accompanied by the rattle and clank of hailstones. But as with most summer storms, the violence passed quickly, leaving scattered leaves and distant grumblings in its wake. Mrs. McCabe stepped out into the steamy evening to check her little patio. A couple of her chairs had been knocked over, and her geraniums looked dejected, as though they took the storm's abuse personally. She started to descend her steps but sensed a movement in the wisps of steam rising from the ground. She squinted, and there, just beyond the thin stand of trees at the edge of her yard, Mr. Pritchard hunched over a shovel, digging into the wet earth with an anger that would put the recent storm to shame. Slowly and silently, she backed into her house, softly closing the door behind her. The chairs could wait.

On Sunday, a hammering at the door startled Mrs. McCabe while she ate her lunch. She clapped her hand to her chest as if that could slow the pounding of her heart. She pushed her chair back and yelled, "Who is it?" as she shambled to the door. When you are an elderly woman living alone, you didn't take too many chances.

"It's Maynard Pritchard, from next door."

She opened the door, and, without preamble, he said, "I want to know who ran over my dog."

Mrs. McCabe considered her answer. On the one hand, she felt he had a right to the information. On the other, she didn't want to be an accessory to murder, which seemed a likely outcome if he were to meet the driver in his current state.

"Well, now, I am not a hundred percent sure. I'm old, you know. My eyes aren't so good." This was a total fabrication. Well, the old part was true. But she knew exactly who did it, and her eyes were perfectly fine.

Mr. Pritchard glared at her, and she got the distinct feeling he did not believe her. But who goes around calling old ladies liars?

"I tell you what. Let me do some asking around, and I will get back to you."

"You? You never leave your house. How are you going to do some asking around?"

"I leave sometimes," she huffed.

"Hmphf," he answered. "I thought you said you saw the whole thing?"

"Well, I did see the whole thing, but some details are a bit blurry."

"Listen. Someone killed my dog, and they should have to pay for that. You can't just go around killing people's dogs and get away with it."

"I agree. But I wouldn't want you to go accuse the wrong person."

He narrowed his eyes. "Fine. You go do what you have to do, but you find out anything, you tell me, you hear?"

"And by the way," she called to his retreating, T-shirted back. "You don't have to knock so loud. You almost gave me a heart attack."

"Well, you're old. Not sure how good your hearing is."

Touché. He got her on that one. She watched him stomp off down the sidewalk and into his yard. She gave him a few minutes to get back to his house, then she grabbed her purse and walked over to Violet's.

7

Violet

June 1969

Violet scrubbed her bathtub, vainly attempting to erase the stubborn stain around the drain. She stopped and cocked her head—was someone knocking? The *thump, thump, thump* came again. Someone was rapping lightly on her door. If her album hadn't finished and the tonearm hadn't swung back to its cradle, she never would have heard it. She sighed, stood up, and wiped her hands on a rag. She opened her front door to find Mrs. McCabe with her hand raised to knock again.

"Mrs. McCabe! What are you doing here? Is everything all right?"

Mrs. McCabe waved away her concern. "I walked over here, didn't I? Grab your purse and let's go."

"Where are we going?"

"We are going to talk to the boy who killed Mr. Pritchard's dog."

"We are? You and I are going to go to talk to someone who not only hit a dog, but left him in the road to die?"

"Yes, we are."

"No, I don't think we are."

"We have to. Mr. Pritchard is going to find out sooner or later who killed his dog, and can you imagine what he'll do then?"

"I don't think it's our place—"

"All right. If that's your opinion. It's a young boy, but I guess that's fine with you." Mrs. McCabe turned to go.

Violet groaned. "You can't do that."

"Do what?" Mrs. McCabe blinked her faded blue eyes at Violet.

"Make me feel guilty."

"I'm not making you feel anything. I am simply pointing out the possible consequences of your actions. Or, in this case, inaction." She took a step. "I mean, you're probably right. We shouldn't get involved. If Mr. Pritchard beats that teenage boy to a pulp, well, I guess he had it coming."

Violet clenched her fists. "Can I change at least?"

"You look fine."

"I've been cleaning a bathroom."

"We're not asking the boy on a date."

"Just give me a minute to put on some clean clothes."

"Well, hurry up. I am old and don't have all the time in the world, you know."

Violet took ten minutes to wash the smell of cleanser off her hands, change out of her house-cleaning clothes, brush her hair, and tie a kerchief around it. She took a minute to consider what one should wear when confronting a dog killer, but tried to hurry as she feared if she dawdled too long, Mrs. McCabe would trudge into her bedroom and help her dress. She wouldn't put it past her. After donning light-blue pedal pushers and a white blouse, she joined the old woman in the living room.

Mrs. McCabe told her to grab her keys because she was driving.

"Where exactly are we going?"

"The boy who was driving that car lives at the other end of the street. I know who he is, as he has been tearing up and down this road ever since he got his driver's license. And possibly before."

"Is it that gray Ford Falcon?"

"I don't know what kind of car it is, but it's old and gray. Two-door. At least I think it has two doors, as it generally speeds by too fast for me to count 'em."

"Yeah, I have seen him going by."

"Long-haired boy, right?"

"That pretty much describes every boy everywhere."

About a dozen houses down the street, Mrs. McCabe told Violet to turn into a driveway. Violet saw the gray car parked among a cluster of scrub oak trees. The house itself was a ramshackle, light-brown mobile home with rust-brown trim. Which might have simply been rust and not trim. Violet was not sure. The hitch was still attached to one end of the house while the steps—which were free of any sort of balustrade—stood a good six inches away from the trailer. Trees crowded the yard, elbowing each other for space and laying down a dense carpet of leaves and pine needles that had evidently never met a rake.

Mrs. McCabe opened her door, but Violet hesitated. The old woman gestured for her to go. "What are you waiting for? An invitation?"

"Do you have a plan for this?"

"Plan? We are going to ask that young whippersnapper if he killed Mr. Pritchard's dog."

"We are? We? As in you and me?"

"Well, I don't see anyone else here, do you?" She made an exaggerated show of looking around the car, into the floorboard, and the back seat.

"This just seems . . . ill-advised. What if he gets angry?"

"What if I do?"

Violet had to concede the point.

She crunched through acorns that littered the yard like confetti, shooting a sidelong glance at Mrs. McCabe to make sure she didn't slip. The two women reached the bottom of the steps. Mrs. McCabe motioned her ahead.

"I have to go up there?" Violet asked.

"I'm old," she said.

"I have noticed you seem to be old when it suits you," Violet said.

"Some things I can do, some things I can't. Or shouldn't. Climbing rickety stairs and falling and breaking a hip is something I shouldn't do. Making my own lunch is something I can do."

Violet resignedly climbed up to the door and knocked tentatively.

"I can't even hear that, and I am right here."

"You're old."

Mrs. McCabe glared at her. Violet did not want to admit the old woman was right. Her knock had been too soft. She didn't hear any sound of movement inside and felt emboldened by a thin ray of hope that no one was home, so she knocked again, more loudly this time, needing to put on a good show for Mrs. McCabe. With luck, no one would come, and they could slink back home. But she heard some shuffling. *Damn*, she thought. She backed down the steps as the door opened.

A young man—although calling him a man was being generous—swung the door open. A lock of thick, blond hair swooped across his forehead in an impressive wave, and he stared at them from under its shadow. Ball caps gave less coverage.

"Well, well. If it isn't Speedy Gonzales himself."

"Pardon?"

"You're the owner of that car, right?" Mrs. McCabe pointed to the Falcon.

His eyes narrowed a bit. "Uh, yeah."

His frown reminded Violet that neither she nor Mrs. McCabe were particularly well-suited to defending themselves against a young, able-bodied fellow, even if he was on the skinny side. What if he decided to chase them off? Or worse?

"And you killed a dog down the street and around the corner the other day, didn't you?"

"What? No way! I would never do that." His slightly belligerent expression slid into surprise.

"Young man, I saw you with my own eyes. I was going out to my mailbox, and you came flying down the road. As you always do. You barely slowed down as you took the turn, and then a dog ran out in front of you, and you hit it. And you kept on going like it didn't matter."

"I have no idea what you are talking about, lady."

"I am talking about how I saw you—and I could see your pretty little blond head behind the wheel, so I know it was you—kill that poor dog."

The young man thought about this for a minute.

"I, uh, I don't think that was me. You must have me mixed up with someone else."

"Really? How many other long-haired, blond hippies in gray cars come down this street?"

"I don't know. I only know it wasn't me."

"It was you. It was yesterday. At around ten when the mail comes. He had just come down the street, and then you came roaring down like all the demons of hell were after you." Mrs. McCabe stood glaring at him, hands on hips.

"Oh, shit." Realization washed all the color from his face. He plunked down on the steps and put his face in his hands.

"Language, young man. There are two ladies present."

"Oh God. I remember feeling a thump. I swear to you I had no idea. I thought it was a bump in the road. I never saw a dog or heard anything." He looked up at them, his face childlike and vulnerable. "You sure about this?" There was hope in his words—hope that something could still prove he wasn't the one who hit the dog.

"I am as sure as I have ever been of anything."

He put his face in his hands again before looking up. "I am really, really sorry. I would never have left it if I had known. And I would have stopped if I saw the dog. I swear to you, I didn't know." His eyes traveled from one woman to the other. "Was it your dog?" he asked, his voice tremulous.

"No, it was my neighbor's. But if he had come down here, I am afraid he might have strangled you with his bare hands. He was rather fond of that dog, even if I don't quite see why."

"Look, lady, I really am sorry. But I-I can't bring the dog back. I don't know what I am supposed to do here."

"First, you apologize. To Mr. Pritchard, the dog owner."

The kid's face paled even more, which Violet would not have thought possible.

Mrs. McCabe waved away his unspoken concerns. "We'll

go with you so you don't end up in an unmarked grave in his backyard."

"Jeez, lady, you're not helping."

"Let's get one thing straight. I am either 'Mrs. McCabe' or 'ma'am.' I am not 'lady' or 'broad' or any other term for a female that your little head can come up with."

He swallowed. "Yes, ma'am."

"Then you are going to do chores for him for as long as he needs you."

"Yes, ma'am."

"So we are clear?"

"Yeah."

"Excuse me?"

"Yes, ma'am."

"That's better. Now, let's go."

"Now?" he yelped.

"Do you have something to do more pressing than this?"

"Uh, not really." He looked as though he were trying to come up with something, but Mrs. McCabe's sharp gaze allowed no room for prevarication.

"Are you underage?"

"Pardon me?"

"Do you live with your parents? How old are you?"

He lowered his eyebrows. Or eyebrow. His hair obscured one of them. "I'm seventeen. And yeah, I live with my mom and stepdad."

"Do you need to ask permission to leave the house?"

He looked offended. "No."

"Then let's go. Get in the back seat."

He followed them to the car in a daze, and Violet felt a little sympathy for him since she had so recently found herself in the same position. She kind of wanted to bow out of this little scenario. Maybe she could park her car and say goodbye to the two of them when she got home. On the other hand, she thought the kid was being honest when he said he didn't realize he had killed Mr. Pritchard's dog. And accidents are called accidents for a reason. She didn't want Mr. Pritchard punching the kid in the face, or killing him, both of which she thought were real possibilities. Maybe she should go to keep the peace.

They parked in Violet's driveway, and, as they got out, Violet decided she should learn his name for any police reports that might come out of this.

"I'm Violet."

The kid's voice cracked and quavered. "I-I'm Tommy. Jeffers."

"I'd say nice to meet you, but I guess not under these circumstances."

"Are you her, uh, daughter or something?" He tilted his head towards Mrs. McCabe, who was struggling to get out of the car but waving off any offers of assistance.

"Oh, God, no! I mean, no, I'm her neighbor. I live here, Mrs. McCabe lives there—" She pointed at their houses in turn. "And Mr. Pritchard—that's the man who's, uh, who owned the dog—lives there."

He nodded blankly, and Violet wasn't sure he had comprehended what she said.

Mrs. McCabe strode across her yard and into Mr. Pritchard's, eyes forward, completely confident Violet and Tommy followed in her wake. She kind of reminded Violet of an elderly, imperious mama duck.

"I'll do the talking. Stand behind me. And maybe behind Violet."

Mrs. McCabe did not turn to witness his response, but he nodded an emphatic agreement anyway.

Because there were handrails—at least Violet assumed that was the reason—Mrs. McCabe mounted Mr. Pritchard's steps and knocked. With quite a lot of force for an old lady. Then she stepped down and waited.

"What in blue blazes is it now?"

He yanked the inner door open with his usual rancor.

He stood studying the three of them through his screen door. "Is this going to be a regular thing? You knocking on my door and giving me bad news?"

"I certainly hope not because I don't find your company at all enjoyable," Mrs. McCabe said.

"I could say the same."

Violet eyed Tommy and wondered how much paler a person could get.

"This is Tommy—" Mrs. McCabe glanced at the boy, who looked as if he might pass out. "Jeffers, right?"

Tommy moved his head up and down almost imperceptibly. Violet thought she could actually discern his heartbeat pulsing rapidly in the vein in his neck, like a tiny hummingbird under the skin.

"Tommy, this is Mr. Pritchard, who as far as I know has no first name other than Mister."

Both men waited, one quaking in fear, the other bristling with irritation. "I said my name to you earlier today."

Mrs. McCabe waved his comment away as inconsequential. She wasted no time explaining why they had come. "He's the one who killed your dog." Violet flinched, wishing Mrs. McCabe had phrased that a little more gently.

Mr. Pritchard straightened to full attention. His face

flushed, starting at pink, working its way to burgundy, and finally arrived at a fine, mottled purple. He and Tommy had covered quite a lot of shades in the last ten minutes.

"Now hold on there," Mrs. McCabe said, holding her hand up. "I have talked to him, and he didn't realize he hit your poor dog. He didn't see it. He was going too fast—" She turned to glare at Tommy. "Which he will—as of today—stop doing. Right, Tommy?"

Tommy gave his frightened, nearly invisible nod again.

"He feels quite bad. He wants to do chores for you to help make amends. Maybe some yard work or something."

Mr. Pritchard's beard bobbed up and down, and he said through clenched teeth, "That is not going to bring back Fred."

"No, it won't. But nothing will. And at least you will know he is doing something to make up for your loss."

Mr. Pritchard moved his gaze away from the boy to Mrs. McCabe. "Do you have any idea what I do for a living?" he asked.

"None, because you have never bothered to enlighten me."

"I am a handyman. Do you see anything around here that needs doing?"

Mrs. McCabe inspected Mr. Pritchard's trailer and yard. "Well, now that you mention it, your place does look mighty spick and span. But maybe he can do things you hate. Mow your grass, clean your bathtub." This elicited a little squeak from Tommy, though Violet could not tell whether it was because he hated cleaning bathtubs or because he was petrified at the thought of being inside Mr. Pritchard's house without witnesses.

Mr. Pritchard considered this. He glanced again at Tommy.

"You honestly didn't see Fred?"

Mrs. McCabe pushed Tommy forward, and he took a few small steps towards Mr. Pritchard, looking like a convict approaching the gallows. He attempted to speak, but all that came out was a choked croak. He cleared his throat and tried again. "Um, no." Mrs. McCabe poked him in the back with a bony index finger. "Sir."

Mr. Pritchard dropped his eyes. "He tore the screen on the back door. I didn't even know he got out. I think he must have taken off after a squirrel or a cat." His face was working its way back through the red color wheel and was now a more gentle fuchsia.

"You can mow my grass every week. I don't have anything else for you to do." He thought for a minute. "You can trim her hedges and mow her grass and fix her back fence." He nodded at Mrs. McCabe without taking his eyes off Tommy. "Are you handy with tools?"

"Um, no. Sir. Not really. I know my way around engines. I can work a lawn mower. Sir."

"Well, that probably means you're not an idiot and can figure things out. Give me a week, because I can still hardly look at you."

Tommy nodded eagerly, now looking like a convict who just had his sentence commuted.

"That OK with you?" Mr. Pritchard asked Mrs. McCabe.

"Fine by me."

"All righty then. Let's try going a week or two without knocking on my goddamn door, shall we?"

Violet offered to give Tommy a lift home, but he said he'd walk. Mrs. McCabe extracted a promise from him that he would not drive like a maniac up and down their road and pointed out that children lived on this street.

Violet did not think the warning was necessary. She thought Tommy might go the rest of his life without ever exceeding the speed limit again. But perhaps some things did need to be spelled out. The thought of Arabella crossing the street as a car came speeding down it at the same time made Violet feel ill. She walked Mrs. McCabe back to her house.

"Remember that conversation about what old people can and can't do?" Mrs. McCabe said, pausing at her little porch.

"Yes."

"I can walk myself to my own front door."

"Yes, ma'am." But she stopped and watched Mrs. McCabe mount her steps. "Mrs. McCabe?"

"Yes?"

"I didn't think we should get involved, but I think you did the right thing. I think you helped everyone."

"Hmmpf," Mrs. McCabe said. The screen door swung shut behind her like an audible exclamation point.

As Violet walked to her house, she found herself smiling and realized she hadn't thought about her circumstances since Mrs. McCabe knocked on her door. And even before that.

And she only felt a little guilty about it.

How about that? she thought.

★

A few days later, Violet was working in her backyard, tending to a few tomato plants growing in pots lining her small patio, when Tommy appeared at Mrs. McCabe's. Mrs. McCabe showed him her toolshed and set him to work on some shrubs, then disappeared into her house. Violet doubted ten minutes had passed before Arabella bounced over and introduced herself and began peppering him with questions as he clipped hedges on the side of the trailer that faced Violet's house.

"Do you have brothers and sisters?"

"One older brother."

"What grade are you in school?"

"Going into twelfth."

"What's your favorite subject?"

"I don't know." He stopped clipping the branches and regarded Arabella.

"Do you like to read?" she asked.

"Not really."

"Oh. Do you like movies?"

"Yes."

"What's your favorite movie?"

"*2001: A Space Odyssey*. Why do you ask so many questions?"

She shrugged, not the least bit offended by his terseness. "It's how I learn things. Why don't you ask any questions?"

"I just did," he said, and his lip twitched a little.

Arabella laughed. "Well, you could ask me how old I am and stuff like that."

He went back to clipping. "I have a feeling you are going to tell me whether I ask or not."

"I am seven years old, and I live over there. I have a baby brother. And Miss Violet is my best friend."

"Isn't she a little old to be your best friend?"

"See? You can ask questions! I don't like seven-year-old people. They are annoying."

"You don't say," he said.

Violet hid a smile as she took a few ripe cherry tomatoes into the house. She came back out a few minutes later with a cold pitcher of lemonade, some plastic cups, and a plate of cookies and headed to Mrs. McCabe's backyard.

"Afternoon, Tommy. How are you doing, Miss Arabella?"

"I am fit as a fiddle," Arabella said with her toothless grin. "That's what my dad says when he means 'good.'"

Violet put the tray down on Mrs. McCabe's little patio table. "Are you thirsty?" she asked Arabella.

The little girl bobbed her head. Violet noticed Tommy glancing at the pitcher out of the corner of his eye. "It's for you, too," she told him. He gave a slight nod but continued working. Violet decided he must not think her as authoritative as Mr. Pritchard and Mrs. McCabe. She couldn't blame him.

She turned to Mrs. McCabe's door and knocked.

"What?" The annoyed voice preceded the annoyed face in the screen door.

"I brought lemonade and cookies. I thought you might like some."

"Hmmmfff," Mrs. McCabe said, but her face brightened at the sight of the sweating pitcher of lemonade with its tinkling ice and bright, swimming slices of lemon. "Well, I hate to see your effort go to waste." She pushed open the screen door and walked down her steps with care. "Take a break, Tommy. I promise I won't bite. Much."

"OK," he mumbled. He peered up as he gathered some

clipped branches and caught sight of Mrs. McCabe glaring at him, arms akimbo. "I mean, yes, ma'am."

They had the lemonade and cookies in the deep shade of a clutch of river birch trees that trembled in the sunlight. And Violet forgot for a moment that she did not want to be making new friends.

8
Violet

June 1969

After their lemonade-and-cookie break, Mrs. McCabe shuffled to her back door. "Will you let the young man get his work done in peace?"

Arabella smiled up at Mrs. McCabe. "Can we come in? I want to say hi to Clyde. I bet he misses me."

"Guess I walked into that one," the old woman muttered.

Violet started to back out, having no real desire to spend more time with Mrs. McCabe, but Arabella dragged her along with her. "Come on! Clyde misses you, too."

"I will come in and say hi to Clyde, though I highly doubt he's given me a passing thought," Violet said. "Then I have things to do."

Clyde obligingly came out when Arabella called. He looked around with his squinting eyes, then stalked over to the little girl and rubbed his scarred face against her scabbed knee.

"Tommy seems to be doing a satisfactory job," Violet said.

"How difficult is it to trim a hedge?" Mrs. McCabe said, settling into her chair.

"Well, I just mean, he showed up, and he's working hard."

"He showed up because I scared the bejesus out of him. As did Mr. Pritchard."

Violet gave up trying to make polite small talk.

Arabella sat cross-legged on the floor, and Clyde rubbed his battered head against her legs.

"You know what Mr. Pritchard needs?"

"A vigorous shaking?" Mrs. McCabe said.

Arabella didn't miss a beat. "A new dog. It's been over a week now. I have Tabitha, and I love her, but if something happened to her, I would want another cat. I like having a pet."

"Well, I am sure he will get another one day. When he's ready," Violet said.

"I was thinking we could get him one," Arabella said. Clyde's rumbling purr provided a pleasant background hum.

"Oh, I don't think that's such a good idea," Violet said. "I think someone should pick their own pet."

Arabella shrugged, neither disagreeing nor agreeing. Violet thought for one so young, she had a knack for observing silences. Not that she couldn't talk your ears off. But there had been times when she would let a conversation lull lay like a comfortable blanket. And now, she was petting Clyde in mute serenity. Violet didn't know if she was capitulating or plotting.

"I think that's a wonderful idea," Mrs. McCabe said.

Violet's head shot up. "You do?"

"I do," Mrs. McCabe said. "I am betting Mr. Pritchard will think he doesn't need another dog. So I think we ought to take the initiative."

"Oh, Mrs. McCabe. That could really go terribly wrong."

But Mrs. McCabe's eyes gleamed with a mischievous light. "What do you think, Arabella?"

"Yes! We should do it!" she said enthusiastically.

Violet tried a few more protests, but once again, she was carried along on the tide of Mrs. McCabe's whim. And the tide swept Tommy along with it.

Mrs. McCabe opened her back door. "Tommy! Put away your gardening tools and come with us. We need you for more important matters." Violet did not hear his reply because Mrs. McCabe did not wait for it. Instead, she closed the door and turned to Violet and Arabella.

"Let's go," she said.

"Whoa. We're going now?" Violet asked, incredulous.

"No time like the present! I am an old lady. We don't know how many tomorrows I have left." She exchanged her slippers for sturdy black shoes and picked up her purse. She turned to Arabella. "Call your mother and ask if it's OK if you go with us. The phone is there. You know your phone number, right?"

"Yes, ma'am!" Arabella ran to the phone, clearly delighted.

Mrs. McCabe pointed at Violet. "You're driving," she said.

"I am? Oh, no, I don't think this is—"

Mrs. McCabe cut her off. "We are going with or without you. So is Arabella. So if you think it's OK to let her ride with an eighty-year-old woman with slow reflexes or with Mario Andretti there"—she thrust her thumb towards her back door as Tommy came through it—"well, I guess that's OK."

"Mrs. McCabe," Violet said, exasperated.

"So if you want to keep her safe, go fetch your handbag."

Arabella hung up the phone. "She said yes! She was happy Miss Violet was driving."

Violet eyed Arabella suspiciously—could she possibly be

manipulating her as deftly as Mrs. McCabe? Was the old lady giving lessons?

"Come on! Chop chop!" Mrs. McCabe said. "Tommy, wash your hands! Quick like a bunny!"

Violet glared at her, hoping to stop the avalanche that was Mrs. McCabe once she got rolling. Tommy washed his hands, and they headed out the door.

"Seriously, Mrs. McCabe! This is not a good idea."

"Possibly. Possibly not. But we are going. With or without you."

Violet let out a moan of frustration and went to her house to grab her purse. Perhaps she could dissuade them on the way there and avert what she thought would surely be a disaster. When she came back out, the three were standing next to her car. Tommy had a plastic cup of ice water in one hand and was brushing bits of leaves and twigs off his shirt with the other. They all climbed into Violet's car.

"I have no idea where I am going."

"I do," Mrs. McCabe said.

She directed Violet to turn here, turn there, go straight. Between directions, Violet interjected her opinion. But she might as well have been talking to the steering wheel for all the good it did. After her many objections fell on deaf ears, she gave up. She had no idea what else she could do in the face of a single-minded Mrs. McCabe, an enraptured Arabella, and a timid Tommy.

Mrs. McCabe ordered Violet into a parking lot which was attached to a pet store.

"Best to be prepared," Mrs. McCabe said as she handed Tommy a few bills to buy a leash. When he returned, Mrs. McCabe resumed her directions. Violet parked her car in front of a squat, ugly brick building. As the four people entered the lobby, a wall of smells greeted them. Violet identified urine, feces, and wet dog with undertones of an acrid disinfectant.

A plump woman Violet thought to be in her late twenties with a short bob and bangs sat behind a counter. It was an unfortunate choice of hairstyle, giving her the appearance of a helmeted, baby-faced football player. Her cheek rested on her palm as she stared intently at a book.

Mrs. McCabe walked up to the counter in her customary no-nonsense fashion. "We want a dog."

"Have you lost your dog?"

"No, I have not lost my dog. Did I say I was trying to find a dog?"

The woman vacillated between looking hurt and offended, unable to decide which one to latch on to. Violet put a calming, gentle hand on Mrs. McCabe's arm.

"Mrs. McCabe, if you will allow me." She turned to the young woman. "Hi. I am Violet. What is your name?"

"Uh, Bonnie."

"Bonnie, we are checking to see if you have any dogs available for a friend." Violet sent up a prayer that there would be no adoptable dogs, and they could go home and forget this whole escapade.

"Yeah, we do." Bonnie rummaged around on her desk and pulled out a piece of paper. She consulted it for a minute. "I'd ask you what you were looking for, you know, boy, girl, old, young, etc., but we only have three available."

"What's the youngest? Age? Boy or girl?" Mrs. McCabe interjected.

"Let's see. We have a girl who we think is about a year old. But . . ." she trailed off.

"Yes?" Violet said encouragingly, hoping there would be something they couldn't conceivably take.

"Well, she's not friendly. And she's not, well, that cute, either."

Arabella stepped forward, putting her fingertips on the counter and standing on tiptoe to see over it. "What will happen to the dog if we don't take it?"

Bonnie shifted her gaze away at the question. "Well. Um, ahem, well, they are uh, usually, uh, euthanized."

Violet felt like channeling Mr. Pritchard and cursing.

"So they will kill her, right?"

Bonnie pursed her lips. "Well, maybe. But someone else might take her."

Arabella didn't bat an eye. "We'll take her."

"Arabella, Bonnie just said she wasn't friendly."

"Fred was mean, and Mr. Pritchard loved him."

The woman stood and picked up some keys from the counter. "Oh, she's not mean. I'll show her to you. You have to wait here. No one's allowed in the back."

She disappeared through a door, igniting a cacophony of barking and cage rattling. She soon reappeared with a dog . . . or a facsimile thereof. The creature wore a collar and an attached leash, but Bonnie carried her until she got in front of the little group. She set her down on the concrete floor.

She was a pitiful specimen of a dog. Her hair was wiry; she had an underbite. Her bulging eyes didn't quite meet the gaze of the people gathered in the foyer. And she trembled in every part of her skinny little body.

Arabella rushed forward. "Oh, you poor thing!"

Violet put out a halting hand. "Stop. Don't ever go up to a dog you don't know. And if they are scared, it's even more important. Go slow. And ask permission. Bonnie, has she ever been aggressive?"

"Never. She's afraid of everything."

Violet turned to the group. "I definitely don't think this is the right dog for Mr. Pritchard." Relief surged through her. They could turn around, go home, and let the idea die a natural death.

Tommy started laughing.

"What's so funny?" Mrs. McCabe said.

"She looks like Mr. Pritchard."

They all turned to consider the dog, who was doing her best to melt into Bonnie's legs. Tommy had a point. The wiry hair that was neither brown nor gray nor blond did look like Mr. Pritchard's beard. He also had slightly bulging eyes and a slight underbite. Of course, she usually saw him when he was angry.

Arabella peered up at the taller people around her. "See? She's meant to be."

"I don't know, Arabella. Mr. Pritchard seems to require . . . a tougher dog. A guard dog. I don't think he'd like us bringing him this poor, wretched thing."

"May I pet her, please?" Arabella asked Bonnie.

"Yeah, sure."

"Are you sure she's gentle?" Violet asked, taking a step forward.

"Oh, yes. I've given her a shot and she practically licked me to death out of gratitude."

Arabella put out a hand, and the dog cowered at first, then sniffed it. She gave a cautious, trembling wag of her body. Arabella moved closer and stroked the dog's head. The dog gazed up at Arabella, and Violet knew it was now a lost cause. The dog was coming home with one of them. Arabella hugged the dog. "Sadie, you are going to a new home, and you are going to be so happy. I just know it."

"Sadie?" Violet asked.

"Yep, her name is Sadie," Arabella said with certainty.

Violet could think of no argument she hadn't already put forward.

Bonnie handed the leash to Tommy.

"Oh, by the way. She kind of doesn't walk."

"What do you mean she doesn't walk?"

"The vet said she's capable of it. She just chooses not to. She stays wherever you put her."

"You've got to be kidding," Violet said. "This is really not the dog for Mr. Pritchard."

"She just needs some love, don't you, Sadie," Arabella said, scratching the dog behind the ears. The dog leaned into her hand and looked up at Violet with her sad, bulging eyes.

"Oh, for heaven's sake." Violet put a hand over her eyes, defeated. She told Tommy to keep a sharp eye on the dog and Arabella. Bonnie went behind the counter, pulled out a form and a pen, and slid them over to Violet. She looked it over, realizing whoever filled it out would be the official owner of the dog. Violet held the pen out to Mrs. McCabe.

"I seem to have forgotten my reading glasses," Mrs. McCabe said, patting the pockets of her house dress. "How about you fill out the form and I'll pay the fee?"

Violet glared. Then resignedly filled in the blanks. The information at the top of the page said the dog—Sadie—had been recently spayed, flea-dipped, and was up-to-date on her shots. Violet, satisfied they had everything in order—well, except for the fact that they should not be doing this at all— turned to Bonnie.

"You seem to like animals. You were patient and gentle with her. Why are you working here?"

"I am studying to be a vet tech. I thought this would be a good place to learn."

"Do you like it?"

"No. No, I don't. It's hard seeing all the dogs come through and—" Her eyes dropped to Arabella. "And you know."

"You should find a job at a vet's or somewhere else."

"Give me a piece of paper. And a pen." Mrs. McCabe reached an open hand across the counter. Bonnie, like everyone else, instantly obeyed. Mrs. McCabe wrote furiously for a minute, then slid the note across to her. "This is my vet, Dr. Carlson. He takes care of my cat. He's a kind man. Been in practice for years. Maybe he has an opening or knows someone who does. Tell him Mrs. McCabe sent you."

"Yes, ma'am. Yes, I'll do that. And thanks!"

"I thought you needed your glasses," Violet said to Mrs. McCabe.

"Well, I didn't *exactly* say I needed them."

Tommy reached down and scooped up the dog. As they turned toward the door, Violet glanced back and said, "You have very lovely hair. You should grow it longer." Bonnie smiled a tentative smile, putting her hand to her hair.

Mrs. McCabe gave a low snort as they stepped outside into the hazy sunlight. "Well, that was tactful. And much needed," she said before the door closed all the way. Violet winced, hoping Bonnie could not hear over the yaps and yelps of the dogs. She risked a glance back, and Bonnie smiled and gave them a little wave.

Violet told Tommy to take Sadie to the grass in case she needed to do her business. Which she did, and Violet took this as somewhat of a good sign. When she was done, Tommy picked her up and carried her to the car.

When Violet pulled into her driveway, she saw that Mr. Pritchard's was empty. Was she relieved that they would not be presenting him a dog at that moment? Or was she dismayed to have to put it off?

Mrs. McCabe directed them like the cast of a Broadway play: Tommy would go back to work on Mrs. McCabe's hedges, Mrs. McCabe would keep an eye and ear out for Mr. Pritchard, and Arabella would run home and tell her mom all the goings-on of the day then come back to keep Sadie company at Violet's. Violet now had a phone, so Mrs. McCabe would call her when Mr. Pritchard pulled up. Meanwhile, Violet would contemplate how she had managed to get tangled up in all of this when all she wanted was to hibernate for a while and find her footing. She wondered if they were doing the right thing or if she was going to end up with a dog she did not need. Or want. She stood in her driveway, blew out a breath, and studied the dog, who did not meet her eye.

"Well, I don't think you're the one who should be avoiding looking at me," she said and gave the leash a little tug. "Come on, Sadie, let's go."

Sadie remained seated. Violet sighed, scooped her up, and carried her into her house.

A little after four p.m., Mrs. McCabe called. She sounded . . . cheerful. "Showtime!" she sang out.

Arabella had been sitting on the floor, showering the dog with affection. At first, the dog did not appear to know what to do except cringe. But when Arabella stopped petting her, the dog tentatively pushed her nose into Arabella's hand. Arabella laughed with delight. Now she clipped the leash onto the dog's collar and encouraged her to follow her to the door. But Sadie still wouldn't walk. It's like she knew she had been one or two walks away from a death sentence, Violet thought as she lifted her up.

They met Mrs. McCabe in her front yard. Tommy joined them, wiping his face with a towel. Mrs. McCabe turned to him. "You take the dog and stay around the corner of Mr. Pritchard's house. We'll go knock on the door."

It was a little late to be objecting, but Violet's profound doubts resurged. "Are you sure we are doing the right thing?"

"I have a hunch. And so does Arabella, right?" Arabella bobbed her head up and down. "And one should trust their hunches."

Mrs. McCabe knocked on the door. Violet again noted she had no trouble mounting the steps.

"Hellfire and damnation. Is this going to be a daily thing? Can we just go back to pretending we don't know each other?"

Mr. Pritchard stood in the doorway, behind the screen, hands on hips, surveying the three females at the bottom of his steps.

"We can do that right after we give you a little present," Mrs. McCabe said.

Violet noted Arabella's wide, gap-toothed grin brimming with anticipation. She prayed Mr. Pritchard didn't crush her feelings too much when he slammed the door on them.

"I don't need any presents. I have everything I need. Except peace and quiet. And that I will gladly accept."

Mrs. McCabe ignored him. "Tommy! Come on out."

Tommy came around the corner of the house carrying Sadie, who was trembling more than ever at the angry voice. *Oh, this is a terrible mistake*, thought Violet as she realized that this was probably a dreadful ordeal for the dog. *God, I feel bad for her, but I do not need a dog.*

Tommy strode up the steps and thrust the dog at Mr. Pritchard, who looked thoroughly bewildered.

"What in seven hells..." He had no choice but to grab the dog before she fell. Tommy retreated quickly, stepping back behind Mrs. McCabe. He had nearly a foot on her in height but still managed to look like he was hiding behind her. "Can someone please tell me what in tarnation is going on?"

"This is your new dog," said Mrs. McCabe. "She's not meant to replace Fred. But you needed a dog. She needed a home. So there you have it."

"This is a dog? Sorriest excuse for a canine I have ever seen. And I don't need a damn dog. Appreciate the thought, but take her back and get the hell off my property."

Arabella climbed up the steps and reached a hand out to the shaking dog. "Please, Mr. Pritchard. Do you know they were going to kill her if we didn't take her? They call it youth-something. What was it, Mrs. McCabe?"

"Euthanasia."

"That's the word. But it's just a big, fancy word for kill, and she's too nice to die. She needs someone to love her. And you need someone to love."

"Oh, for Chri—Pete's sake. Really. I didn't even want Fred. I found him at someone's house when I was doing a job. Had him tied up outside, and he was mangy and thin. So I told him if they didn't take care of him, I would. Couldn't stand to see him like that. But I don't need to do that again."

Arabella was not convinced. "Maybe you don't need to, but Sadie needs you to."

"Sadie?"

"That's her name. She kind of whispered it to me."

"Listen, I know it's a tiny imposition," said Mrs. McCabe, "but we just wanted to do something nice for you. Why don't you keep her overnight, and if you don't want her, we will talk about what to do tomorrow?"

"No. Absolutely not. Take her back. I don't want the da—the darn dog."

Violet bit her tongue, deciding now was not the time to tell Mrs. McCabe and Arabella I told you so.

"Have it your way," Mrs. McCabe said. "We'll take her. Tomorrow. Violet here is not set up to take care of a dog. So if you can keep her tonight, we'll go buy some supplies tomorrow." Violet's head turned so sharply to look at Mrs. McCabe, she was sure she pulled a neck muscle. Mrs. McCabe ignored her.

"And what if I say no?"

"Just one night, Mr. Pritchard. I bet you still have Fred's things. Violet and I will go early tomorrow."

He narrowed his eyes. "One night. Tomorrow, she's yours."

Violet said, "Just so you know, she's gotten her rabies shot, and she's been flea-dipped. And she's spayed. She's healthy. She's just a little scared."

"A little, huh? If this is a little scared, I hate to see a lot scared."

Did Violet detect a softer note in his voice? Also, he had spoken a sentence or two without cursing. Were those good signs?

"I will keep her tonight, but you better go do some shopping because it's ONE night. ONE." He turned and fumbled with the handle of his screen door. Once he got it open, he walked in and kicked the inner door closed with his foot.

Mrs. McCabe turned. "Well, I think that went rather well."

"You do, do you? You seem to have a nice backup plan that I notice doesn't include you."

"I've got Clyde. Don't think they'd get along. You mark my words, that dog is in her new home. Shall we?" She motioned to her house. "I'll pour us all some iced tea, and we will have a little nibble of something. Arabella, how about you help me?"

Violet stood for a minute, mouth agape. *Who on earth is this person, and what happened to Mrs. McCabe?* Mrs. McCabe turned around. "Well, come on and close your mouth. You look like a carp standing there."

The foursome drank their tea on the back patio in the shade of Mrs. McCabe's river birch trees and Mr. Pritchard's tall pines.

"Do you think we should go to the pet store now? We still have time," Violet said.

"Nope."

"Do you really think he is going to keep that dog?"

"I do. In spite of his gruff appearance, I think he's a big old softie."

Violet was skeptical and took a sip of tea. "I don't see that at all. But I do see dog ownership in my future."

9

Mr. Pritchard

June 1969

Maynard Pritchard stared at the dog he had set down on his dark-blue living room carpet. She remained where he had placed her, like a stuffed animal. She kept her stumpy tail firmly tucked between her legs and her head lowered, but watched him with sad brown eyes.

"Jesus Christ on a dog biscuit," he said. Sadie trembled.

"Yeah, I know I sound scary. Fred thought so, too. But he got used to it. I don't think there's much hope for you. I don't understand how in seven hells I ended up with you in my house." He shook his head. "I mean, I never said yes. And come to think of it, I actually said no." Sadie stood there.

"Fine. Let's see if you're hungry." He plodded into the kitchen and took out Fred's bowl that he had hidden under the sink so he wouldn't be reminded of the damn dog every time he came in to eat. Holding it, the heaviness of Fred's loss weighed on his chest again. He did not want to get all wrapped up in another animal. Or person. Nope. Tomorrow, he would march over to that young woman's house—no use dealing with the old lady. He had a feeling she would talk him into another dog if he tried to discuss it with her. He would take Sadie, carrying her if she was still choosing not to move her damn legs, and hand her back and be done with her and all of them. What in the hell happened to his quiet little street where no one bothered him? Perhaps he'd stick a sign on his door threatening to shoot anyone who knocked on it.

He put the dish on the counter and filled it with a scoop of dry food. He started to place it on the floor, but stopped, deciding to make it a special meal like he used to with Fred. The dog looked like she could use some fattening up. He retrieved a container of leftover country fried steak gravy and poured it over the pellets, and stirred it around with a spoon. Glancing back at Sadie, he noted she still stood where he left her. He rolled his eyes, set the food on the floor, and gave her a chance to walk over. He filled another dog bowl with water and set it down. She didn't budge. She hadn't even turned around. There must really be something wrong with her. They got him a sick or crippled dog. Jesus Christ in a bicycle basket.

He picked her up, taking care to be gentle because he didn't want to make whatever was ailing her worse. He placed her in front of her food, but she just watched him. He eased down onto the floor, his back against the cabinet, and pushed the dish towards her. "Here. It's good. I promise."

She stared at him.

"Come on, dog. Sadie. I don't know what you've been through, but I am not going to beat you. So eat."

Stare.

He reached up to the cabinet and fumbled blindly for the spoon. Once he grabbed it, he scooped some food, making sure to get a bite with lots of gravy. He held it to her nose. She took a tentative sniff. Then another. Finally, with a delicate, diffident thrust of her head, she took the food from the spoon and chewed. He ladled some more. She ate some more.

"Good dog," he murmured. Did her back end almost wag? Was her tail not quite as tucked under as before? He continued spoon-feeding her and talking softly to her.

"I swear if you ever tell a living soul I did this, I will call you a goddamned bald-faced liar. Not that it would matter, because no one on God's green Earth would believe mean old Maynard Pritchard would get down on the floor and spoon-feed a damn dog."

He scraped up the last bit of food, and she took it as gently as she had the first. He gripped the dish, holding it in front of her, and she licked the last traces of crumbs and grease from it, showing a little more enthusiasm than when they started. When she was done, he spread his hands wide, palms up, and said, "All done. Now what?"

She crept forward tentatively. "Well, damn. You can move. Come on."

She lay down on her stomach, inching nearer, reminding him of a soldier commando-crawling under barbed wire. When she got close enough, she extended her head and put her chin on his thigh, continuing to stare at him with her chocolate-brown eyes. He reached out and petted her wiry head, and stroked the silky fur around her ears. She pushed closer to him.

"What in the hell happened to you that you're afraid to even move?" he asked her.

After a while, he eased her head off his leg. "Gotta make my own dinner now, dog. Else I might run out of gravy. You wouldn't want that now, would you?"

He placed Fred's bed in a corner of the kitchen, and said, "Come on, here ya go." She stared.

"This is getting a little old, but I'll put up with it for a bit." He reached down and picked her up and moved her onto the bed, stroking her head until she curled up into a tight ball. He moved about the kitchen, pulling out pork chops, tenderizing them, throwing on some salt and pepper, putting them in a skillet. Next, he boiled water and poured in rice. While that cooked, he opened a can of green beans and threw them in a saucepan. The whole time, Sadie gazed at him. He couldn't tell if she was curious or fearful. Maybe both, he thought. After the pork chops were done, he stirred some flour into the grease and drippings, stirring until it was smooth. Then he added milk. Not that he would ever tell anyone, but he could make a mean gravy. He ate at his table, carrying on a conversation with the dog. He finished eating and cleaned up the kitchen, and Sadie still didn't move anything but her eyes.

"You're gonna get cramps all curled up like that."

He went into the living room and turned on the TV. Sadie stayed where she was. He got up, cursing, picked her up with one arm and the bed with the other, and settled her down next to his easy chair. A couple of shows later, he caught himself nodding off and decided it was bedtime. He turned off the TV.

"Guess it's time to see if you know how to do your business outside. Probably should have done that sooner. Fred used to tell me when he needed to go." He didn't even bother to call her or try to get her to walk. He carried her out his back door, to the little side area near his shed where he had taught Fred to go. And for the first time, she moved around a bit. She sniffed here and there, circling once or twice, then took a dump. When she was finished, he patted her on the head and told her she was a good dog. She wagged her back end a tiny bit. He started to walk away, and she took a few steps, but stopped. He turned to see what she would do, and she squatted and peed.

"Well, you're not half bad as far as dogs go," he told her. "At least you know where to do your business." She took a step. "Well, come on, if you're done." He slapped his thigh, and she walked towards him, slow and tentative. She would not go up the stairs into the house, so he gathered her up and lugged her back inside. "Well, we'll work on that," he told her. He realized he had just implied they had a future together. "Well, someone can work on it. Maybe there is some hope for you after all. With the right person."

He set her down on her bed and moved her water closer. He locked up the house, turning off lights as he exited each room. Before he made his way down his narrow hall, he checked the stove. Satisfied everything was in order, he headed to his bedroom. He undressed down to his T-shirt and underwear and threw his clothes in a hamper. After brushing his teeth, he lay down on the bed with a tired sigh. He'd installed kitchen cabinets at a customer's house, put up some shelves at another. Fixed a lawn mower at another. Then came home to find his neighbors thrusting a dog at him. They were mentally deluded. He would start putting his foot down about their knocking on his door.

He wondered how the dog was doing in the living room. She was quiet as a mouse pissing on cotton. She was still pretty scared, he reckoned, and he speculated again about what her life had been like to make her so terrified. Well, he knew about life kicking you in the teeth, that was for sure. He thought of her as he'd seen her before he turned the lights out. Curled up in a ball on the bed, watching him, bracing herself for life's next kick in the ribs. He cursed under his breath, threw the sheet off, and plodded off down the hall, flipping the light switch on as he went. The shaft of light from the hallway fell across her body, and he could see she hadn't moved so much as a paw. He stood looking at her for a minute or two, hands on hips. Finally, he lifted her up and carried her back to the bedroom. "Goddamn dog," he muttered. He placed her on one side of the bed and walked around to the other, popping his hand around his doorjamb to turn off the hall light as he went. Climbing under the sheet, he relished the feeling of his muscles sinking into the mattress, letting go of the tensions they had held all day. He sensed the minuscule movement of Sadie creeping across the bed. She curled into herself with her back against his side.

"I can't believe I am doing this. You ever tell, you're banished."

Sadie gave a little canine sigh and settled into sleep. It wasn't long before Maynard's snores mingled with the dog's deep breathing.

10
Violet

The next morning, Violet vacillated between hiding from Mr. Pritchard and peeking through the windows at what she could see of his yard. At any given moment, she expected him to come stomping up her steps or bang angrily on her door. Every little noise made her jump. She did what she always did when she was anxious: housework. She threw clothes into the washing machine, made banana-nut muffins, vacuumed (and if she missed a knock because of the roar of it, well, she couldn't help that, could she?), tidied the kitchen, finished another square in her afghan. Then made lunch. As she washed her dishes, she caught sight of Mr. Pritchard's grizzled head. She inhaled sharply and jerked back behind the curtain. But she couldn't resist craning her neck around the gauzy fabric to get a better view. He stood near the end of his lawn, beside a line of trees that separated his property from the one behind him. Then he knelt on one knee and patted Sadie on the head. Sadie looked up at him and—Dear Lord! Was the dog actually wagging her tail? Violet squeezed her eyes shut, shook her head, and looked again. The scene had not changed. "Noooo!" she said out loud. Not in protest, but in disbelief. Did she dare hope that Mr. Pritchard had himself a new dog? She turned off the water she realized was still running and dried her hands. *Well, I'll be doggone*, she thought, smiling. Then her grin faded. Now she would have to admit Mrs. McCabe was right.

She took some muffins across the street. Caroline had just gotten Allen down for his nap, and Violet told her to sit and rest while Violet set out the muffins and some iced tea. Caroline heaved a huge sigh as she sank into a kitchen chair.

"They say you forget about labor pain and that's why you get pregnant again. But apparently, you also forget how completely exhausting a newborn is." She took a long drink of tea. "It's so nice to sit! So tell me about this dog and Mr. Pritchard."

"I swear, I think Mrs. McCabe is a witch. I keep finding myself doing things I have no intention of doing. Although I do believe it was Arabella's idea." They both glimpsed out the window to the backyard where Arabella was talking animatedly to . . . no one. At least no one outside they could see.

"Please tell me he was OK with the dog."

"I wish I could. He did not seem to appreciate having a dog quite literally thrust on him. But on the other hand, he didn't hand her back. And I honestly can't say why. I had no hope this would work."

"Arabella has an almost scary intuitive sense about people. She has guessed things or sensed things about people that would make you think she can read their minds. My in-laws are long-time friends with another couple. They do everything with them. Play cards, cookout, go to the movies. One day, Arabella was visiting when the friend, Mrs. Mullis, was over. After she left, Arabella asked my mother-in-law why Mrs. Mullis was so sad. My mother-in-law laughed and said she wasn't sad. Two weeks later, my mother-in-law called and said the Mullises were getting a divorce. Turns out Mr. Mullis had been having an affair. Nobody else saw anything different about Mrs. Mullis except Arabella, but she had only that week found out about her husband's infidelity right before Arabella was there. And that's just one example. It's crazy."

"Well, she may have been right on target this time as well. I looked out the window this morning, and there was Mr. Pritchard out in the yard with the dog, and—did Arabella tell you what the dog was like?"

"A bit. She said the dog was really scared."

"Petrified would be a better word. And when I say petrified, I mean like the petrified forest. She doesn't move. I have never seen a creature so frightened in my life. I thought it would take her weeks to get even a little friendly or open to anyone. But this morning? She was wagging her stumpy little tail. Seriously. Not a whole lot, but I saw a definite wag. He can't give her back now, right?"

"With him? Who knows? I would hope not. To tell you the truth, I think there's a teddy bear trapped in that grumpy old body."

Violet snorted. "Maybe you have some ESP thing going on like Arabella because I sure don't see it. Although come to think of it, Mrs. McCabe said the same thing."

"Well, he helped with Mrs. McCabe. He fixed her window, and he's probably the one who trimmed her hedges."

Violet was quiet for a minute, considering this. "I kind of want to go over and ask him how it's going, but I also don't want to give him a chance to push the dog on me."

"If I were you, I would stay away. Keep in your house. Close the door, pull the shades."

Violet laughed. "I think that is a plan."

Violet hurried back across the street, hoping Mr. Pritchard didn't spot her. As she reached the edge of her yard, a car drove slowly around the corner where Mr. Pritchard lived, coming to a near stop, then accelerating again. When it got to her, it stopped. A young man—a GI, judging by his haircut—leaned out his open window. "Excuse me, miss," he said, his accent immediately placing his hometown as somewhere around New York City. He tilted his head towards the blond driver. "We are supposed to be meeting a property manager at 822 Magnolia. But we are having trouble seeing some of the house numbers."

Violet met his eyes, and her heart thumped. His eyes were warm and brown and kind and—and nothing, she told herself. He's a good-looking guy. No big deal. Answer his question—what was his question?—and move on. "I am sure it's that one." She pointed to the empty trailer next to the Fitzgeralds. "They are 824. The numbers go down in that direction."

"Got it. Thanks. I didn't want to walk into the wrong house," he said, the aforementioned eyes crinkling at the corners with his smile.

Violet could not help but return his smile. "That would be embarrassing. Are you thinking of moving?" she asked. Merely making friendly conversation. Nothing more.

"Well, we are thinking about it. I'm Nick Battaglia, by the way." He held a hand out the window.

Violet shook his hand as Harry waved from his side of the car. "I'm Harry Cisse," he said, ducking his head so he could see her.

"Good to meet you both. I'm Violet Wentworth."

"You live here?"

"Yes, I do. Just moved here last month, as a matter of fact."

"Ah. How do you like it?"

"It's nice. A quiet street, mostly." *Until lately*, she thought to herself.

"Sounds good. It was a pleasure to meet you, Violet Wentworth. We'll let you get on with your day."

He gave her a little two-fingered salute, and Harry steered the car into the next driveway. She completed the trek to her front door and wondered what had happened to the quiet street she had moved to and if it would ever return.

11

Tommy

July 1969

A few days later, Tommy was trimming suckers off one of Mrs. McCabe's trees. He had no idea why he was doing it. Wouldn't they just turn into branches? What was wrong with that? But Mr. Pritchard had told him to do it, so here he was. Mr. Pritchard had also been the one to tell him they were called suckers, which seemed an odd term for something that actually grew out of the tree rather than something that was growing on it. The tree grew near Mr. Pritchard's backyard, and, as Tommy worked, the man emerged from his house and entered his shed. He hauled out a sawhorse, some wooden boards, and some tools. Tommy paused and straightened, curious. Mr. Pritchard scowled at him.

"Don't you have enough work to do over there?"

"I'm just about done here. Sir."

"Speak up. Can't hardly hear you." Mr. Pritchard put a board on the sawhorse and pulled out a measuring tape.

Tommy cleared his throat and swallowed. "I'm about done here. Sir."

He stretched out the measuring tape and, without looking up, addressed Tommy. "You ever do any woodworking?"

"Uh, no. Sir."

"Well, a boy ought to know his way around woodworking tools. Come on over here."

"Yes, sir."

Tommy put the clippers in Mrs. McCabe's small, orderly shed and replaced the padlock on the door, figuring he was done for the day. He walked over to Mr. Pritchard's, stepping across a blanket of brown pine needles.

"Now, let's see. I am between projects and not sure what I am going to make next. Does your mother need anything?"

Tommy's mind blanked. "I can't think of anything."

"Bookshelves? That's about the easiest thing to start with."

"Not really. She doesn't read much and has some shelves for all her little doodads."

"Hmm." Mr. Pritchard thought for a minute. "How about a vegetable bin?"

"A what?"

"You know, a bin for vegetables. Onions and potatoes and such."

"She doesn't actually cook much." Tommy was feeling a little embarrassed for his mom and her lack of interest in reading and cooking.

"Well, what does she like?"

"Makeup," Tommy blurted out. He cast about for something else, trying to picture his mother at home. What did she do when she was not working? She watched TV, but she had a TV stand. Then he thought of another thing. "She reads magazines," he offered.

Mr. Pritchard rubbed his beard. "Yes. Yes. That would work. Easier than a vegetable bin, too. So we'll make her a magazine rack."

He disappeared into the shed and came back with a dowel, a couple of clamps, and some nails. He held up two boards he had brought out earlier. "These are going to be the end pieces."

He measured one and pulled a pencil out of his shirt pocket and made a mark. He stuck the pencil behind his ear and did the same with the other board. Then he handed the tape measure to Tommy.

"You measure."

Tommy was confused. "But you just did that."

"Always measure twice. Maybe three times. Will save you a shitload of trouble later."

So Tommy measured, self-conscious, his fingers fumbling and unsure. Then Mr. Pritchard measured the widths of the two boards and made marks on them. Tommy noticed that the measurements of one end of a board did not match the other. He said as much.

"Glad you picked up on that. We are making the top ends a little wider than the bottom."

"OK." Tommy could not picture how that would look, but he didn't want to ask.

When Mr. Pritchard handed him the hand saw, he inhaled sharply. He knew he would screw it up. He said as much.

"Yeah, ya might. So what. I got plenty of wood."

He showed Tommy how to hold the saw, how best to move it to cut through the wood. "Your first goal is to not cut off any body parts. Second goal is to make a nice, clean cut. You do that, and it's good."

Tommy gripped the handle of the saw, hefting its weight in his palm. He tentatively ran the serrated edge against the wood and felt the friction and heard the rasp of the teeth. He exerted more force, and the wood began to separate. His mind closed around this one pinpoint of awareness as he concentrated on cutting through the board, following Mr. Pritchard's instructions, but also intuitively gauging the right pressure to apply. Everything else faded into the background. This concentration, this focus, was what he experienced when he was driving or working on an engine. He thought he could get to like this.

12

Mr. Pritchard

July 1969

On a Sunday morning when birdsong filled the air and a bright blue sky soared overhead, Tommy showed up to work with a black eye that he tried to conceal with his long hair. Mr. Pritchard took note, but said nothing at first. He set Tommy to work sanding the wood for the magazine rack. Tommy worked quietly, asking fewer questions than usual. They took a break for refreshments, and Mr. Pritchard waved his glass at Tommy.

"Get in a scrap with someone?"

Tommy's hand moved to his eye, seemingly of its own volition, and as soon as he realized it, he stopped its progress and shoved it into the pocket of his jeans.

"Uh, something like that."

Mr. Pritchard narrowed his eyes. His instincts were humming, and they weren't singing about a fight among boys. As they had begun working together, Mr. Pritchard had asked him a question or two about his family. He had learned Tommy had an older brother who lived on his own and that Tommy couldn't wait to move out and follow in his footsteps. He had gathered—more from what was unsaid than what was said—Tommy didn't get along with his stepfather.

"I'm going to ask you a question, and I hope you'll be straight with me. Did your stepfather do that?"

"What makes you think that?"

"A hunch." Mr. Pritchard took a long swig of ice water. "Did he or didn't he?"

"I don't want to talk about it."

"I sure understand that. But I want to know if the son of a bitch is hitting you or not. Then we can quit talking."

"Yeah, he blows up sometimes. It's not a big deal."

"You two don't get along, do you?"

"I can't stand him," Tommy said in a voice so subdued that Mr. Pritchard almost missed it.

"Is he home now?"

Tommy's head jerked up.

"No. You can't say anything to him! He won't like it!" Tommy's vehemence raised his voice so that Mr. Pritchard had no trouble hearing that time.

"Well, that's not what I had in mind. I want to have a word with your mother. When he's not there."

Tommy visibly relaxed, but he still regarded Mr. Pritchard with suspicion.

"I don't think that's such a good idea, either."

"Maybe, maybe not. But I want to talk to her, and I think I can convince her not to mention it to your jackass of a stepfather."

"He plays poker on Monday nights. She's usually home. But really, it's fine. I can handle it."

"I'm sure you can. Still don't mean things can't get better."

Mr. Pritchard took a last swallow of water without meeting Tommy's eyes. He set his glass down. "And Tommy?"

"Yeah? I mean, yes, sir."

"Drinking won't solve your problems."

"I don't know what you're talking about."

"Maybe that's just aftershave I smell on you sometimes. Let's get back to work."

On Monday evening, Mr. Pritchard left his house for a little stroll. As he headed out the door, he glanced at Sadie. "You know, if you were any sort of decent dog, I'd take you for a walk." She peered back at him, head low, and gave a tiny wag of her tail.

"Never mind. We'll work on it." He patted her head, and she wagged harder.

He walked down the dirt road, through the elongated shadows of trees, golden light spilling through the gaps and glinting off the occasional flying insect. When he arrived at Tommy's house, he surveyed it for a minute. It was in sorry shape. Possibly the sorriest home on a street full of sorry homes. It sagged as if its unhappy family weighed it down. He took in the rust stains, the yard left to its own devices, the splintered steps with a crevice so big between them and the door you could lose a small child. Mr. Pritchard shook his head, squared his shoulders, and knocked on the door.

Tommy answered it, eyes widening when he saw who was on his doorstep.

"This really isn't a good idea," Tommy hissed.

"We'll see," Mr. Pritchard said and stood on the steps, grim and immovable as a mountain.

Tommy slumped in defeat. He pushed open the screen door, and its torn netting flapped. Mr. Pritchard stepped into the cool, dark house.

"Can you call your mother?"

Tommy tried one more time. "Seriously, Mr. Pritchard. Everything is fine. So my stepdad gets mad sometimes. It's not a big deal."

"I have an idea. Trust me."

Tommy seemed as trusting as Sadie when she first arrived. But he finally called over his shoulder, "Ma! Mr. Pritchard is here, and he wants to talk to you."

Tommy's mother came out of a back bedroom, patting her hair, smoothing her skirt, and putting on a thousand-watt smile. She wore a purple miniskirt and a paisley blouse, and leather string was tied around her head. Her blond hair hung down past her shoulders. She could almost pass for a teenager. Almost.

"Oh! You're the fella my Tommy's been working for, ain't that right?"

"Yes, ma'am."

"I'm Jenny," she said, thrusting out her hand and adding a dimple to her smile.

"Pleased to meet you. I am here to offer a solution that I think will work for all of us."

Jenny smiled vaguely. "A solution? What on earth do we need a solution for?" She turned her head and blinked at him, three or four long blinks. Flirtatious blinks. He plowed on, ignoring it.

"I need an assistant. A boy Tommy's age needs a steady job. And he also could use a safe place to live. I'm offering both."

Jenny laughed, but her darting eyes hinted at some inner turmoil. "What on earth are you talking about, Mr. Pritchard? Tommy has a great place to live. Right, Tommy?"

Mr. Pritchard checked Tommy's reaction. Tommy stared at him as if he had spoken in tongues. Now he considered his next move. He had summed up Jenny in that first minute: her voice dripped Southern honey, her clothes whispered hippie, but the crow's feet around her eyes signaled fast-approaching middle age that she seemed to be trying to avoid at all costs. He wondered if maybe she would think it a tad more convenient to not have a nearly adult child around all the time, reminding her of the passage of years. *Should I take that approach?* But no. That would probably wound her ego a bit. And imply she didn't love her son, which she obviously did. No, he would just come right out and say what the problem was.

"Mrs.—I'm sorry, I didn't catch your last name. But, ma'am, let's be honest. We both know who gave Tommy that black eye. I am not making judgments. It's hard for a man to take over a household where another half-grown man who is not his blood lives. So I am proposing Tommy come live with me. He'll be right down the street. He'll still go to school. I'll make sure of that. And he'll work with me. He'll learn a trade. And if he goes on to do something else with his life, well, he'll have some handy skills to use around his own house one day."

Jenny's facade crumbled, and her eyes filled with tears. "Tommy? What is this all about? Did you ask him to do this?"

Tommy turned to his mom, dazed. "No. I had no idea he was going to say any of this."

"Are you that unhappy here?"

Tommy hesitated, looking from his mother to Mr. Pritchard. Mr. Pritchard gave him a tiny nod. Tommy took a deep breath. "I am, Ma." He winced as a tear slid down her cheek. "It's not you. It's him. He doesn't like me, and I don't like him."

"But to move out? That seems a bit much." A little nervous laugh fought with her teary eyes. "We could talk to Ernie. We'll work it out."

"Ma. We could try this and see how it goes. Without mentioning why to Ernie. You know how he gets. And I will come see you. When he's not here. I'll come a lot."

"Oh, Tommy. I only wanted a happy family. I wanted someone to take care of us." She swallowed and brushed a tear away with the edge of one finger, careful not to smudge her mascara. "I thought you got that in a fight at school."

"I didn't want to tell you the truth. Ernie's nice enough to you, but me and him don't get along. And as long as he doesn't treat you bad, I thought I would just put up with it."

"Oh, Tommy! You should have told me!"

"I know, Ma. But I didn't want to cause more problems." He turned to Mr. Pritchard. "You really mean this? You want me to come live with you?"

"Yep."

"I want to give it a try, Ma. I promise I'll come see you. And I'm almost grown anyway. I only have a year left of school."

Jenny stepped towards her son. She placed her palm on his cheek and smiled a watery smile. "I love you, you know. I may not have been able to give you everything, but I've tried my best."

Tommy blushed at the public show of affection. Mr. Pritchard studied the knickknacks on a nearby shelf as if he were thinking of buying one. "I know, Ma. I know."

"I still think we should talk to Ernie. Give it one more try as a family."

"Ma," Tommy said, swallowing. "I ain't ever gotten in a fistfight at school. Ever." His voice was so soft that Mr. Pritchard had to stop himself from leaning forward to hear. He didn't want to intrude on the moment.

"What?" Jenny frowned. "But . . . oh. Oh, Tommy. You should have told me." Mr. Pritchard had a feeling that deep down, she had known what was going on and had hoped the situation would right itself. But Mr. Pritchard could only see it deteriorating as Tommy asserted his independence more and more. Two roosters in a small henhouse rarely worked out. Each had to prove he was the top bird.

"It wouldn't have helped," Tommy said. "And it might have made things worse. One day, I am going to have to hit him back. I can't keep lettin' him hit me."

Jenny's eyes slid away from her son's. She stared at the wall, and in her face, Mr. Pritchard could see scenario after scenario play out. And none of them were good. Jenny pulled a tissue out of a box that sat on a table next to the sofa. Mr. Pritchard winced at its orange and brown crocheted cover. Jenny dabbed at her eyes. "If this is what you want to do and you promise to come see me, I guess we'll do it. When will you . . . move your stuff over there?" They both looked at Mr. Pritchard.

"No time like the present."

Jenny sighed, but nodded. Tommy disappeared into his room and threw everything he could into a couple of garbage bags, re-emerging a few minutes later. Jenny had a hard time meeting Mr. Pritchard's eyes. He placed a large and gentle hand on her arm.

"You're doing the right thing. I promise I'll take good care of him."

She bobbed her head in acknowledgment and turned to Tommy. "You make sure you come see me, Tommy, you hear?"

"I will, Ma. I promise."

Mr. Pritchard took a bag and slung it over his shoulder. Tommy unwittingly mimicked his movement, and they set off, out of the house and down the dusty street. "Mr. Pritchard?" Tommy asked.

"Yes?" Mr. Pritchard replied, ignoring the ever-so-slight quaver in the boy's voice.

"I just, uh, want to ask . . ." Tommy cleared his throat. "Why are you doing this?"

"I had a stepdad once. I know what it's like to get knocked around by the so-called man of the house."

"Were you able to get away?"

"Yep."

"How did you do it?"

"Lied about my age and joined the Army. And promptly got sent over to a war."

"I could do that." Tommy's voice held a note of excitement.

Mr. Pritchard stopped walking and turned to face him. "Over my dead body. Believe me. I know how you think because I used to be you. You think war is all about proving yourself, about adventure, about being a hero. Well, it ain't any of that. It's mind-numbing tedium interrupted by gut-wrenching fear and seeing things you can't ever, ever erase. It's blood and guts, and trust me, those words do not convey a tenth of what it's actually like to see someone nearly cut in half and trying to hold their insides in. About what it's like to be sprayed by your buddy's blood. About what it's like to live when your buddies die."

"What did you do?"

"I was a waist gunner." Mr. Pritchard started walking, and his beard tilted up a little as he pursed his lips. "I shot other planes down. Other men who were just like me. Young, stupid men who, like me, thought they would go to war and come back a hero. Young men who had no beef with me but were simply obeying orders. You go to war as one thing, you come back as something else, and it ain't ever what you thought it would be."

They finished the walk without talking, and Mr. Pritchard wondered if the boy had listened to anything he said.

As they arrived at Mr. Pritchard's trailer, Tommy broke the silence.

"Just so you know, you didn't have to talk to my mother. I can take care of myself," Tommy said.

"I am sure you can. But why stay there if you don't have to? And I could use the help. Win-Win."

13
Violet

July 1969

As summer deepened, the days strung themselves together in an endless chain of muggy heat. Violet spent less time outside tending her tomatoes and sitting on her patio, but she ventured out enough to notice Tommy was becoming quite a regular at Mr. Pritchard's house. And at Mrs. McCabe's. She often saw his car in Mr. Pritchard's driveway and glimpsed the teenager ducking in and out of one house or another. Between the two of them, they seemed to be keeping him busy.

One steamy morning, as Mrs. McCabe was making her daily trek to her mailbox, she spotted Violet returning from the grocery store. She ambled over to Violet as she lifted bags out of her trunk.

"I can't get rid of him."

"What are you talking about?"

"That Tommy kid. He's here morning, noon, and night. Doesn't he have a home? A family?"

Mrs. McCabe continued ranting, using her hands and her mail to emphasize her point, but not to help Violet as she struggled to carry two bags to the door. Violet fumbled at the door latch, managing with difficulty to turn it. She pushed the door ajar with her foot and entered the house, Mrs. McCabe right on her heels.

Violet set the bags on her counter. "I have more to bring in. Are you going to follow me or just wait here?"

"I'll wait here."

"Make yourself at home," Violet said. Mrs. McCabe settled herself in a kitchen chair, completely unfazed by Violet's sarcasm.

She brought in the rest of her groceries and listened to Mrs. McCabe as she put them away.

"Seriously. He has trimmed hedges, weeded my garden, painted the porch railings, changed some light bulbs. Meanwhile, he comes to the door and asks if there's anything else. I have to talk to him. I moved here so I wouldn't have to chat with people."

"Yes, I understand that feeling," Violet said, turning to look deliberately at Mrs. McCabe.

"Wasn't he supposed to be helping Mr. Pritchard?" the elderly woman continued.

Violet wondered how a smart woman like Mrs. McCabe could be so oblivious to pointed barbs. The thought occurred to her that perhaps she was willfully oblivious. *Something I should cultivate*, Violet thought.

"Mrs. McCabe, you were right there when Mr. Pritchard offered up your yard as a place for Tommy to work off his debt. Also, I am sure he will find something else to do one of these days. He's young, and he must have friends. But in the meantime, he's doing things for you that you might find difficult. Enjoy."

"Enjoy my foot. He bangs, he talks, he needs water."

"Speaking of which, can I get you something to drink, Mrs. McCabe?"

"I don't want to be an imposition, but I am a bit parched."

Violet plucked a glass out of the cabinet. "Tea, lemonade, or water?"

"Lemonade?" Mrs. McCabe said. "Now lemonade is a fine beverage for a hot day."

"Sooo . . . lemonade?"

"Well, why not?"

Arabella's shave-and-a-haircut knock sounded at the door. When Violet called for her to come in, the little girl bounced into the house, dragging her energy with her like a wake that rippled out to the corners of the room.

"Hi, Miss Violet! Hi, Mrs. McCabe! It is soooooo boring when Allen is napping. When do you think he will actually do something?"

"I hate to tell you, but it might be a few more months," Violet said.

"How old is he now?" Mrs. McCabe asked.

"He was born at the end of April, a week before my birthday. I thought that was a neat present, but now I am not so sure."

"So he's about two, almost three months old, right?"

"Yes."

"Well, soon he will start laughing. And you can make funny faces and play peek-a-boo, and he will think you are the best thing since sliced bread."

"Really?"

"I promise."

Violet observed this exchange as she poured three glasses of lemonade. It was just a few weeks ago that Violet would have bet Mrs. McCabe to be more likely to growl at children than become chummy with them. Maybe trick them into an oven or something. But reassure them? No, she had not seen that coming.

"Mrs. McCabe, did you and your husband and your kids live here?" Arabella asked as she flipped through Violet's stack of *Life* magazines.

"In this neighborhood? No, just me."

"But you lived in Edenton in a different house?"

"Yes, Flynn and I moved to Edenton twenty years ago. Give or take. But in a different house."

"Where did you grow up?"

"I grew up between here and Charleston. Out in the country. Then I lived in Charleston for a while. Then Charlotte. Then Washington, D.C. Then Charleston again. Then Flynn retired and we moved to Edenton, which is where he grew up. Then after my daughter passed, I moved here."

"After all that traveling, Edenton must seem a bit . . . dull," Violet said.

"Who wants excitement at my age? I wanted a small place I could easily take care of. And I wanted to be left alone. Although that isn't working out so well."

"I know what you mean," Violet said, her voice as dry as a cornstalk in winter.

"What does 'barnstorming' mean?" Arabella interrupted. She held up a *Life* magazine with its cover photo of the gray, pocked surface of the moon and the headline, "Barnstorming the Moon."

"Well, that's a good question," Violet said. "That's what they call it when people give aerial shows. Not like the Thunderbirds you see at the Air Force base, but smaller planes. I think they got the name because they are usually out in the country and the best places to land are farms. With barns."

"So what does 'barnstorming the moon' mean?"

"Well, you know the astronauts are taking a trip to the moon soon, right?"

Arabella nodded.

"So I guess it is a kind of aerial stunt, in a way. Like the old pilots from years ago, they will fly to the moon, do their thing, then fly home. Does that make sense?"

"Men on the moon!" Mrs. McCabe harrumphed. "They are going to get themselves ki—" Her eyes flitted to Arabella. "Er, carried away."

"I think they have made things very—" Violet also glanced at Arabella. "Organized. Very, very organized."

"Well, I hope so."

"Will you watch it, Mrs. McCabe?" Arabella asked.

"Yes, I guess I probably will. The whole world will be." She shook her head. "Landing men on the moon," Mrs. McCabe said again. "I can tell you when I was your age, I could never have imagined anything close to such a thing."

"Nor could I," Violet said.

"Miss Violet?"

"Yes?"

"You still don't have a TV, do you?" Arabella asked.

"Well, no, I don't."

Arabella's eyes twinkled, and she jumped up.

"I have a great idea! We should all watch it at my house together!"

"Oh Arabella, that's a wonderful idea, but I am not sure

your mother would want us all there with the baby and all. I believe they said it might go quite late."

"I will ask her! I will tell her you don't have a TV, and Mrs. McCabe has one but doesn't have anyone to watch with, and I will promise her that I will help with the chores and Baby Allen for the rest of the week. Or the month even!" She picked up her glass of lemonade, drained it, and said, "Gotta go!"

And she was out the door before either of the two women could object further.

14
Caroline

July 1969

Outwardly, Caroline tried to appear interested and open-minded as her daughter's proposal for watching the moon landing tumbled out like a white-water river. Inwardly, she began concocting excuses.

"And if we invite Miss Violet and Mrs. McCabe, we have to invite Sadie and Mr. Pritchard and Tommy, or they will feel left out!" Arabella finished.

Just as Caroline was about to enumerate all the reasons why they couldn't host their neighbors, she saw her husband's face light up. George Fitzgerald was a NASA buff. He watched every launch he could and read as many magazine and newspaper articles as he got his hands on. He had already expressed his excitement about the upcoming lunar landing. Caroline remembered his face when he talked about the moon mission earlier in the week. He had looked like a little boy on Christmas morning. Now, he was more enthusiastic than ever at the thought of sharing the event with others. Caroline almost won him to her side when she pointed out how long the coverage might go. Even George had to admit they might be in for a late night. Caroline explained how they would pay for getting the children off schedule for the whole week beyond. He listened, nodding, but she saw that when he glimpsed his daughter's pleading eyes, his thoughtful expression melted into one of tenderness. She braced herself for defeat.

"Sweetheart," he said, taking her hand. "This is the most incredible thing that has ever happened in our lifetimes. Arabella is going to remember it forever. And she will either remember it as the time her parents made her miss the biggest event of this century, or the time they invited friends over and had a Lunar Landing Party. It's one night. We'll all work hard to keep Baby Allen on schedule and tell everyone to not be too loud when he's sleeping," George said.

"Lunar Landing Party? You've given it a name?"

Her husband grinned, the dimple in his left cheek making an appearance. The dimple that had made Caroline fall for him.

"And it is summer. It's not like it's a school night."

Caroline considered her daughter's face alight with hope, then her husband's dimpled smile awash with anticipation. She vainly fished for any other obstacles she could present to her husband.

"Everyone can bring a dish so you don't have to do everything," George said, putting an arm around her waist and pulling her close.

"Please, Mama?" Arabella hugged Caroline's legs and stared up with pleading eyes. "It will be the best day ever! And you don't want Violet to miss it, or Mrs. McCabe to watch it alone!"

Caroline raised a hand in defeat. "I know when I am outnumbered! We'll have a little party. Emphasis on 'little.'

Arabella, can you get me a piece of paper and a pen? I need to start making a list."

Arabella's whoop of joy swallowed Caroline's request. George's arm tightened around Caroline, and Arabella hugged them both. Caroline couldn't help but laugh. *One night*, she told herself. Surely she could manage to be social for one night?

"Yay! It's going to be the best night ever! Everyone will be together watching it! And we get to stay up late past our bedtime!"

"So we really are inviting grumpy Mr. Pritchard?" Caroline asked, raising an eyebrow.

"We can't leave him out. And he's not so bad. He just likes to act all cranky."

"From what I hear, he must be as superb an actor as Gregory Peck. And I don't know about a dog . . ."

"She's very sweet. I promise she won't hurt a fly or have an accident in the house."

"Well. If you're sure she doesn't jump or bite or . . . anything."

"She hardly moves."

"Oh, poor thing. I guess that would be OK. Are you sure he will come?"

"I think so."

"Well, that will be as momentous as the Lunar Landing."

Arabella headed to the door.

"Where are you going?" Caroline asked.

"I've got to go tell Miss Violet the good news. And when I get back, I am going to look up 'momentous'. Then I am going to make invitations."

And before Caroline could answer, Arabella had skipped out the door and halfway across their front yard.

15

Violet

After Arabella left, Violet had headed outside, wrongly thinking she could do some weeding around her front porch before the heat built up. So now here she was, dripping sweat and deeply regretting her decision.

"Miss Violet! Miss Violet!! Guess what?" Arabella ran up to her, a smile as wide as the sea lighting up her face.

"Goodness! Did you win a million dollars?" Violet stood, took off a gardening glove, and ineffectually fanned herself.

"No! That would be good, but this is really good, too! My mom said we could have the Lunar Landing Party!"

"Whoa! It's a party now? And with a name?"

"My dad came up with the name. But if we are going to invite you and Mrs. McCabe over, we should also include Mr. Pritchard and Tommy. So that many people kind of makes a party, right?"

"Well, I guess it does, but I am not sure I would count on Mr. Pritchard coming."

Arabella's reply was lost in the rumble of a moving truck trundling down the street. It stopped in front of the empty house next to the Fitzgeralds, then lurched into reverse and backed into the driveway. The brakes squealed, and the truck rocked to a halt. Two men jumped out of the cab, shoving and pushing each other and shouting good-natured insults as they went around to the back of the vehicle. One of them raised the roll-up door of the cargo space, sending the ratcheting sound echoing across the sunstruck neighborhood.

"Ooooh! New people!" Arabella clapped her hands.

Violet shaded her eyes against the glare of the sun. "I wonder if those are the guys I saw the other day."

"You met them?"

"Well, I did meet two men who were looking at the house."

"Let's go over and see!" Arabella grabbed Violet's hand and tugged her in the direction of the trailer next door.

Violet balked. "Oh, Arabella! I can't meet new people like this. I am a mess!"

"No, you're not! And besides, you said you already met them."

As Violet mentally fumbled for other arguments, a car pulled up and parked in front of the moving truck. A man got out, and Violet immediately recognized Nick, the GI who had asked for directions. As he closed the car door, he turned and saw Violet and Arabella. He waved and began walking over.

Oh, no. I'm hot and sweaty and my hair is curling up and I look awful. Then she stopped herself. *Wait. Why should I care?* She squared her shoulders and allowed Arabella to pull her towards Nick so that they joined him where Violet's yard bled into the sandy road.

"Hi! Violet, right?" he said, his eyes smiling into hers and making her aware of every drop of sweat that trickled down her body and every frizzed hair that caught the sun. She wondered if she looked like a frayed Q-tip.

"That's right. And this is Arabella."

"Hi, Arabella! Nice to meet you. I met your mom the other day when we were looking at the place."

"Oh, I'm not her mother," Violet said.

"Oh. Oh. Sorry." A sheepish expression crossed his face, but was it her imagination, or did he also look glad?

"Understandable mistake. She lives next door to you, as a matter of fact."

He held out his hand to her. "Pleased to make your acquaintance, Arabella. I'm Nick."

"Hi! Are you moving in?"

"I am, indeed. Along with my buddy Harry."

Displaying exceptional timing, the aforementioned Harry yelled from the porch, "Hey, Nick! Is this how it's going to be? Me doing all the work?"

"If I have any say about it, yes," Nick shouted back. He winked at Arabella. "Want to come meet him?"

She bobbed her head, and the three crossed the road.

The third man came out of the house. "It's hot as blazes out here."

"Kid alert!" Harry said.

"What is a kid alert?" Arabella asked.

The dark-eyed man leaned down conspiratorially. "It means that some people who tend to use bad language have to watch themselves now."

"You mean they say bad words?" Arabella's eyes widened.

"I am sorry to report they sometimes do. I promise, though, that we will be on our best behavior while in your company. Right, Harry?"

"Who, me? I am always a gentleman, especially in front of the ladies." He bowed deeply towards Arabella. She giggled.

"And who do we have the pleasure of talking to?" Harry asked.

"I am Arabella Constance Fitzgerald."

"A lady's name if ever I heard one. I am Harry Cisse." He waved his hand at the man who had just come out of the house. "And this is our friend and number-one furniture wrecker, Roger Charnock." Roger was shorter, with brown hair and black-framed glasses.

"I dented one table. One!" he said as he gave Violet and Arabella a little wave.

"And this is Violet . . . Wentworth, right?"

"That's right."

"Miss Violet is my best friend," Arabella said.

Nick grinned. "Well, you can tell a lot about someone by the company they keep. So if you're friends with Violet, she must be a remarkable person."

"She is." Arabella looked at Harry and Roger. "She lives across the street." She pointed. "And I live right there, with my brother, mother, and father. But my brother is only two months old, so he doesn't do much."

"Well, enjoy that while you can," Nick said. "I am the third of seven brothers and sisters, and life was a lot simpler when they didn't do much."

"Seven! That sounds pretty neat!"

"It has its ups and downs. And it may have had something to do with why I joined the Air Force."

"You're in the Air Force? So is my dad. What do you do?"

"I am a mechanic. I work on the airplanes."

"My dad works in the hospital, and sometimes he drives an ambulance, and sometimes he stitches up people."

"I would say that's a good father to have. And a good neighbor. Never know when you might need medical attention."

"My dad took out my stitches here." She pointed to her forehead where a small scar peeked out of her hairline.

"Well, that looks like it might have hurt."

"It did, but I really don't remember it too well. I was little."

"So, a long time ago," Harry said solemnly.

Arabella nodded. "A loooong time ago. I was two."

"We seem to have matching scars." Harry bent down and pointed to a similar scar on his forehead.

"Oh, wow! It is like mine!"

"Yes, but my dad did not take out my stitches."

Violet watched the exchange, amused. She liked the way Nick and Harry talked to Arabella, bantering and joking around with her and not excluding her in favor of talking to an adult.

"I hate to say it, but we better get to work," Nick said. "Harry and I promised Roger lunch since he works for food." He lifted a box out of the truck and thrust it at Harry. "Arabella, one day, I'd love to hear the story of how you got your scar."

"How about me? Wanna hear mine?" asked Harry.

"Do I have a choice?" Nick asked as he grabbed another carton.

"Nope!"

Violet and Arabella said their goodbyes, and as they walked back to Violet's, Arabella said, "They seem nice."

"Yes, they do."

"Maybe we should invite them to the Lunar Landing Party."

"That is a question for your mother," Violet answered. And chose not to examine how her heart seemed to skip a tiny beat. *It must be the heat*, she told herself.

16
Nick

July 1969

After the men unloaded the last items, Harry threw himself down on the sofa that sat in the middle of the living room.

"I don't know how you made it through boot camp," Nick said, crossing his arms and looking down at his roommate. "You work for an hour and relax for two."

"This is not relaxation you see before you, but an empty tank. I need refueling. Feed me, and I will be raring to go."

"Let's go, Rog. We won't get anything more out of him until we stuff him with pizza."

They returned the rental truck and then drove to a local pizza place that hugged the edge of the base.

"I can't believe you guys are abandoning me to the barracks," Roger said as a waitress brought three beers to the table.

"Feel free to come over anytime," Nick said.

"Especially when it's time to mow the yard," Harry said with a tip of his beer and a wink.

"Sure you don't want to change your mind and live the carefree life?"

Nick shook his head. "Nope. I am looking forward to

living off base. First thing I am buying is a grill. I shall be King of the Backyard Barbecue. Roger, we'll be sure to let you know when we fire it up."

Roger snorted. "First thing you will need is a lawn mower. And mowing the lawn in the summer here? I give you a month before you wish you were back on base."

"Not likely, Rog. I've been looking forward to this for a long time."

"Well, I hope so, for your sake." Roger raised his mug. "Here's to the city mouse becoming a country mouse."

They laughed and clinked their glasses.

Nick and Harry drove Roger to the barracks and picked up Harry's car. When they returned to their new home, Harry headed to his room, declaring himself done for the time being.

"What happened to 'raring to go'?" Nick called to his retreating back.

"Refueled. Now need rest. Underestimated the capacity in the old engine."

Nick shook his head as he heard Harry rummaging around, presumably looking for his bedding. Snores soon emanated from the room. Well, let him enjoy his break. Nick enjoyed the alone time. He pondered the boxes stacked haphazardly around the kitchen and living room. He had to laugh that a boy from Brooklyn was moving into a trailer in South Carolina. Beyond his back window stood a swath of piney woods, and, through their tall, straight trunks, orderly rows of emerald corn plants gleamed in the sun. It was so different from where he had grown up, he might as well be in a foreign country. He grew up running with his friends on the sidewalks and city streets that led to the crowded apartment where he lived with his family. Here, you had to drive to the store. There, you could walk and buy your groceries at the market, your bread at the baker's, and your meat at the butcher's. He did kind of miss the proximity of everything at home. And he missed his favorite hot dog and hamburger joint that was right at the end of his block. But he liked it down here in the South. His first encounters with Southerners were some of his fellow trainees at his Texas boot camp. He would have sworn they were hamming up the accent. But one day, after graduation, he ventured into town to a little restaurant for breakfast, and a middle-aged woman with towering blond hair brought a glass of water to his table and said, "How y'all doing this mornin'?" with a drawl so thick you could pour it on pancakes. He grinned at her in delight.

"I'm doin' good. How about you?" he said, hoping to engage her in conversation so he could listen to her some more.

She regarded him for a minute and then became the first person to ask the question he now got all the time when meeting new people not in the Air Force. "Y'all aren't from around here, are ya?"

He chuckled. "You can tell, huh?"

"You're like a rooster in a henhouse with that accent. Kinda stands out. New York?"

"Guilty."

"Aw, don't worry. We are used to people from all over here, being next to the base and all. What can I get ya, hon?"

Some things on the menu baffled him. Biscuits and gravy? Grits? He ordered scrambled eggs and bacon, to be safe. But he did not join the Air Force to be safe, so he did go out on a limb and order a side of biscuits instead of toast.

They had been delicious. The golden, crisp top hid the fluffy, white center that was soft as a cloud. It was heaven. Heaven, with butter on it. He declared himself a fan.

Thinking about that waitress made him think of Violet. Her accent was not as twangy as the ones he heard in Texas, but she definitely sounded Southern. But it was softer. Or maybe that was her voice. Low. A little husky. He shook his head and tried to push her from his mind. Instead, he thought of how, after ten years of living in barracks, he had a place of his own. He liked seeing the woods beyond his back door. He had a yard for the first time in his life. A driveway instead of a parking lot. Neighbors who weren't all GIs like him. He thought he might enjoy this. Let Roger have his doubts. Nick would have his backyard.

He made his bed and unpacked a few things in his bedroom before tackling the kitchen. He had unpacked the plates and silverware before Harry stirred himself and wandered into the room, yawning and scratching his abdomen.

"Well, well. Rip Van Winkle has woken up. Too bad I saved some work for you."

Harry grinned. "Man, you should have taken a rest, too. Gotta love a lazy Saturday."

Nick pushed a box towards him with his foot. "Today is not supposed to be a lazy Saturday, pal. But as long as you're well rested, maybe now you can get busy."

"Slave driver."

Harry ripped the tape off the carton and set about putting some dishes away. Nick did the same with his, and in no time, they stowed the kitchen items in their cabinets and drawers.

A knock sounded at the door, and the men exchanged glances.

"You expecting anybody?"

Harry shook his head. "Nope. You?"

Nick shrugged and answered the door to find a man about his age standing on the stoop along with the little girl he'd met earlier in the day. He carried a cloth-wrapped basket, and she clasped a couple of pieces of construction paper.

"Hello. I'm George Fitzgerald, your neighbor. And I believe you met Arabella."

"Nice to meet you. I'm Nick Battaglia. Arabella, good to see you again. Care to come in? It's still pretty hot outside."

George and Arabella stepped into the air-conditioned trailer, and Harry introduced himself. George held up the cloth-covered dish. "My wife sent these. Biscuits, with a jar of jelly. Best she could do on short notice."

"Aw, she didn't have to do that. But I gotta tell ya, I had my first biscuits when I first joined up and was stationed in Texas. Love at first bite! I can't think of anything your wife could have sent over that would have made me happier."

George laughed. "I grew up in North Carolina, and whenever I was stationed somewhere out of the South, biscuits were one thing I sorely missed."

Arabella leaned towards her father, cupped her mouth, and whispered. Or at least Nick thought she meant to whisper. He heard it plainly enough. "See? I told ya he talked kind of funny."

"Arabella!" George said, giving her a rather stern look. He turned to Nick. "Sorry about that."

Nick laughed. He bent down towards Arabella. "I am from New York. We all talk like this. And can I tell you a secret?"

Arabella nodded with two large dips of her head.

Nick leaned closer and whispered, "When I first moved here, I thought people here talked funny."

She grinned at him. "Mr. Harry doesn't talk funny. Well, he sort of does, but not like you."

"Harry is from Ohio. Different funny."

George cleared his throat. "I think Arabella has something to ask you."

Nick raised his eyebrows in question.

Arabella gave each of the men the invitations she had made. "We are having a Lunar Landing Party next Sunday. We want you to come."

"You are very welcome to come, but we understand if you have plans," George added.

"Plans? Not really. I would love to come. Harry?"

"I'm a go for that!"

"May I bring something?" Nick asked.

"Some people are bringing a dish, but you just moved in. You don't need to go to any trouble."

"If everyone else is chipping in, then I better chip in, too. Can't let the neighbors show me up. And I can actually cook a thing or two," Nick said, grinning.

Harry leaned forward. "Don't let him fool you. Nick here is an excellent cook. It's why I agreed to be his roommate. What time should we be there?"

"We are starting at three o'clock. I understand you met Violet, across the street. She'll be there, so at least you'll have one or two people you've already met."

Nick welcomed that news, but kept his face and voice neutral. "Great! We'll see you Sunday."

As he watched them walk away, he thought what a friendly street he had moved to.

17

Dominico Battaglia

1942-1969

Nick never had a life plan when he was growing up. No ambitions beyond running the streets with his friends. As the third child of seven, he—like the other children from sizable families in the neighborhood—did not receive much personal attention, but he did get a lot of freedom. As long as he got his work done and was home for supper, he could play stickball in the street, smoke in the alleys, whistle at the girls who giggled as they sashayed by. Nick earned himself a reputation as one of the neighborhood's worst troublemakers. That he was also a charming one kept him just on the right side of real trouble. He exasperated his teachers, maddened the shopkeepers, worried the parents of the girls in the neighborhood, yet he could grin at them and flatter them and walk away unscathed. To the girls themselves, his infectious smile and bad boy reputation proved irresistible. He strutted around with his cigarette pack rolled up in his sleeve, his thick, dark hair slicked back with a little wave at the top. Very James Dean-like. He didn't dwell on it, but he figured he would probably end up like James. Dead at a young age, mourned by all the girls who knew him. After all, twenty-four seemed old enough. Anything beyond that was getting old, and what was there for a thirty-year-old man? Bills, backaches, bad knees, and a brood of kids all needing new shoes at the same time. In other words, drudgery.

One of the highlights of his days—though he would never admit it to his friends—was time spent with his grandmother. She roped him into her kitchen, saying she needed help because she wasn't as young as she used to be. Since she seemed quite able-bodied, he suspected she recruited him to keep him out of trouble. Not that he minded it. In fact, he truly enjoyed listening to her stories of growing up in Italy, of the voyage to America, of starting a new life in New York City. And as she talked, she instructed him on how to make the breads and sauces that had populated his childhood. The two of them worked together in the crowded little kitchen, redolent with garlic and yeast and dough, creating meals that he would later realize had been the embodiment of her love for her family.

When he was seventeen, two events changed the course of his life. First, his grandmother passed away, leaving him without his anchor. And second, he met a beautiful girl who swept him away.

He met Giulia when he attended his best friend Tony's sister's wedding. The February nuptials featured a Valentine's Day theme, with the church decked out in red flowers and white ribbon. He wore a dark suit—out of style and a tad short in the arms and legs—but he still turned heads. He was used to his effect on girls—and sometimes women—and didn't think too much about it. Until he saw one of the bridesmaids coming down the aisle.

A vision in red walked down the path between pews. The scarlet of her dress accented her delicate features and huge dark eyes. As she made her way to the altar, their eyes met, and Nick decided Cupid must exist, for her eyes shot an arrow straight into his heart. At the reception, he asked her to dance. She said yes, and from that moment, they were hardly apart.

Giulia DeSanto lived across the river in a wealthy suburb in New Jersey. Tony said her family owned a sprawling house with a huge green lawn and a swimming pool, but she liked the excitement of the city enough to put up with his family's cramped apartment and had started coming to stay with them. Tony thought she was crazy. He'd joke that he would gladly switch places with her.

"Why didn't you introduce me before?" Nick asked Tony.

"Because I knew you'd ask her out, and you're a no-good bum, so I tried to hide her from you."

"Looks like I found her anyway," Nick said with a grin.

In a way, Giulia was like Nick—always flirting with trouble and managing to hover just this side of catastrophe. But she pushed further than he ever did. She thrived on danger—throwing her head back and laughing on roller coasters, flinging her arms out on the back of a cousin's speeding motorcycle, or leaning out the window of the passenger seat of drag-racing cars. She once walked toe-to-heel on the ledge of an apartment building roof, and his heart seized up with fear. But she merely laughed and jumped down, hugged him, and called him an old woman.

She loved to party and could drink some of his friends under the table, which astonished everyone since she didn't weigh much over 100 pounds. But the longer they dated, the more he observed she was rarely without a drink. She carried a flask in her handbag for "medicinal purposes," as she laughingly called it. Sometimes, he caught her looking pensive, which she would instantly shake off when she realized he was looking at her. She would never tell him what, if anything, was wrong. But he sensed that behind the luminous face she presented to the world lay a pool of darkness, deep and untouchable. He recognized this dichotomy even as they talked, or danced, or made love. And yes, they made love. She was his first, but he suspected he wasn't hers, a notion that troubled him but one which he could not bring himself to ask her about. She never mentioned a former boyfriend. He never heard of one. But maybe everyone wanted to be polite and not talk about it in front of him. It also bothered him—admittedly after the fact—that she had been the one who brought him up to her aunt and uncle's apartment when no one was home. Leading him by the hand up the stairs to the third floor, laughing over her shoulder as she glanced back at him. He loved her boldness. But it also unsettled him.

These were all things he questioned when alone, but when he was with her, her laugh, her smile, and her manic joy pushed his doubts away. When she looked up at him with her dark eyes, full of mischief, when she laid her head upon his shoulder, when they danced and her warm, lithe body pressed against his, he experienced a bliss that carried him through the times his uncertainty nibbled at him.

They dated almost a year. They did everything together, and sometimes Giulia's little sister, Talia, would tag along. She was three years younger, coltish, unfinished, full of questions. Nick did not mind too much. In her sister's presence,

Giulia's brashness softened. She was gentler, more tender. Nick enjoyed seeing that facet of her.

The seasons passed. Spring came, and Nick and Giulia rode in open cars with friends, balmy breezes weaving the smell of her perfume with tendrils of the dank smells of the city. Summer arrived, and they lay on sandy beaches crowded with other beachgoers and splashed in the cold Atlantic waters. In the fall, they walked through Central Park, crossing the Bow Bridge and watching autumn-stained leaves drift onto the surface of the lake. When Christmas rolled around, Nick thought of asking Giulia to marry him, but he hesitated. Her frenetic pursuit of thrills attracted him and repelled him. Some invisible hand held him back. He was torn, unable to make up his mind, so he talked to his father about it without mentioning why he worried about her.

"Dominico, rushing into things can land you in a heap of trouble. Taking your time hardly ever does," his father said. "You're young. Give it time. If you love each other, the love will only grow."

He was surprised at the relief that coursed through him at his father's words, and he thought perhaps waiting would give Giulia time to mature and settle down a bit. He would put off the proposal for the time being. His vision of a Christmas engagement melted into a summer one. Or maybe even an October one. He imagined proposing to her on the Bow Bridge of Central Park, him kneeling, her hands to her mouth with delighted surprise, surrounded by glowing, autumnal trees.

That would also give him time to save money for their own place. When Nick had graduated from high school, he got a job in his cousin's auto repair business. He liked the work and began thinking of opening his own shop one day. New York City teemed with automobiles, and there would be no shortage of customers for a competent and honest mechanic. As he walked home from his job one day in January, he shook his head at how practical he had become. *If only Nonna could see me now.*

He ran up the four flights to his family's apartment, the exertion chasing away the cold that sank into his bones during the long hours at work. He hung up his cap and coat on the tree next to the door. "Ma! Pop! I'm home!" He headed to the bathroom to get cleaned up, but his father came into the hall from the kitchen.

"Nick. I need to talk to you. Come in here." His father's characteristic smile was gone, replaced by deep frown lines. Nick's heart clenched. Something was wrong. He followed his father into their cramped living room, filled with lace and Jesus statues. Madonnas watched him with sad eyes from every vantage point. A bleeding, mournful Jesus gazed heavenward.

"Son." His father put his hand on Nick's shoulder. "Dominico, you had better have a seat."

"Pa, I haven't washed up yet." A terrible fear at what his father had to say rose up in his throat. If it couldn't wait until he'd cleaned up, it must be terrible. Had something happened to one of his siblings? His mother? But where was the rest of the family? Wouldn't they be here, too, to hear what his father had to say? Nick sat, dread pressing him into the sofa cushions.

"It's Giulia. It's bad news, son. She fell from the bridge and—" His father's voice grew thick and soft, softer than Nick ever remembered it. "I'm afraid she didn't survive, Nicky."

The words did not make sense. It was as if they had been poured from a pitcher and now lay on the floor at his feet in a nonsensical heap. His brain worked to put them in order. "Giulia fell? From the Brooklyn Bridge? How does someone just fall from the Brooklyn Bridge?" A memory of Giulia on the wall of a building flashed across his eyes: Giulia, arms outspread, backlit by a warm, spring sun, rays picking out red highlights in her dark hair. Her laugh drifting to him on the thread of worry he hoped would anchor her to the structure.

"They say she was with her sister. Fooling around."

"That poor girl," his mother said, standing in the doorway, twisting a dish towel in her hands, the crease between her eyebrows deep as a canyon. "And her poor sister. It's just awful."

All the times he witnessed her reckless behavior, he had pictured her falling, crashing, tumbling, but somehow he still never thought anything would happen. His shock paralyzed him, muted him, but another emotion wove through his numb psyche: a sense of inevitability. Could anyone who courted danger as relentlessly as Giulia avoid getting stung by it eventually?

The attendees at her funeral sat in the pews, heads bowed in heavy sorrow. Everyone wept, their pain palpable on the cold winter air, ponderous with the scent of roses. After the service, at the wake, and in the days following, they murmured about how sad, how tragic, that one so young should die so suddenly, so needlessly. Nick at first tuned them out, but he caught a fragment here, a piece there, of something other than grief. He began to hear murmurs that her death was not a random accident after all.

He approached Tony and asked why people were saying Giulia's death was not accidental.

Tony at first dismissed the talk. "Come on, Nicky. People talk. They make up shit. They can't let anyone rest in peace." But as Tony spoke, his eyes drifted away from Nick's. Nick pressed him.

"Nick, she fell off the Brooklyn Bridge. You really think that was an accident?" Tony finally snapped.

"It could have been," Nick said. "She was always doing crazy shit."

"I gotta go," Tony said and tried to pull away.

"Tony." Nick grabbed his arm. "If you know something, ya gotta tell me. Don't you think I have a right to know?"

Tony fell into troubled silence, looking up their street at the housewives going in and out of shops, their bags growing heavier with each stop.

"A right? Maybe you do, Nick. But once you know something, you can't unknow it. You sure you want that?"

"Yes, I do."

Tony studied his friend, and his shoulders sagged.

"OK. Have it your way. But you better sit down."

Nick's heart skipped as he remembered his father telling him to sit before he broke the news about Giulia's death, and he had a sudden urge to flee, to say never mind. But he knew the not knowing would eat at him. He had to find out the truth. *How bad can it be?* he wondered. How bad can anything be after the horrible fact of knowing Giulia was no longer on this earth?

They sat on the nearest stoop.

"You want the truth, here's the truth. She left a note," Tony said. "She planned it. She didn't fall. And Talia wasn't with her. My aunt and uncle spread that story around so it sounded like an accident. If the priest knew, she wouldn't get a proper burial, you know?"

Nick sucked in his breath. Closed his eyes. Breathed the shock in and out. He wanted to say no, that she could not have taken her own life. "What did the note say?" Nick asked.

"Nick, don't ask me that. It's bad. I don't want you to remember her this way. Remember the good stuff."

"Tony, she killed herself while she was my girl. You don't think I'm going to be asking what I could have done for the rest of my life?"

"Trust me, Nick. You don't want to know this. But I can tell you it wasn't about you."

"Tony, please."

Tony looked up at the sky. He took a deep breath and dropped his head, staring down at the concrete walk beneath his feet. His eyes met Nick's. "I'll tell you. But you can't tell anyone. Not a soul. Do I have your word?"

"I swear on my grandmother's grave."

"She said her father—" He broke off, then started again. "She said he . . . did things to her. He . . . had sex with her."

Nick's breath left his body. The world—the world he thought he had known—shifted around him, a kaleidoscope with an added fragment that changed everything. He was glad he was sitting. "Shit, Tony. Are you serious?"

"She said it had been going on for years, and that's why she liked to come to Brooklyn so much. She said she hated him and hated herself, and she was a bad person and didn't deserve to go on living."

"How could he do that? Jesus Christ, Tony."

"Believe me, we're saying the same thing. My dad confronted her father, and they almost got into a fight. My aunt and mother begged them to stop. If the priest hadn't been coming over, I don't think they could have stopped them. But now my family's not talking to Giulia's family. Talia has come to live with us."

"Did he—has he done the same thing to her?" Nick remembered Talia, three years younger, pretty in her own right but plainer when held next to the flame that was her sister.

"I have no idea. But she came willingly enough. She's not going out much. People think she's devastated with grief. Which is part of it. But Ma is worried about her."

Nick ran a hand across his eyes, then through his hair. He sat for a long moment, arms on his thighs, staring down at the pocks in the sidewalk, the cement comprised of different colors of beige that blended to make one color. Something he had never noticed before.

Tony lit a cigarette and passed it to Nick. Nick took a long drag.

"Nick, I am sorry."

"I am sorry, too. You knew her longer."

"You were in love with her, though."

"I was. But I also felt a . . . I don't know how to describe it. Like she would burn herself up somehow, someday. You know? She did everything like . . . well, fast. Frantic. She reminded me of a candle that's burning too bright and will run out of wick. I am shocked she's dead and yet . . . I am not that surprised. Does that sound insane?"

"No, I kinda understand what you mean. I always thought

she was a bit crazy in the head, but I had no idea what made her act the way she did."

"I had no idea either, Tony. None. All these months and she had that secret burning her up. And I didn't suspect a thing. I feel like I shoulda known. Shoulda been able to do something."

"Don't do that, pal. Don't blame yourself. It won't bring her back, and it won't help you."

Nick snorted, a sharp, bitter sound. "Suddenly you're a wise, old man?"

Tony gave him a wry, sad grin. "It's what my dad said to all of us. But it sounded like good advice."

Nick spent the next few weeks adrift. He went through the motions of his life, there but not there. His mother fretted; his father scrutinized. His siblings treated him as though nothing had happened, but their sidelong glances spoke of their concern. He took long walks, leaving his neighborhood so he wouldn't run into people he knew. Sometimes he walked near the span where Giulia had ended her life as if he could find some answers there. The soaring bridge formed part of the background of his life, and he had rarely given it any more thought than the streets and sidewalks he traversed every day. But now he studied its stalwart towers and delicate web of cables. He wondered what she had thought as she climbed. Did she hesitate? Or was her mind irrevocably made up? If someone had stopped her, would she have tried another day? Had she been afraid when she launched herself into the air? Had it hurt? He hoped she hadn't died in pain.

After a few visits, he began avoiding the bridge as much as possible. He took to riding trains to other boroughs and walking new streets, taking in new sights. On one bitter cold day, he found himself in Manhattan. A biting wind swept down between the buildings and pushed people along to their destinations, leaving the avenues mostly deserted and giving him an eerie feeling of being alone in the vast city. He walked, hands shoved deep into his coat pockets and shoulders hunched against the frigid gusts.

When his hands and feet became numb with cold, he decided to take the train back home, but as he turned a corner to head to a station, a flash of color caught his eye. He stopped and found himself looking at an Air Force recruiting poster featuring a handsome man in dress blues. "The Sky is No Limit!" the caption declared. He stared at it and, for the first time in his life, considered leaving Brooklyn. He could leave all this behind him and see the world.

He went in.

Later, his mother wept, but his father clapped him on the back with pride. Serving one's country was honorable. And the Air Force, his father said, would make a man out of him.

He had been excited about the possibilities, and that sentiment lasted as long as it took for him to be processed into boot camp. When they shaved his dark hair into a pile on the floor, when his sergeant demanded "Yes, sirs" and "No, sirs" and nothing else, when he rose before dawn day after day for drills and inspections, he questioned whether he wouldn't have been better off sticking with his job back in Brooklyn. But he would be lying if he said he wasn't proud of himself when he graduated boot camp. Getting through hell couldn't be much harder, he thought.

The reality of the Air Force did not quite match the promise on the poster. At least not the way he interpreted it. Instead of the world tour he had been hoping for, he got a weather tour. And a bad weather tour at that. He baked in San Antonio for basic training and tech school. The South Texas spring was like the worst heat wave in July in Brooklyn, except back home, he wasn't carrying packs and doing drills in broiling heat that lasted months instead of days. He went from San Antonio to Wichita Falls, where he roasted some more, then froze when the seasons changed and the winter wind rushed unhindered across the open prairie. They told a joke at the base that there was nothing between Wichita Falls and Canada to stop the gusts except a barbed wire fence and a tumbleweed. The wind blew constantly—blistering currents in July and arctic blasts in February. He put up with Wichita Falls and its winds for three years and was then sent to Vietnam, where the monsoonal rains did their best to rot him from the feet up. He never felt dry. The damp pervaded everything: his clothes, his bedding, his letters from home.

He did not fight on the front, but instead serviced airplanes that hauled everything from Slim Jims to live animals to dead soldiers. He asked for a combat assignment, but he was told they needed him where he was. He never did see action, though he did lose friends—a cargo plane carrying some of his buddies crashed in the fetid, steaming jungle. A few got transferred to battle units and didn't come back. He counted himself both lucky and unlucky—lucky to be alive, unlucky to not be part of the action.

From the steam bath of Vietnam, he next went to Goose Bay, Labrador. Just like San Antonio taught him about real heat, Goose Bay taught him about true cold: a bitter, finger-freezing frigidity with blizzards blasting the short days and long nights. When summer finally came, he rejoiced—only to be kept inside by hordes of man-eating mosquitos that might give New York City rats a run for their money.

And now, he found himself in a real-life version of Mayberry. The weather was a little better. Hot and muggy for sure. Mosquitos definitely. And there wasn't anything to do around here except an occasional movie. But so far, this rated as his best assignment.

After nearly ten years of living on bases, he wanted a change. He asked some of his buddies if they wanted to go in together to rent a place, and Harry jumped at the opportunity. Nick had scoured the paper for an affordable place to rent and found the single-wide trailer in Ashford, backed up against a wedge of pine woods that separated the neighborhood from the farms beyond. Something in his city boy imagination awoke as he contemplated the stands of lofty pines interspersed with hardwood trees that formed the back border of the property. He liked the way the sun shone on the needles of the evergreens, how the trunks of the trees shot up so tall and straight. He paid his deposit on the spot without consulting Harry, who had, in truth, told him if the place boasted a bed, a toilet, and a kitchen, he'd be good.

★

His first morning in his new home confirmed his belief he had done the right thing. When he awoke, he padded into the kitchen to get his coffee and gazed out the window. The sun peeked over the horizon, its rays shooting through the trees and a rising mist that wound around them. The beauty almost took his breath away. He was happy to be where he was, he realized. Giulia was now a ghost he had made peace with. He had been glad to get updates from home and learn Talia was doing OK. Kind of a party girl, Tony wrote in a letter, but she wasn't as reckless as her sister had been. He hoped she was not flayed by the same misfortune that had ravaged Giulia. Over the years, he had met some soldiers who had fought in Vietnam who reminded him of Giulia—they wore recklessness like a second skin and brushed up against danger like a hand passing over a candle flame. Nick knew that one day, they might not pull their hand back fast enough. But he didn't know how to help, so he steered clear. The guilt over Giulia's death had accompanied him for years, but time and experience had helped find a path beyond the self-reproach. He had learned three things: one, he had been no more than a kid himself; two, you can't rescue someone when you don't know they are drowning; and three, you can't save someone who doesn't want to save themselves, they'll just pull you down with them. He'd be happy to do what he could for his friends and family. But he would not let himself get tangled up with someone who might drag him down into their own murky depths.

18
Violet

July 1969

"Come in," Violet called, recognizing Arabella's knock over the strains of "I Heard It Through the Grapevine."

Arabella let herself in and skipped over to Violet, who sat at a sewing machine in a corner of the living room.

"I didn't know you could sew."

"I picked up a thing or two from my mother. She insisted I take her old sewing machine when she got a new one, hoping I would follow in her talented footsteps. But the best I can do is make curtains and tablecloths. Although I did make an apron once."

"So what are you making now?"

"Curtains for my bedroom."

Violet snipped a thread and pulled the fabric away from the machine. "What do you think?" she asked Arabella, holding up the curtain.

Arabella examined the white cloth with a border of blue, red, and yellow flowers along the bottom. "Ohhhh! That's pretty."

"Why, thank you."

Arabella brandished a stack of papers she clutched in one small hand. "These are my invitations to the Lunar Landing Party. Here's yours. I drew a violet on the front." She handed Violet a folded piece of construction paper. The cover featured an Arabella-original drawing. She showed Violet the rest. "Here's a cat for Mrs. McCabe, a dog for Mr. Pritchard. For Tommy, I made a car. I already gave Mr. Nick and Mr. Harry their invitations. They both had airplanes on them. I wanted to do something different for each of them, but I don't know them well enough yet."

Violet smiled. "I'm sure they're happy with them anyway."

Violet opened hers. Inside, Arabella had written the date, time, location, and reason for the party. "Well done, Arabella. If you ever need a job, perhaps you can be social secretary for Mrs. Nixon or something."

"What's a social secretary?"

"Someone who is very good at arranging social engagements. Like Lunar Landing Parties, for example."

Arabella's eyes widened. "I could get a job having parties? That would be perfect!"

Violet laughed. "You would be a natural. Are you really going to ask Mr. Pritchard?"

"I wouldn't want him to feel left out."

"I think you should be prepared for him not to come."

"Oh, I think he'll come."

"You do, do you?"

"Yes. Because Sadie's invited, too, and she needs to meet people and learn there are more good people than bad. I don't think she knows that."

"Well, then, I hope he comes for her sake," Violet said,

though she actually hoped he'd come for Arabella's sake. "Are you going to deliver the rest now?"

"Yes! You want to come with me?"

Violet weighed the awful heat outside with wanting to somehow press upon Mrs. McCabe and Mr. Pritchard how important this was for the little girl.

"Sure."

"Yay!"

They headed to Mrs. McCabe's first. The elderly woman opened the invitation and peered at it. "Oh, I don't know, dear. I think that's too late for me. And more people than I have seen in one place in years."

"Oh, but you have to come. My dad says it's going to be a momentous event. And I don't think people should watch momentous events alone. Plus, it wouldn't be a party without you! And it would be a way to say thank you to everyone for helping when you were sick. And we have new neighbors you should meet."

"You sure have a long list of reasons for why I should come."

"So will you please? Pretty please with a cherry on top?"

"I can't think of a good reason to say no. Though I am trying."

"Yay! That means yes! We will see you at three o'clock on Sunday!" As Violet turned to follow Arabella out the door, she saw Mrs. McCabe shaking her head, but a small smile played around the corners of her mouth. Violet thought perhaps Arabella did not need her help after all.

★

As they headed over to Mr. Pritchard's, Arabella spotted Tommy in Mrs. McCabe's backyard, staking her tomatoes.

"Tommy!"

He turned, flipping his blond bangs out of the way. "Hey, Bug."

"Listen, we are having a Lunar Landing Party Sunday. You know, for when the astronauts land on the moon."

"I could have figured that one out."

"Well, anyway, we want you to come! Please say yes! Everyone is going to be there."

He straightened up and used his forearm to push his hair out of his eyes. "Who is everyone?"

"Me. Miss Violet. Mrs. McCabe. Mr. Pritchard."

"Mr. Pritchard is going to your party?" Tommy narrowed his eyes.

"Well, I haven't asked him yet."

Tommy gave a short laugh. "I'll tell you what. If Mr. Pritchard comes, I'll come."

Arabella grinned. "You got it."

Next, they knocked on Mr. Pritchard's door.

"Whaddya want?" He appeared at the door, eyebrows drawn together in a fierce chevron. Violet frowned at him, but he took no notice of her.

"I came to see how Sadie was doing. Do you need anything for her?"

"She's doing OK. And I don't need a da—um, a cotton-picking thing."

"Can I see her?"

He exhaled in capitulation. "Fine." He called for her, and Arabella exchanged a disbelieving look with Violet as his voice took on a softer tone. He caught their astonished expressions. "You tell anyone, I'll deny it to my dying day."

Arabella grinned at him. "Cross my heart! I won't tell a soul! Right, Miss Violet?"

"My heart is crossed," Violet said, struggling to keep her face solemn.

Sadie emerged from behind a chair, head low, her creeping walk bringing her slowly toward the door. Arabella stretched her hand out and let Sadie sniff her the way Violet had taught her. Sadie nuzzled her palm, and Arabella giggled. She stroked the dog's head, and Sadie tilted it so Arabella could scratch the sweet spot behind her ears.

"She's doing really well, Mr. Pritchard."

He grunted.

"I think she likes it here."

Grunt.

"I think it would be good for her to meet other people. I think it would help her stop being afraid of everything."

"Well, I'm not sure if she will ever stop."

"Well, maybe she could be a little less afraid." She continued petting Sadie's head. "We are having a Lunar Landing Party on Sunday, and we want you to come and bring Sadie."

"What in the he—tarnation is a Lunar Landing Party?"

"The astronauts are supposed to land on the moon, and we are all going to watch it at my house. Maybe the more people Sadie meets, the more she will realize we are not all bad."

Mr. Pritchard grunted again. "Well, I don't know about that. Not really a party kind of fella."

"Tommy said he'd come if you come."

"He did, did he?"

"Yes. I think he thinks he can get out of it that way."

"Hmmphh."

"He doesn't think you'll come."

"Is that a fact?"

"It is. He even laughed when I told him you might."

"Seemed mighty sure of himself, huh?"

"Yes, he did. You should come. You know. For Sadie. And you can change her name if you want."

He looked down at the dog and shook his head. "No, I think she's a Sadie all right."

Arabella smiled at him. "Hope we see you on Sunday!"

"Well, possibly you will. Just to confound Tommy. Thinks he knows everything."

Arabella grinned at him and turned to go. *Forget White House social secretary*, Violet thought. *Arabella could be a diplomat and negotiate world peace.*

19

Violet

July 1969

The day of the moon landing arrived like any other July day in the South: hot, steamy, and stifling. The sultry, motionless morning felt like the world was holding its breath in anticipation of the historic event that was to take place later that day. She wondered what the three astronauts up in space were thinking. What was it like to wake up thousands of miles from Earth? She shuddered at the thought. She'd much rather watch it on TV than experience it in real life.

Four days before, she had watched the liftoff of Apollo 11 with Caroline and Arabella. The TV displayed the white rocket standing upright in the arms of the launching apparatus—a structure that looked no sturdier than Arabella's tinker toys. When they showed far shots of the rocket with smoke billowing around it, Arabella asked if the smoke was OK. Caroline said yes, but told her she needed to keep questions to a minimum so they could hear.

"T-minus sixty seconds and counting," the announcer said. "Neil Armstrong just reported it's been a real smooth countdown. . . . We have passed the fifty-second mark."

When they got to twelve, the announcer started calling off the seconds as they flicked by on the screen, then fire bloomed underneath the rocket. Violet sat transfixed, hand over her mouth, praying nothing would go wrong. Clouds of steam, more massive than before, billowed out in all directions, and the rocket rose straight into the sky. A little thrill passed down Violet's spine at the majesty of the moment.

"Liftoff! We have liftoff!"

"Is it good, Mama? It looks like it's going so slow. Like it could fall over like *thunk*." Arabella held her hand up, fingers pointing to the ceiling, then bent it abruptly at the wrist.

Caroline placed her hand over her heart, relief relaxing her features. "Yes, the launch is good. It doesn't look like it, but the rocket is actually going very fast. It's already gone two miles in one minute."

"I don't really know what that means."

Caroline put her hand on Arabella's head. "No, I guess you wouldn't. But the launch was a success. That's what matters."

"Thank goodness," Violet added. On TV, the rocket soared ever higher, breaking away from the bounds of Earth and heading for the moon.

Now the day had arrived when the astronauts were supposed to step onto the moon's surface. Violet walked over to the Fitzgeralds' a little before three.

"I came a little early to see if you needed any help before everyone else gets here," she said when Caroline answered the door.

"I could probably find you something to do. Come on in. And this is George."

"We finally meet! I'll have to shake your hand later," George said, holding up a hamburger patty by way of excuse.

Violet set the green bean casserole she had brought on the counter. "My special dish. Practically my only dish. I am not the best cook," she admitted sheepishly.

"I am sure it will be delicious," Caroline said.

"We'll see what you say after ten potlucks and ten green bean casseroles. What can I help with?"

Caroline shrugged. "Ask him. He's in charge of the cooking."

"If you don't mind getting out ice and putting them in the glasses, that would be great," George said.

"Ice duty on a hot July day? I can live with that."

A few minutes after three o'clock, Arabella looked out the front window and clapped her hands. "Mrs. McCabe is here!"

George opened the door as Mrs. McCabe climbed up the steps. She carried a large, foil-covered bowl in both hands, and her pocketbook dangled from one elbow.

"You gonna help me with this or just stand there gawking?"

"I'll take it," George said amiably as he took the dish in one hand and held the door with the other.

"That's some kid you have there. Smart, but runs on a bit. Wouldn't take no for an answer about this shindig."

He laughed. "Sounds like her. She wouldn't take no when she asked us if we would host it."

"If I remember correctly, she had a rather enthusiastic ally," Caroline said. She came around the corner, wiping a hand on her apron, and held it out to Mrs. McCabe. Mrs. McCabe shook it gingerly. "It's good to see you."

"Potato salad," said the elderly woman, nodding at the dish George carried into the kitchen.

"Oh, that's lovely, Mrs. McCabe," Caroline said. "Why don't you sit here." Caroline motioned to George's easy chair.

"Don't mind if I do." Mrs. McCabe shuffled to the chair and sank into its overstuffed embrace.

At fifteen minutes after three, a knock sounded on the door. George answered it again. "Nick! Harry! Come in. So glad y'all came!" Violet's heart lurched in her chest, and she chastised herself for it. *So he's handsome. That doesn't mean you have to melt like a stick of butter in the noonday sun,* she told herself.

"Glad to be here," Nick said, handing a dish to George. "This is a pasta dish I threw together."

"Oh, you didn't have to do that," Caroline said. "We know you just moved in."

"It was no problem. So nice of you to invite us."

George went around the room, making the introductions. "You know Violet Wentworth."

"Ah, yes, we met," Nick said. Heat flooded Violet's face, and she knew she was blushing. Thankfully, George moved on to Mrs. McCabe, and everyone's attention went with him.

"This is Mrs. McCabe, who lives next to Violet. You met Arabella. And this is my lovely wife, Caroline, there in the kitchen." Caroline waved a bag of hot dog buns in greeting. "Everyone is here except Mr. Pritchard and Tommy."

Arabella tugged on her dad's hand. "Can I run across and get him?" she said in her not-quite-whisper.

"I think you better leave well enough alone. If he's going to come, he'll come. If not, maybe we should let him be."

"But sometimes people just need a little encouragement."

"Where did you hear that?"

"From you!"

Everyone laughed.

"Well, if they don't come soon, perhaps you can go give some encouragement," George told her.

Violet suppressed a smile as she caught Arabella surveying the room, her face alight with happiness. Caroline was asking Nick about where he grew up. Mrs. McCabe sat in front of the TV. Harry went out to help George with the grill. She really hoped Tommy and Mr. Pritchard would come.

George and Harry came in after a few minutes. "Got the charcoal ready, and I'll fire it up soon. Figured we'd eat about five o'clock, if that's OK."

Caroline put out deviled eggs, cheese, and crackers for people to munch on until dinner was ready. George fiddled with the antenna, turning it this way and that, trying to get the clearest picture. Mrs. McCabe directed him. "No, no, turn it back again! No, that's too far. Stop! Right there!"

The party was underway.

20
Tommy

July 1969

Mr. Pritchard generally didn't put Tommy to work on Sundays. Sometimes they spent time on a woodworking project, but if he had nothing else to do, Tommy worked on his car. Which is what he was doing when Mr. Pritchard came down the steps carrying Sadie. Tommy heard the soft *thunk* of the trailer door and gave a cursory glance in that direction, then shot up, banging his head on the hood.

"Ouch," Tommy exclaimed, rubbing the top of his head.

Mr. Pritchard stood on his stoop, gazing straight ahead. He wore a blue, short-sleeved shirt with a darker blue, diamond print and a pair of dark-gray slacks. His hair and beard were neatly combed. Tommy had never seen him so dressed up.

"You're going to swallow a fly if you leave your mouth hanging open like that," Mr. Pritchard said, though he didn't look at Tommy as far as Tommy could tell. Instead, he kept staring at the houses across the street.

"Where are you going?"

"Why, to the Lunar Landing Party across the way there."

"You're going?" Surprise made Tommy's voice squeak.

"Looks like it." He straightened his collar with his free hand, still holding Sadie with the other. "Guess you better get ready. Heard you were going to go if I went."

"I . . . but I . . . um," Tommy said. "I'm not dressed. I'm all sweaty."

"Yeah, well, you got ten minutes. I'll take Sadie around back and let her do her business. Also, when you come back out, bring the two bags of chips and cookies on the counter."

Tommy stared at him, mouth still agape in spite of Mr. Pritchard's warning about flies. Finally, he clamped his mouth shut, threw the wrench in the toolbox, closed the lid, and slammed his hood. "I can't believe you're going."

"How often do you see a man land on the moon? Figure we should mark it somehow. You got nine minutes."

"I can't believe Arabella told you I'd go if you did."

Mr. Pritchard kept his eyes straight ahead, surveying the neighborhood. "Eight minutes and thirty seconds."

Tommy threw up his hands in frustration and brushed past Mr. Pritchard, still shaking his head. Did he just glimpse a ghost of a smile buried in that no-color beard? He set his toolbox on the floor inside the front door and started peeling his shirt off as he walked to the bathroom, where he took the fastest shower he'd ever taken. He toweled his hair on his way back to his room and threw on his best shirt and jeans. As he brushed his hair into its swoop, he hoped it would dry at least a little bit on the short walk across the street. He gave one last peek in the mirror before heading to the door, then remembered the bags. He made a quick U-turn and grabbed the bags and was back outside in what he thought had to be under eight minutes. He squinted in the bright, hot sunlight.

Mr. Pritchard leaned against a tree in the front yard with Sadie at his feet. She had assumed her usual posture, with her head ducked down, but her eyes peered up and at him, and she gave a tiny wag of her tail. A frisson of joy bloomed in his chest. Knowing the dog was happy to see him felt like an achievement of sorts.

"I'm ready," Tommy said.

Mr. Pritchard scooped up Sadie, and the trio marched across the street. Mr. Pritchard started whistling a tune Tommy didn't recognize. Tommy gave him a sidelong glance. He had never known him to whistle before. Not for the first time, Tommy thought adults were really weird.

21

Violet

July 1969

Violet decided neither Mr. Pritchard nor Tommy were going to come after all. She hoped Arabella would not be too disappointed. But at a quarter to four, a sharp rap sounded at the door. Arabella jumped up, clapping her hands and nearly upsetting Mrs. McCabe's little plate of deviled eggs and crackers that rested on the end table next to her.

"It's Mr. Pritchard and Tommy!"

Arabella flew across the room and opened the door to a well-groomed Mr. Pritchard and a damp Tommy. Mr. Pritchard carried Sadie. Tommy carried two paper bags. Each looked as if he were trying to out-awkward the other. As they hovered uncomfortably in the doorway, they reminded Violet of two little boys ready for their first day of school.

Arabella grabbed Mr. Pritchard's free hand.

"You're here! I knew you'd come!"

"You did, did ya? Then why do you look so surprised?"

"That's not surprise, silly. It's happiness!" And she threw her arms up in an expression of joy.

"You're going to scare the dog."

Arabella leaned forward, ratcheting her excitement down a notch or two. "Hi, Sadie! I am so glad you came! How are you?" Mr. Pritchard set Sadie on the floor, and she pressed against Mr. Pritchard's leg, but she wagged her tail as she gazed up at Arabella. After a few more pats, Arabella turned to Tommy and peered up at him with her snaggletoothed grin. "I'm glad you're here, too."

George came over to greet them, saving Tommy from replying—but not from blushing.

"Come on in. I'm George. Arabella's father."

Mr. Pritchard shook George's hand. "Maynard Pritchard. And this is Tommy Jeffers. He's kind of my apprentice."

"Tommy, pleased to meet you."

Mr. Pritchard took a step into the room, but Sadie remained still. Mr. Pritchard sighed. "Dog's not fond of walking." He bent down and lifted her up again and carried her to a spot near the sofa. "You sure you're OK she's here? I had orders to bring her." He directed a pointed stare at Arabella.

"And we had orders to invite her."

"Not surprised."

George went around the room and made the introductions one more time. He collected the bags from Tommy and took them to the kitchen.

"Thank you so much, Mr. Pritchard and Tommy," Caroline said.

Man and boy nodded. Violet wondered if she should take Tommy under her wing. Spending too much time with Mr. Pritchard might deprive him of the capacity for polite speech altogether.

George brought a couple of kitchen chairs into the living room for Tommy and Nick, who had given up his seat on the sofa to Mr. Pritchard. Mr. Pritchard had objected, saying he wasn't that gosh-darned old, but he sat.

George served soft drinks to everyone. Mr. Pritchard turned to the TV with interest.

"What's going on now?" he asked with a nod to the TV.

"Armstrong and Aldrin are in the lunar module, and they've separated from the command module," Nick answered.

Tommy shook his head. "I have no idea what you just said."

Nick laughed. "The command module is the main spaceship. Kind of the control center of the whole mission. The lunar module is the part they will land on the moon. After the moon part of the mission is over, they will fly the lunar module back, dock with the command module, and head back to Earth."

"Oh, OK. Got it."

"So the two pieces just separated, and they should be starting the countdown to landing soon. I was telling Mrs. McCabe about how fast they had to go to get into orbit when they took off." He turned back to the elderly woman. "Just to get into orbit, the rocket had to reach seventeen thousand miles per hour. Then they increase their speed to twenty-four thousand miles per hour during their second orbit of Earth. They have to go that fast to break away from Earth's gravity." Violet listened to the conversation with curiosity. She had followed the space program for years—who hadn't?—but she didn't always understand everything. She had meant to read the *Life* magazine articles that had inspired Arabella to throw this shindig, but she hadn't gotten around to it. Nick's explanation gave context, and his enthusiasm was contagious.

That's why she was listening, she told herself. That's the only reason.

"How fast do jets travel?" Tommy asked. Violet smiled. Tommy didn't often speak up, but this sparked his interest.

Nick said, "Well, a fellow broke the record a couple of years ago, and it still stands: a little over two thousand miles per hour."

Tommy blinked. "Wow. How do you know all this stuff?"

"Mostly Uncle Walt."

Tommy frowned in confusion, but Violet chuckled. "He means Walter Cronkite, I believe, Tommy."

"Yes, I watch everything I can. And read about it. I'm kind of a NASA nut."

Violet listened as Nick explained a little more about space travel to Tommy. He was patient, but not condescending. Violet had a soft spot for Tommy. She knew he was now living at Mr. Pritchard's, a fact that made her burn with curiosity. She could not picture how that had come about. She had surmised Tommy didn't have a happy home life and had taken note of his black eye and his reluctance to talk about it. She remembered his ramshackle trailer where everything looked like it needed pruning, patching, or polishing. But living with Mr. Pritchard? Perhaps he was a teddy bear as Mrs. McCabe and Caroline had both suggested. She shook herself out of her reverie and tuned back to Nick and Tommy's conversation.

"That got them into lunar orbit yesterday," Nick continued, "and here we are."

"So it's only Armstrong and Aldrin who will land on the moon?" Tommy asked.

"Yes. Michael Collins will stay on board the main spacecraft."

Caroline blew out a breath. "I don't know which is scarier: stepping into the vast unknown that is the moon, or being all by yourself in a spaceship."

Violet agreed with her, but the men did not.

"I think it would be way worse to be Collins because you're left out of all the fun. Imagine getting that close to the moon but not being able to walk on it like your colleagues," George said.

"You say fun, I say terror," Caroline said with a smile at her husband.

George glanced at the TV. "OK, everyone, I think they are about ready for the landing."

They crowded around the television, and George turned up the sound. The screen showed a countdown superimposed over a picture of an insectile-looking contraption set against a black sky and gray, cratered moon. When the countdown hit 13:04, a voice from NASA said, "Coming up on one minute." Walter Cronkite's familiar, comforting voice clarified. "One minute to ignition, and thirteen minutes to landing."

"Is that the spaceship?" Arabella asked, looking at the screen.

"That's the lunar landing module Nick was talking about," George said, not taking his eyes off the grainy, black-and-white screen.

"What's the beeping noise?"

"That's the way their communications work. Now, Arabella, I think you're going to have to hold off on your questions. They are going to be saying a lot of things you won't understand, and I don't understand it all either. But the more we listen, the better we'll be able to follow. OK?"

Arabella tried to be quiet, but as the picture changed, she stage-whispered, "Why does it look different?"

"Shh. Sometimes they show live pictures, and sometimes they show an animation. They can't show everything because only Michael Collins is in the command module." Arabella's pale eyebrows drew together, and Violet knew a question—or many—was bubbling up in her head and fighting to spring out. But Arabella studied her father for a minute as he turned his focus back to the TV. Violet hid a smile behind her hand. She noticed Nick watching Arabella as well, but he was not hiding his amusement. He glanced up, and their eyes met, and Violet found herself dropping her hand, sharing her grin with the new neighbor.

Walter Cronkite spoke up again. "I don't know if we could take the tension if they decide to go around again."

"That's the truth!" George agreed.

After another minute, George, Harry, and Nick let out a whoop.

"What happened?" Mrs. McCabe asked. Violet had trouble deciphering the static-ridden transmissions from NASA's Mission Control Center and was sure Mrs. McCabe did, too.

"It's a 'go' to land!" Nick said.

A few minutes later, the tinny voice from Control Center came through. "Eagle, Houston, you're go for landing . . . three thousand feet."

Violet clenched her hands as the suspense of the moment flooded the room. She felt a rush of gratitude for Arabella, because if it weren't for her, she would not be watching this at all. She couldn't believe she had been going to miss it.

They watched, rapt, as the arm of the module drifted over a silver-gray expanse marked by craters and boulders. Beyond it, only a few stars showed in the jet-black sky. The countdown ticked off the feet from the surface: one hundred feet, then seventy-five. The screen switched to a control panel, and after a second or two, an aqua button lit up in sharp contrast to the dull, dark gray of the surrounding console: Lunar Contact! The choppy stream of data reports from the astronauts kept coming as they guided the module to the right place, but their television screen still showed a simulation. But then the words LUNAR MODULE HAS LANDED ON THE MOON flashed on the television. Everyone, even Mr. Pritchard and Mrs. McCabe, broke out in cheers. Violet sagged with relief.

"Man on the moon!" said Walter Cronkite, sounding like Arabella in his utter, childlike delight.

"We copy you down, Eagle," said Mission Control.

"Houston," said one of the astronauts, and Cronkite interjected in complete wonderment, "Aw, jeez."

The astronaut continued speaking. "Tranquility Base here. The Eagle has landed."

"Roger, Tranquility. We copy on the ground. You got a bunch of guys about to turn blue. We're breathing again. Thanks a lot."

Everyone laughed. On screen, Cronkite took off his glasses and rubbed his hands together, looking as amazed and awed as the neighbors gathered in the Fitzgerald living room. "Wally, say something. I'm speechless," Cronkite said.

Mrs. McCabe shook her head. "I thought flying airplanes was something. Telephones. Automobiles. But I'll be darned if I ever thought I would live to see the day when a man landed on the moon."

Mr. Pritchard appeared as awestruck as everyone else. Next to him, Violet asked, "Well, what do you think of that, Mr. Pritchard?"

"Craziest dad-blamed thing I've ever seen."

"I'd have to agree with you."

George stood. "I think that's all for now. How about we get dinner ready and eat? We can watch some more when they get closer to the moonwalk."

Arabella tugged at her father's arm. "Aren't they going to get out and walk around?"

George chuckled. "Yes, they are, but it's not like getting out of a car. They have to run a bunch of checks on their equipment, and then they have to put on their spacesuits. It will take a while."

"Oh," Arabella said. "I didn't understand a lot of that."

Violet took her hand. "I didn't either. But I do know that two men are on the moon even as we speak, and that is pretty incredible. How about we help your mom get stuff ready?"

George and Harry took the hamburgers and hot dogs out to the grill, while Violet and Arabella helped Caroline set out condiments, the dishes everyone had brought, as well as napkins, plates, and flatware. Before long, Harry and George carried in the trays of grilled meat, and the mouthwatering aroma wafted through the room.

Seven adults plus Tommy, Arabella, and Baby Allen crowded the Fitzgeralds' small kitchen and living room. They bumped elbows, balanced plates on laps, joked and laughed, buoyed by the amazing thing they had just witnessed.

Nick's pasta dish that he "threw together" turned out to be the hit of the party. Everyone oohed and aahed over the cannelloni. He blushed and grinned. Violet's heart gave a little flip. *Oh no, you don't! We are not having any of that nonsense.* He was good-looking for sure, with a nice smile and gorgeous cheekbones. *But no. No. And no.*

"My grandmother was a great cook," Nick said. "She used

to pull me into her kitchen to keep me off the streets. I guess I learned a thing or two."

"Don't let him fool ya," Harry said around a big bite of cannelloni. "He cooks all the time. And his food is molto delizioso! Did I say that right?"

Nick grinned. "Close enough."

"Look at this spare tire I'm getting. I tell ya, if he were a little prettier, I'd marry him."

"If you were a lot prettier, I'd ask."

When everyone finished, they pitched in to clean up, except Caroline, who gave Allen a bottle. Harry and George scraped the grill. Violet did the dishes, and Tommy dried them. Mr. Pritchard put away food with Caroline directing him here and there. Surprisingly, he looked quite comfortable in the kitchen doing kitchen things. Arabella wiped the table with a sponge. Nick took out the trash. Mrs. McCabe offered to help, but Violet waved her offer away and told her if she can't relax when she's nearly eighty years old, when can she? After everything was tidied up, George brought out a deck of cards.

"Looks like we'll have a bit of a wait, so I thought we would entertain ourselves with card games."

At first, they played concentration, four people at a time. Nick sat next to Violet, and she found herself overcome with self-consciousness. She gave the game her best effort in spite of her discomposure, but she needn't have bothered. Arabella beat everyone. She had a prodigious memory ("Except when it comes to chores," Caroline said.) and won several games in a row. She finally sat out and let the others play. Mrs. McCabe and Mr. Pritchard did not participate. Mrs. McCabe said she could hardly remember her own name, much less a card she had just seen. Mr. Pritchard just shook his head. Still, he watched, and Violet thought perhaps he was not scowling as much as usual.

After concentration, they played blackjack, and Mrs. McCabe allowed herself to be cajoled into taking part. And she won. She said it was beginner's luck, but everyone could tell she handled the cards adroitly. They switched to poker, and George managed to lure Mr. Pritchard to the table. Violet thought Mr. Pritchard well suited to that game, as his continuous frown made it hard to judge if he had been dealt a good hand or a bad one.

A little after eight o'clock, Caroline served homemade peach ice cream along with the cookies Mr. Pritchard and Tommy had brought.

"Never had peach ice cream," Nick said. "This is wonderful."

"There are lots of peach orchards around here. Keep coming over, and you can have peach pie, peach cobbler, peaches and cream," Caroline said.

"Peach salad, peach burgers, peach spaghetti," George added.

"Don't listen to him," Caroline admonished.

"Well, this is delicious, so I am not going to complain."

After the ice cream, Caroline put Allen down for the night as the poker game resumed. When she emerged from the baby's room, she caught Arabella trying to stifle a huge yawn.

"Bella, come here," she motioned to the child. "Why don't you take a little nap?"

"I'm not tired."

"That yawn says otherwise."

"I don't want to miss anything."

"And you won't. I absolutely promise I will wake you up before the astronauts walk on the moon."

"Why is it taking so long?"

"They have to make sure their suits are perfect." George knelt in front of her. "It's awfully dangerous out there on the moon. They want to make sure they do it right."

Arabella reluctantly agreed, and she lay down on the sofa with her head in her mother's lap. Caroline stroked her hair, and, in spite of her protests, Arabella fell asleep in minutes.

Caroline let her sleep for almost an hour. When the moonwalk seemed imminent, she shook her gently awake. Arabella rubbed her eyes, but then shot up, instantly alert.

"Did I miss anything?"

"Not a thing, Bella. Not a thing. It's been a little boring as they went through all their checks."

They gathered around the TV again, and six hours after the actual landing, the astronauts opened the hatch of the lunar module. Aldrin gave directions to Armstrong, and the announcer explained that Armstrong couldn't see much with all his equipment on, so Aldrin had to verbally guide him.

"Oh my goodness!" Violet placed both hands on her cheeks.

"Dear Lord, please keep them safe," Caroline murmured.

"OK, Houston, I'm on the porch," Armstrong said.

"That's a funny porch," Arabella whispered.

"And we're getting a picture on the TV," said a chipper voice on the broadcast. A few minutes later, the gathered neighbors gasped as the shadowy leg of Neil Armstrong dropped down from the module. The shadows made for murky viewing, but they were able to discern a ghostly form making its way down the ladder. Violet hardly dared to breathe as Armstrong explained the ladder collapsed too far but was OK. Then Walter Cronkite said, "There's a foot on the moon. Stepping down on the moon!"

"Surface appears to be very, very fine-grained. It's almost like a powder," said Armstrong. Violet shook her head in disbelief. They were listening to a man talk to them from the moon.

Walter Cronkite seemed to be thinking the same thing. "Armstrong on the moon. Neil Armstrong, thirty-eight-year-old American, standing on the surface of the moon," he said, his voice full of wonder. "On this July twentieth, nineteen hundred and sixty-nine."

"That's one small step for man. One giant leap for mankind," said Armstrong, the end of his sentence punctuated by static.

Neil Armstrong wore a bulky white suit and helmet with a huge glass faceplate. His appearance gave Violet a sense of the danger in their mission. They were stepping out into air they couldn't breathe, and temperatures that could cook them or freeze them. But Armstrong's voice calmly described how he could kick up the surface material, that it was like powdered charcoal, sticking in fine layers to his boots.

The picture scrambled for a minute, and they all cried out in dismay, but it resolved in seconds.

"Okay. It's quite dark here in the shadow and a little hard for me to see that I have good footing," Neil said. "I'll work my way over into the sunlight here without looking directly into the sun."

Every once in a while, the picture garbled. Arabella glanced at George, and he caught her eye. "It's not our end, sweetheart! That's coming from up there. Not a thing I could do to fix that signal." He grinned at her.

Neil started talking again. "This is very interesting. It's a very soft surface, but here and there where I plug with the contingency sample collector, I run into a very hard surface, but it appears to be very cohesive material of the same sort. I'll try to get a rock in here. Just a couple."

"It has a stark beauty all its own. It's like much of the high desert of the United States. It's different, but it's very pretty out here. Be advised that a lot of the rock samples out here, the hard rock samples, have what appear to be vesicles in the surface. Also, I am looking at one now that appears to have some sort of phenocryst," Neil said.

"Phenocryst," said Astronaut Wally Schirra in the CBS studio. "Typical of volcanic rock."

"Glad he explained that," Mrs. McCabe said dryly. But she was as mesmerized as the rest of them. The only one who didn't appear riveted was Arabella. She watched the TV for a minute, then gauged the reactions of the surrounding adults before turning back to the broadcast. Violet realized that if you still believed Santa could fly around the world with a team of reindeer—and she assumed Arabella did—then flying to the moon may not seem like such a stupendous feat.

Armstrong had disappeared from the camera's view, but just as Violet was wondering where he was, he bounced into the picture and past the lunar module. Someone on the TV whistled and said, "Hey! Look at the bounding step!"

"He's moving funny!" Arabella said.

"That's what low gravity will do for you," George said.

"Boy, it looks like fun, doesn't it?" said Walter Cronkite.

"What's going on?" Arabella asked.

"So the other astronaut, Buzz Aldrin, is going to come out and walk on the moon, too," George said. "They have to wear these things called portable life support systems, and right now, Neil is watching Buzz's so he can come down the ladder safely."

"Oh. OK."

"OK. Now I want to back up and partially close the hatch," Buzz said. "Making sure not to lock it on my way out."

They heard laughter. "A pretty good thought," Neil said. Violet and the little group laughed along with the TV announcers.

Buzz continued, "It's a very simple matter to hop down from one step to the next."

Neil answered, "Yes. I found I could be very comfortable, and walking is also very comfortable."

"Oh, there he is!" Arabella pointed as Buzz Aldrin backed down the ladder. "I kind of know what I am looking at now."

The announcer explained the ladder did not compress the lunar dust as much as they thought it would, so the last step was much bigger than they expected. Buzz pushed off the steps and jumped lightly down. Then he leapt up the ladder again. He looked so weightless, Violet feared that if he let go, he could float away.

"That's a good step. About a three-footer," one of the astronauts said.

"Isn't that something! Magnificent sight out here."

"Magnificent desolation," Buzz Aldrin said.

"Like walking on a trampoline," Walter Cronkite said.

After the moonwalk ended, George turned the volume down. "Well, I can say that was the most exciting thing I have ever seen in my life."

"I will second that," Nick said, clapping him on the shoulder.

Harry turned to Mrs. McCabe. "Mrs. McCabe, I imagine you've seen a lot of things in your life. How did this rate?"

"All I can say is that it sure beats all I have ever seen."

Violet turned to Caroline and Arabella. "Arabella, I owe you one. I would have been sitting at home reading a book if you hadn't had this idea. Caroline, thank you so much for opening your house to all of us." She surveyed the room and kitchen. "That was something else. But now I think we ought to clean up and get out of your hair."

Everyone jumped up—except Mrs. McCabe, who rose a little more slowly—and cleaned up the living room and kitchen, washing glasses and returning chairs to their rightful places, all the time talking about what they had seen and heard.

"Who knew the moon's surface would be like powder?"

"Did you see the way Neil was kind of bouncing? That was far-out!"

"That was funny when he said he would make sure he didn't lock the hatch. Can't believe they are calm enough to make jokes from the moon."

The neighbors began to drift away. Mr. Pritchard scooped up Sadie, and he and Tommy were the first to leave. Violet lent Mrs. McCabe her arm and told her she would see her across the street. Nick jumped up and said he would escort them both.

"We'll be OK, Mr. Battaglia," Violet said. "It's just across the street."

"Please, call me Nick. And my mother would never let me hear the end of it if I let two ladies go out this late alone."

Violet laughed. "This is Edenton, Nick. The worst thing that can happen is a cat runs across the street and scares us."

Mrs. McCabe took his arm. "I, for one, would be happy for the company. Come along, young man."

Violet sighed, and Caroline grinned at her and shrugged. Violet shrugged back and followed the two out the door. "I'll check in tomorrow, Caroline. Just to make sure there wasn't a mess we left that we didn't see with our moonstruck eyes."

Darkness stretched out around them beyond the reach of the one streetlight. Violet admitted to herself she was glad Nick was helping Mrs. McCabe across the uneven ground. When they reached the road, Nick stopped. He pointed at the crescent moon. "Hard to believe there are two men up there right now."

Violet made a show of looking up at the heavens, but she found herself picturing Nick instead of the silvery sliver: his strong profile, his dark hair. Her heart thudded in her chest, and she chastised herself again. She was going to have to make it a point to stay away from him. She really did not need any entanglements. She blinked, and the waxing moon slid into focus, glowing in a field of stars in the summer sky. She pushed Nick out of her mind and let the wonder of the night's events fill her.

"Just beats all," Mrs. McCabe said, her voice low and full of awe. "Just really beats all."

22
Nick

July 1969

Nick stared at the moon, imagining what it would be like to walk on its surface, thousands of miles from Earth and other people. He couldn't. Was it exhilarating? Frightening? Both? He shook his head and dropped his gaze down to Mrs. McCabe and Violet. A streetlamp illuminated Violet's upturned face, and he felt the same electric jolt that had run through him when he first saw her. He wanted to push back a strand of dark hair that brushed her cheek. He wanted to watch her green eyes light up as they had while watching the moon landing. He could barely stop himself from stealing glances at her throughout the evening. And she seemed quite immune to him. He had become a cliché, he thought. The once-upon-a-time charmer who had now encountered and desired the one girl who didn't swoon at his feet. Since Giulia, he had dated a few girls, but none had lasted more than a few months. These brief relationships nagged at him. He liked to think he had recovered from his early heartbreak but hadn't met the right person yet. Still, he worried the cuts Giulia's death had inflicted on his heart pierced too deeply and left irreparable damage. *Stop. You are getting way ahead of yourself. Besides, Violet probably thinks you're an idiot or a show-off for spouting all those facts earlier.* He had wanted to cut short his explanations, but couldn't. Nervousness made him chatty.

Mrs. McCabe tugged on his arm.

"Well, that's enough moon gazing. Some of us need our beauty sleep."

"Not you, Mrs. McCabe," he said. "You get any more beautiful, and you'll have me falling head over heels for you."

"Oh, pish! That charm doesn't work on me. I am far too old." But Nick could tell she was pleased.

They crossed the road, and Violet started to say her good-byes. "Thank you, Nick, for seeing us home."

"Where do you think you are going?" Mrs. McCabe asked.

"Um, home?"

"I need you to open my door. Nick will be busy keeping me from falling down those steps in the dark."

"I think he can manage the steps and the door, Mrs. McCabe."

"Think how bad you would feel if while he was unlocking the door, I fell down. Plus, you'd have to take care of me again." She stopped walking and let go of Nick's arm as she rummaged in her handbag. Nick noticed she wasn't the least bit wobbly. She pulled a key ring out of her purse, separated a key from its mates, and held it pinched between her forefinger and thumb as the rest jangled. When Violet hesitated, Mrs. McCabe thrust it in her direction. Violet grabbed the key with a heavy sigh.

"I can never decide whether to leave the porch light on so I can see or if I should keep it off because of the bugs," Mrs.

McCabe said as Violet fumbled at the doorknob in the dark. Nick finally heard a *click*.

"I'll bring you a bug light," Nick said.

"Well, thank you, young man. That is mighty kind of you. Not that I am out after dark very often."

Violet pushed the door ajar and dangled the keys for Mrs. McCabe to take back. "Now can I go home?"

"Not so fast, missy."

"What am I waiting for?"

"It's late, and it's dark. Our nice, new neighbor here can see you home safely. I'll feel better knowing he walked you to your door."

Nick watched, amused, as Violet opened her mouth, closed her mouth, opened it, and then pursed her lips. "Fine. If that will help you sleep. I know how you worry about me all the time."

Mrs. McCabe stepped into her house and turned on her porch light, bathing Nick and Violet in the spill of it. Moths appeared almost as soon as the pool of yellow did, fluttering around them and batting against the fixture. "Yes, dear. I do." She turned to Nick. "Thank you for seeing us both home. I'll leave my porch light on for a few minutes," she said. And closed the door.

As they walked down the steps and across the yard, Nick leaned towards Violet and whispered, "That is the tiniest bulldozer I've ever seen."

Violet laughed and said, "That is quite an accurate description. She has bulldozed me into several things against my will. I find myself doing things and thinking, how did I get here?"

"If she ever took up a life of crime, we'd all be in trouble."

"But possibly rich. She always manages to come out on top somehow. Thanks for walking me home. Completely unnecessary, but I know you had no choice in the matter."

Violet had stopped at the opening in her fence. He wanted to make a joke about Mrs. McCabe not being happy if he didn't walk her all the way to her door, but he sensed a firm goodbye in her thanks. He would have liked to talk to her longer, but told himself to take his time. Some things were worth waiting for.

He walked away, whistling "Moon River." When he got to the end of Violet's driveway, he turned, checking to make sure she got into her house. She was pushing her door open, but she paused and turned. He gave her a little salute, and she saluted back. He resumed whistling as he crossed the moonlit, sandy road.

PART

2

August-September 1969

23
Violet

Arabella began school in mid-August, but she still managed to pop over and visit in the afternoons between her school and Violet's work. Violet was surprised at the little lift she felt each time Arabella came bouncing in, like she scooped up beams of sunlight and then scattered them around Violet's trailer when she came in. Violet knew, too, that Arabella called on Mrs. McCabe, and that also made her glad.

Violet had kept to her promise to avoid Nick. Since their schedules didn't mesh, this wasn't too difficult. Life carried on, and not altogether unpleasantly. She now went long hours without thinking about her past until some little reminder flashed into her mind as suddenly as a curtain being flicked aside. Along with the memories came a stab of sadness, sometimes double-edged with guilt. But one day, she had a memory of *before*, a good memory, and she smiled at it like it was an old friend instead of a foe. She closed her eyes and enjoyed the vision and realized she might actually be healing.

A few weeks after school had started, Violet opened her door to find Arabella quivering with excitement. She studied her, narrowing her eyes and putting her hands on her hips. "You look like the cat that ate the canary. What have you been up to?"

"I've got a secret!"

"Not for long. I have a feeling it's about to burst out of you."

Arabella skipped in, and Violet closed the door behind her.

"I found out when Mrs. McCabe's birthday is! It's next month! September sixteenth!" Arabella said, flopping herself on Violet's sofa.

"And?" Violet said cautiously.

"We should throw a surprise party for her."

"Oh, boy. She's almost eighty years old, Arabella. I am not sure a surprise party is good for her health."

"Well, we could make it so we don't jump out at her. A little, quiet surprise, not a big, loud one. I saw her birthday in her huge family Bible. I told her she should have a party, and she said she's never had a birthday party. Never! In her whole life!"

"I could see how that would get you thinking. But chances are she doesn't want one at this late date."

"I think she would be happy to have all her friends with her, don't you?"

"Well, you'd think most people would, but I am not sure about Mrs. McCabe."

Someone knocked on the door, and they exchanged looks.

"You don't think that's Mrs. McCabe, do you?" Arabella asked in her typical stage whisper.

"Don't worry," Violet said, ruffling Arabella's hair as she walked by her. "I am pretty sure she couldn't have overheard us."

When she opened the door, she caught her breath. For it was not the diminutive Mrs. McCabe on her porch, but tall, good-looking Nick.

Arabella jumped up.

"Mr. Nick! I am glad you are here. I want to ask you something."

"Well, I guess you better come in out of the heat," Violet said, wondering why on earth he had popped by. And why did her body have to betray her whenever he was around? Her heart took off at a gallop, her cheeks flushed. She stepped aside, struggling to take deep, even breaths as he strode in, and his presence filled her small living room all the way to the corners.

"All right, little Miss Arabella. Ask away."

"Mrs. McCabe's birthday is September sixteenth. She told me she has never even once had a birthday party. I was thinking we should have one for her. A little one, because Miss Violet said a surprise party might not be good for her health. Don't you think that's a great idea?"

Nick leaned down to Arabella.

"I do think it's a great idea. And how about this: I just bought a grill, and I have been thinking of asking all the neighbors to come over. What if we do a cookout at my house and make it a surprise party for Mrs. McCabe?"

Arabella jumped up and down. "Yes! That would be perfect!"

"Are you sure about that?" Violet asked Nick.

"Absolutely," he said. "You have a calendar?"

Violet collected her kitchen calendar and handed it to Nick. He studied it for a minute and said, "I think we can make Sunday, September fourteenth work, don't you?"

Arabella nodded and clapped her hands, letting out a little whoop of delight.

He returned the calendar to Violet and knelt in front of Arabella. "Remember those gorgeous invitations you made for the Lunar Landing Party? Think you can do some for this?"

"You bet!"

"You can just call it something like Nick and Harry's Backyard Barbecue. Don't mention her birthday, of course. I feel confident you can make sure she comes, Arabella. We'll get everyone else to come fifteen minutes earlier. So, let's say three forty-five for them, and you can tell Mrs. McCabe to come at four." He turned to Violet. "Maybe you can walk with her? To make sure she arrives at the right time?"

"I will try," she said. "I am sure she will argue with me."

"I appreciate you taking one for the team. I hate to make her bring a dish, but do you think that will make her suspicious if we tell her not to?" Nick asked.

"I'll tell you what. I'll drop my dish over earlier, and we'll say you're taking care of everything."

Nick nodded. "Excellent idea!"

Arabella said, "I better do the invitations. Bye, Mr. Nick! Bye, Miss Violet!" She skipped out the door and across the road. Looking both ways, of course. Violet watched to make sure.

24
Violet

August 1969

Violet closed the door after watching Arabella cross the road. "There's something about this street that keeps making people do things they hadn't intended to do."

Nick grinned. "Or maybe doing them in a way they hadn't expected. I really did intend to have a barbecue. And this will be a nice thing to do for Mrs. McCabe."

"Yes, it will. I just hope we don't give her a heart attack."

"I think it probably helps that she'll know we're all going to be there."

"Good point. So. I don't think you came over to plan a party for Mrs. McCabe."

"Ha! I almost forgot. I was wondering if I could borrow a casserole dish? We're having a cookout in my unit, and I need one to bring my contribution."

"Surely you have one? Didn't you bring one to the Lunar Landing Party?"

"I did. I dropped it and broke it. I haven't had a chance to buy a new one. I'd blame Harry, but he wasn't even home."

Violet chuckled. "Of course you can borrow mine."

She walked to the kitchen to fetch the cookware in question, talking over her shoulder. "I hope it didn't have hot food in it when you dropped it."

"Thankfully, it didn't. It slipped when I was washing it. I did tell Harry I wasn't going to replace it, that I was cutting back on the time I spent cooking. You should have seen his face. You want to scare Harry? Tell him you're going to deprive him of food."

"I say, keep him guessing. You're spoiling him."

"That I am. But I do love to cook."

"You could always cook for me." Violet wanted to clamp her hand over her mouth, though it was too late. The words were out in the room, and she couldn't get them back. Her face burned. She fumbled, trying to clarify what she meant. "I mean, I don't really like cooking, and I am not that good at it. I often eat eggs for dinner when I am off from work because it's quick and easy. When I am at work, I eat there." *Violet, shut up!* She knew she was babbling, as if the torrent of new words could push her foot out of her mouth. But instead, those six words hung in the air like a brightly colored banner, and all her explanations were like neon arrows pointing to it.

Nick just smiled. "Maybe I should send you over a plate. I better head back. Thanks for this." He held up the dish. "I'll return it soon in case you need it for Mrs. McCabe's party."

He strode out the door. Once the door closed, Violet leaned against it and groaned.

25

Nick

As soon as Violet closed the door behind him, Nick began kicking himself. *I'll send over a plate.* Possibly the stupidest thing he'd ever said to a woman. He had the perfect opportunity to ask her out, and instead, he made an idiotic offer like she was an invalid. The dish had been an excuse. He could have gone next door to the Fitzgeralds and borrowed one. Or hopped in his car and bought a new one. He had not counted on Arabella being there, and her presence had thrown him off. And after Arabella left, Violet had opened a door and laid down a welcome mat, and he had bowed politely and turned away from it.

On the other hand, she had backpedaled so fast, maybe she didn't want to go out with him. Maybe it was best he had not asked her for a date.

He entered his house and shook his head. What on earth was going on with him? He had never been this tentative about asking a girl out before. And he had been turned down before. It wouldn't kill him if he got turned down again. So why the hesitation?

When he thought about it, he realized his wavering stemmed in part from the fact that he liked this neighborhood. If he were to ask her out, would that make any get-togethers awkward? It would definitely make things a little uncomfortable if she said no. But even more so if she said yes, and they went out for a while but then broke up.

He shook himself and realized he had walked to the fridge, opened it, and was staring into it blankly. *OK, Nick. You either need to ask her out or decide not to. Quit the waffling.* He pulled out some sausage and slammed it on the counter. *That's all well and good, but I still don't know which one to pick.*

26
Violet

August 1969

The next day, Arabella was back with a fistful of invitations.

"Can you look at these and make sure I got everything right? I was going to ask my mom, but Allen has a cold. He's really gross right now."

"I imagine he is." Violet held out her hand and examined each paper. All but one made it clear it was a secret, surprise birthday party for Mrs. McCabe. The one that omitted that information simply called the event a backyard barbecue. And Arabella had included the different times appropriately. Violet handed the invitations back. "These are perfect. Good work!"

"Thanks! Want to go with me to deliver them?"

"Sure. Why not?" She wanted to see Mr. Pritchard's reaction. And to throw in some encouraging words to help ensure Mrs. McCabe's attendance.

"Let's do Mrs. McCabe first!" Arabella extracted Mrs. McCabe's invitation and handed the rest to Violet.

"Will you come, please?" Arabella asked after Mrs. McCabe had perused the folded piece of paper.

"I don't know. Sounds like a lot of fuss and bother, if you ask me."

"You have to come, Mrs. McCabe! You had fun at the Lunar Landing Party, didn't you?"

"I can safely say it was more fun than watching paint dry." Mrs. McCabe looked up at Violet. "What about you? Are you going?"

"I don't think I have a choice, do I, Arabella?"

"Nope!" Arabella shook her head, and her pigtails flew around her face. "So can I tell Mr. Nick you are coming, Mrs. McCabe?"

"Well, why not. It's not like I am doing anything else on a Sunday afternoon."

When she told Mr. Pritchard, he snorted. "You're gonna give the old lady a heart attack."

His remarks did not ruffle Arabella in the slightest.

"We have it all worked out, Mr. Pritchard. It's going to be a gentle surprise!"

"More's the pity."

"What does that mean?"

"Never mind."

Tommy grunted when she handed him his invitation. Violet once again thought she needed to have him over for dinner before he forgot how to speak altogether. But when Arabella asked him, he said he would come. He had not lost the power of speech yet.

27
Violet

September 1969

Mrs. McCabe could not have asked for a more magnificent day for her birthday party, even if she had known she was having one. A gentle sun spilled a buttery golden light on leaves dulled to yellow-green by the ebbing of summer. Violet lay in bed for a few minutes, watching dust motes swirl in a sunbeam, and realized she hadn't thought of that time in ... how long? Guilt pierced her, dagger-sharp. "I'm sorry," she whispered to the sunbeam. "I'm sorry I haven't thought of you lately." She knew she was healing, but even the healing hurt. She pushed it all away with the blankets: the grief and the guilt. She was getting better at that.

She spent the morning catching up on laundry and grocery shopping. A little after one, she threw green beans and mushroom soup into her recently returned dish. She had planned to make something new, but she had not had time to find a new recipe. Well, maybe next time.

After she slipped the dish into the oven, she retreated to her bedroom to change. She stood in front of the closet, one hand on the doorknob, the other on her hip, considering her choices. She reminded herself she was only attending a casual, neighborhood cookout on a warm but pleasant day. But the picture of a certain dark-eyed man kept popping into her head. She shoved the image away. *No*, she thought. *I want to be comfortable and confident, but I am not trying to please anyone.*

In defiance of her rogue thoughts, she chose a pair of brown pedal pushers and a beige summer sweater. The top had a high neck but short sleeves. It was one of her least favorite outfits. The colors did not suit her at all. *It's only friends and neighbors. No big deal.*

Satisfied, she returned to the kitchen. She took the casserole out of the oven and sprinkled canned onion rings on top and returned it to the top rack to brown. Earlier in the week, she thought of an idea for Mrs. McCabe's present. When Nick returned her dish, she had handed him the wrapped gift and asked if he could keep it at his place until the party. He said sure. Then stood there, amused.

"What are you smiling about?" She tried to sound neutral but was afraid her defensiveness enveloped her words like poisonous tendrils.

"I've never seen you in your uniform."

She glanced down. "Oh." She blushed. "Lovely, isn't it?"

"Actually, you make it look pretty good, if you don't mind my saying so."

She drew her brows down. "You must be blind as a bat in a thunderstorm." But her flush deepened.

"I'm serious. You could wear that at a fashion show and people would run out and buy it. Like Mrs. Kennedy's hats. Excuse me. Mrs Onassis."

She fumbled around for something to say and came up with nothing. "You are surely exaggerating. But speaking of this uniform, I have to get to work. Thanks for holding on to this for me."

"Not a problem. Thanks for lending me the casserole dish. I'll see you Sunday."

After she closed the door, she had scrutinized her dress. *He's full of baloney*, she had thought. *I look like a pink sack of potatoes*. Still, she'd headed off to work with a spring in her step.

Now, she brushed her hair and scraped it into a bouncy ponytail. Satisfied, she pulled the casserole out of the oven and covered it in foil. Before she walked it over to Nick's, she checked her appearance one more time in the mirror, smoothing a stray hair and tugging the bottom of her sweater. She retrieved the casserole and, wearing her oven mitts, carried it on a trivet to Nick's. She crossed the street, hoping Mrs. McCabe wasn't peeking out her windows.

When she got to the door, she had no choice but to kick it to announce her presence. When Harry opened the door, a flare of disappointment blazed in Violet's chest like an ember in a dying fire. She mentally berated herself. She was not some fresh-faced teenager, and she shouldn't be acting like one. Also, Harry was a nice guy. She quickly arranged her features into a bright smile and gave him an extra chirpy, buoyant hello, then wondered if she had overdone that. Then chastised herself for all this second-guessing and overanalyzing. He invited her in, and she placed the prepared dish on the counter. Harry made a show of checking to make sure Mrs. McCabe was not outside, looking high and low and side to side, making her laugh. He saluted her before holding the door wide open. "Coast is clear, Agent Wentworth. See you in a few!"

Back at her place, she tidied the kitchen and made a point of not checking her hair and minimal makeup one more time. At two minutes before four, she headed out to accompany Mrs. McCabe.

Mrs. McCabe was coming down her steps, holding the handrail with a tight grip as she lowered herself to the next tread.

"Hello, Mrs. McCabe. Are you heading over to Nick's?"

"That I am."

"Shall we walk together?"

"It's a free country."

Violet gritted her teeth.

Mrs. McCabe studied her as they began walking across the lawn. "Is that what you are wearing?"

"Yes. What's wrong with it?"

"Honey, you look like a brown paper lunch bag. A used one. You should be showcasing your assets on a lovely crystal tray. Or at the very least a decent plastic one. Not hiding them behind a dull, brown wrapper."

"We are just going to a backyard barbecue."

"Mm-hmm. I'll tell you what. I'll make your excuses, and you run back and put on something more attractive."

"Mrs. McCabe. I'm fine, honestly.

"You're not fine. You're running," she said, looking straight ahead as they traversed the road.

"What do you mean, I'm running?" Violet said, bewildered. She was walking quite slow to keep pace with Mrs. McCabe.

"Nick is interested in you, and that has you scared. I didn't live to be this old without learning a thing or two."

"I don't know what you are talking about."

"Oh, yes, you do. I can see it in your eyes." They got to the edge of Nick's yard. "I don't know what has happened in your past, but whatever it is, it is just that: past. Meanwhile, you have a fine young man who is quite interested in you. You could do a lot worse. And you aren't getting any younger."

"He's not interested in me," Violet protested.

"Oh, yes, he is. I see him staring at you all the time. Looking away when you look at him. One of you ought to get on with it and ask the other out, for Pete's sake. It's exhausting to watch."

Violet thought of a thousand things to say, but all her words lodged in her throat. Damn Mrs. McCabe for making her feel flustered. It was none of her business. They arrived at Nick and Harry's, and Violet struggled to reclaim her equilibrium.

She knocked, and Nick opened the door, and Violet's heart gave a little flip. *Damn it! Stop that!*

He blocked the opening and grinned at Violet, giving her a tiny nod, a gesture she took to mean everything was ready. A strong aroma of bread and garlic wafted out the open door, and Violet's mouth watered. Violet motioned for Mrs. McCabe to go ahead of her, and Nick offered his arm to their guest of honor. She took it and stepped over the threshold. As she entered the room, everyone yelled, "Surprise!" Mrs. McCabe appeared, for the first time since Violet had known her, at a complete loss of words. She surveyed the room, taking in Nick by the door, Mr. Pritchard and Tommy and Sadie near an easy chair, Harry near the kitchen. And the Fitzgeralds front and center with Arabella radiating happiness.

"What is this?" Mrs. McCabe asked.

"It's your surprise birthday party!" Arabella shouted.

"Well. Well." Mrs. McCabe observed the colorful balloons and streamers hanging from the walls and light fixtures. A paper banner with "Happy Birthday" printed in primary colors was taped to the wall behind the sofa. "Well," she said again.

Violet had waited behind her and now moved into the room. She turned to say something to Mrs. McCabe—but the thought evaporated like steam in a desert. Mrs. McCabe's pale-blue eyes were . . . watery.

"Mrs. McCabe. Are you all right?"

Mrs. McCabe cleared her throat. "I, uh, I'm fine. I don't know what to say." She regarded Arabella. "But I think I know who to thank."

Arabella grabbed her hand and pulled her to the easy chair. "This is your throne for today! And here"—she picked up a handmade, glittery, paper contraption from a nearby table—"is your crown! You are the birthday queen."

Mrs. McCabe bent forward, allowing Arabella to put the crown on her head. Everybody started chattering at once, and Nick asked Mrs. McCabe if she wanted something to drink.

"I'd like iced tea, but I am not sure a Yankee like yourself would know how to make it."

Nick grinned at her. "Just so happens Caroline and George brought a pitcher."

"I'll fetch you a glass," said Caroline.

"You're smarter than you look," Mrs. McCabe said to Nick.

"Um, thank you. I think."

Caroline brought the tea, and Mrs. McCabe thanked her. "I have to admit, y'all surprised me," she said. "And I didn't think I could be surprised at my age."

"Arabella told us you had never had a birthday party," Caroline said. "And, of course, it was her idea to throw you one. Better late than never, right?"

Nick brought out several plates of appetizers: crisp toast points with bruschetta—the source of the heavenly garlic smell—savory stuffed mushrooms, and brightly colored skewers of antipasti. Everyone swarmed the table, chatting and eating at the same time. Eventually, the guests drifted to their seats. Arabella leaned into her mother and cupped her hand around her mouth and her mother's ear. "Can Mrs. McCabe open her presents now?" Arabella's muted voice still had more stage than whisper to it.

Caroline laughed. "I think she heard you, so I guess that's next on the agenda."

"We got you presents!" Arabella announced. She handed Mrs. McCabe a box. "This one is from my mama and daddy and me. And Baby Allen, I guess."

Violet thought Mrs. McCabe was going to get misty again, for she gazed at the gift on her lap for a long time. But when she looked up, she smiled. "It's been a long time since someone gave me a birthday present. Thank you, Arabella. And Caroline and George. And Allen, too."

She tore the paper to reveal a round cookie tin. Mrs. McCabe pried the lid off and exclaimed in delight. "Are these your pecan sandies?"

"They are, indeed. I hope it's OK. We all thought you might like useful gifts and not more knickknacks or something like that."

"This is absolutely perfect!"

Tommy was next. He thrust an envelope at her, not quite meeting her eyes.

She opened the flap and read a handwritten note that promised three visits from him to do yard or handy work. Violet held her breath, remembering Mrs. McCabe's complaints about him being around too much in the summer, but she was at her most gracious.

"Tommy, this is so thoughtful. Thank you."

"You're welcome," he mumbled. He moved back to a wall and tried to melt into it.

Mr. Pritchard stepped forward and handed Mrs. McCabe a long, narrow box wrapped in brown butcher paper, and Violet wondered if they could hold off sniping at each other in honor of this special occasion. Mrs. McCabe eyed him suspiciously, but took the package and opened it. Inside were two beautiful wooden spoons polished to a golden glow.

Mrs. McCabe was speechless for the second time that day. She stood for a long minute looking at the burnished spoons, rubbing her finger along one. "Did you make these?" she asked Mr. Pritchard.

"Yeah, but don't go making a big deal about it. Just a little something I made with scraps."

Mrs. McCabe took a long moment to answer. "They are truly beautiful. You are kind of . . . well, an artist."

"Let's move along," Mr. Pritchard said, looking around the room as if for liberation. "Violet? Nick? Harry?"

Nick came to Mr. Pritchard's rescue. "This is from Harry and me."

Mrs. McCabe took the proffered envelope, and inside was a piece of paper. "This entitles the bearer of this letter to a home-cooked Italian meal, delivered to your home." She squinted up at Nick. "Which one of you is doing the cooking?" she asked.

"Definitely him," Harry said, pointing his thumb at Nick. "But I am a crackerjack delivery boy. Service with a smile is my motto!"

"In that case, I accept!"

Harry put his hand over his chest. "Mrs. McCabe. You wound me. You don't think my cooking skills are up to par?"

"No, and I believe you're the one who told me that."

"Then it was probably true."

"I think we have one more," Nick said and retrieved a large bundle from a nearby coat closet. He handed the package to Violet, who handed it to Mrs. McCabe.

"Well, aren't you the devious one! How did you sneak this over here?"

"I have my ways."

Mrs. McCabe tore the wrapping. "What is this?" she asked, staring down at a riot of color that peeked out of the paper.

"It's an afghan."

Arabella helped tug the wrapping away, revealing a crocheted blanket made up of vivid squares of colored yarn.

"Did you make this?"

An unexpected wave of embarrassment flooded Violet, and she suddenly understood Mr. Pritchard's haste in moving to the next gift. "I did. I've been working on it for a while. I had no idea what I was going to do with it, so when Arabella told me about your birthday, I thought maybe you would like to have it."

"Oh, but surely you made this for someone?"

"I really didn't. And it's not perfect. It has quite a few flaws. I am trying to improve, so you're actually getting a practice afghan. So don't get too excited."

"Don't be bad-mouthing my blanket, young lady!" Mrs. McCabe ran her hand over the expanse of yarn. "It is so beautiful. Thank you, Violet."

The softness in her voice took Violet by surprise, and the disparity between that and her usual abrasiveness left Violet feeling unmoored.

"Can I help with dinner?" She jumped up from her chair and joined Nick, Harry, and Caroline setting out buns and potato chips and a choice of salads and condiments.

"I'll start the burgers and hot dogs," Nick said, pulling a tray of prepared meat out of the refrigerator and heading for the back door.

"Oh. I was hoping for one of your Italian dishes," Mrs. McCabe said.

"Trust me. There'll be a little Italian in the burgers."

People milled about, talking and nibbling chips. Violet watched in wonderment. How did this reclusive, reserved road turn into . . . this? Mr. Pritchard whispered something in Caroline's ear, making her laugh. Mrs. McCabe bounced Baby Allen on her knee as Arabella leaned over them both, playing peek-a-boo with him. Tommy and Harry chatted about airplanes. Violet realized the quiet sensation inside her was . . . contentment. Something she had thought she would never feel again.

Nick brought in the grilled food, and everyone heaped their plates to overflowing. George threw up his hands after taking a bite of hamburger, declaring himself outclassed as a cook and Nick his permanent replacement.

After dinner, Nick and Arabella disappeared inside, and a minute later, they reappeared. Nick carried a pan with cupcakes, and Arabella carried one with a lit candle, her small hand cupping the flickering flame. Nick started them singing "Happy Birthday" with his strong baritone, and Mrs. McCabe beamed.

As they ate their cupcakes, Violet pulled a piece of paper out of her pocket. "I almost forgot! I got a letter from Bonnie."

"Bonnie?" George asked.

"She's the one who helped us adopt Sadie. At the pound."

"I remember her! She was nice. What did she say?" Arabella asked.

"I'll read it. 'Dear Miss Wentworth, I just wanted you to give my thanks to Mrs. McCabe. I called her vet, and he hired me as a technician! I really like it here. He says I have a nice touch with the animals. We have some sad stories here, too, but not like the pound. And here there are a lot of happy stories of animals we help. So thank you very much! Love, Bonnie. PS: Hope the little dog is OK.'"

"Aw. That's nice. Wonder if she changed her hairstyle," Mrs. McCabe said.

"What?" George asked.

"Never mind," Violet said.

She refolded the letter and tucked it away. The temperature had dropped into the sixties with a freshening breeze. Warm, rich light slanted between the stand of pines at the end of the yard and fell across the group of neighbors as they sat in an assortment of outdoor furniture. The chairs creaked to the background chorus of crickets and frogs, birdsong and human chatter. A lawn mower droned in the distance, perfuming the air with the scent of cut grass.

Mr. Pritchard finally stood up. "We better go. Boy's got homework," he said. "Good burgers. Thanks." He turned to Mrs. McCabe. "Happy birthday. You don't look a day over seventy." She glanced at him sharply, but Violet saw the glint of amusement in his eyes.

"Neither do you," Mrs. McCabe said with a sweet smile.

"For your birthday, I'll let you get away with that."

George got to his feet, "Guess that's our cue. Come on, little Party Planner. Time for a bath, a book, and bed. A short book!"

Arabella hugged Mrs. McCabe. "Happy birthday, Mrs. McCabe. I hope you enjoyed your party!"

"I did, Arabella. And you were right. Every person should have at least one party in their lives just for them."

The little girl skipped after her parents.

"Can I help you clean up?" Violet said, folding up her lawn chair and propping it against a tree.

"I think we're good. But I'll be happy to walk you across the street," Nick said as he and Harry began folding the rest of the chairs.

"That won't be necessary, but thanks," Violet said.

"Speak for yourself," Mrs. McCabe said. "I am now eighty years old. That sandy road is hard to walk on."

"You're not eighty until Tuesday."

"I might not make it until then if I fall in the road."

Nick ducked his head to hide his amusement. Violet gave up. The three walked up the steps into the back door, and Violet retrieved her dish. At one end of the sofa lay Mrs. McCabe's presents.

"Ah! I forgot I had presents!" Mrs. McCabe said, sounding as delighted and childlike as Arabella. "See? We need help carrying all this," she added.

Violet still thought she could manage, but she didn't argue, knowing she would lose. Nick scooped up the stack of presents—the blanket and the boxes with the wooden spoons and cookies. Violet took the envelopes, and Mrs. McCabe took one of Nick's arms—never mind that they were full. They set off in the waning light of the day.

Nick deposited the stack of goodies onto Mrs. McCabe's sofa. "Can I help you with anything else?"

"Just see Violet gets home safely."

"Yes, goodness knows what I might encounter in the fifty feet from here to my house," Violet said.

Nick held the door open for Violet. "Milady." He turned to Mrs. McCabe and gave a little bow. "Happy birthday. Hope you enjoyed your party."

"My dear boy, it was the best birthday I've had in years."

A silence descended after Nick closed Mrs. McCabe's door, and he and Violet walked the short distance to Violet's porch. Above them, wispy clouds had turned cotton-candy pink against the deep turquoise sky.

"Pretty sunset," Nick said.

"Yes, it is," Violet agreed.

They stopped at Violet's steps.

"Violet," Nick said.

Violet turned and met his dark eyes, and her breath caught.

Nick cleared his throat. "Uh, um, would you go out to dinner with me?"

Violet wondered if it was possible for you to flush and have all the blood drain from your face at the same time. She opened her mouth to say no, to tell him that she did not want to get involved with anyone, that it wasn't personal. But what came out instead was a breathless "Yes."

Nick looked comically surprised for a second. "Oh. You will?"

Well, she couldn't exactly say no now, could she? She didn't trust her voice, so she just nodded.

The smile that spread across his face at her words made her knees wobble. "OK. OK then," he said. "What nights are you off?"

"Wednesday is my usual day off, and I also get Sundays or Tuesdays, although this week, I got both. I can sometimes work the early shift on Saturdays. Oh, and this Tuesday, I am thinking of bringing dinner to Mrs. McCabe. It being her actual birthday and all. So Wednesday?" Was she babbling? She felt like she was babbling.

"Would six thirty work for you?"

For a moment, she forgot how to breathe. "Yes, six thirty will work."

"I'll come by and pick you up."

She opened her door and could not stop herself from turning to watch him go through her gateless fence. He must have felt her gaze because he also turned. He gave her a little salute. "Until Wednesday." And he walked off, whistling "Cupid" by Sam Cooke.

28

Violet

September 1969

For the next seventy-two hours, Violet understood what people meant by walking on air. Her feet did not seem to touch the ground. She felt light and giddy. Bubbly, for goodness sakes. When was the last time she'd felt bubbly? She could not stay still. So she cleaned. Since she had moved in only four months ago, her home was quite tidy. But she wiped down her spotless counters, scoured her already scrubbed bathtub, mopped her shining floors.

At night, she lay in bed pondering this new development. She tried to tell herself to slow down, but her heart had wrested the steering of her life away from her brain. Logic was no longer in charge. She liked him. There. She admitted it. He was handsome and charming and pleasant to be around. She was torn between hoping she'd enjoy their date and hoping she'd discover something in his personality that would help her put a stop to future ones. She did not think her heart was ready for a relationship, in spite of how it thumped when she saw him.

She didn't tell anyone Nick had asked her out. Not Mrs. McCabe when she took her pizza for her birthday dinner.

Certainly not Arabella when she dropped by for a visit after school. And she didn't see Caroline, although she didn't think she would have told her either. Not yet. She wanted to try out this new experience alone, without comment from other people. Even a person as good-natured as Caroline.

When Wednesday evening arrived, she started getting ready early, knowing she would dither about what to wear. She tried on skirts and dresses and cursed her wardrobe's slim pickings. She should have done more clothes shopping, she thought. Although, to be fair, she had not been in the right frame of mind.

She settled on a purple-and-white floral mini dress. Its long sleeves might be a little too much for the still-warm weather, but it was the most cheerful and date-like thing she owned. She grinned at her reflection as she thought Mrs. McCabe would be proud of her for wearing purple and not the drab brown outfit she had worn Sunday.

As she brushed her hair until it gleamed, she wondered what they could talk about. She was not ready to delve into the last two years. Or the two years before that. Maybe she would ask questions about his childhood, where he had been since joining the Air Force. If she kept control of the conversation, perhaps she could keep it in safe waters.

She gazed at herself in the mirror, turning her head this way and that, checking her appearance. *Not bad*, she thought. Her heart sank when she checked the clock. She still had a quarter of an hour. So she waited. For fifteen long, restless minutes. Each one ticked by with excruciating slowness. She paced. She plumped pillows. Straightened knickknacks. Finally, the hum of an engine in her driveway rescued her from making sure her books were perfectly aligned. Her heart began to pound. She waited a couple of beats after his knock to open the door, taking a few deep breaths to quell her anxiety. *He's just a guy*, she reminded herself. *Just an average, ordinary guy*. She opened the door. Just an ordinary, handsome, thoughtful guy who threw parties for old ladies. So much for the deep breaths.

They drove to Ricci's Restaurant. He held the door open for her, and she walked in, instantly charmed by the little dining area. Taper candles had been nestled in wine bottles, their flickering flames glinting off the kaleidoscope of colored wax that dribbled down the sides. Soft music played in the background.

"This is beautiful. Have you been here before?" she asked as the hostess seated them.

"I have a confession," Nick said after thanking the hostess. He leaned towards her. "I had not been here before, but I came last night to check it out. I swore the staff to secrecy."

Violet burst out laughing. "And here you are, ratting yourself out!"

"I am. The pressure was too much."

"So I guess it was good?"

"It was good. Not my grandmother's level of good, but for an Italian restaurant far from any Italians, it will do."

"What about Mr. or Mrs. Ricci?"

"I met Mr. Ricci yesterday, and when he said, 'How y'all doin', I figured he is at least a generation or two removed from Italy. Possibly many more."

"Oh dear."

"Shhhh. We'll let him think he's keeping my secret, and we'll keep his."

"Sounds like a plan."

They perused the menu and ordered their food. Violet noted how he made eye contact with the waitress, mentioned her name as he talked to her, always said "thank you" and "please." While working as a waitress, she had come to appreciate the people who treated her like a human rather than a faceless servant. Once they'd ordered, Nick turned his attention to her, and her worries about what to talk about drifted away like the smoke rising from the candle. He told her stories about his Brooklyn childhood and the trouble he got into. She told him about beach days on the South Carolina coast. He told her about snow; she told him about hurricanes. The dinner flew by—and he was right. The food was delicious. They finished the meal with cannolis and coffee. Violet realized she had been oblivious to the other diners who came in and out as they sat and ate and talked. When she finally glanced around, Mr. Ricci—who had come over and checked on them once or twice and looked about as Italian as Barney Fife—was placing upside-down chairs on the tables.

"I think we may have worn out our welcome," she whispered.

Nick scanned the dining room. "Guess that's our sign. Shall we?" He stood and held out his arm.

Mr. Ricci ambled over. "Did y'all enjoy your dinner?" he drawled. *Definitely not an Italian accent*, Violet thought, suppressing a giggle.

"We did," Nick said. "Thank you. Hopefully, we'll be back, if the lady agrees to go out with me again."

"Well, I hope the little gal says yes. Y'all have a good one, ya hear?"

They got to the car and burst out laughing. Violet said,

"If he's Italian, he's definitely from Southern Italy." And they laughed again.

When he pulled into her driveway, he walked around and opened her door and escorted her to her porch.

"I have to admit, it's strange to take a woman out who lives right across the street. Haven't done that since high school."

"I know what you mean," she said, instantly regretting the small confession as it skirted too close to topics she would like to avoid for now. Fortunately, he did not pick up that thread.

"I wasn't lying when I told Mr. Ricci I hope to go back. Or to another restaurant. If you'd like to go out with me again."

She gazed up at him, trying to find something she didn't like about him that she could latch on to, but, instead, she pictured him talking to Arabella with patience and interest and handling Mrs. McCabe's bristly personality with aplomb; she remembered how he talked to the hostess and waitress at the restaurant. How he talked to Tommy. "Yes," she said. "I would love to go out with you again."

Even in the dark, his smile shone brilliantly, and Violet melted.

"Well, I would like to say Friday or Saturday, but you're working, aren't you?"

"I am actually on the lunch shift for Saturday. I get off at four."

"Great," Nick said. "Will six thirty work for you again?"

"I'll be ready."

He pecked her on the cheek, and she went into her house, leaning against the door, breathless and bowled over, her cheek burning with the warmth from his lips. She heard him walking back to his car, whistling "That's Amore."

On Saturday, Nick took her to the only Chinese restaurant in town. Another date or two, and they would be out of places to dine out, Violet thought.

Again, they talked effortlessly and laughed at each other's jokes, and, again, the world narrowed to the space around them. After dinner, the waitress brought ice cream and fortune cookies. Nick cracked his open first and held the tiny slip of paper between his thumbs and forefingers and chuckled.

"He who throws mud loses ground," he read.

"Your cookie has a point," Violet said as she snapped hers into two pieces. "Running in circles gets your shoes worn down on one side," she said.

They laughed at the absurdity of the fortunes but agreed they each held a certain wisdom. "Makes me look forward to opening more," Nick said, digging his spoon into his vanilla ice cream.

Violet smiled, but the tiny printed words sparked a feeling of unease she couldn't put her finger on. She pushed the thought aside and enjoyed her dessert. Still, the little saying kept popping back into her head.

Later, he walked her to her door again and took her hand in his, enveloping it in warmth. The rough calluses on his palm contrasted with his tender grasp. "I'll call you."

"OK. I had a nice evening." Her heart did the now familiar flip-flop.

"I did, too," he said, squeezing her hand. She smiled at him, and he leaned down and brushed her forehead with his lips. A bare whisper of a touch, but her skin radiated from it.

"Sweet dreams," he said and walked away, whistling "To Know Him Is to Love Him."

She grinned as she stepped inside her house, realizing she had been waiting to hear what he would whistle.

As she washed the makeup from her face, the words of the fortune cookie ran through her mind. She stopped and thought. *Is that what I have been doing? Running in circles? Not actually dealing with anything, but simply scurrying around and around and around it? Wearing out one side of my life?*

Maybe it was time to switch directions.

PART

3

November-December 1969

29
Violet

November 1969

Thanksgiving arrived, clothed in brown leaves and wood smoke and crisp, cold air. Violet had barely reached the top step of the Fitzgerald porch when Arabella flung open the door. Violet smiled, knowing the girl had probably been watching at the window for the first guest to arrive. Violet entered the house, pushed along by a glacial gust of wind. She carried her casserole dish and placed it on the counter.

"Well, Arabella. Aren't you lovely!" Violet said as she took off her coat.

Arabella twirled, showing off her red top and green, white, and red plaid skirt and matching plaid hat. "Don't you think I look like Ann Marie in *That Girl*?"

"As a matter of fact, you do. Very professional."

Arabella took Violet's jacket, her grin crinkling her nose.

Violet turned to Caroline. "This is a sweet potato casserole. It will need to go in the oven for about five minutes or so to toast the marshmallow topping."

"Will do. Just remind me when it's time. And what happened to your famous green bean casserole?"

"I am branching out into new territory."

"Well, whatever you brought, I am glad to see you. My brain is all scattered hither and yon. I don't know if I am coming or going. George is actually a big help, but he also wouldn't care if we ate peanut butter and jelly sandwiches on paper plates."

"What can I do?"

Caroline consulted her list. "Let me check. The turkey is in the oven. George made some appetizers. Not peanut butter and jelly sandwiches, thank goodness. You can put that pot of creamed corn on the stove and keep an eye on it. I'm finishing the mashed potatoes."

"You didn't have to do this, you know."

"Ha! Tell that to Arabella!" But Caroline laughed. "Really, I don't mind. Who knew I would actually enjoy this kind of thing? I always avoided being the hostess in the past, but here I am, hosting all the time now."

"And doing a marvelous job, I would say," Violet said.

"Why, thank you, Violet. I do appreciate that!"

A knock sounded at the door, and Nick and Harry tramped in.

"Oooh!" Arabella said. "What do you have?"

"Risotto in the bottom dish and mushroom ravioli in the top," Nick answered, balancing his stacked dishes.

Arabella made a face. "I don't know what risotto is, but I know what mushrooms are. Ew."

Nick grinned at her. "Don't knock it until you've tried it, kid. And risotto is the best rice dish you will ever taste."

"Violet, Caroline, good to see you both." Violet's heart had skipped a beat at the sight of him. They had been dating for two months and had managed to keep it a secret for the first few weeks. But it had been getting awkward, so Violet finally told Caroline, who had squealed like a girl in high school. "To think I was wondering how I could get you two together! You make such a cute couple." Slowly, the word had spread. The first time she had seen Mrs. McCabe after she found out, the elderly woman had snorted.

"Don't say anything," Violet had warned her.

"Me? What on earth could I possibly say? I guess I could say I told you so, but I won't. I could even say that dressing in a brown paper bag didn't help you run away from love, but I won't. No, I'll just keep my mouth shut."

"I wish," Violet had retorted.

This Thanksgiving gathering would be the first time the neighbors had met since she and Nick had started dating. Violet hoped it wouldn't be too weird.

Harry placed some sodas on the counter. "Can't say I made these myself like my show-off chef of a roommate, but I bring them with glad tidings."

Caroline took them from him. "Any contribution is welcome."

Mrs. McCabe arrived with a pumpkin pie and whipped cream. After handing off the dessert to Caroline, she settled into George's La-Z-Boy with a happy sigh.

Tommy came next, carrying a bakery box of cookies and a slightly embarrassed expression. He mumbled his greetings to everyone as he presented the cookies to Caroline. "They're store-bought," he said apologetically.

"That's fine, Tommy! I am glad you didn't go to any trouble. I am sure you're busy enough with school," Caroline said. "Are you sure your mother doesn't mind you being here?"

"Yeah." His eyes darted to Mrs. McCabe. Cleared his throat. "Yes, ma'am. She was worried I wouldn't be OK with it. But she and Ernie are going to his mother's house, and I don't hardly know her. I only met her once."

"Well, we are glad you can be here."

Tommy's face turned a light shade of pink, and Caroline hid her smile. "Where's Mr. Pritchard?"

"He's coming. Told me to go on ahead since I was ready."

"I wonder if he will show up. Maybe he's had enough of us," Violet whispered to Caroline. But ten minutes after Tommy arrived, Mr. Pritchard came, a cloth-topped basket hanging on one arm and Sadie tucked under the other. He handed the basket to Caroline. "Biscuits," he said. Caroline smiled at him. She started to open her mouth to say something, but Mr. Pritchard scowled and headed into the adjoining living room. His expression forbade any fuss over his contribution.

George emerged from the bedroom, freshly showered and smelling of Old Spice, and set out appetizers. "Dig in!" he said. Everyone crowded around the kitchen table, oohing and aahing over the smoked salmon mousse on crackers and the deviled eggs speckled with paprika and parsley. Nick sat beside Violet. They did not hold hands or touch, both feeling a little shy in the company of the neighbors, but Violet felt his presence next to her as strongly as if he had put his arm around her and drawn her close. She looked around the room and realized she was enjoying herself. That she liked these people. Even Mrs. McCabe had grown on her. Who would have thought that would happen?

30
Caroline

November 1969

On the Saturday evening after Thanksgiving, Caroline and George sat in their living room, reading and enjoying a quiet moment at the end of a busy day. They had decorated the tree in the afternoon. Caroline decided Arabella was old enough to hang her favorite ornaments: iridescent glass partridges perched on the branches of the tree with little clips. She smiled as she remembered the look of disbelief on Arabella's face when Caroline handed them to her and nodded at the tree. Caroline also let her set up the nativity scene. Arabella had artfully arranged the figurines around the Baby Jesus and wound up the little music box that played "Silent Night." When George plugged the lights in, Caroline smiled to see Arabella gazing at it with utter delight. Even Baby Allen stared in stupefied amazement at the silver tree that glowed in different hues as the mechanical wheel next to it revolved through its cycle. The family ate dinner as the colors splashed across their living room in steady rotation. Arabella had been reluctant to go to bed and leave all the decorations, but after Caroline put Allen down, she told Arabella she could read for half an hour. Caroline left her propped up in her bed, sur-rounded by her stuffed animals, reading *The Wind in the Willows*, promising to come back in thirty minutes to tuck her in.

Caroline had settled on the sofa with her own book, occasionally glancing up to admire the tree, when suddenly the lights in the house flickered and went out. A scream vaulted her out of her seat.

"That was Arabella," she said, heart hammering as she headed to her daughter's room. She and Arabella almost collided in the dark hallway. Caroline grabbed the girl's shoulders.

"Bella, are you all right? What happened?"

"My lamp went out, and when I sat up to turn the other one on, I saw this blue light come out of the wall. It was so fast, I wasn't sure I'd actually seen it, but then it did it again. Right where I was sitting."

George pushed past them to investigate. He looked into her room and shouted, "Out! Everyone out. I'm getting Allen. Go to Nick and Harry's. Now!"

Caroline's heart hammered in her chest. She scooped Arabella up, hesitating, torn between getting her daughter to safety and making sure George got Allen. *George will get him*, she told herself and ran to the door and into the yard. Seconds later, George caught up with her, Allen squalling in his arms. They ran to Nick and Harry's, and George banged on their door with one hand and held Allen against his chest with the other. Nick opened it, taking in their disheveled state and trying to hear what George was saying over the angry and bawling Baby Allen.

"Call the fire department! Our house is on fire," George said.

Harry had appeared behind Nick, and he immediately turned to the phone as Nick ushered them all in. Harry dialed the operator and told her they needed a fire truck and gave the address.

"They're on the way," he said.

Caroline set Arabella down and took Allen from George. "Stay in here where it's warm," George said. "I'm going to go out and make sure the fire trucks find us."

Nick grabbed two coats and handed one to George. "I'll go with you."

Caroline bounced Allen on her shoulder and kissed his downy head, trying to comfort him, but her brow was creased with worry.

"Do you have something I can wrap him in?" she asked Harry. "I can't stay in here."

Harry fetched a blanket as well as two more jackets. One he wrapped around Caroline's shoulders, and the other he wrapped around Arabella's.

"It's a little big, but it will keep you warm."

"Thanks, Mr. Harry." Her voice sounded tiny and small and unsure.

They joined George at the edge of their yard, and Caroline gasped when she saw that flames now framed the windows of Arabella's room, the curtains blazing brilliantly in the dark night. A sob burst out of Arabella. George picked her up.

A minute later, the rising and falling wail of a siren pierced the night. Lights pulsed beyond the distant trees and houses, growing closer, until two fire trucks emerged at the end of the street and roared towards them. Nick and Harry ran to the road to wave them down. One truck pulled into the yard, and firefighters jumped out and began pulling a hose to the house. One of them asked the men if anyone was in the house.

"No, we are all safe," George answered.

"Daddy. What about Tabitha?" Arabella asked after the fireman walked away.

"I am sure she's laying low, well away from the fire. I doubt she'll come to the firemen, so let's let them do their work, and then we can search for her."

A minute later, Violet rounded a fire truck that had parked between her house and the Fitzgeralds'. She stopped and let out a chilling cry that made Caroline briefly forget her own fear. Violet covered her mouth with one hand and gripped her abdomen with the other and began sobbing. She looked around wildly and spotted the Fitzgeralds. She ran towards them, reaching out a hand to cup Arabella's head.

"Oh my God, are you all right?" Her voice teetered on the edge of hysteria, her eyes frenzied, her breath coming in short gasps.

George reached out his free arm. "Violet. It's OK. We're all OK." He rubbed her shoulder.

Nick appeared at her side. "Violet, why don't you and Caroline and the children come inside? We'll stay out of the firemen's way."

Nick's eyes slid to Caroline's, and she nodded her agreement.

Violet barely seemed to comprehend what Nick was saying, but she allowed herself to be led to the house, face stricken and tears spilling down her cheeks. Nick put an arm around her shoulders.

"Arabella, you want to go inside with me?" Caroline asked. Arabella shook her head and clung to George's neck.

"She's OK. I'll keep an eye on her," George said.

As Caroline turned to follow Nick and Violet, a fireman walked over to George, eyeing Violet's receding back as he did.

"Sir, is this your house?"

"Yes."

"And you're sure no one is in there?"

"Positive. It's just me, my wife, and two kids, and we're all accounted for," George said, his face awash by the red lights of the fire truck.

"What about her?" He nodded towards Violet.

"She's a neighbor. Lives over there. I don't know why this upset her so much."

The fireman nodded and went back to his duties. Caroline shivered with the cold and decided it was a good thing for Allen's sake she was going inside. She'd barely noticed the chill in her horror at seeing her house on fire.

Later, George would tell her how a third truck drove up and several men donned masks and went to the door of the house. One immediately turned around and ran over to George.

"It seems the door is locked. You got a key? Or we could use an ax."

"Oh," George said. "I locked it?" He fished in his pocket and pulled out a set of keys, separating one and handing it to the fireman.

He described how the men with masks went in, and after a few minutes, Arabella's blackened, smoldering mattress flew out her broken window, and she had buried her face in her father's shoulder, crying. Other debris followed. Her toy chest. Stuffed animals. Other things he couldn't identify.

Mrs. McCabe, Mr. Pritchard, and Tommy joined them, Mrs. McCabe asking breathlessly, fearfully, where Caroline and the baby were. Relief flooded their faces when George told them they were waiting comfortably inside Nick's house.

"Where is Violet?" Mrs. McCabe asked, looking around. "Her car is in her driveway."

George shook his head. "She came out, and she kind of went hysterical when she saw the house. She started crying. Nick took her into his house."

"Well, that's right odd," Mrs. McCabe said. "That doesn't sound like Violet at all."

They all agreed it did not.

Caroline came out, and when she glimpsed the gaping black hole that was Arabella's window and the burnt pile of her belongings on the lawn, she clapped her hand over her mouth.

"Oh, George!" She took a deep breath and moved to George's side.

He put his free arm around her and pulled her close. "It's going to be OK. We are safe, and that's the important thing."

"I know you're right, but oh God."

"Is Allen sleeping?"

"Yes, he is. Nick is keeping an eye on him. And Violet. What on earth happened to Violet?"

"I don't know. How is she now?"

"She's calmed down now, but she's just staring into space." A fireman came up to them.

"I'm Chief Underwood. We got the fire out, though we

are still looking for hot spots. You're mighty lucky. I think most of the mobile home will be OK. Usually, these things go up like a stack of kindling, but there were a lot of stuffed animals in the room where the fire started. Between those and the mattress, they created enough smoke to keep the flames from spreading. And your closing the door helped. Although you didn't have to lock it." But he was smiling. "Can you tell me what happened?"

George told him about the blue flame Arabella had seen. "Sounds like an electrical problem. We will inspect it tomorrow. For now, we'll make sure we douse all the hot spots."

"Can we go in and get some of our belongings? Clothes? Diapers?" Caroline asked.

"Ma'am, I'm going to have to say no. It's not going to be safe for civilians. And honestly? I don't think you will want any of that stuff. The house was full of smoke, so everything is going to reek to high heaven. Some things may be damaged by the heat or from soot. Anything you can salvage from inside the house will need to be cleaned."

George thanked him. He glanced at Caroline. "You should probably take Arabella inside. She's shivering like crazy. I'll wait here until the firemen are done. Then we'll need to find a place to stay."

Caroline could not stop replaying what might have happened to her daughter. To her family. She took Arabella from George and hugged her hard. She kissed her forehead, pressed her warm weight against her chest, inhaled her dewy scent of baby shampoo and powder. Once back in Nick's living room, she relished the bright warmth and the lingering aroma of dinner as welcome counterpoints to the dark night outside and the smell of her home going up in flames. As if sensing her thoughts, Arabella began to cry again, and Caroline patted her back. Mrs. McCabe patted Caroline's.

"It's going to be OK, Bella," Caroline told her. "We are all OK."

The men tramped in, bringing a rush of cold air and the sharp tang of smoke and allowing the red glow from the fire trucks to spill into the house. The door remained open long enough for Caroline to see the emergency lights switch off, first one truck, then another, leaving only headlights to pierce the darkness. She thought of her house sitting in the dark next door and wondered how bad it would look tomorrow. Tears stung her eyes.

"Can I get anyone some coffee?" Harry asked.

"I'll take one," Mrs. McCabe said and walked over and touched Caroline's shoulder. "You all can stay at my place."

"Or you can stay here," Harry said.

"We appreciate it, everyone. Truly. But they have emergency housing at the base," George said. "Nick, Harry, if I could just use your phone."

"Sure, George. If you want, there's one in the bedroom," Nick said. George followed him down the hall as Harry pulled out mugs.

Caroline glanced at Violet, who huddled at the kitchen table, looking as pale and shaken as Caroline felt. Her silence reverberated through the room, and Caroline could see everyone shooting glances at her, though, for now, they allowed her time to collect herself. Until Mrs. McCabe finally broke the silence.

"Violet, honey, are you OK?" Caroline thought this was a ridiculous question. Violet was clearly not OK, but what else does one say in situations like this?

Violet raised her head, dazed. She blinked. "I'm fine," she said. Then with more certitude, "I'll be fine. How are you, Caroline?"

"I'm not sure, honestly. In shock, I guess."

Violet pushed herself out of her chair, going to Caroline and Arabella and wrapping them in a hug. "I'm sorry I freaked out. I am so glad everyone is OK."

George came out, rubbing the back of his neck with his hand. "We have rooms, courtesy of the U.S. Air Force. Caroline, they will meet us at the guest housing on base. The sergeant I talked to said they could probably find us a larger place in a day or two. Also"—he placed his hand on Caroline's shoulder—"they have some baby supplies: diapers, clothes, bottles. Stuff that people have donated when they moved."

Caroline slumped with relief. She hadn't realized how worried she'd been about what they'd do about Allen.

Violet said she had some clothes that would probably fit Caroline, and she left to get them.

The Fitzgeralds stood, and Caroline handed Arabella to George and scooped Allen up off the sofa. They filed out of Nick's house and stood in the cold, smoky night. Allen stirred, but settled back into sleep against Caroline's shoulder.

"Daddy?"

"Yes, Bella?"

"Can we find Tabitha now?"

"Yes, of course we can." He turned to Nick. "You have some flashlights we can use?"

"Sure. Be right back." He came back with two and handed one to George, who headed to the front door. The firemen had closed it. He pushed it open and called softly.

"Tabitha! Here, kitty. Come on, girl."

A shadow dashed past him and stopped on the porch at the sight of Nick. She was a tuxedo cat, and when George shone the flashlight on her, her white socks and bib glowed in the dark. George laughed with relief. Caroline, watching with Arabella, warned her to stay quiet. "You might scare her away. She must be pretty spooked."

"Tabitha, come here." George crouched down and held out a hand. Tabitha stretched her neck and sniffed his hand. "Atta girl. Come on. It's OK. It's all over." As he talked to her, Caroline watched intently to see if she was all right. Her fur stood on end and had an oily sheen. And she was panting. She tentatively moved closer to George, and Caroline saw her white patches were smudged with soot. But she appeared unhurt. She rubbed her whiskers against George's hand, and he stroked the side of her face before reaching down to pick her up. She struggled for a minute, but he held her and crooned to her and settled her into a comfortable position in the crook of his arm.

Mrs. McCabe, who had disappeared into her house when Violet went to hers, reappeared carrying her old brown-and-blue afghan. "For Arabella," she said. "Well, well, you found Tabitha. That is good news. You're going to need a cat box. I have an old cardboard box and some litter I can give you. And some cat food. Nick!"

"Yes, ma'am!"

"Come with me. I need some strong arms."

George gently placed Tabitha in the back seat of the car.

She crouched in the footwell, pressing into the space under the seat.

Violet joined them with a bag she handed George. "Caroline, hopefully this stuff will fit. A few tops and pants. Oh, and a pair of sneakers."

Mr. Pritchard stepped up, also carrying a bag. "Some clothes for George. Probably not a good fit, but better than nothin', I reckon."

"Arabella, since nothing here is your size, I guess we will go shopping tomorrow. Get you some new things."

"I don't mind wearing these clothes for a while."

"Well, you might in a day or two."

The neighbors hugged them, and Caroline took a last glance at the dark, lifeless hulk that just hours ago had sheltered her family. Violet gave Caroline one last hug as George eased himself behind the steering wheel. Caroline climbed into the car with Allen on her lap. Arabella sat in the back, petting Tabitha. Before Caroline closed the door, she overheard Nick ask Violet if she was really all right.

"I am, Nick. I really am. But I think I need to be alone for a bit."

"You got it," he said. But Caroline detected a note of worry in his voice.

31

Violet

November 1969

Once inside her house, Violet pushed the door closed and squeezed her eyes shut against the tide of panic she had been battling since seeing the fire trucks. She leaned forward, hands on her thighs, heart racing, heat flushing her face, breathing in great gulps of air. She wondered if she was having a heart attack.

Her mind roiled. She needed to get away, to think, to figure out what she was feeling. She would go home, she decided. And realized this was the first time in months that she had thought of her parents' house as home. Somewhere along the line, this little trailer had become home to her.

Her heart slowed, and the tightness in her chest loosened its grip, allowing her breathing to return to normal. She washed her face and changed into her nightgown. When she climbed into bed, the tears came. Sobs wracked her body, and she allowed herself to weep until she was empty. She remembered doing this in her parents' house, but she had used her pillow to smother the sound. Here, she could cry aloud, and no one would hear. The thought both relieved and disheartened her.

As the fear and grief receded, fatigue filled the space they left, leaving her spent and wrung out.

She thought of what Mrs. McCabe had said before her birthday party two months ago. "I don't know what has happened in your past," she had told Violet. "But whatever it is, it is just that: past." She had been wrong. Those days, those events, were not behind her. They were here with her now. She had a vision of Marley in *A Christmas Carol*, with his chains forged from the things he had done while alive. She had her own bonds that constrained her, weighed her down. She dragged them with her wherever she went.

As the minutes slowly ticked off the night's passage, sleep eluded her. She managed to sleep a couple of hours, but awoke before dawn with sandpaper eyelids and a desolate heart. She plodded into the kitchen and made coffee and, while it brewed, stared out her back window at the dark sky just starting to lighten. As she listened to the hiss and rumble of the percolator, she considered her decision to go home. Was it running away? Wasn't it time to be done with that? But no. This time she wasn't fleeing or hiding. She was facing her past head-on. She had only a vague concept of what this meant, but the idea felt right.

Thus resolved, she sat down at her kitchen table with coffee, pen, and paper. She quickly wrote a letter, folded it, and sealed it into an envelope. After washing her mug, she packed a suitcase. As she mindlessly pulled clothes out of her dresser drawers and off hangers, she made a mental note to call Turner's later and tell them a crisis had come up and she would be away for a few days. She didn't know how long she needed, but she certainly couldn't afford more than that. Damn. She might have to dip into her savings at the end of the month. Well, she'd deal with all that later.

She slipped out of her house, hoping no one would see her toss her suitcase into her back seat. She scanned the street to make sure no one was out and crossed the road. After a moment's hesitation, she slid the envelope into Nick's mailbox, her hand hovering uncertainly over the little door. She should have been more definitive in the letter. She should let him off the hook. Dating him was a mistake. She wasn't ready. She thought she would never be ready. How could she be? She thought about retrieving the letter and writing a new one, but her neighbors would start stirring soon, and she didn't want to talk to anyone. She remembered it was Sunday, so no one would check the mail. She raised the little red flag, hoping Nick or Harry would notice it.

She returned to her car. As she opened the door, she scraped together some courage and looked at the house across the street. She sucked in her breath. It wasn't as bad as she had feared. The fire had transformed Arabella's double windows into a lightless maw. Sodden, blackened belongings lay in a pile in the yard below broken panes. The front door had streaks of soot above it, but the rest of the house appeared intact. She hoped the damage inside was not too terrible. Regret pinged at her. She should be here for Caroline. Help her out. But she couldn't. Not just yet. She had some thinking to do. And some remembering.

32

Violet Donnelly Wentworth

1946-1966

At eighteen, Violet could see her whole life spread out before her, a red carpet of possibilities and plans she would tread with confidence and determination. She would marry her high school sweetheart, Sam. She would go to college and earn a degree in English or literature. She would land a job teaching. In a few years, she and Sam would have two, maybe three, children. They would grow old together and stay in love forever and one day find themselves sitting in rocking chairs on their front porch, laughing and reminiscing at the ups and downs and twists and turns their lives had taken. She had expected twists and turns. She had not expected a cliff.

Violet had known of Sam Wentworth most of her life. They had never been friends or traveled in the same circles. Although they started at different elementary schools, they had gone to the same church. Back then, he was a towheaded boy she barely knew, fidgeting in the pews, squirming in Sunday school, dodging among the adults as they chatted when the service was over. If she thought of him at all it was with annoyance. *Why can't he simply sit still and behave?* she wondered. In junior high, he made a name for himself as an athlete. Football, track, basketball. She made a name for herself as a brain. She took the top classes, made the top grades. Won a statewide essay competition. Their orbits barely touched.

He took notice of her when she went with friends to see a track meet in the spring of their freshman year. The girls cheered their team on, but Violet held a book open on her lap, and she looked down at it more than she did at the runners. He told her later he had spotted her right away and kept looking to see how much she watched the events and how much she read. After his best event—the four-hundred-meter—he glanced her way and saw her dark head bent. He sauntered over to the bleachers.

"Must be an interesting book."

Her head shot up, and she regarded him with confusion. Her girlfriends dissolved into a wriggling mass of giggles and nudges. "It is. *A Midsummer Night's Dream*."

She studied the Greek god in front of her in his tank top and shorts, long, lean muscles shiny with sweat, the early spring sun glinting off his cropped, blond hair.

"Shakespeare?"

"You've read it?" she asked.

"Well, to be honest, no. But I know of it. Do I get any points for that?"

"Not much," she said. But the corners of her mouth turned up ever so slightly.

His teammates called him over for the next event. "Be right there," he shouted. He turned.

"I'm Sam Wentworth," he said.

"I know," she said.

He grinned. "Yeah?"

"I might have heard of you."

"And you're Violet."

Her heart skipped a beat at the thought that he knew her name. She had always believed herself invisible to the popular kids. But here was her name, rolling off the lips of this golden boy.

"I'll talk to you later, Violet. Now I must run. Literally."

As he ran the next event, she found herself reading less and watching more. At the end, when he came in first, he caught her looking and waved and grinned at her. She raised her hand slightly, her chortling friends making her self-conscious.

That began his pursuit of her, which she, at first, resisted. But he wore her down with a campaign of sweet gestures. He left gifts on her porch. His first gift was a bouquet of wild violets in a small jug. The next, a bird's nest which she hoped was not a current home for anyone. Another time, a mason jar of acorns. A pressed frond from a fern. The simple presents charmed her more than she cared to admit. After a month, as summer burst forth, she agreed to go out with him.

They became the high school dream couple: she dark and pretty and bookish, he blond and handsome and athletic. Many a girl gave Violet a scornful glare for catching one of the best-looking jocks, although no one was more surprised than she. She had never been one to aspire to dating an athlete. She generally thought of them as shallow and not terribly bright. But Sam made her rethink her preconceptions. Underneath his sportsman's facade lay a kind soul and a canny mind.

They married a month after graduation. The memory of the moment when she walked down the aisle shone more crisp and clear than any photograph. She recalled everything, from the smiling faces turned towards her to the dust motes that danced in a sunbeam that struck Sam's fair hair and turned it into a burnished halo. Most of all, she remembered his face, boyish, young, hopeful, full of love. Full of kindness. She didn't know then that those qualities could be stolen. Eroded, possibly, but not appropriated and destroyed.

He had hoped for a track scholarship, but, while he had been good, he hadn't been quite good enough. Without the monetary award, college was not in his cards. He shrugged at the change in direction. His intelligence manifested itself differently than hers. He did not enjoy spending hours with books as she did. She sometimes wondered if he hadn't felt some relief when his path veered away from college. He continued working his high school job at a local horse farm, driving tractors, mending fences, clearing trails in the woods for riders. Violet enrolled at the local technical college for some general classes for the fall and got a job in a department store in the women's dress section, where she tried to steer matronly women to more flattering clothes choices. Between their two paychecks, they rented a small house. They moved in, and Violet unpacked her wedding gifts with a swell of happiness. She carefully placed her dishes, pots, pans, flatware, and glasses in the cabinets, stopping often to admire them and think, *These are mine and Sam's. They are ours, and we are each other's.*

After the wedding, they made love almost every night. Afterward, they lay naked in the summer heat, skin damp with sweat. He made her feel so beautiful that her initial shyness slowly slipped away. A fan whirred in a feeble attack on the breathless, humid air. A chorus of crickets sang outside the open window. They talked and planned and joked and laughed. They ate cold chicken and chocolate cake in bed, both young enough to relish the pleasure of the rebellious act.

Sam worried that their paychecks would not cover their expenses. He told Violet he was going to look for another job, that as much as he enjoyed working outside, they needed more money. She knew the last thing he wanted was to follow in his parents' footsteps into the textile mill. That would be a last resort.

To help out, she sought ways to be thrifty. Her mother had despaired of teaching her to cook. Violet would rather read a cookbook than employ anything she gleaned from it. But now, her mother taught her about buying bargain meats and tricks to stretch them. Chicken in stews and bread crumbs added to ground beef made those meals more filling and generated leftovers. She evolved into a passable cook, but had no illusions that her abilities went beyond that. She didn't quite fall in love with cooking, but she liked knowing she was making something Sam would enjoy and saving them a few cents in the process.

After several weeks of job hunting, a local hardware store hired him as a salesman. His experience at the farm helped. He could converse about anything from paint to lumber to nails—but his comfort with the products did not extend to the customers. Violet sensed a chord of discontent when he talked about a customer demanding a refund on something they had obviously damaged themselves. But the owner, Mr. Wilkinson, said a happy customer will go home happy, an unhappy one will stop and tell everyone they meet. "Keep 'em happy," he instructed. Violet understood Mr. Wilkinson. Her manager lived by the adage "You get more flies with honey." Violet enjoyed the challenge of working with cranky women. Turning a situation around and bringing a smile to a grumpy customer's face gave her a sense of accomplishment. Sam thought it a waste of his time. Violet shook off the rude interactions like water off a duck. With Sam, they soaked in and fed a little streak of resentment she tried to soothe.

Money was tight. Violet did not enroll in the spring semester classes as she had planned, and they celebrated a lean Christmas. Violet minded the first more than the second. She had everything she needed and some of what she wanted. She didn't need a lot of gifts. But Sam brooded about it. He wanted more money, more opportunity, but wasn't sure where to go for it. Early in the new year, one of his high school buddies came back from boot camp and shared his experience in the Army. The training. The discipline. The possibilities. And planted a seed Violet tried to stamp out. But Sam's eyes lit up when he talked about it.

"Just think, Vi. We could travel. See the world. I could get some training for something more useful than finding the right hammer for some idiot." He gazed into the distance. "When I was little, I used to say I wanted to be a soldier. I drew pictures of battles. Played with toy soldiers. Used sticks as rifles." He looked at her. "This could be our ticket out of here, Vi."

She watched her husband with dismay as the seed sprouted and grew. She tried to tell him that as a private, he wouldn't get paid much more than he made now. But he saw opportunities: travel, glory in war, promotions. And a way out of a dead-end life.

They fought that spring of 1964. They fought about money, about his desire to go into the Army, about new purchases. When their decrepit car defied his attempts to keep it running, she had to admit they needed to replace it. But they could not afford it. By the time their first anniversary came, the tension wore her down, and she relented. He enlisted in the Army the next day. She was relieved when he told her he didn't have to report for months. They had time. Buoyed by the promise of the future, he, too, gave a little and allowed her parents to lend them enough money to buy a secondhand car. He didn't want to leave her with the unreliable one. In the meantime, she put aside her worries, wanting to make the best of the few months they had before he left for basic training. She donned the costume of the stoic wife, but she never wore it comfortably.

He departed in May 1965, on a day awash with the sunshine and green leaves of the coming summer. They kissed and clung to each other, but both held on to the optimism of youth. They were young, strong, indestructible. He had a fair chance of being sent to Vietnam, but Americans were not heavily involved there. They did not see the quagmire that lay ahead.

Violet adjusted to her new role as a soldier's wife. When she joined his parents at graduation, she walked with a straight spine fortified by pride. Sam, beaten down and built back up in boot camp, walked with the confidence won by triumph over hardship.

After basic training, Sam received artillery instruction for eight more weeks. Violet held out hope he would be assigned to a base in the States, where she could join him. The idea of living somewhere else began to tantalize her. She liked her little town, but she also wouldn't mind seeing something of the world.

But his orders came through for Vietnam. Violet's heart nearly stopped at the news. But she straightened her shoulders and talked herself out of her fears. *He'll be fine*, she told herself. *It's just an assignment.* The newspaper reported the United States was sending more troops as South Vietnam lost ground to the Communists. *But the American soldiers will soon have this turned around*, she thought. *He'll be home in no time.*

He had fifteen days' leave before shipping out. He and Violet spent every minute together. If he had any fears, he didn't share them with Violet. Nor did she share hers with him. They created a bubble that neither their past arguments nor future worries penetrated—at least for those two weeks. They had dinners with family, outings with friends, visits to his old boss and favorite teachers, but mostly they whiled away their time in bed. Violet would have been embarrassed to admit how much time she spent naked and lounging in the sheets. And liking it. She blushed thinking about it.

Far too soon, the fifteen days passed, and the bubble burst. He boarded an airplane and left Violet staring out an airport window at the plane taking off with her life on board.

She threw herself into nesting. She cleaned the house from top to bottom as if someone with the plague had died in it. She made curtains. She hooked rugs. She even learned to refinish furniture after finding a couple of old, worn nightstands at her grandparents' house. She resumed reading—something she had sorely neglected during her first year of marriage. She became a regular at the library, checking out classics from Shakespeare to Dickens to the Brontës. She worked. Her busy schedule helped the time go by, but she had the strange sensation that the days were flying by but the months were not. The feeling unsettled her.

Somehow, one season gave way to another, then another, until the end of summer arrived and with it a phone call from Sam. He had been injured and was coming home two months early.

"Just a little injury to my shoulder," he reassured her. "I'm fine."

Violet put aside a niggling worry that he did not sound fine. He sounded grim and not that happy to be coming home. She hoped his wound wasn't worse than he was telling her. But she would find out soon enough. Her Sam was returning to her.

33
Violet Donnelly Wentworth

1966-1967

On the appointed day, Violet waited at the airport, shy and uncertain. It had been so long since she had talked to him, laid her head on his shoulder, made love with him, she could barely remember.

As soon as he came down the boarding stairs, she spotted him, slim and handsome in his uniform, arm in a sling. Her Sam. Her heart soared. Tears she didn't know were forming spilled out of her eyes, down her carefully made-up cheeks. She walked across the tarmac, and he dropped his duffel bag. They met halfway, and he threw his good arm around her waist and pressed her against him. He buried his face in her hair. She wrapped her arms around his neck and breathed in the scent of him—soap and Sam and a new smell of cigarettes. She felt as if she'd been holding her breath for eleven months and could finally exhale. He leaned back and peered at her, studying her face. Gradually, they became aware of their families waiting a few feet away. They broke apart, and everyone rushed in and hugged him and clapped him on the back. Someone grabbed his bag, and they exited the airport in a loud herd.

Sam told them he had been shot in the shoulder, but it was healing well. Violet asked him how it happened, and he brushed it off.

"Doesn't matter. I'm home now, right?"

Violet expected their new life together to have some bumps, but reality turned out to be more difficult than she imagined. They ground against each other like gears that did not mesh, creating friction and sparks. He didn't notice the changes she made to the house—all the little things she had done with her own two hands to make the house homier. She pushed her resentment away, telling herself he'd been gone a long time. He was short-tempered, responding irritably to even the most innocuous questions. She decided he was probably tired and, after a rest, he would be better.

But then came the flashbacks and nightmares.

A week after Sam got home, he was dozing on the sofa on a Sunday afternoon. Violet dropped a pot in the kitchen sink, the metal clanging against the porcelain. As she picked up the pot, she heard a *thump* and shouting from the living room. She peered through the kitchen door. Sam crouched on the floor, motioning with his hands. "Down, get down! She has a rifle!"

"Sam!"

"Shoot her!" he shouted. "Shoot her, goddammit!"

Violet stood stunned, still holding the offending pot, staring at Sam, who looked over his shoulder and yelled.

"Sam!" she said again.

She crossed the room and touched his arm, and he jerked around and grabbed her wrist.

"Sam! Ow! That hurts! What is wrong with you?" She tried to pull her arm away, but he tightened his grip. He was looking not at her, but through her. She didn't know what to do. She said his name again, tears pooling in her eyes. Something shifted in him. His eyes fell to his hand gripping her wrist, and slowly he relaxed his fingers until she pulled free. She backed away from him, pulling her throbbing arm to her chest. He rose, pushing up on the sofa cushion with trembling hands.

He dropped onto the sofa, his forehead glossed with sweat.

"Sam," Violet said, her voice softer. "What happened?"

He shook his head. "Sorry. I woke up and didn't know where I was for a minute."

"Oh, honey," she said, moving closer.

"Don't," Sam said. He stood. "I need to get out for a while."

He grabbed his coat and the car keys and took off in their car before she could summon any more words. She stared at the front door he had slammed, a barrier to the world and now a barrier between them. She became aware that she still held the pot. Angry, red imprints circled her wrist like bracelets. She walked back to the kitchen.

Sam did not come home until after she went to sleep. She lay for a long time in the bed alone, thinking of what had happened. About what Sam said. Had it been a dream or something more? Had there been a girl with a rifle? Did someone shoot her as he had ordered? What had Sam gone through over there?

She wasn't sure what time he came home, but she woke in the middle of the night to hear him snoring softly beside her. Relief at having him by her side flooded through her, and she sent up a silent prayer of thanks and fell back asleep. In the morning, she awoke to weak December sunlight streaming through their window and casting rectangles of light on the worn hardwood floor. Sam lay on his back, face slack in slumber, and tenderness filled her heart even though he reeked of whiskey. They would get through this, she thought. They were Sam and Violet. For better and for worse.

With Sam now home, Violet pictured a holiday season brimming with happiness and new family traditions. Getting a tree. Hanging stockings. Buying presents. They did all that, but a tension stitched their days together, a patchwork quilt of merriment and melancholy, irritability and appeasement. She found herself wishing Christmas and New Year's were behind them, and they could slip into a soothing routine. Perhaps then Sam would get used to being home.

But he didn't.

She knew he was trying. His shoulder healed. He got his job back at the hardware store, and on the surface, he seemed like his old self. But he had more episodes like the one he had the week after coming home. He didn't have them too often, but when he did, they disturbed them both. In spite of his protestations, she could tell whatever happened to him during these times was far deeper than waking up and not knowing where he was. He went through the same motions, shouted the same words. He would not tell Violet what he saw. Once when she asked, he had turned on her.

"I don't want this ugliness in your head. It's bad enough it's in mine."

His voice held such venom and vehemence, she didn't ask again.

She discovered that loud noises would trigger an occurrence, and she learned not to get close to him when that happened. He had nightmares that jolted them both from sleep—and again, she found it best not to touch him when he was in the throes of one. Often, he would leave after an incident. Usually to a bar, she surmised, as he would come home later and pass out, stinking of alcohol.

Six months after he got home, she confronted him about his drinking.

"I need to have a drink or two to sleep, Violet." His voice was angry, defensive. She left it.

There was some truth in what he said. On the nights he drank, he didn't have nightmares, usually. But she watched with concern as he spent more and more time away from her and more and more time drinking. She found an empty vodka bottle under the seat of their car and others stuffed into the trash.

Eight months after he got home, she approached him again. She waited until a day when his mood was sunnier than usual. They had gone to her parents' for dinner—a pot roast with vegetables and chocolate pie for dessert. It had been one of the better times they'd had since his discharge. The summer heat reminded her of their honeymoon week, and maybe it reminded Sam of it, too. When they got home, he put his arms around her and nuzzled the little space between her neck and collarbone. Hope surged in her. They'd made love in the time he'd been home, but a gap existed between them. This time felt different. They kissed and took each other's clothes off all the way to the bedroom.

Afterward, Violet snuggled against him like she used to. Her relief filled the room, an almost palpable presence. She gently broached the topic.

"Sam. I worry you might be drinking too much."

He instantly stiffened.

"Don't get defensive," she said, making an effort to stuff her words with affection and understanding, willing him to understand not just what she said but how she said it. "I am not accusing you or anything. I only want to let you know I am worried about you. I love you, Sam. I love you so much. And I wish I could help you get better."

He pulled her closer to him, and he rolled over to his side so they were chest to chest. His shoulders shook, and she realized he was crying. She held him and told him over and over again that it was going to be all right. She loved him. He loved her. They would survive this. He stopped with a ragged breath.

"I love you, too, Vi. I'm sorry this has been so hard for you."

"Shhhh." She placed her hand on his cheek, stubbled with a day's growth of beard. "It's OK. It's been hard on you, too."

The next morning, he declared he was going to quit drinking and see if he could get his farm job back. "I hate that goddamn store." Months ago, she would have flinched at his language, but now his cursing around her was commonplace.

As it turned out, the foreman at the farm had broken his leg about the time Sam's shoulder healed. At sixty-seven, he decided now would be a fine time to ease into retirement. Mr. Patterson, the farmer, hired Sam to replace him but told him Old Red would stay on, so he would have to work with him when his leg got better. Sam liked Old Red, so Mr. Patterson and Sam shook on it. He was as happy as Violet had seen him since before he left for Vietnam. Perhaps they were finally getting back on track.

Life stayed on an even keel for a month or more. Sam still had flashbacks and nightmares, but the physical demands of his work helped him sleep better, and they came less often. Violet and Sam fell into a routine of work and dinners with their parents. They made love occasionally—sometimes with fierce passion, sometimes with quiet tenderness. Violet was content. She still occasionally suspected he was drinking. Was that alcohol she smelled on him? Was he sleeping heavily because he had a hard day at the farm or because he passed out? She didn't dare ask, afraid her words would crack the fragile shell of their relationship.

In late September, as she rummaged for some soap in the cabinet under the bathroom sink, she unearthed an old bottle of shampoo. The liquid inside had turned thick and gloppy. She threw it away, but considered the messy cabinet. She knelt on the floor and pulled out the extra rolls of toilet paper, a tin of shoe polish, other bottles of forgotten toiletries, an old half-used tube of toothpaste, and her sanitary napkins. As she replaced the items that were still useful, she paused, studying the sanitary napkins, sitting back on her heels as she tried to remember when she had last needed them. More than a month had gone by, she realized. She, whose periods rolled in as regular as the tides, had not had her period since at least early August. *Well,* she thought as a little niggling feeling of excitement began to grow. *Well.*

She waited another week or so before she told Sam. He acted thrilled, and yet . . . she sensed something reserved about his response. Several more weeks passed before they told their parents. All were over the moon, but was Sam's smile a little strained?

She asked him about it one night.

"I'm happy, Vi, I am. But it's a big step. I just wonder if we can afford it."

"We'll make it work. Other people do."

"I know." He pulled her into an embrace, his lips brushing her hair on the top of her head. "But I also . . . I still have the flashbacks."

"But they are getting better." She leaned back and peered up at him. "You're healing, Sam."

"Yes, I am getting better." But his eyes did not meet hers.

A week later, Sam didn't come home from work. She fretted, telling herself he got held up at the farm even while her imagination took off with images of tractor accidents or chainsaw mishaps. She hovered on the edge of calling Mr. Patterson, but she didn't want to look like a nagging wife. And Sam would hate it. Finally, at eleven, he stumbled in drunk.

"Sam! Where have you been?"

"Shorry, Vi." He laughed at his own mistake. When he continued, he enunciated carefully. "I mean sorry. Went out with some of the guys. Joe's birthday. Just the one time, I shwear. Swear." He leaned down for a bleary kiss, but she ducked under his arm.

"Hey, Vi, don't be like that!"

"I'm not, Sam. I'm fine. You go on to bed, and I'll be there in a minute after I turn out the lights."

She took her time, wiping down the kitchen counter, checking the stove, and, finally, turning off the lights. When she heard the bedsprings, she went into the bathroom. She used the toilet, washed her face, brushed her teeth, leaned against the door. When she came out, he was asleep.

She climbed in bed next to him and lay awake, trying not to cry. *Please let it be just this one time,* she thought.

He went out more and more with "the guys." He promised to call if he was going to be late, and sometimes he did, and sometimes he didn't. When he didn't, she'd find herself standing at their front window, in the dark, waiting for headlights to come down their road and light up the sycamore that stood sentinel in their yard. She paced. She choked back tears, not sure if she was crying from worry or self-pity. Or both.

She confronted him again, but gingerly. Did she take the gentle approach out of a desire to gently persuade him or to avoid a fight? She didn't know.

"Sam, you're going out a lot with your friends. I miss having you here," she said softly.

He eyed her warily, already on the defensive. "A man's gotta blow off steam."

"I know. And you work hard. But maybe you could cut back a little? I mean, you're going to be a dad soon."

His temper flared. "So you become a dad and your life ends? Some of the other guys are dads. You think their wives are nagging the hell out of them every time they go out?"

She recoiled and blinked at him. She didn't know how to tell him she worried he couldn't control his drinking, that it seemed to be all or nothing with him. When was the last time he'd had one beer?

At times, he was fine. Other times, he wasn't. He would go a week and come straight home. Violet sank into those days, pulling a blanket of pretense around her. *This is how it will always be,* she told herself, refusing to look further than this day, this meal, this moment. On those evenings, they worked on the nursery, painting, fixing trim, setting up furniture Violet got from her parents. They lay in bed at night discussing names. She reeled off a long list of them—most of which he shuddered in mock horror until she hit him with a pillow. In those moments, she could ignore the worry fraying the edges of her happiness.

The next week, he would stay out late, and she returned to staring and pacing and cleaning. He usually came home after she was in bed. If she was awake, she pretended she wasn't. Drunk Sam was not the Sam she loved, and she did not want to talk to him. She did not like to see him stumble or hear him slur. She squeezed her eyes shut and counted the minutes until he passed out.

The week of Thanksgiving was a good one. He came home every night, and they had dinner together. When the holiday came, they went to his parents' house on Thanksgiving Day and her parents' the day after. He was on his best behavior for his mother. He seemed so much like the old Sam, her heart swelled. He joked. He tried to help his mother clean up, although she batted him away and told him to go sit with his father and let the women wash up. His father offered him a beer, but he declined. His father drained can after can, occasionally calling one of his daughters or his wife to bring him a new one.

They enjoyed a pleasant dinner at her parents' the next day. Her brother Jerry and sister Betty and their spouses and kids filled the house with effervescent noise. But as they moved into the weekend, she worried what it would bring. But they Christmas-shopped together, ate dinner together... Violet was buoyed.

On Sunday night, as they got ready for bed, Violet felt a flutter in her abdomen, bringing a gasp to her lips. She pressed her hand across her stomach.

"You OK?" Sam had been turning back the bedspread. Now he straightened up, concern drawing his eyebrows together.

Violet's face transformed with wonder. "I think I just felt the baby move." She crossed the room to him and took his hand and held it to her belly, but the baby lay still. She slumped with disappointment. Sam put his arms around her. "Don't worry. It will move again." She leaned against him, feeling his warmth and strength, luxuriating in how their bodies fit so neatly. *Please let us stay like this forever,* she thought.

On Tuesday, he didn't come home from work. She ate her dinner with only her growing anger for company. After she finished, she took her plate to the sink and considered what remained on the stove. Instead of storing the leftovers in the refrigerator like she usually did, she threw the extra pork chops and mashed potatoes in the trash. Her dismay at the waste battled with the satisfaction she got from her little act of defiance.

She tried to make a normal evening of it. She watched a little television on the black-and-white console her parents had handed down to them when they bought a color set. After a while, she realized she had no idea what she had just seen. She opened a book to read, but she could not absorb the words. Her mind just kept turning to Sam. He had been home well over a year. Wasn't it time he moved on? She went to bed, determined to sleep, determined not to worry. But sleep eluded her, and, instead, she lay awake planning what she would say to him the next day. It was time she put her foot down.

He got home after midnight, stumbling to bed as usual. How he managed to get up for work, she had no idea. But he did. She made his breakfast and bit her tongue to keep from lashing out at him. Now was not the time.

That afternoon, she rubbed spices into a chicken for dinner, wondering if he would be home to eat it. Relief mixed with dread when she heard his car crunch the gravel in their driveway. He entered the house, sweeping off the brimmed hat he wore at work.

He pecked her on the cheek as he went by.

"I'm gonna take a quick shower," he said.

She gauged his mood. Not cheerful, but not sullen either. But did it matter? She was going to have her say regardless.

By the time he came back in, she had slipped the chicken in the oven and was slicing a cucumber for their salad.

"Bradley's horse got away from him again," Sam said. Bradley was Mr. Patterson's seventeen-year-old son. "Kid has butterfingers when it comes to holding on to a rope. They need to give him an old, tired mare who won't go running off since he can't control the young gelding he was given."

Sam told her more about his day as the food cooked. Violet attempted to meet his small talk with chitchat of her own, but all she could think of was how she wanted to bring up last night. And the other nights. But she knew any discussion would go better on full stomachs.

They finished eating, and Violet stood to clear the table.

She took the plates and silverware to the sink and turned to study him.

"Sam, I need to talk to you."

"Oh, boy. Here it comes," he said, but he grinned at her. She winced, knowing he was expecting her to ask him to pick up his clothes or smoke outside now that she was pregnant and the surgeon general had warned about the ill effects of smoking. She inhaled deeply and plowed on.

"Sam. It's about your drinking." He rolled his eyes and sighed. She hurriedly continued. "And staying out at night when I want you—need you—home."

"Oh for God's sake, Violet. Not this again."

"Yes, this again," she said. "It will be 'this' again until you stop, or at least cut back. I'm tired of making a dinner for two and only I am here to eat it. I am tired of worrying about you and wondering if you're OK."

"No one asked you to worry. I'm fine."

"You're my husband, Sam. I love you. I can't help but worry." She paused, gathering her courage. "I think you drink too much."

He snorted. "You should see Joe. Man, that guy can throw back some whiskey."

"I don't care about Joe. I care about you." She stepped over to where he sat in his chair, pushed back away from her, arms crossed. "I want you at home, Sam. I miss having you here."

He shifted his eyes away. "Fine. You want me to stay home, I'll stay home. I'll cut back on drinking. Just stop nagging me about it."

He stood, and his chair clattered against the wall. Violet flinched. Sam headed for the door.

"Where are you going?"

"To have a smoke. You don't want me to smoke in the house anymore, so I'm going outside. Maybe I can think of something that will actually please you."

The door closed behind him as his barb found its mark. Would it have been better to leave it alone than to have this anger and resentment boiling up between them? Before, only her resentment permeated across their home like a noxious miasma. Now it had doubled.

Sam was true to his word and came straight home for the next couple of days. Violet made his favorite meals, hoping to cajole him into better spirits. She asked her manager at the store to keep her on the day schedule, claiming her pregnancy wiped her out by evening. Her manager wasn't happy as their busiest weeks lay ahead. But Violet thought she should make the house as welcoming as possible when Sam got home. She made her own vow that she would not ask—nag, to use his word—about anything else for a while. She wouldn't say a word about his clothes, about how he splashed water all over the bathroom when he shaved. She would even tell him he could smoke inside, especially on chillier evenings.

She worked Saturday morning, leaving Sam in bed asleep. They only had the one car, which she usually left for Sam while she took the bus to the department store. She didn't mind the walk from the bus stop, and most places she went were on the bus line. When she neared her house a little after four p.m., the sun was throwing long, last rays across the road. She pulled her coat tighter about her as a sharp breeze whipped down the street. She ducked her head and didn't notice her dark house until she reached the empty driveway. She sighed. *He could be running errands.*

She changed out of her work clothes into more comfortable slacks and flat shoes and set about making dinner. She attempted to concentrate on her task instead of worrying about Sam, but without much success.

At five, the car pulled into the driveway. She debated what tack to take: Confrontation? Nonchalance? She closed her eyes, praying he was not drunk.

"Hey, Vi," he said, tossing the car keys on the counter. "How was your day?"

OK, so he was playing the good husband. She would play the good wife.

"Busy. Lots of husbands coming in for Christmas gifts." She flipped the meat she was frying. "Is ham OK for dinner?"

"Anything you cook is fine by me," Sam said.

They tiptoed around each other, delicately trying to gauge the other. They weren't fighting, at least, thought Violet. But they weren't exactly enjoying themselves either.

They sat down to eat, and Violet smelled the alcohol on him. She kept her head down, sawing at her ham with a knife, chewing slowly, buying time, knowing she couldn't ignore the odor wafting off of him. But she didn't want to break the tense treaty that lay between them like a sheet of thin glass, ready to break into fragments at the least amount of pressure. But hadn't he broken it when he went out drinking?

Finally, towards the end of the meal, when she thought she could use her knife on the tension in the room, she said quietly, "You've been drinking, haven't you?"

His eyes narrowed. "Yes, I have," he said, his voice tight. "I had a few drinks with the guys, and here I am at home for dinner."

She nodded, tried to arrange a believable smile on her face. She began clearing the table. He had a point. He HAD come home. He didn't appear drunk. But her sense of unease lingered.

He pushed back his chair. "I'm going out for a smoke."

She shrugged and scraped the plates, watching bits of ham fat and green beans fall into the garbage can. She began washing the dishes and, after a few minutes, looked down to discover she had been scouring the same plate the whole time. She hated this antipathy between them. She made a decision. She dried her hands and left the rest of the dishes for later. She wanted to talk to him. To try to make things right between them.

She opened the door quietly, willing herself to be brave, to go talk to him. He leaned against the trunk of their car, the light of his cigarette waxing and waning as he took a drag from it. Then he lifted a narrow, rectangular bottle to his lips and took a gulp. Her heart shattered.

"Sam."

He turned with a start. "Shit, Vi. Are you spying on me now?"

"No. I came out to try to make up with you."

"So now what? You going to yell at me because I took a little drink?"

"I don't know, Sam. What should I do? Let you drink and pass out every day?"

"And why not? What is so bad about that? Then I won't have to remember. You have no idea what it is like in my head. None. The shit that won't go away. The shit that wakes me up at night. I can't fucking take it." He lifted the bottle and drank again, draining what was left. He studied the empty container for a minute before hurling it against the sycamore tree, the explosion of breaking glass rending the quiet night.

A sudden fury rose in Violet. "No, I don't know because you won't tell me. You won't let me help. You just drink yourself into oblivion. Well, I've had it, Sam. I've had it up to here."

She stumbled into their house. She had a wild urge to get away. This time she would be the one to leave. She grabbed her coat and the car keys and headed outside as he came in.

"Where are you going?"

"I'm going for a drive, Sam. For once, I'm the one who needs to get away."

She was out the door before he could say anything. And what would he have said? Stay? Go? She was afraid to find out.

She drove aimlessly at first. In the cold, December darkness, she passed few cars and no people. She found herself slowing a little when she drove by houses with lit windows, peering at the little tableaus laid out in the bright squares. A family at dinner. A couple watching TV. A figure walking from one room to another. She wondered if they were happy families or if they all had their secret pain like she did. Like Sam did.

Her anger evaporated, leaving sadness in its wake. She drove to the outskirts of town. After making a few turns, she found herself at a landing at the marsh where Sam had proposed to her. She turned the engine off and remembered their dating years. They used to drive out here and kiss and cuddle and daydream, their background music provided by frogs and insects calling across the flat expanse. Sometimes they just stared out at the moonlight as it painted a silvered path on the water between patches of reeds, her head on his shoulder, his arm around her.

Goddamn the Army. Goddamn Vietnam.

She wept.

How could she get them back on track? What could she do? She brushed at her face, succeeding only in leaving wet smears. When the cold had wrapped around her and made her shiver, she started the car. She drove back home slowly, still bereft of answers, remnants of tears drying on her cheeks.

When Violet approached her street, a red, pulsing glow caught her eye. She frowned. Was that someone's Christmas lights? She turned onto her road, squinting at the odd light, thinking it looked familiar, trying to puzzle out where she had seen it before. She got closer, and the puzzle clicked into place. The lights were from a fire truck. Her heart began to hammer. She prayed the fire was at someone else's house. God, what an awful thing to think, but she couldn't help herself. What if she had left the stove on? She had been so distracted. But she was always diligent about turning the burners off. No, it had to be another house. Or possibly a brush fire in the field across the street.

As she drew nearer, the possibility of it being another house diminished with each wide yard she passed. And then, her house loomed in front of her, fire trucks assembled in a half arc around it. Her heart thudded, dropped, stopped. Furious flames whipped at the black sky. Flames from her house.

She slammed on her brakes and jumped out of her car. Someone told her later she had left it running, the door open. She was oblivious to anything but finding Sam. She yelled his name, scanning the crowd of firemen and neighbors gathered in the road and in her yard, searching for him, but he did not appear. He did not come to her side and reassure her. Take her in his arms so they could comfort each other as their home succumbed to the blazing conflagration. When she didn't find him, when he didn't rush to her side, she looked at the house and began to run. A fireman grabbed her and held her back. She screamed. She hit him. Where was Sam? Maybe he had left? Had taken the bus? Had a friend come to pick him up? That must be it. He was in a bar. For the first time since he had come back from Vietnam, she was relieved to think he was out drinking.

The fireman's words broke through her shouts. "Ma'am, is there someone in the house?"

"My husband. My husband was home, but he must have gone out. He couldn't be in there."

The fireman left her in the care of a neighbor. Someone brought her a blanket and a cup of hot coffee she held with shaking hands. Someone else got her parents' phone number and went to call them. They arrived, breathless, anxious, and coaxed her into their car to keep warm. Over and over again, she craned her neck to see if Sam was coming. Some other men arrived in dark cars, not in fire gear. Once she ascertained neither one was Sam, she turned away from them and continued waiting for him. *He should arrive soon*, she thought.

The firemen carried on with their work. The flames appeared to be winning the battle at first, but eventually the water won out and the house lay before her, a smoldering, blackened ruin in the red lights of the fire trucks.

And still Sam did not come.

34

Violet Donnelly Wentworth

1967-1968

On the morning after the fire, Violet sat at her parents' kitchen table in the rumpled clothes she had been wearing the night before. She had kept vigil all night, expecting Sam to storm into the room at any moment to make sure she was OK. He would hear about the fire while he was at a bar. Or he would see their devastated house when he went home. He would be frantic with worry. But instead of Sam, two policemen knocked at her parents' door, wearing grim expressions as they swept their hats from their heads. They had found a body, they said in soft voices as if that would lessen the destruction of their words. A positive ID would be made using dental records. They did not need to explain why.

Their pronouncement punctured the bubble of hope she had wrapped around herself. Somewhere in the back of her mind, she must have considered the possibility. But if she had, she had quashed it before it became fully formed. Even after she understood what they were telling her, her consciousness shied from the knowledge as if it were a sharp blade that could cut her to the bone. *No,* she kept thinking. *No, it can't be true.*

Violet spent the next two days curled up in bed, her back to the door, refusing food, refusing comfort. Her mother brought her meals on trays, then took them away again, untouched. At the beginning of the third day, her mother came in and sat on the edge of the bed. She rubbed Violet's shoulder gently.

"Violet. I understand how devastated you are. But you have to eat. You have to take care of the baby."

The baby. Had she even thought of the baby? She hadn't thought of much of anything. Her thoughts, if she had any, crawled sluggishly, ill-formed, illogical.

"I—" she started, and stopped. The words jammed in her throat, a jumble of ideas unable to find form and passage. "I'm not hungry."

"I know, sweetheart, but you need to eat something."

"Mom." Tears thickened her voice. "I shouldn't have left him. It's my fault he—" Her voice broke, and she cried. Again. Her eyes and her face were swollen from crying. Her head ached.

"Oh, honey. It's not your fault. You couldn't have foreseen that a fire would break out after you left the house."

"But if I had been there—"

"You don't know what would have happened."

The police returned, hats in hand. The body was Sam's. Violet sat on her parents' sofa, but that did not keep her from swaying. Her father grasped her hand, a modicum of his strength seeping through the conduit of his squeezing fingers, steadying her.

"The firemen found him in the bedroom," one policeman said. "The fire started in the living room. The cause appears to be a cigarette that fell onto the sofa, although they are still running tests. It probably smoldered for a bit, and your husband didn't realize it had fallen. It would have created a lot of smoke. That's what gets people," the policeman said.

"So he didn't . . ." She couldn't form the words.

"No, ma'am." He understood her unfinished thought. "It was smoke inhalation. That also explains why he couldn't get out. He most likely lost consciousness."

Violet wondered how much Sam had to drink before he went to the bedroom. But did it matter now? The thought that he might have been unaware of the fire and that he hadn't been overtaken by flames eased her mind. She closed her eyes. She couldn't believe she was thinking about which was a better way to die. For Sam to die.

After the police left, Celia took her daughter's hand. "You see, Vi? If you had been there, you might have died, too."

"I wish I had," Violet whispered.

"Oh, Vi." Her mother's shoulders slumped.

"And I don't think I would have. He'd been drinking, Mom. He was always drinking."

"But that is not your fault either."

"No, but I could have been more patient." She turned and looked at her mother. "Just a few days ago, he told me drinking was the only way he could cope. I never told you about his horrible nightmares and flashbacks. They were terrible. He's"—a sob escaped her—"Was so tortured, Mom. I should have been more understanding."

"Oh, honey. I am so sorry." Celia enveloped her in a hug, and Violet cried into her mother's shoulder, tears welling from an endless pool.

She ate. Woodenly, without tasting anything. But she ate.

Friends and neighbors and fellow church members came bearing the usual casseroles, but also made humble offerings of clothes and household goods to replace the things Violet had lost. If Violet had been present in mind and not just body, she would have noted the generosity, the swell of kindness towards her. But she was not present. She was still at the fire. She thought she would always be at the fire.

The day before the funeral, Celia went alone to the store and bought Violet underwear, bras, pajamas, and a black dress for the funeral. Violet was indifferent.

Three and a half years almost to the day since her wedding, Violet buried her husband. Carrying a child who would never know him, never feel his strong hand, never ride on his shoulders, never hear his voice read a story. Her loss was an abyss that swallowed her whole.

The memories of the funeral encapsulated themselves in snapshots, a lurching slideshow of disjointed images: a closed, flower-draped coffin alone at the front of the church, holding both Sam and her future, both soon to be buried in the earth; a sad sea of faces blending together; the pallbearers carrying their terrible burden down the aisle; her legs almost giving way and her father's tightened grip on her arm to keep her from stumbling.

At the graveside, bouquets and sprays of flowers surrounded the grouping of chairs as though they were onlookers themselves. The lowering sky pressed cold, damp air onto the funeral-goers, onto the rows of graves spreading out beyond the one that would soon be Sam's. The pain in her heart weighed a hundred pounds. A thousand. She didn't know how she would bear it.

Two days later, Violet found blood in her underwear. Hours later, she lay in a hospital bed, everything lost to her. Her home. Her Sam. Her baby.

Violet did not understand how she kept breathing. How the sun kept rising. How people on the television kept talking and moving. How had the world not stopped? The loss of Sam had gutted her. She wouldn't have thought she would have any more capacity for grief. But losing the baby showed her sorrow was limitless.

Her doctor prescribed a sedative, and Violet spent those first days after her miscarriage in a haze. She slept, and, when she didn't sleep, she stared at the few belongings she had left—objects from her childhood that she had not taken with her to her new home: some of her books, a carved wooden pelican, a beach snow globe her grandmother had given her. She had meant to move these last items when they had new shelves to put them on, but in the aftermath of Sam's return from Vietnam, she hadn't thought of them. And here they were, remnants of a life torn asunder.

After a few weeks—the exact number got lost in the fog of her days—her mother refused to refill her prescription. A day or two later, she refused to bring any more food to her room. Violet would barely have noticed except her mother would stand in her doorway and tell her she wasn't leaving and she wasn't going to stop talking unless Violet came to the table for dinner. Violet heaved herself off the bed, parked herself at the table, and woodenly lifted fork to mouth. She tasted nothing. She ate T-bone steaks and brussels sprouts with equal heedlessness. Next, her mother told her she wasn't doing her laundry anymore. Again, Violet didn't care if she wore the same clothes for days, but her mother refused to go away unless Violet got up and carried her laundry to the washing machine.

Her thoughts floated in some remote realm. They were sailboats bobbing on a far horizon. Stars transmitting from distant galaxies. She thought about arguing with her mother. She thought about killing herself. She thought of going for a drive. These ideas would form and float beyond her grasp before she could act.

Against her will, Violet began to come back to life. Gradually. Unwillingly. Eventually, a day came when she went for a walk. The day was an unseasonably mild one in late February in the first year Sam did not tread the earth. When Violet woke in the morning, she lay in bed, staring out her window. Early buds sprigged the trees like tiny birds. The sunlight spread across her parents' yard, warm and welcoming. A bird sang. She had a sudden desire to move, to stretch her legs, to feel the sun on her shoulders.

She got dressed and ate breakfast and told her mother she was going for a walk. Her mother kept her face expressionless, but nodded. Violet stepped outside, and a breeze interlaced with warmth lifted her hair. She walked. Violet had at least one foot in the world again, though it would be a long time before she felt a resident of it.

A year unreeled around Violet, filled with all the firsts of mourning: the first holiday without Sam, the first season change, the first birthday. An endless parade of days to be gotten through. And then came the first anniversary of the fire.

The date loomed, an insurmountable wall, another divider of her life with Sam and her life without him. The first year had passed miserably, and each milestone broke her heart a thousand times, but those days connected her to Sam. She feared the second year would drag her away from him. It would plant him firmly in the past and carry her into her unknown future until one day, she would look at him as though from the wrong end of a telescope. One day, would he disappear forever?

The Saturday after Thanksgiving, she trudged home to her parents' house from work. She had returned to her retail job in July, finding that her biggest challenge was smiling politely all day. The anniversary of the fire was Monday, and the date weighed more and more heavily on her shoulders, on her heart, as it pulled closer. When she entered the kitchen, tired from the effort of being polite and pretending the anniversary of the worst day of her life was not days away, she found a visitor sitting with her mother at the table. She had never seen him before. His lean legs, crossed at the ankles, stretched under the table and almost to the other side. His neat afro haloed a strong jaw and hard eyes. Her mother stood when Violet entered, her hip knocking the table, clinking the salt and pepper shakers, uncharacteristically rattled. Violet was puzzled. The man drew his legs in and unfolded himself to a standing position, nearly bumping his head on the light fixture above the table.

"Violet," her mother said. She cleared her throat. "This is Michael Hoyle." Pause. "He served with Sam in Vietnam. He wanted to speak to you."

Violet sucked in her breath. Her world wobbled, then steadied. Anguish had drowned her for months. Now the grief played hide-and-seek, coming out of the shadows and slashing her with a fresh laceration when she least expected. It could happen at the grocery store, in the post office, on a patch of sidewalk. In her mother's kitchen. Anytime. Anywhere. Still, this was a particularly deep gash.

"I'll leave you two to talk," her mother said.

Celia's back disappeared through the doorway to the living room. Violet turned to the stranger and motioned for him to sit. "I see my mother has supplied you with refreshments." She waved her hand at the half-empty iced tea glasses and plates dotted with leftovers of cookies and crackers and cheese.

"Yes, ma'am."

"You don't have to call me ma'am. I think I am younger than you."

A tiny, crooked smile tilted one corner of his mouth. "Habit."

"So what brings you here?"

"Well, first, I am sorry for your loss. I was at the funeral, but I didn't get a chance to tell you that. It tore me up when I heard about Sam."

She nodded, lacking the energy for niceties.

"Second, I don't know if Sam told you much about what happened in Vietnam."

"He told me nothing," she said, unable to keep the words from riding a note of bitterness out of her mouth.

It was Michael's turn to nod. "Thought that would be the case." He leaned forward, setting his elbows on the table, tenting his fingers, resting his chin lightly on his thumbs.

"All of us have trouble talking about Nam, I think. Some bad things happened there. I am sure you've heard some news reports of some of them in the last year. Since our tour. It's another world over there." He paused, rubbed his hands together, clasped them, tented them again. "I thought you should know because it really messed some of the guys up. It might be easier knowing... why he came back so... different."

Violet considered this. She almost didn't want to know. But she pictured herself a week from now. A month. No, she had to learn the truth. "Go on," she told Michael.

"Our unit was on patrol, looking for Viet Cong, trying to flush them out. By then, we had been conditioned to kill anything that moved. We'd be walking through that steaming jungle, not knowing if Charlie was in front of you, behind you, beside you. Once they were above us, in the trees. All you knew was they were out there and they wanted to kill you. No way to describe how it feels to know someone wants you dead. Our unit had been ambushed a couple of days before. We had been lucky. A few injuries, but no fatalities. But we were jumpy from it. Anyway, on this patrol, I was in the rear. Sam was in front. Suddenly, the jungle gave way to a little clearing with a few huts. Sam gave the signal for everyone to stop and be quiet, which we did, looking for signs of life. We crouched behind trees and shrubs, not talking, using hand signals. Then a girl came out of a hut."

Violet had a sudden urge to stop him. To hold up her hand and tell him she didn't want to hear anymore. She had a crazy vision of her putting her hand over his mouth and felt a bubble of hysterical laughter rise up in her throat. She pushed it down. He kept talking, cracking something open that would never close again.

Michael continued. "I couldn't see much from where I was. But Sam yelled that she had a rifle and to fire. Everyone near the front fired their weapons. In a barrage. From what I understand, a woman ran out of the hut, and they shot her, too. And shot up the hut for good measure. After a minute or two, the firing stopped, and we waited again. Nothing moved. We approached cautiously, some of us keeping a lookout in the rear, others approaching the huts, rifles ready, to make sure no one else was hiding. There were a few more people in the hut, all shot. All women and children." He paused and swallowed. His eyes slid away. Slid back to Violet. "The girl with the rifle was no more than ten or so. Lying in the dirt, sunlight on her face and dark hair, blood everywhere. And beside her was a pitchfork. Not a rifle. When we searched the huts, we didn't turn up any weapons at all."

Tears pricked at Violet's eyes. *Jesus God*, she thought. No wonder Sam had nightmares. Had he worried she would have judged him if he told her? Would she have? Or could he simply not bear to think of what had happened?

Violet pictured the girl—spun a hundred news photos of Vietnamese children into one. Black hair parted in the middle and tied loosely at the nape of her neck, high cheekbones, bronze skin. Was the woman who ran out her mother? Running out to save her child?

Michael filled the silence she left. "And we covered it up. We returned to base and told the officers that we had surprised some Viet Cong. Implying soldiers, not women and children. We thought . . . I don't know. Some of the guys said the only good Charlie was a dead Charlie. Most of us didn't feel that way at all. But whatever we had done, whatever we would do, we couldn't bring those people back, so what would an inquiry do? Slow us down, ruin our reputations, and still those people would be dead. And I think some of us supposed if we didn't think about what happened, it would go away. But it never did. As time went by, I came to believe telling the truth would have been better. Something about covering it up seemed to make it grow and fester." He took a gulp of tea and then swished the amber liquid around the glass. "I don't know if my being here and telling you all this is the right thing or not. I thought about it for a long time before I decided. But I thought if you understood what Sam had been through, it might help you . . . have some peace, I guess. I imagine he, of all us, might have carried more guilt since he gave the order to fire. But he was just doing his best in a tense situation. He was a good guy. He would never have wanted to hurt those innocent women and children."

"No, no, he wouldn't have." She pictured pre-war Sam from high school leaving thoughtful, little gifts for her. She remembered post-war Sam, crouching in the living room, fear radiating from him in ripples she could almost see. "He had flashbacks about that," she said quietly. "He would yell, 'She has a rifle.' He would never explain afterward. He had a lot of nightmares."

"I'm sorry," he said.

"Do you?"

"Pardon?"

"Do you have nightmares? Flashbacks?"

He nodded. "A little. They are getting better. I see the girl, after. The bodies in the huts. Sometimes they get up and walk towards me, hands out, blood streaming from their wounds." Michael shook his head. "Sam wasn't the same after it happened. Before, he would joke around. Everybody liked him. He was easy-going. Fun to be around. But after? He shut down when we weren't on patrol. Didn't talk much to anyone. Quit joking around. And on patrol? He always insisted on going first, and he got a little reckless. He made the rest of us nervous, and we were already pretty jumpy. Then he got shot and sent home."

"How did he get shot?"

"Sniper. He got lucky. We had stopped for a break. He had been leaning on a tree. The break ended, he straightened up and got shot in the shoulder. I am fairly sure if he had still been leaning, he would have been shot in the head. Two more guys in our unit were shot and killed. The rest of us opened fire and shot the hell out of the jungle around us. We got the sniper."

Violet pondered that. She wanted to ask about the sniper. Perhaps a lone soldier, facing a squad of enemies in the jungle. Had he been young like Sam? Scared like him? But that, she decided, she did not want to know. She thought of Sam, evading such a close call only to come home and die a year later.

"Thank you for telling me about this."

He looked down at the table. Ran a finger along a crease in the plastic tablecloth. "I hope it gives you peace. I figured it's better to know more about what happened to him than not. Covering things up just seems to make them rot." He regarded her, and she read the question in his eyes. Had he helped? his eyes asked. But she didn't know.

35

Nick

November 1969

Morning glided in slowly, nudging Nick out of a fitful night's sleep. He opened his eyes, stretched, then sat up with a start as the events of the night before flooded his consciousness: the fire at the Fitzgeralds' house, Violet's dramatic reaction. He swung his feet to the floor and wondered how they were all doing. Perhaps later, he could check on Violet. Possibly take her something to eat. And as for the Fitzgeralds, he imagined they would be by to look at their house in the light of day.

He padded into the kitchen, careful not to wake Harry, though in truth, a freight train coming down the hall might not rouse him. He cleaned the percolator they had left sitting the night before. He filled it with water, added the coffee grounds to the basket, and plugged it in. Once done with that, he grabbed a jacket and slipped his shoes on. He'd get his Sunday paper while the coffee percolated.

As he headed down the driveway, he stopped and studied the house next door. He was surprised that it wasn't worse. Arabella's window was broken and haloed by soot, the room blackened beyond recognition. Scorched, saturated debris lay strewn about the lawn. The rest of the mobile home appeared to be in fair shape, all things considered. He hoped they could salvage some of their belongings and, maybe, the trailer itself.

When he got to the mailbox, he noticed the flag was up. Odd. He hadn't mailed anything in a few days, and he didn't think Harry had. He took the paper from the green tube and opened the mailbox above it. A white rectangle lay tucked inside with a single line of writing inscribed in its center. No stamp, no address. He pulled it out and saw his name on the front. His heart sank. He couldn't imagine anything good coming from a letter left in his mailbox.

Once in the house, he threw the paper on the counter and ignored the freshly brewed coffee. He tore open the flap of the envelope and cautiously removed the folded letter inside. He glanced at the name on the bottom. Violet. Just as he thought.

Dear Nick,

I want to apologize to you and to everyone for last night. And for also not being truthful with you all about what brought me to Edenton.

You see, I was married before. Two years ago, my house caught fire, and my husband died. There's a lot more to my story than that, but I don't have time to tell you the long version right now. The last two years have been long and hard. I thought I had moved to Edenton to heal, but I think I was doing more hiding than healing. The fire at the Fitzgeralds shook me to the core, as you probably noticed. I decided to go home for a little while. I needed to go back to where all this happened and face my past.

Please feel free to share this with our neighbors. I won't be hiding anymore.

I am not sure where this will leave us. I like you, Nick, a lot. But I am a pretty broken person. I think I will need some time, and then we will have to figure out what the future holds.

Perhaps this letter raises more questions than it answers. I don't know. But it's all I can do right now.

Violet

Nick finished the letter and stared out at the strip of woods behind his house. The stubbled cornfield lay beyond the lacework of bare branches. It was a view Nick had not yet tired of, but he did not see it now.

He remembered his vow about not getting tangled up with someone who might drag him down the way Giulia had. He remembered how happy it made him to be with Violet. He cursed silently and refolded the letter. Why couldn't life just be easy? Just once in a while?

He had some thinking to do.

36

Violet

November-December 1969

Violet pulled into her parents' driveway and sat in the car, gathering her strength. She had no idea what to say to them. *Hey, Mom and Dad. The long-awaited nervous break-down has arrived.*

Although she had just been here two days ago when she celebrated a slightly belated Thanksgiving with her family, she looked at the house with fresh eyes: the porch where Sam had left his little gifts, the swing where they had held hands, the light fixture next to the door standing guard against anything more than kissing on those dark summer nights when fire-flies danced on the honeysuckle-scented breeze. And beyond those old memories, the newer ones: the places Sam had been but wasn't, the pained eyes and pitying click of tongues from friends and neighbors, the bed where she had curled up and wanted to die. She had thought a change of location would help her heal. Or had she? Maybe she had just wanted to get away from the swirl of memories.

She took several more deep breaths. She couldn't sit out here forever.

Entering the house through the kitchen, she was transported back to her childhood. She remembered charging in from playing in the cold and being greeted by the mouthwatering smell of a stew simmering on the stove. A different season clicked into place, and she recalled scampering in after reveling in the sun on a summer day, blinded in the darkened house where blinds were drawn against the heat. The house had been cool and dark and smelled of cookies.

Now, her mother stood at the stove, wrapped in a floral-print robe, flipping slices of sizzling bacon with a two-pronged fork. Her mother jumped at the door opening and put her free hand over her breast.

"Violet! You gave me a start! What on earth are you doing here? Are you all right?"

She put the fork on the counter and moved towards Violet, studying her daughter's face, taking in the suitcase in her hand. Violet pecked her mother on the cheek. The two women bore a strong resemblance—same dark hair, green eyes, wide smile. Worry lines etched Celia's face between her brows and at the corners of her mouth. Violet thought she was probably getting those, too.

"I'm fine, Mom. Why don't you finish cooking, and I'll take my suitcase upstairs. When I come down, I'll tell you everything. Dad is here, right?"

"Yes, he is. He's shaving right now. We were going to go to church, but we can always go to the evening service." Her mother's mouth pursed with concern.

"Seriously, Mom. I am OK. Your bacon is going to burn." But her mother didn't turn back to the stove until Violet herself turned away.

Upstairs, she pushed open the door to the room she and

Betty had shared. It had lain dormant through the passing years, a space in hibernation. The frilly curtains still framed the dormer windows. Two twin beds rested against opposite walls, both covered with the same chenille bedspreads that had seen the girls through high school. Her little desk. Their dresser and vanity with its giant round mirror. The room comforted her and depressed her equally. Her childhood embraced her here, but so did the loss of her planned future. As she placed her small suitcase on the desk, her father's heavy steps thudded and creaked on the stairs. When she heard him thumping into the kitchen, she slipped into the one bathroom in the house and closed the door. She breathed in the minty scent of her dad's shaving cream on the damp air. How long could she put off going downstairs? She splashed water on her face and fixed her hair. Used the toilet. Washed her hands. Stared at herself in the mirror. *Go on. Go down there and get it over with,* she told her reflection.

Her father sat at the table, his bulk dwarfing the spindly straight-back chairs. He stood, and the air roiled around him. Tall and barrel-chested, he was his own weather front. He brought in gusts of cheer and loud exclamations, sent drafts swirling in whatever room he entered. James Donnelly would never be overlooked. He wrapped her in a bear hug. "Vi! I haven't seen you in hours!" He held her at arm's length.

"Dad," she admonished, but love softened her voice.

James grinned and sat back down, picking up a chicken salt shaker—her mother had a thing for chickens—and sprinkled some granules over his eggs.

"Violet, you want some breakfast?" Celia asked.

"No, thanks, Mom. I ate at home," she lied. She didn't

think she could handle food on her churning stomach. "You go ahead and eat though."

Violet let them eat before she delved into the deep topic of the state of her life. Normally, she would ask about Jerry and Betty and their families, but she had just seen them. Was it only two days? It seemed like a lifetime. She asked, instead, if her mother had started Christmas shopping, which got Celia talking about some sales at Woolworth's where she found some great deals for the grandkids.

Her parents finished their breakfast. Her father pushed his plate away and leaned back. "So, Vi. What brings you here? Not that you aren't welcome anytime, but we can tell something's wrong."

As she drove through the miles of lonely swamps and autumn-wrapped fields, Violet had rehearsed what to say to her parents. Truth is, she didn't know why she was here, but knew she had been pulled back as surely as if a rope had reeled her in. So no words came. But tears did.

Her father held one of her hands in his beefy one while her mother fetched a box of tissues. They let her weep. They had gotten used to her crying spells after the fire. With an effort, she got herself under control.

"I have made friends," she told them, wiping her eyes. "On my street. Nice people. We've done things together— watched the moon landing. Had a birthday party. And everything has been . . . better than I expected. I was doing really well. And then last night—" She put her hands over her face as if to shut out the memory. "Last night, my neighbors' house across the street caught fire. I panicked when I saw the fire trucks. I didn't want to go out and face whatever was going on, but I couldn't not go out. A fire truck blocked my view, and when I came around, the house was on fire. It all came back to me. That night. I was so scared that someone had been . . . left in there. But they were all fine. Still. It was all just . . . too much. Especially with the anniversary coming. I thought I was healing. I thought I was getting better. But I feel like I did two years ago." She wept.

Her mother waited until her crying stopped before speaking.

"Oh, Violet. Sweetheart. I thought it was too soon for you to move away from family."

"Nonsense," James interjected. "You saw a fire. And right around the same time yours happened. That would bring it all back for anyone. You're getting better every day, Vi. I see it. You might not remember how hurt you were back then. You couldn't function. But look at you now. You have gone out and found yourself a place to live and made it a home. You have a job. Getting over a tragedy is not a straight line. It goes up and down and sideways. And sometimes it may even feel like you have gone backward. But you haven't."

"Hon, what can we do to help?" Celia asked.

"I don't know, Mom. I felt like I needed to come back here to . . . face it, I guess. I can't explain."

"Well, you're here now," James said. "Stay as long as you like."

Celia stood and began gathering the dishes.

"Mom, let me wash up."

"Oh, honey, I don't mind. You didn't even eat."

"I want to do it. I want to keep busy."

Violet filled the deep porcelain sink with water and squirted in some soap.

"Why don't you guys go on to church? I'll clean up here."

"You sure, Vi?" Her mom wrung her hands, face troubled.

"Yes, Mom. I'll be fine. Dad shaved, after all."

"I take offense at that."

She smiled at him. The tension in the room dissipated a little, leaving more air for Violet to breathe. She loved them dearly, but she would welcome a little time alone to think.

After she finished the dishes, she called her boss at Turner's, telling him she had a family emergency. He surprised her. Told her to take a week, more if needed. Said she was his top waitress. This was news to her. He did usually give her the best tables. But he had never expressed his approval or disapproval. Well, that was a welcome relief. One less thing to worry about.

With that taken care of, she wandered from room to room, driven by a need to revisit these spaces as if taking a walk through her childhood and adolescence. Sam was here, tucked in the memories of more recent holidays, but the presence of her brother, sister, and parents dominated. She brushed the back of the old sofa, which she and her siblings had turned into a pirate ship, a cabin in the wilderness, a car. She touched the chair where Sam had sat with formal stiffness the first time he came to pick her up for a date, and she realized she'd thought about him with a smile instead of a catch in her heart. In this room, they celebrated Christmas, and she had pictured her child running on chubby legs to see what Santa had brought. That one still stabbed at her. She breathed deeply through the pain of it and moved to the doorway of her brother's room. His was the smallest in the house, tucked next to the kitchen. He used to have a sign on the door: "Girls Keep Out!" But he had never turned her away. Not when she was ten and he was sixteen and she wanted attention from her big brother. Not when she was twenty-one and he was twenty-seven and she needed a shoulder to cry on. She went to her parents' room where she had run when thunderstorms crashed over the house or when nightmares drove sleep away. They had been able to fix everything then. Now, they had been as lost as she when the fire took everything from her. They wanted to help her, make her whole, but such a feat was not within their power, no matter how badly they wanted it to be.

Next was her bedroom. She remembered playing dolls and house with Betty. She remembered their fights and slammed doors, with one of them trying to lock the other out. She remembered Betty helping her with her makeup for her wedding.

She had pushed away so many good memories. Tragedy had painted over them with broad, heavy strokes. A reused canvas. But as soon as that thought occurred, another followed quickly on its heels: she could paint over it a third time. She could make new memories. She had already started.

She spent Monday cleaning out her parents' attic.

"I honestly do not know why you're doing this," her mother said.

"I don't either," Violet answered, leaving it at that. Because, frankly, she didn't know. But somehow she knew she needed to swim through the past to get to the future. She spent all day bagging up old clothes and toys and lamps and picture frames for charity. She emerged in time to shower off the dust and cobwebs before dinner. Exhaustion weighed her down, but that was part of the point, she realized.

Violet awoke on Tuesday, the weight of the day bearing down on her chest. Two years ago today since the fire. Since Sam's death. And even though she didn't lose the baby until a week later, she equated that loss with this day as well. She had woken up two years ago, worried about Sam and his drinking, about their arguing and inability to reconnect. But she had never thought the day would hold anything worse than that. She lay in bed, allowing herself to feel, to taste, to hear, to see the memories. An overwhelming sadness swelled within her, but for once, she did not cry.

She heaved the blankets aside and slipped into her clothes before the cold whisked away all her body heat. When she went downstairs to join her parents for breakfast, the air pulsed with things not said. They went through the motions of getting out the butter and cutlery and mugs in a delicate silence, punctuated by mundane comments and the clatter of forks and knives.

Her mother had made extra food. Biscuits, toast, bacon, sausage. Celia's unspoken motto had always been if you can't fix it, feed it. A rush of tenderness for her mother welled up in her as she thought how much her parents wanted to make things right for her but couldn't.

When they sat down, Violet pierced the tension.

"I know what today is. And I know it's awkward to make small talk when we are all thinking about what happened two years ago. So let's just get that out in the open."

"Oh, honey," Celia said. Violet thought—not uncharitably—if she had a nickel for every time her mother had said those two words over her lifetime, she'd be a wealthy woman.

"Mom, it's OK. You have your sewing club, and I don't want you to miss it. I actually want to be alone." Concern etched every line in her mother's face in sharp relief, and Violet realized with a flash of tender sadness she was getting older. She put her hand on her mother's shoulders. "I'm fine. I promise."

"OK. I'll be at Edna's if you need me. Her number is in my address book."

Violet smiled ruefully at Celia's somber expression. "Understood. I will call if I need you. But seriously, Mom, I really think I am better than I have been in a long time."

Her father hugged her as he headed out the door to work. She helped her mother clean the kitchen, and then her mother got ready for her sewing club. Before she left, she hovered, and Violet put her hands on her shoulders. "Seriously. Have fun. Don't worry about me."

Violet watched her leave from the living room window. She closed her eyes and took several deep breaths. She had not lied. Something had shifted inside her, and she felt stronger than she had in two years. And what she was going to do would require all of that strength.

She shrugged into her coat and walked out into the crisp air. Not quite winter, but the chill presaged its coming. She got into her car, put it in gear, and backed out of the driveway.

Her destination lay not far from her parents' house, and yet it was light-years away.

She turned down the familiar street, drove to the end, and parked on the verge. The wind swirled leaves like brown confetti and pushed small, white cloud puffs across the sky. Mackerel sky, her dad once told her it was called because the clouds looked like fish scales fanned out across the heavens.

She had not been back here in two years. Not once. Her parents told her that her former landlord had not yet fixed it or sold it, so it sat as it had when the fire consumed it. She steeled herself and stepped out of the car.

She dug her hands in her coat pockets and tossed her head to clear the strands of hair that blew across her face. Sadness swelled in her chest and pushed up through her heart and her throat and made her eyes sting with tears. Across the small strip of pavement lay her scorched ruin of a house. One corner of white boards remained, easing into gray then into black as they got closer to the yawning window they had once framed. The brick supports of the porch were intact and only slightly smudged by soot, but charred debris covered its floor. The frame of the house still stood, but jagged holes showed where the roof had burned and fallen. The window glass was gone, as was the entire front door. One could easily imagine it as a monstrous face, with blackened, sepulchral eyes and mouth.

A wave of sadness threatened to sweep her away, but she bore up against it and remembered. The day they had found the house and their giddiness at having a place of their own. The days they spent painting, flinging dollops of color at each other. How he used to grab her by the waist and swing her around. The burnt pork chops. The broken heater in January that forced them to snuggle under blankets by the fireplace in the living room until the landlord fixed it. The time she killed a wolf spider and the dozens of babies it had been carrying on its back scattered everywhere, and she went screaming out of the house and called Sam from a neighbor's, telling him it was a life-and-death emergency. The days of doing ordinary things: waking up next to each other, eating dinner together, snuggling in bed before going to sleep. The long stretch of loneliness when he had been in Vietnam. Then the time when he returned and she could no longer find the ordinary things, when the days brimmed with fighting, yelling, crying, worrying. Long silences and constant anxiety. She faced all the memories, watching the Movietone News of her life play before her mind's eye. She had not allowed herself more than a glimpse of that time in the intervening years. Had turned it off, like a TV show. But now she reviewed it all.

She tore her eyes away and gazed at the sycamore tree that still stood sentinel. Against what? Maybe it wasn't a sentinel at all, but an observer. *It will be here long after this house is gone. More gone,* she corrected herself. She wondered if there was still glass at the base of the tree where Sam had thrown the liquor bottle. She hoped no children played barefoot here. Her eyes followed the thick trunk up into its lacework of branches outlined against a sky swept clear by the gusts. To the right of the tree and above the ruin of her house, a fat crescent moon shone in the day-bright blue sky, and Violet remembered the last time she had contemplated the moon. It had been the night of the lunar landing, walking across the street with Mrs. McCabe and Nick. She gazed upward and thought of the men who had walked on the surface of that distant half-disc. How they had exploded from the earth and hurdled through space with no certainty of what they would discover and no assurance they would return home. They had pushed the boundaries of what men could do and just . . . did it. Could she push her own boundaries? All she had to do was put one foot in front of the other and take hold of the hands offering to help her, to friend her, to love her. All she had to do was break through the grief that bound her and take a chance on life again.

37
Violet

December 1969

Violet returned to her parents' house with new resolve. She headed straight upstairs and packed her suitcase. She was ready to go home. Her home.

She pulled the sheets off the bed, straightened the room. She ate a sandwich she did not taste as her thoughts tumbled one over the other. Her mother rushed in the door, hair in slight disarray from the wind in spite of the headscarf she had worn. She placed her hands to her reddened cheeks to warm them.

"Goodness, it's blustery outside."

"Mom, I'm going to go home. Today. Now."

"Are you sure, sweetheart?" Celia said, looking up from unbuttoning her coat. "You can stay as long as you like. This all seems so rushed."

"I know. But I am sure I've gotten what I needed. And I can't stay away from work forever."

"Well, surely you can stay for dinner."

Violet said the one thing that would convince her mother not to fuss about her leaving before she ate. "I'd like to get home before dark. I'll stop by the shop and see Dad on the way out of town to say goodbye."

She gathered up her suitcase, purse, and coat. Her mother waited in the living room, eyebrows still knit with worry. She stood when she heard Violet come down the stairs.

"Are you sure about this, Vi?"

Violet kissed her cheek. "I am. Try not to worry. I'll call you when I get home," Violet said, hugging her.

"You do that. And drive safe." That directive wrapped up so many more messages: take care, be well, be happy, lock your doors, don't talk on the telephone in a thunderstorm. The words swaddled all of her mother's worries and wishes for Violet's health and well-being in one little package. Violet met Celia's eyes, and fondness filled her heart rather than her old teenage irritation. *How differently we see the ties of love as we get older,* she thought. What once used to seem like manacles now seemed like life preservers, keeping her afloat instead of dragging her down.

"I will, Mom."

As she had promised, she stopped by her dad's print shop. His employees raised their heads. "Vi! Good to see you!" "Hey, Vi! Looking good!"

Her father stepped out of his office on the heels of that last sentence. "Mel, I heard that."

"Sorry, Mr. Donnelly! I just meant—"

But James cut him off. "I'm kidding, Mel. I know what you meant." He turned to his daughter. "What brings you here, Vi? You sure have gotten into a habit of popping in unexpectedly."

Violet grinned. "I have, haven't I? But I am here now to tell you I decided to head home. I think I got what I came for."

"And what was that?"

"A few steps forward."

"That's my girl. I was a little worried about you."

"I know you were."

"You realize you can spend so much time waiting to feel better that you forget to live your life in the here and now. You can only put things on hold for so long."

"I think you're right, but I don't think I could have seen that before."

"Come here and give your old dad a hug." She melted in his embrace, enjoying a moment of being his little girl. Then he held her at arm's length. "You better get going. Don't be a stranger. And drive safe."

"Mom already commanded me. I don't dare disobey her."

She waved goodbye to Mel and Jasper and Fenn, men she had known her whole life. They tipped their caps at her and told her to drop by anytime. "We like looking at your mug better than your old man's," Jasper called after her.

She made one more stop before heading out of town.

She found his gravestone among hundreds of others. An ancient live oak spread its nearly bare branches overhead. The wind had died down, but the temperature had plummeted. Violet shivered as she stared at the gray stone marker.

Samuel John Wentworth
U.S. Army
February 5, 1946—December 2, 1967
Beloved husband and son

She had not wanted the line about the U.S. Army. Everyone else may have been proud of his service, but she held the Army responsible for his death. They had broken him and left him depleted and desolate. But she didn't have the energy to argue when she had gone with his parents to order the marker.

She wished she had a grave for her child, but she had lost it too early.

"Sam." She knelt and placed her hand on the icy stone. "I came to ask you if it's OK to move on. I started dating someone. I know it sounds stupid to say you'd like him, but I think you would." She stopped, looking up at the lacy scaffolding of branches holding up the indigo sky and framing the sickle moon. "I've missed you, Sam. I've been angry and sad and scared and numb, but most of all, I've missed you." She sniffled. Swallowed. "It's not fair, what happened to you. All of it." She plucked at a dormant blade of grass. "I've realized you're not coming back. I guess it's time I got on with my life. I feel guilty about that. So I came here so you could make me feel better. Though I don't know how you're going to do that. I'd say send me a sign, but I don't really believe in that." She stared at the sliver of brown resting in her palm, drained of life, of vibrancy. But maybe not of hope. The grass comes back. Not this blade. But others like it. She tipped her hand and let it drift to the ground. She rose, brushing the bits of dirt and leaves from her slacks.

"I will always, always love you, and I am going to try and remember my bright, golden Sam. Not that I will forget dark, shattered Sam. He was you, too. I understand that now."

She stood a while longer, giving thanks for the good times they had together, however brief. She said a final goodbye and walked back to the car.

She drove home on a highway that cut through a slumbering coastal plain. Under the darkening sky, woods huddled up against marshes that, in turn, gave way to fallow fields. Swamps lay tucked here and there, hiding impenetrable obsidian depths as dusk surrendered to night. Violet did not turn on the radio but traveled in silence, the hum of the engine and murmur of tires on pavement offering a soothing soundtrack. The moon accompanied her, playing hide-and-seek among the trees as the road unfurled in front of her headlights.

About twenty-five miles outside of Edenton, on the outskirts of a small town, a road crew stopped the cars in her lane. Someone had apparently hit a light pole. The car had been towed away, but the men were directing traffic around the downed pole. She waited idly, but not impatiently. She glanced around. To her left, small brick homes lined the street, marching up to a cinder-block gas station that squatted on the corner. Its window signs proclaimed "Boiled Peanuts" and "We Have Worms!" A small theater dominated the other side of the road, its marquee jutting over the sidewalk. Huddled next to it, like a small child, was an unremarkable brick building. The windows were lit, though her view was blocked by white, ruffled curtains. A sign proclaimed "Breakfast! Lunch! Dinner!" *They are enthusiastic about their meals,* she thought. Her eyes traveled up to neon letters glowing above the door. She blinked. Once. Twice. Three times. Stared disbelievingly. Then she started laughing. A happy sadness swelled in her heart.

"Thank you, Sam," she whispered into the windshield. Even though she didn't believe in signs.

She accelerated as a man waved her along. Behind her,

the sign flickered. The name of the restaurant—"Nick of Time"—glimmered in her rearview mirror.

Night had fallen when Violet reached home. The yellow glow of the bug lights Nick had installed at both her house and Mrs. McCabe's shone like beacons as soon as she rounded the corner near Tommy's house. *Tommy's old house,* she corrected herself. She pulled into her driveway and shoved the gear shift into park. *Home,* she thought. *I'm home.*

She felt conspicuous as she lugged her bag into the house. She remembered Saturday night and knew the neighbors must be wondering if she had gone around the bend. First crazy, then missing. Sort of. Well, she'd deal with that over the next few days.

The house smelled stale the way houses do when they sit empty. She'd only been gone three days, but it seemed longer. Her house seemed to agree.

She turned up the heat, unpacked, lit a few candles to freshen the air. She called work and told them she was back. Her boss said he would call tomorrow with her hours for the rest of the week. Told her he was good for the next couple of days but would definitely need her for the weekend. She was relieved. She had someone she wanted to talk to the next day. She wrote a note and slipped into the night and stuck it in that someone's mailbox.

38
Nick

December 1969

Nick drove home from his job, exhaustion pinning him into his seat. He had not slept well since the Fitzgerald fire and Violet's departure. His eyes were grainy and his movements slow. At work, he'd dropped wrenches and tripped over lifts, and by midday, his coworkers started calling him Jerry—as in Jerry Lewis. He hoped the nickname didn't stick.

He also hoped he could get a decent night's sleep tonight, but since he still didn't know what he was going to do about Violet, he doubted he would. To make matters worse, when he pictured Violet's face, Giulia's emerged, superimposing itself over Violet's features. Instead of Violet's green eyes, he saw Giulia's brown ones. Instead of Violet's wide smile, he saw Giulia's impish one. It felt like a warning to him. But yet . . . they were so different. Giulia had been a live wire, shooting beautiful, deadly sparks into the lives around her until she burned herself out. Violet . . . he had to think hard to push Giulia's ghost out of the way. He had always sensed the streak of sadness in her, but that streak ran through something more . . . steady. He liked her self-sufficiency. He liked her music. The way she talked about books. Her sense of humor. How sweet she was to Arabella and patient with Mrs. McCabe. Except for the occasional eye roll. If he wasn't so tired, he would have smiled over that. Maybe a shower would rinse off his melancholy mood along with the workday grime.

The shower failed to revive him, so he lay down thinking how good it would feel to close his eyelids, which rasped over his eyeballs with every blink. Sometime later, he woke with a start, confused. Why was he dressed in his bed? He sat on the edge of his mattress, trying to clear the grogginess that prevented coherent thoughts from forming. Slowly, the world began to make sense. It was Tuesday. He'd lain down after a shower. He looked at his clock. It was almost seven. He got up and made his way into the living room, where he found Harry reading the evening paper.

"You've got mail, Gloomy Gus." He pointed his chin toward the kitchen table.

"Thanks, Happy Harry."

"It was special delivery."

Nick frowned. "What do you mean?"

"No stamp. No postmark. Methinks your ladylove doth dropped it off."

"Harry."

"Don't shoot the messenger."

"I'm not. I'm thinking of shooting the pain in my ass who lives here."

Harry remained unperturbed. "Want me to open it for you?"

"I think I can manage."

"Want to tell me what's going on?"

"What do you mean?"

"Only that her car disappears and you mope around for days. And that was after her crazy reaction to the fire next door."

Harry reminded Nick of a relentless younger brother, always wanting to know what was going on. Nick thought he had gotten away from that when he joined up. "I told you what happened. She was married before, and her husband died in a fire."

Harry whistled. "Yes, that explains her reaction Saturday night. But next question."

"How about we move straight to no questions."

"No can do, Nicky boy. I feel an obligation to help my roomie out. So here's the question: why aren't you with her? Helping her?"

"Harry, for one thing, she went home to see her parents for a few days. And for another, she told me in no uncertain terms Saturday that she needed time alone."

"Do you like her, Nick?"

"Yes. No. I mean, yes, but there's . . . there are reasons I don't want to get involved."

"And they would be . . ."

"Private."

"Nahhh. I'm not buying it. I want to know why you have this gorgeous gal who is clearly crazy for you and you're not trying to close the deal."

"She's not a piece of real estate, Harry."

"No, she's a living, breathing, groovy girl who's going to get away."

"It's more complicated than that."

"Complicated, my ass. Girl likes boy. Boy likes girl. Boy asks girl to go steady. Where's the complication?"

"I am not sure she's ready after . . . after what happened."

"So you are going to wait until all conditions are perfect?"

"Harry, can you just leave it?"

Harry put his hands up in surrender. "Hey, man, I am offering my totally objective and wise help. I'll say one last thing. Sounds like there might be two people who feel they aren't ready. But no one will ever be completely, perfectly ready. We all have our shit to bear."

"I think that was two, maybe three things. And the last was poetic. You should go write it down."

Harry grinned and tipped an imaginary hat. "Bonus advice because it's Tuesday!" He rose and walked to the fridge. "I guess I will have leftovers because you don't seem to be standing at the stove and cooking."

Nick ignored him and retrieved the letter as Harry rummaged around through leftover containers and beer bottles. He recognized Violet's handwriting.

He took the letter back to his bedroom, tore open the sealed flap, and pulled out the single sheet of paper. It had very little writing on it.

Dear Nick,

It has been a long three days. I have done a lot of thinking, a lot of revisiting my past, and I believe I have made a giant leap forward. Or ten leaps.

I would like to invite you to dinner tomorrow (Wednesday). Nothing fancy, because, well, it's me cooking. But I'll make a nice dinner and we can talk. If you can't make it, please leave me a note in my mailbox. If you can make it, is 6:00 good? If I don't hear from you, I'll assume you're coming.

Love,

Vi

He released a breath he didn't know he was holding. He inhaled, exhaled, and imagined dinner tomorrow. The ghost of Giulia appeared. And was she joined by the ghost of Violet's husband? He needed to give Violet space. He knew how important it was to have time to grieve and heal.

Harry knocked on his door.

"Yes?" Nick said.

Harry cracked the door and peeked in. "I'm not thrilled with the choices. I am going to make a pizza run. Want anything?"

"Sure, I'll have a slice or two. And Harry?"

Harry raised his eyebrows in question. "Get enough for tomorrow night too. I won't be cooking then either."

As Harry opened his mouth, Nick stopped him. "Just zip it, Harry," he warned.

Harry grinned widely, but then pursed his lips and made a zipping motion across them. But he winked at Nick as he turned back down the hall. *Little does he know,* thought Nick.

39
Violet

December 1969

As soon as Violet's eyes opened Wednesday morning, she thought of Nick and wondered what he thought of her note. If he got her note. Her incredibly stupid note, she now thought. Why hadn't she told him to call her either way? Or at least with a yes? But she knew the answer to that. She had been afraid to talk to him. She had not been ready to hear his voice and had definitely not been ready to hear a no. He must think she's crazy. She glanced at the clock. He had probably not left for work yet, and she was not going to check her mailbox until he was gone. Well, she had other things she could do. She started by throwing her laundry in the washing machine, taking a detour by the living room window to see if Nick's car was in the driveway. Which it was. As she ate her breakfast and cleaned her house, she peeped through the curtains every now and again. She avoided looking at the Fitzgerald house. The sight of the damage still caused her heart to seize up. As she was polishing the coffee table, a car engine rumbled through the quiet morning. She checked the window in time to see Nick's car disappearing up the street.

Shaking slightly, she forced herself to stroll, not sprint, to the mailbox. She hesitated before opening the little door, thinking, *Please, please, please*—and sent up a prayer of thanks when she found it empty.

She worked extra hard on her house until no speck of dust dared to land on her furniture. She did a grocery store run. Finished her laundry. She almost checked her clock to see if it was working because the hands ticked by so slowly. And the longer the day dragged on, the more her doubts crept in. Perhaps he had other plans. Maybe he hadn't seen her note. Possibly he didn't think she deserved a reply. Why had she left the invitation so open-ended? God, she could kick herself.

She made chicken and dumplings for dinner. A simple dish, but tasty. While the chicken simmered, she dressed. After her first date with Nick, she had added some new outfits to her wardrobe. Now, as she got ready, she walked the tightrope between looking attractive but not looking like she was trying too hard. Even though she was trying very, very hard, indeed.

She returned to the kitchen and mixed the batter for the dumplings, plopping them by spoonfuls into the bubbling broth. After they had fluffed up, she sprinkled paprika and parsley on them. She heated a can of green beans. Retrieved the salad she'd made earlier from the fridge. Set the table. She opened a bottle of wine and thought how depressing it would be if she had to sit and eat all this alone.

The sky outside deepened to navy streaked with fading fuchsia. A dog barked, the sharp tone echoing through the silent house, reminding her to put on a record. Something soft and mellow. She searched through her albums and found Sam Cooke, and remembered Nick whistling "Cupid" after he walked her home from Mrs. McCabe's birthday party. Was it too presumptuous? Too eager? *The heck with it,* she thought, and slipped the album out of its sleeve and placed it on the turntable.

"You Send Me" melted into "Only Sixteen," and night slid in, chasing away the sunset. The clock read 6:12. She sighed, closed her eyes, and was resigning herself to dinner alone when a knock sounded at the door, sending her heart into a gallop. She smoothed her slacks and straightened her top and took several deep breaths before answering.

Nick stood on her doorstep, hair damp and face smooth, and her heart swelled at the thought that he had taken pains with his appearance just as she had.

"Hi, Nick. I am glad you came."

Nick bowed his head in acknowledgment.

"Please, come in," she said, amazed at how discomfited she felt. She stepped back and held the door. She motioned for him to follow her. His presence filled her kitchen. She swore she could feel the warmth radiating from his body even though he stood feet away from her. Hoping to look busy instead of nervous, she checked the dumplings and green beans, poking the first and stirring the second. She turned and spotted the wine and poured two glasses, relieved to have something to do. This was more awkward than their first date.

"Have you spoken to George and Caroline? How are they?" she asked as she handed him his glass.

"They are doing well. They've come by the house every day and have been able to salvage a few things. They were pretty lucky."

"They were."

"The trailer is going to be OK. They have to rebuild

Arabella's room and replace some carpeting and a few other things, but . . . well, it's amazing, all things considered."

"I'm so glad." She felt relief for her friend but also a pang of guilt for not being here for her. She would find some way to make it up to her. She shook those thoughts away for now. "I hope you're hungry. Everything is ready."

She brought the food to the table and dished out the steaming chicken and dumplings. Unsaid words lay between them, thickening the air. She wondered if talking first and eating later would have been a wiser choice.

"Looks wonderful," he said.

"Old family recipe," she replied. "One of my favorites."

"It's delicious," he said, taking a bite. Was it her imagination, or did he seem a little distant? There was something off about him. Something she couldn't put her finger on. Had her behavior the other night made him question his feelings for her? *Well, why wouldn't it?* she wondered. She'd acted like a crazy person.

As they ate, music played in the background, candlelight flickered on the table, and uneasiness wove threads of tension around them. At first, they made stilted small talk, but as they compared Thanksgiving memories, she found the conversation flowed a little more smoothly. He reminisced about one Thanksgiving when it snowed, and he and his siblings were so excited to play in the snow in November. She shared the story of the Thanksgiving after her grandmother died and her mother could not pull herself together to make a meal, so Violet and her sister reheated some leftover gravy and biscuits, and that became their holiday dinner.

He complimented her again on her cooking, and she waved it off. "It's not that hard," she said.

"Maybe, maybe not. But it was very good. I think you sell yourself short in the cooking department."

She began to think maybe this would be OK after all.

As they cleaned up, she worried about how to talk to him about . . . everything. She became tongue-tied as he stood next to her at the kitchen sink. She washed a dish and handed it to him. He dried. Her hand brushed his, and she almost dropped a plate.

After she wiped down the table, she squared her shoulders.

"I guess I can't put this off any longer," she said with a weak laugh. *Great segue, Violet. Really smooth.*

"Violet, you don't have to tell me anything, you know. You don't owe me an explanation."

"I think I do. Let's go into the living room," she said, leading the way. Sam Cooke had played itself out long before. She placed a John Coltrane album on the turntable. Something soft and soothing. They sat on the sofa. "The things I haven't told you feel like a huge presence between us," she continued. She drew in a breath. "There is a lot more to the story than was in the letter." And she told him. About how she and Sam were high school sweethearts, about Sam's service in Vietnam, about how he came home so changed, so traumatized. She described his drinking. Their fights. And, finally, how she had left him the night of the fire to get away from him. How a dropped cigarette smoldered on the sofa, and, after he went to the bedroom, it flared into a conflagration that consumed the house and him. "I am sure he was more passed out than asleep. If I hadn't stormed out"—she paused to get past the break in her voice—"he wouldn't have died."

Nick listened without interruption, sometimes looking at her, sometimes looking down at the floor. She could not read his face, nor gauge his reaction, but she plowed on, determined to tell him everything.

"And also . . . I was pregnant. I was almost four months along. And a week after the fire, I lost the baby. So I literally lost everything. Including myself for a while. For the last two years, I have wished for nothing else but to go back and do things differently. I would have been more patient with Sam. I wouldn't have stormed off that night."

"Violet," Nick said, his voice gentle. "I am so sorry."

She stared down at her lap, where her hands lay folded like nesting birds.

"So that's the story. My life laid bare." She paused. "I think one of the hardest things for me to come to terms with—and one of the hardest things to say to you—is that I blamed myself for two years. But when I saw the fire at the Fitzgeralds' house, I may have freaked out, but something also clicked, though I didn't realize it until a day or two later. I suddenly saw how accidents can just happen. I still feel ashamed that my last words to Sam were 'I need to get away.' I still feel guilty I left him that night. I still feel guilty that I didn't think about the baby more. I understand it was all an accident, but it's still hard to accept."

"Violet, you did the best you could under the circumstances."

"I suppose you're right. But I keep thinking I should have been more understanding. Looking back, I was such a shrew."

"What about Sam?"

"What do you mean?" She looked at him.

"I mean, where is his responsibility?" He sat back against the sofa. "Look. I have my own story that taught me I can't be responsible for someone else's desire to self-destruct. When

I was seventeen, I had a girlfriend. Her name was Giulia."
He told Violet about how beautiful she had been, and how
broken, and what had broken her. And how she had taken her
own life and how he blamed himself for not knowing—or
trying to find out—what lay beneath her shimmering surface.
"And Giulia's death almost dragged me down with her." He
stopped and looked at Violet. "And that is why I . . . I can't do
this, Violet."

Violet's heart contracted, and her breath caught in her
throat.

"What do you mean, Nick?" she said, keeping her voice
low because she couldn't breathe.

"I think we need a break. Back when Giulia died, I vowed
I wouldn't get into another relationship where I needed to
rescue the other person."

"Rescue? You think I need rescuing?" A wave of anger
cascaded over her, replacing her fear of losing him like a
sudden summer storm. Did he think she was laying all this
before him because she wanted to be rescued?

"I think I put that badly . . ." Nick started.

"No, no, I think you put it perfectly." She stood stiffly,
smoothed her skirt, and steeled her spine. "If you think I need
someone to rescue me, then you're right. We need a break.
Because you don't know me at all." She crossed the room to
the door and held it open. She needed him to leave. Now. She
was shaking with fury. "Good night, Nick."

"Violet, listen . . ." He rose and moved closer, hands out
in supplication. But what could he possibly ask for? He had
made himself quite clear. She felt tears rising in her eyes, and
she did not want him to see what might look like another
sign of weakness.

"Good night."

He sighed and walked out the door.

Violet resisted the urge to slam it, and instead closed it quietly but firmly as he walked down the steps. Then she burst into hot, angry tears, her hand over her mouth in case he was still close enough to hear. Did he really think she was some helpless, swooning female, succumbing to the vapors when things got rough? And what if she did need help? A shoulder to cry on from time to time? He was just going to cut and run? How had she misjudged him so badly?

40
Nick

December 1969

As Nick walked up his driveway, he saw Harry's car was gone, and he sent up a silent thanks for small blessings. He certainly did not want to talk about how he and Violet had apparently just broken up, nor about how he had stuck his foot so far into his mouth he would taste shoe leather for weeks. He had meant what he said about needing to step back. He had not meant to say it so tactlessly.

He walked into his house, flicking on lights, and threw himself on the sofa. He shook his head. Had it only been a few days since the fire? It seemed like a lifetime had gone by. He remembered her face that night, the anguish, the shock. And then he thought about what she had told him tonight. Giulia's death had overwhelmed him with the double-edged sword of grief and guilt. But over the years, he had made peace with her suicide, forgiving her, forgiving himself. He knew that at eighteen, he had been too young and too inexperienced to understand that her behavior had been triggered by abuse. It never occurred to him to look beyond the face she presented to the world.

But Violet . . . she had been married to Sam. Had been tied to him in ways he had not been tied to Giulia. Plus, she had a far better understanding of what was ripping him apart than Nick had ever had about Giulia. That kind of guilt could drag you down, but she had been rising to the surface. Until the fire.

She was right. She did not need rescuing. And he hadn't really meant it that way. One of the things he admired about her was her independence. She possessed a quiet strength that drew him to her from the minute he met her.

He stood and went to the fridge. He reached in and grabbed a beer, but the memory of Violet's story flashed into his brain. He put it back, closed the door, and poured a glass of water instead.

Why did he feel so . . . unsettled? He had made a decision, and usually, acting on a decision gave him a sense of calm. But he was anything but calm. He tried to consider the problem logically: One, he had decided he would never involve himself with someone who would drag him down. And what had led to that resolution? His realization that you can't save someone if they are just going to pull you underwater with them. Two, Violet was putting her life back together. She wasn't drowning, but was she ready for a relationship? She probably needed more time to recover from the tragedies she had suffered. So it was a good thing he had said they should take a break. Although he had not intended a permanent break. Or had he? Maybe subconsciously he had.

Following the trail of logic did not settle his emotional chaos. He sighed and put his glass next to the sink. He went to bed, but sleep eluded him. He shifted from one position to the next, hit his pillow, tangled his sheets. And yet for all his spinning and turning, his mental turbulence far outpaced his physical restlessness.

He'd done the right thing. For both of them. She needed to heal. And he needed . . . what? Not to be a part of her healing? Whoa, surely that wasn't it. He stared at the popcorn ceiling, partly illuminated by the streetlight. Was he simply running away? So many questions and thoughts tumbled about in his head, he had trouble catching hold of any of them.

Airplane engines were so much easier to figure out than life.

41

Violet

December 1969

The next morning, Violet called Mrs. McCabe to get Caroline's phone number. She was long overdue in checking on the Fitzgeralds. Also, if she were completely honest with herself, she wanted to hear a friendly voice. She just had to put up with Mrs. McCabe first. When Mrs. McCabe didn't answer, Violet's heart clenched with anxiety—had something happened? She flicked aside the curtain in her front window and saw Mrs. McCabe's car parked in her driveway. Violet threw on a jacket and walked over to her elderly neighbor's house.

"Violet! You're back! I'm glad to see you," a robustly healthy Mrs. McCabe said as she opened the door.

"You are?"

Mrs. McCabe ignored her question and pushed the door wider. "Come on in."

"I just wanted to see if you had Caroline's phone number. I tried to call you, but the phone kept ringing."

"I must have been in another room," Mrs. McCabe said. "Do come in. You're letting all my heat out."

"Do you have her number?"

"I might. I need to find it though. Why don't you come in while I hunt for it? You look silly standing out there on the doorstep."

Violet sighed and stepped in.

"I'll fix you a glass of iced tea. You look tired. A little tea would be just the thing."

"Mrs. McCabe, I'm fine. Don't go to any trouble."

"No trouble at all. I'm a mite thirsty myself." She waved Violet over to the sofa, and Violet once again felt like a sheep being herded by a very skillful sheepdog.

"Nick came by and told me about your ... husband," Mrs. McCabe said, the clink of glasses punctuating her statement. "And the fire. Sounds like you went through a really rough time."

"Mrs. McCabe, I don't want to talk about it."

"Did I say you had to?" Mrs. McCabe set a glass in front of Violet and motioned for her to sit. "I thought I would do the talking. I want to tell you a story. About me. What brought me here."

"I already know about your children." Violet sat, deciding the fastest way to get what she wanted and go home was to humor Mrs. McCabe. "I am very sorry they died so young."

"Well, indulge an old woman." And she began. "Once upon a time, there lived a young girl who never wanted to be a lady. She liked collecting bugs and climbing trees and running around in her father's old breeches. As you probably realize, that girl was me."

In spite of herself, this description of Mrs. McCabe's youth intrigued Violet and caught her attention.

"I never wanted to court, and I certainly never wanted

to marry," Mrs. McCabe continued. "But what other options were there for a girl of a certain upbringing in the years before the Great War? My father died when I was fifteen, and my mother's dearest wish was that my sister and I would make good marriages so she could rest easy. I rebelled at first, but I soon realized no other viable alternative lay open to me. I despaired of finding someone I could actually tolerate— and who could tolerate me. You may have noticed I can be a bit . . . opinionated. I was the same, even way back then. But I found Flynn. It did not start off as a head-over-heels kind of courtship, but instead grew quietly and slowly but quite steadily. He possessed a pleasant disposition, and he respected my opinions. So when he asked me to marry him, I said yes. We got along well, he and I. As you know, we had two children, and we built a marvelous life together. We traveled, we laughed, we lived. We survived two world wars, the Great Depression. And then he died. Oh, how I missed him. That would have been enough to break my heart, but Fate was not done with me yet. I try not to be fanciful or superstitious, but through all the world's trials and tribulations, we had always been lucky. So I felt Fate was exacting the price for our favorable fortune. Silly, I know. But it's hard not to look for answers—even far-fetched ones—when life keeps handing you some very bitter lemons. First, Flynn died. Next, Willis was killed in a car accident, and finally Irina died of cancer. And I was left alone. So I decided I was finished. I would wait for Death to come to me. Well, I've been waiting eight years, and here I still am. The pneumonia I came down with in June might have done me in, but you and Arabella saved me. I wasn't all that happy at first, since I've been ready for the Grim Reaper to come calling for several years. And I thought

I was through with people. I figured, what's the use? Why become fond of new people when they will go away and leave you? But you kept coming to visit, and you brought Arabella. I found you a bit annoying at first, but to tell you the truth, I kind of started looking forward to seeing you both. And I began to realize I wasn't quite ready to give up the ghost yet."

"Well, I am glad we could help, but why are you telling me this now?" Mrs. McCabe's story riveted her, but Violet was too depleted to . . . what? Console Mrs. McCabe?

"I will answer your question with another. Why did you move here?"

"I was trying to get over my . . . husband's death. I found it hard to live among all the memories of him. They were everywhere I turned."

"Yes, I know that feeling well. But were you actually attempting to get over his death?"

Violet's eyes slid away. She plucked at a nub on the brown sofa. Her shoulders slumped in defeat. "No, I don't think I was." Her voice was almost a whisper. She waited for Mrs. McCabe to scold her and give her a lecture. She'd endure it, then ask for Caroline's number and leave.

She almost jumped when Mrs. McCabe reached out a hand and patted her knee. "And that's okay. That's what you needed. But you have to recognize when it's time to move on."

"But if I move on—" She stopped.

"You'll betray your husband?"

Violet was horrified to find tears filling her eyes, far too fast and too copious to blink away.

"That's how I felt for a long time," Mrs. McCabe said. Violet heard the squeak of a chair and the creak of old joints, and a tissue appeared before her downcast eyes.

"But honestly. None of my family would have wanted me to shut myself off from the world the way I did. Do you really think your husband would have wanted that for you?"

Violet thought of Sam—the before-war Sam—and knew he would never have wanted that. The image in her head clicked like a slideshow. After-war Sam would not have wanted it either, she realized. He had never wanted to hurt her or cause her suffering. And for the first time, she thought of what living in his hell must have been like. He had his own torments and, piled on top of that, the guilt that he couldn't be happy. Couldn't make her happy. And she cried harder. Mrs. McCabe stayed silent, occasionally handing over a tissue when needed.

Minutes passed, and Violet's sobs subsided. One last fresh tissue was proffered before Mrs. McCabe leaned back into her chair.

"Do you feel better now?"

"Not particularly," Violet said, her voice quavery and still thick with emotion. "I went home these last few days to face things. To lay them to rest. And I thought I had. When I drove back here, I thought I was ready to take on the future. Ready to move on. Why am I still crying about it?"

"Grief is like a broken road, with patches of weeds and potholes and switchbacks. And one you'll be traveling for a while longer, I'm afraid. But along the road, there are also rest stops and friends and nice things to see. There is no reason you can't enjoy the more agreeable parts of the journey even as you negotiate the bad. And there is no reason you can't have a little company, too. Like me and Caroline. And perhaps a certain gentleman friend."

"If you are thinking of Nick, I think that boat has sailed. Or to stick with your metaphor, that car has driven away."

"Oh, I find that hard to believe. That young man is crazy about you."

"Maybe he was once, but I think that's over," Violet said, and told Mrs. McCabe the more recent events.

"Pishposh," Mrs. McCabe said. "You had an argument. A spat. Happens to everyone."

"But he said he didn't want to get tangled up with anyone who was, well, as messed up as I am."

Mrs. McCabe rolled her eyes. "First of all, what's he going to do? Find a teenage nun who's been locked away in a cloister? Actually, scratch that. That person would be a mess. No one escapes this life without some battering and bruising. Feel free to tell him that. And second, bully for you for setting the record straight. You don't need rescuing. You need love and support. There's a big difference. And if he can't see that, or if he can't deal with the latter, good riddance to him. Now drink some tea. I think you need it."

Violet took a few large gulps. The cold liquid soothed her hot, dry throat. "I probably need to get going."

"Didn't you want Caroline's telephone number?"

Mrs. McCabe reached for a little floral book that rested on the table next to her, in front of the black kettle phone. She scratched some figures on a piece of scrap paper and handed it to Violet, who rose and smoothed her skirt and threw her last tissue in a small trash can near Mrs. McCabe's chair. She went to the door and turned to Mrs. McCabe and swallowed hard. "Thank you, Mrs. McCabe."

"Don't mention it." But she smiled brightly at Violet, and Violet realized Mrs. McCabe was her friend after all.

She walked back to her house in the light of a weak December sun. The tree branches were bare, the grass brown, but the sunlight shone on the green needles of the pines. Woodsmoke tinged the air, and, for the first time in two years, Violet thought the scent comforting and cozy instead of distressing and disturbing. She walked to her house with a little lighter step, but suddenly she stopped. "Why that . . ." she trailed off. That tricky old woman had the address book right next to her all along. Violet closed her eyes, shook her head, and gave a little chuckle.

42
Nick

December 1969

Nick fumbled with his keys as he struggled to unlock the door, the persistent ringing of the telephone making him clumsy. He realized part of his rush was because he thought it might be Violet. He pushed the thought away. She'd been seriously angry. Which meant she probably was not the one on the other end of the line.

The lock clicked, and he ran for the phone, huffing a breathless, "Hello?"

"Nicky, Nicky, Nicky!" A laughing voice came through the receiver. Definitely not Violet's, but whose? Then it registered.

"Talia DeSanto? Is that you?"

"It is, Nicky! You'll never guess where I am!"

"The Rose Diner?" he said as he tossed his keys on the end table.

She laughed. "Not even close!"

"Donnie's Pizza?"

"Still ice-cold, Nicky."

"All right. I give up. Where are you?"

"I'm in Charleston."

"Charleston? As in Charleston, South Carolina? What are you doing there? In December, no less."

"I came down with a girlfriend who's from here. I thought it would be a lark, but it's a ghost town. There is nothing to do. So I thought, hey, Nicky lives in a Carolina somewhere. Surely he's not that far away. So I called your parents and got your number. I thought I'd drop by."

"Sure, sure. I'd love to see you. How are you going to get here? Do you have a car?"

"Yes, we came down in mine."

"Won't your friend mind?"

"Nah. She's cool. I told her I wanted to visit an old friend for a day. I'll drive down tomorrow, have lunch, and spend a few hours with you. Are you free in the afternoon?"

"I probably can be. I have some leave saved up." He gave her his address and the directions off the highway. And his work number in case he was still there when she got into town.

"It will be terrific to see you, Flyboy," Talia said.

"You, too. But you do know I am just a mechanic and I don't actually fly?"

"Mechanic Boy does not have the same ring to it."

"How about Mechanic Man?"

"Maybe when you grow up enough. I'll see you tomorrow. Flyboy." She emphasized the "boy," and he couldn't help but chuckle.

After he hung up the phone, he thought, *Well, that was a surprise.* He tried to recall the last time he had seen Giulia's little sister. He remembered he had seen her on one of his visits home, and that had been what? Seven years ago? She had been eighteen, blossoming into adulthood and looking as beautiful as her sister had. Now she would be twenty-five. He marveled that he actually anticipated seeing her instead of dreading it as he would have seven years ago. Also, her impending visit took his mind off Violet. Sort of.

He changed into civilian clothes and headed back to the base to buy groceries. Hopefully, his boss would let him take some leave for the afternoon, so he got food for lunch. And provisions for dinner just in case. If she didn't stay that long, Harry would at least be happy.

The next morning, Nick felt a little lighter. He found himself looking forward to seeing someone from home. He liked living where he was, but he still got homesick from time to time.

His boss told him to go ahead and take the afternoon off. It was a Friday, in December. It was a slow time.

He arrived home and began pulling out the fixings for lunch. He had done a lot of the prep the night before. He was chopping the previously poached chicken breasts for chicken salad when the phone rang. "Well, here I am, in beautiful, tiny Edenton. It's so small! Do they roll up the sidewalks at seven around here?"

He laughed. "More like five."

"What on earth do you do for fun?"

"It's not like we did that much in Brooklyn."

"Perhaps, but we could go to Coney Island or walk around the city and gawk at people. Anyway, I am here, at the little Chinese restaurant you told me about."

"And I got the afternoon off and am here to wait on you hand and foot."

"That is super! I'm famished! Be there in two shakes."

Before long, the roar of a car engine—a powerful car engine—signaled Talia's arrival. He went to the door and whistled. Talia stepped out of her blue Mustang. She grabbed her purse and shut the door with her hip, glancing up at Nick's expression of appreciation.

"Is that for me or the car?" she asked as she sashayed across his lawn, exaggerating the swaying motion of her hips.

"Both." And he meant it. The car was impressive, but little Talia had grown into a lovely woman. Her straight, dark hair brushed her narrow waist, and her short dress artfully displayed long, shapely legs. *She must have men following her all over the city,* he thought.

"Still the charmer, I see." She climbed the steps and hugged him, then stood back, looking him up and down. "And also still handsome!"

"And you look lovely as always," he said.

She kissed him on the cheek. "I bet you say that to all the girls who come visit you from Brooklyn."

"I swear to you on my grandmother's grave, you're my only visitor from Brooklyn I have said that to."

"Let me guess. I am your only visitor from Brooklyn!"

"A parade of Brooklynites could come through here, and I bet you'd still be the only one I'd say that to. Come on in."

She squeezed by him as he held the door open. "Don't you mean, 'Come on in, y'all'?"

"I haven't quite picked that up yet. I sound like an idiot when I say it."

"You sound like an idiot? Never!"

"I already made your lunch. You don't need to flatter me."

She surveyed his living room and kitchen. "I've never been inside a trailer. It's not half bad."

"It's a place to lay my head," Nick said.

"It's cute. It doesn't blow over in a high wind?"

"Not so far. Would you like to eat now?"

"You bet! I am starving! Trish's mother served grits for breakfast. Ick."

"I kind of like those."

"I should have brought you my portion. You can have them. Hope you have something better for my lunch."

"Chicken salad sandwiches and fruit salad. Sound good?"

"Heavenly!"

Nick finished mixing the chicken salad and scooped some onto two slices of bread. There was an easy comfort between them, which Nick thought was odd considering their bond was built on the death of her sister. He had never known if her father had done the same things to her as he did to Giulia. That was not a question one could ask. He hoped he hadn't. *Sick asshole,* he thought. He pushed the thoughts aside. "So tell me about that car. Did you rob a bank?"

"The bank of Vito."

Nick turned to stare at her. "You're talking to your father again?"

She shrugged. "Only when I need money."

Her words gut-punched him. It was not his place to approve or disapprove of her actions, but he did not like knowing she and her father had reconciled. She sensed his reproach. "I'm kidding. Don't look so stern! I haven't talked to that asshole since Giulia died. We had trust funds he had set up when we were born. I was able to access it when I turned twenty-one. For about one whole second, I thought of telling him to shove it, but then I thought, 'Tal, are you nuts?' Why should I suffer?" She grinned. He glimpsed Giulia's smile in there. They both radiated a devil-may-care attitude, but Talia's possessed a hard edge. Nick sensed that if you got too close, you would cut yourself. But maybe that was why she was still here and Giulia wasn't. "Anyway, you like the car?"

Nick raised his eyebrows. "Let's just say if you want to leave it here, it's OK by me."

"You would look marvelous in it," she said as he placed a plate in front of her. "Not as marvelous as me, but not too shabby."

She told him about her job as a retail buyer, which she loved. He told her about the places the Air Force had sent him.

"So you got a girlfriend?"

He hesitated a hair too long, and she noticed. She put her elbows on the table, rested her chin in her hands, and studied him. "Let me guess. You had one, but you screwed it up?"

"Why do you assume it's my fault?"

She smirked. "So I'm right?"

He leaned back in his chair. "Maybe you should become a lawyer. Cross-examine people in court."

"Come on. Spill the beans. Is she nice? Pretty? How did you meet her?"

"She's very nice," he said, sighing. He realized the truth of his words. She was nice. And smart. What was wrong with him? "And yes, she's pretty." He had always thought her beautiful. OK. He actually found her stunning. "She's a neighbor. And I think that's all I want to say about my love life."

"Oh, I am not letting you off the hook that easily."

"You know, I was looking forward to your visit, but now? Eh."

She ignored him. "So she's your neighbor. How long did you date?"

"Only a couple of months."

"So what happened?"

"I found out she had been married before and her husband died in a fire."

"So?"

"Talia. Anyone ever tell you it's impolite to grill your friends like you're Perry Mason?"

"All the time. Hasn't stopped me yet. So, go on. You discovered she was a widow."

"Well, that makes her sound old."

"I'm waiting."

"So I found out she was still sorting out her life. It seemed like a bad time for her and me to be involved."

"Oh my God. Please tell me you are kidding, Flyboy. That's the stupidest reason for breaking up with a girl I ever heard. We are all working on sorting out our lives every single day."

"I didn't really break up with her. I kind of said we needed a little break."

"Ah. A coward's breakup."

"Talia."

She picked up her fork and speared the last chunk of pineapple. "I just call 'em like I see 'em. So you still like her? Or was that simply an excuse to get out of the relationship?" She popped the fruit into her mouth.

He stood. "Are you done?" he asked, nodding at her now empty plate. "I know I am done with this conversation."

"Hang on a minute." She handed him her plate as she pointed the fork she still held at him.

"I think you still like her. You have that vibe about you, you know? Kind of like a sad puppy. So if you still like her, you should go to her and apologize profusely for being an idgit."

"Thanks for your advice. Forget becoming a lawyer. You could start your own newspaper column for the lovelorn."

"You jest. But I'd be fabulous." She carried her fork and the rest of the silverware to the sink, then crossed to the front window. "So which house is hers?"

"Talia. You are relentless."

After lunch, they talked more, and too soon she said it was time to head back to Charleston. He walked her to her car, and she hugged him and placed her hand to his cheek. "It was wonderful to see you, Flyboy. You look well."

"So do you, Talia. I am glad you are doing OK."

She looked into his eyes for a long moment, an entire world passing between them. "You, too." She slid into the driver's seat. "Seriously. If you like this girl, don't let her get away. You deserve a nice person in your life."

"You never give up, do you?"

"Nope." He pushed the car door closed with a solid *thunk*, and she started the engine. As she backed out of his driveway, he watched her, thinking about what she said. She shifted the car into drive and blew him a kiss. He chuckled and waved. He wondered how Giulia would have turned out had she lived. Could she have put the past behind her? Could Violet? Was it unfair of him not to give her a chance?

He shook his head and strode back into his house.

43

Violet

December 1969

Violet fretted all day about whether she should march over to Nick's and ask him if they had any future. But she kept remembering him saying how he didn't want to get involved with someone who needed rescuing, and her blood would boil again. And under the anger ran a rivulet of sadness about what might have been.

Still. A part of her—a BIG part of her—wanted to make sure once and for all that their relationship was over. She wanted to be able to tell herself she had done all she could.

She was shaking out a rug on her front porch when his car pulled into his driveway. At noon. Which was unusual. Like a teenager with a secret crush, she ducked back into the house before he spotted her, but she peeked at him from behind the curtain. *God, I have turned into that busybody Gladys Kravitz from* Bewitched, she thought. But she wanted to make sure nothing was wrong. She watched for a minute, and he seemed . . . jaunty. He walked with a spring in his step as he mounted the porch stairs two at a time. She wondered if she should go over and talk to him right now and get this . . . this whatever it was out in the open. Were they dating or breaking up? She straightened her shoulders and decided that was what she would do. No time like the present. Well, there was no time like ten or fifteen minutes from now, which is about how long it would take her to freshen up.

She headed to her front door and pulled it open just as a sporty blue car whipped into his driveway. She checked her forward momentum and watched, curious. A tall young woman stepped gracefully out of the car, swinging her waist-long dark hair as she reached into the car and retrieved a handbag. Violet's heart stopped. She once again slipped back into her house to avoid being seen. She eased the door closed and crossed quickly to her front window and watched from behind the curtain, feeling even more like Gladys Kravitz than before. Nick appeared in the doorway, and even from here she could tell he was smiling. The young woman hugged Nick and then touched his face in a very affectionate and familiar way. And Nick . . . he looked down at the stranger in a way that made her think of the way he had gazed down at her. Tenderly. Warmly. Ardently. She pulled back from the window and collapsed against the wall, tears stinging her eyes. It didn't matter that he had essentially broken up with her. It didn't matter that she was still angry at him because of what he had said. It still hurt to see him already smiling at another woman. Hugging her. Getting pats on the cheek. She angrily swiped the tears away, thinking of Mrs. McCabe's words. They'd simply had an argument, she'd said. A spat. Well, apparently Nick had quite easily and quickly gotten over their quarrel.

Fine. She'd survived worse. She could survive this.

44
Mrs. McCabe

December 1969

On Saturday, Mrs. McCabe called Violet because she wanted to know what was going on with her and Nick. As she dialed the number, she thought how it wasn't that long ago when she wouldn't have cared a hoot about what the neighbors were up to, much less actually picked up the telephone to call them.

"Hello?" Violet answered.

Mrs. McCabe could not tell her mood in the two short syllables. "Violet? It's your neighbor. Mrs. McCabe."

"Is everything OK?" Concern colored her voice, and Mrs. McCabe felt a little touched.

"Everything is fine. I was just wondering how things were going."

"What do you mean how are things going?" Perplexity turned Violet's answer into a question.

"With Nick, I mean."

"I haven't heard from him, and I don't think I will."

"Why ever not? You should give him a chance to redeem himself from that thoughtless comment. I mean, we all say—"

Violet cut her off. "He had a date the other day, Mrs. McCabe. I saw it with my own eyes. He's moved on. I'm moving on. I appreciate your concern, but that's the end of the matter. It's done."

Violet didn't quite hang up on her, but she made a quick excuse and left Mrs. McCabe staring at the handset. Nick had a date? When he had just been going out with Violet practically moments before? That did not sound like Nick at all. He was a nice young man. Mrs. McCabe thought she had pretty good instincts about this kind of thing. She was slowly hanging up the phone when a hard knock sounded at her door. At first, she thought it might be Violet, but she realized it was not Violet's firm but polite knock. No. This was much more forceful. Rude, even.

She opened the door, and, sure enough, Mr. Pritchard stood on her stoop.

"Can I help you?"

"I thought you might want this. If you don't, fine."

She frowned, and he stepped aside, revealing an evergreen tree a little taller than she was. She peered at it, then at him. "What on earth?"

"I cut one for me and Tommy. Thought you might like one. If not, I'll give it to Violet or put it in the wood chipper."

"You cut a tree? For me?"

"It was no big deal, so don't go making it one. Got an extra tree stand, and I can set it up for you."

But an idea took root in Mrs. McCabe's head, sprouted and grew.

"I actually have someone who can set it up for me. But if you could bring over the tree stand, I would appreciate that." Then to Mr. Pritchard's stunned amazement, she reached over and squeezed his hand. "You're an angel, Mr. Pritchard. A heaven-sent angel!"

"I'll bring the stand over if you promise not to do that again," he said as he propped the tree against the living room wall. After he left, she picked up her telephone. Again.

Several hours later, Nick was kneeling on Mrs. McCabe's nubby living room carpet, turning a screw in the stand to stabilize her new tree. Bing Crosby's smooth tones filled the little trailer. "All right. How's it looking?" he said.

"Now it's leaning a little to the right. I appreciate you helping me. Mr. Pritchard was going to, but he had a job to go to. I do have one other favor after you finish . . ." She glanced at the clock.

A soft knock sounded at the door. *Perfect*, she thought. Out loud, she said, "I wonder who that could be?"

She answered the door, and Violet stood there. "You need some help with some decorations?" she asked.

Nick jerked his head up and nearly knocked the tree over. Mrs. McCabe regretted the position he was in, under the tree, on his knees. It was very undignified. Although after what he said to Violet, a little time on his knees was probably just what he deserved.

"Mr. Pritchard was kind enough to bring me a tree," Mrs. McCabe said. "But I haven't decorated in years, and with my bad back . . . well, I thought it best if I didn't overdo it."

Mrs. McCabe watched Violet take in the scene: the tree, Nick on his hands and knees, Mrs. McCabe's most angelic face. Violet drew her eyebrows together. Mrs. McCabe wanted to tell her if she kept grimacing, she was going to develop permanent frown lines, but she decided now was not the time. Instead, she took Violet's arm and guided her into the house, closing the door firmly. She called out, "Nick! We have a little help so this should go very quickly."

Nick gave her a weak smile. "Oh, um, hi."

"Isn't this lovely!" Mrs. McCabe clapped her hands together. "Nick got out the decorations when he got here, so once we get the tree straight, we can start. Nick, it's leaning a little more to the left." Nick ducked back under the tree and turned the screws a few more times.

"Perfect!" Mrs. McCabe said.

As Nick rose off the floor, Mrs. McCabe opened a package of glass ornaments, pretending she didn't notice the sudden frost in the air. She knew Violet was working hard to come up with an excuse, so she moved as quickly as her old, creaky joints would allow. She thrust a box of decorations at Violet. "Here you go!" Violet had no choice but to grab the box or let it fall to the floor. But as she grasped the box, she glared at Mrs. McCabe, and Mrs. McCabe resolved that in the near future, she would definitely have to talk to her about her scowling.

For now, Mrs. McCabe turned her back on Violet and rummaged through the other stacks of boxes on the coffee table as she talked. "I remember when Flynn and I bought those," she said, nodding at the ornaments in Violet's hand. "We'd had an argument about some silly, little thing, and we were still all prickly with each other. We took the kids for a Saturday lunch at Woolworth's, and after we ate, we wandered around the store for a bit. Irina found those ornaments and said, 'Look, Mommy! It's like you and Daddy!' Flynn and

I looked at one another, and, well, we made up with our eyes. No words necessary."

She sighed as she remembered that day, so clear in her mind it might as well have been a movie playing. But she noted from Violet's grim expression that her story was not having the desired effect. Maybe Mrs. McCabe should have given them to Nick instead. He might have been more open to seeing six pairs of polychromatic mercury-glass lovebirds on perches. They seemed to be raising Violet's temperature. And not in a passionate way.

Mrs. McCabe pulled out another carton of brightly colored balls. "Nick, here you go." She dived into the boxes again. "Ah! Hooks!" She turned and handed the box of hooks to Nick. Neither Nick nor Violet moved. Mrs. McCabe put her hands on her hips. "What are you waiting for? Christmas?" She laughed and slapped her thigh. "Hahaha! Get it? Waiting for Christmas? That was funny. But seriously. Come on! I'm not getting any younger. This could be my last Christmas. So let's make it a grand one."

She stooped down into her pile of decorations again and hid the little smile she couldn't conceal. Young people! Getting in their own way about everything. She remembered the line from *It's a Wonderful Life*: "Youth is wasted on the wrong people!" It was true. But they had her to help.

Nick and Violet resigned themselves to hanging ornaments. Mrs. McCabe hummed along with Bing as he sang about being home for Christmas. As soon as Nick or Violet finished their boxes, Mrs. McCabe handed them another one.

"So, Nick. Are you going home for the holidays?" Mrs. McCabe asked.

"Yes, I am."

"You must miss your family."

"I do, but I've been living away from them for ten years, so I've gotten used to it."

"You had a visitor the other day, if you don't mind my saying. I don't usually stare out my window at the neighbors, but I was fetching my mail and noticed that snazzy car in your driveway. Tommy would love that!"

Nick chuckled. "So would I. That was a friend of mine from when I grew up." He cut his eyes to Violet, but returned his attention quickly back to the tree as if the placement of the next ornament were crucial to the success of peace negotiations with Russia.

"Must be one lucky fella to have a car like that."

"One lucky gal, you mean."

"Oh? Is this a special someone?"

Nick laughed. "No. She's the little sister of someone I once knew."

"A grown-up little sister," Mrs. McCabe said with a wink.

"She may have grown up, but she's too much like a little sister to me," Nick said.

Mrs. McCabe stole a glance at Violet, whose face had flushed a bit. "Aw, how delightful. What brings her here?"

"She was down in Charleston visiting a friend and decided on a whim to drop by. It's the first time I've had anyone from home visit. Kind of nice, actually."

"What did she think of our little town?"

He grinned. "That it was little."

"It may be an acquired taste," she said. She stood back and examined the tree, which Violet had been steadily and single-mindedly decorating. "Well, it's coming along nicely! But . . ." She cocked her head to one side. "It needs tinsel. Yes, that would absolutely do the trick. But I don't have any." She looked from Nick to Violet. "Would you two mind going to get some?"

"I'll go!" Violet said.

"That's OK. I'll go," Nick offered.

"Why don't you both go? Nick can drive, and Violet can pick out the tinsel."

"It's a run for tinsel, not a bank robbery. I don't think I need a getaway driver," Violet said.

"Nonsense! Errands are more fun with company! You both should go." She grabbed their coats and thrust them at them. "While you're gone, I'll clean up this mess." She waved at the empty boxes.

"I can help you clean up," Violet offered.

"Oh, I can manage," Mrs. McCabe said, herding the two toward her door. "I may be eighty, but I can still take care of myself."

"But you said—" Violet started, but Mrs. McCabe opened the door and guided her out. "I really appreciate this, Violet. I do hate driving at night now, and it gets dark so early. Nick, drive safe."

She closed her door firmly before Violet could lodge any more objections. Once she was assured one or the other would not come back in, she slid a package of tinsel under a sofa cushion.

45

Violet

December 1969

Nick and Violet found themselves kicked out into the literal cold. They stood, a bit dazed, on Mrs. McCabe's front porch. Violet shivered in her lightweight coat, gathering it closely around her, wondering if she should fetch a heavier one. Nick turned his collar up.

"You don't have to drive. I think I can handle this mission on my own," she said.

"I am sure you can. But can you handle telling her"—he nodded his head at Mrs. McCabe's door—"you went alone?"

"Ah, well. Therein lies the rub."

"Why don't we get this over with? You can even drive, and I'll pick out the tinsel. And we don't have to tell the Bulldozer we disobeyed her direct orders."

Violet couldn't help but smile a little. "Sure, I'll drive. My car is closer, anyway."

She ducked into her house and grabbed her purse. When she came out, Nick was leaning against the hood, whistling "For What It's Worth" by Buffalo Springfield. She took a deep breath before climbing in. *This is no big deal*, she told herself. *We're neighbors and need to get used to seeing each other anyway.*

"So where does one find tinsel on a Saturday night in Edenton?" Nick asked.

"Woolworth's. Where else?"

"Of course. Woolworth's."

A thorny silence fell between them. It stretched and grew and filled the car. He filled the car. His presence was almost palpable. She could feel the heat of his body, smell his cologne. *This was such a mistake.*

"Look, Violet," Nick said, his words breaking the silence but not the discomfort. "What I said the other night was, well, idiotic. And I didn't mean it. Really. One thing I have always admired about you is your independence. I know you don't need rescuing."

Violet noted he didn't say anything about how his telling her he needed a break had also been idiotic. She was glad now he'd had company when she had decided to head over to talk to him. She would have made a fool of herself.

"I appreciate that," she said, trying to make her tone nonchalant.

They arrived at the strip mall where the gaily lit Woolworth's crouched at one end, a commercial behemoth next to the other smaller stores. Inside, bright lights shone on a riot of red and green, silver and gold. Tinny Christmas music played over the loudspeaker. Violet headed straight to the Christmas area and scanned the shelves for the tinsel, intent on completing their shopping trip as quickly as possible. Nick stood back, staring up at something. She followed his gaze to a large, plastic Santa on display on top of the shelves.

"At the risk of getting on Santa's bad side, that is the scariest Santa Claus I have ever seen."

She couldn't help but laugh at the face of the maniacally grinning St. Nick. "I have to admit that would have given me nightmares when I was a child."

"Maybe that's the idea. Scare children into good behavior?"

"It would certainly work for me." She went back to looking for the tinsel, and he wandered down the next aisle. "Hey, Violet, come here. Look at this one."

She rounded the end cap, and another Santa sat on the roof of a small house. Except he was a giant compared to the house and appeared to be squashing the structure beneath him. Also, his eyes glowed demonically inside his cheery, red face. "Yikes. That one is worse!"

"Who makes these? What are they thinking?" Nick asked, shaking his head. "I may swear off Christmas."

"Let's get the tinsel before we see another one. Isn't three like a magic number or something?"

"If we see another one, maybe we will be transported to some alternate evil Christmas world," Nick said.

"Here it is," Violet said, holding up a flat rectangle of silver strands. "Do you think one will do?"

"Probably, but let's get two just in case."

She grabbed another pack.

"Quick, before Demon Santa sees us," Nick said.

They quick-walked to the lines of registers, and Nick slapped the tinsel on the counter.

"Did you find everything OK?" the cashier drawled.

"I'll say!" Nick said. "Nice Santas you have here!"

"We do love Christmas around here," the cashier said, missing the sarcasm in Nick's voice. A bubble of laughter rose up in Violet's chest. She bit it back, but suppressing it made it worse. The cashier bagged their purchase and shot sideways looks at Violet as if afraid she was about to go off the deep end. And that made Violet snort. She clapped a hand over her mouth and glanced at Nick and saw his shoulders shaking, his lips pressed tight with the effort of trying not to laugh out loud. He snatched the bag, and they both stumbled outside as laughter erupted from them. Violet almost fell off the curb, and Nick reached out and grabbed her arm, steadying her. His touch, even through her jacket, sent a shock wave through her. She tried to push away the feeling, but when she looked up at him, he was staring at her, his eyes tender. Their laughter had dissolved into something else, something delicate that spun between them like gossamer.

"I'm a fool. And goodness knows, everyone has been telling me that. I should have been there to support you after what you told me, but instead, I ran away, afraid of being hurt. I thought you were like Giulia, but I was wrong. You are strong and sane and facing up to your life. But in the last few days, I decided you're worth it. I like my life better with you in it."

Tears prickled her eyes, but she smiled at him. "I'm kind of a fool, too, so maybe we make a good match."

"You are not a fool. You had every right to be mad at me for what I said. I'd like to promise I will never say anything like that again, but I don't know if I can. So I will just make a vow to try every day to do better." He brushed her cheek with a warm hand, and the touch sent ripples of heat through her. He hesitated a moment, looking into her eyes, waiting, she supposed, to gauge her reaction. She stared steadily back at him. He leaned down and kissed her, his lips soft, sweet.

Delicious. Nick pulled back slightly and gazed into her eyes. She felt as though the world had stopped, that there was nothing in it but the two of them and the bright lights of the five-and-dime behind them. Until she heard a man say, "There are children around, you know." Violet glanced around and spotted an older man walking with a woman, presumably his wife. The woman elbowed him sharply in the ribs. "Hush up! It's sweet. Maybe you can take a page from their book!"

She smiled back up at Nick. "We better get this tinsel back to Mrs. McCabe."

"Right. Or she might send Mr. Pritchard after us."

As they drove back to Mrs. McCabe's, Nick's presence filled the car again, but this time Violet did not want to run away. She wanted to lean into it. She wanted to feel his strong, rough hand in hers, lean her head on his shoulder, wrap herself up in his warmth.

She only had one regret. Mrs. McCabe would be tickled to learn that her plot had worked. She hoped she wouldn't gloat about this.

46
Violet

December 1969

When they returned to Mrs. McCabe's house, the boxes had been put away and the elderly woman was setting up a manger in her little bay window.

"Oh, good! A successful trip, I see." She eyed the tinsel, but her smile said she knew the success went beyond their purchase. She opened the packet and carefully separated fistfuls of the silver strands, handing them to Nick and Violet and taking some herself. The three draped the tinsel over the branches of the tree as Ella Fitzgerald sang some jazzy Christmas songs. Mrs. McCabe smiled the whole time. When they were done, they all stood back and looked at the tree.

"It looks lovely, Mrs. McCabe," Violet said.

"It does. Darn it."

Violet looked questioningly at her.

"I owe all this to Mr. Pritchard."

"Ah," Violet said. *And I owe me and Nick to you.* "You should tell him thanks. Painful as it may be."

Mrs. McCabe grimaced. "I suppose I will."

"We should probably call it a night," Nick said. He held up a hand as Mrs. McCabe started to speak. "Yes, I will walk Violet to her door."

"What makes you think that's what I was going to say?"

"Hmm. I wonder," Nick said as he picked up Violet's coat and held it out for her to slip into. He donned his own coat and tipped a nonexistent hat to the elderly woman. "It's been a pleasure, ma'am."

Mrs. McCabe beamed. "It has been a lovely evening, hasn't it?"

"It has," Violet said. "Good night, Mrs. McCabe."

Nick walked her to her door through cold night air that cut like shards of glass. "It's getting colder," he said.

"It is."

She turned to him after she unlocked her door. He stood close—somehow still generating heat even in the bitter air. Then he bent and kissed her again. He placed one hand lightly on her lower back, a warm butterfly of a touch. His other slid past her cheek to the back of her neck, sending tingles up and down her spine.

"When can I see you again?"

"I'm off tomorrow."

He leaned back in, and she breathed in the scent of him. He kissed her lightly but lingeringly on the lips. "Six o'clock? How about I cook you dinner this time?"

"What about Harry?"

"I'll get rid of him."

"Sounds sinister."

"I'll try to be merciful."

He turned into the night, his breath visible on the cold air as he whistled "Will You Still Love Me Tomorrow."

★

At the appointed time—actually five minutes after the appointed time so she didn't appear too eager—Violet walked over to Nick's. When he opened the door, her heart leapt in her chest. She stepped into his living room and into the mouth-watering aromas of his cooking that filled the house.

"Whatever you're cooking smells wonderful."

"Hopefully it will live up to expectations," Nick said as he took her coat. Her body quivered at his proximity. She had to stop herself from leaning back into his chest. "Harry is very jealous," he said, seemingly oblivious to her inner turmoil.

"Oh, so you didn't bury him in the backyard?"

"No, I sent him to the base to hang out with friends."

She glanced around, noting his lack of holiday decor. "Do I need to call Mr. Pritchard to bring you a tree?"

He raised his eyebrows. "I don't see any lights in your window either."

She sat at a stool in the kitchen as he stirred some sauce. "I guess it just seems like a lot of trouble for just one person."

"Exactly," he said.

"Harry doesn't count as a person?" she asked, raising an eyebrow.

"Not really. Have you seen him eat?"

"Speaking of eating, what are we having?"

"Osso buco with risotto and salad."

"I see why Harry was envious."

"Don't worry. I promised him the leftovers."

When dinner was ready, they sat at Nick's little chrome-and-Formica kitchen table. He had lit candles, opened a bottle of wine. The food was, as always, delicious, but Violet thought she could concentrate better if Nick's knee didn't bump hers every once in a while, or if she couldn't smell his cologne mingling with the scent of garlic and bread. He was far too distracting.

After dinner, she helped him with the dishes. Or started to. As she handed him a plate, he took it from her and their hands brushed and sparks flew. Not literally, of course, but she seriously did not know how she couldn't see fiery particles of light flashing from their touch.

Their eyes met and held. Nick dropped the plate into the soapy water, ignoring the splash that wet his shirt. He dried his hands on a towel and tossed it onto the counter—all without taking his eyes off hers. He wrapped his arms around her and pulled her against him and kissed her. He kissed her deeply and tenderly and thoroughly, and she melted into him. Minutes or hours passed—she had no idea, as her body seemed to float somewhere outside of time.

He broke away and led her to the sofa, where they sat. He kissed her again, then leaned back a little, brushing a strand of hair from her face with a light touch that sent shivers throughout her body.

"I think I owe Mrs. McCabe a great deal," he said, cupping her cheek.

"Oh, I don't think you should tell her that. It'll just encourage her."

"You have to admit she was right when she manipulated our reunion."

"Well, I don't actually have to admit it." But she smiled into his eyes. "You sure you don't have regrets? Or maybe not regrets, but reservations?"

"None. Harry actually did point out that I am not going to find anyone without issues." He took her hand in his and kissed the top of it. "Violet, I had a moment of panic. I hope you can forgive me."

"I can. I already have. I just want to make sure you're ready for this." She gestured with her hand as if "this" were something actually in the room.

"Listen, I've done a lot of thinking," Nick said. "People like Giulia, like Sam, are damaged. The stuff they suffered drilled holes in their souls that became bottomless pits. And you and I could have thrown all our love into that pit until the end of time, and all that would have happened is they would have somehow, some way, at some time, drag us down with them. I have had ten years to think about Giulia and to deal with my guilt that I wasn't a better boyfriend to her. Hell, even a better friend. I struggled with that for years. She was beautiful and the life of the party, and that is all I saw back then. I didn't try to really get to know her, to learn what went on in her head and heart. I could have done better. I felt then maybe I could have saved her. But then one day, this guy I knew, an old tech sergeant, said something that has stayed with me. He had a son who was about my age, and he was always getting in trouble, always drinking and rabble-rousing. I saw how it tore the sergeant up, watching his son get into fights and accidents and, occasionally, jail. I asked him why he didn't stop his son. And he told me something I've never forgotten. He said, 'Battaglia, I have begged and shouted, pleaded and threatened, and none of it has worked. I decided it's his life he's screwing up. He's an adult, and I can't control him. I have pointed him to a different road, but I can't make him get on it. He has to make that turn himself.' I thought that sounded a little cold at the time, but as the years went on, it started making more sense. And I came to realize two things: One, I could have been a better boyfriend for sure. And two, it's not my job to save anyone. To be a friend, to offer support, yes. To rescue? No." He took a deep breath. "So what about you? Are you ready for this?" He made a similar gesture to hers, and she smiled at him.

"I am. When I went home, I was able to settle some things in my mind. I still wonder if I could have saved Sam that night. I am sure I could have just by being there. But in the long run? You're right. It wasn't my job. And it would take a Herculean effort to try. He couldn't find his way out of his own head, and I sure couldn't shine a light in there and show him the way out. But I know—I am starting to know—that Sam would not want me to give up the rest of my life because of my guilt that he lost his." She paused. "I am still struggling with feeling like dating you, feeling what I feel for you, is . . ." she said. "It's just . . . hard to let go. It feels like . . ." She trailed off, unable to find the right word.

"A betrayal?"

"Exactly." God, he understood. How amazing it was to have someone who knew what she was going through. She squeezed his hand.

"It takes time. You've realized Sam would never want you to live your life full of guilt, so that's a giant step in the right direction." He kissed her again, lightly this time. "So, now that we have settled that, you think we can make a go of this?" He raised his eyebrows questioningly, his mouth turning up in his crooked smile.

"Well, since I really like your cooking, I'm going to have to find ways to keep you around, so yeah, I think we can make this work."

"Not what I wanted to hear, but I'll take it." He smiled.

She reached up and kissed him, and he leaned into her, kissing her back, deeply. She sighed a little, thinking she might be able to do without food altogether if he was going to kiss her like that.

PART

4

November 1969-March 1970

47
Caroline

The day after the fire, Caroline and George returned to their house to survey the damage. Caroline wanted to keep Arabella from seeing the wreckage of her room, but Arabella insisted on going in with them. Caroline vacillated, not sure what would be best, but finally decided that Arabella's vivid imagination might fill in the blanks with visions worse than the actual damage, so she relented.

Arabella's room was completely destroyed. What the fire had not consumed, the water had ravaged. Grimy insulation dripped from gaps in the blackened and bubbled walls and ceiling. Sodden ash and burnt debris blanketed the buckled floor. The remaining furniture—what had not been thrown out the window—had been burned so thoroughly, Caroline would not have known what they were except for their positions in the room. There was nothing salvageable at all. Arabella's sole possessions were the pajamas she had been wearing and a couple of stuffed animals she had left in the living room.

Caroline studied Arabella as she stood in the doorway of her ruined room. Arabella swallowed and blinked a few times. Caroline grasped her hand. "We have to get this checked out and see what they can repair. But whatever happens, you will get all-new furniture. A new bed. New pictures for your walls." Caroline found that planning their next moves, making lists of things they would need, helped supplant the terrible visions from the night. She had to face forward, not look back.

Arabella did not answer immediately. She gazed at the room, her head slowly swiveling as she took it all in. Then she peered up at Caroline. "Can I help pick out my new bedspread and stuff?"

Relief at the normalcy of the question swept over Caroline. "Of course you can."

The rest of the house was undamaged from the flames, but the smoke created its own problems. It looked like a giant had taken a handful of fine, black powder and blew it over the interior of the house. Caroline's attempts to wipe away the soot left greasy smears. After experimenting, she discovered a solution of water and dishwashing liquid broke the oil down and made it easier to wipe away.

They continued their inspection of the house. All the carpets, curtains, and upholstered furniture had to be professionally cleaned, and the cabinets and counters and tabletops wiped down. Caroline was relieved that many things could be salvaged and scoured, although her relief was tempered when she opened her closet to pull out a shirt and the sleeve pulled away from the shoulder. The heat had melted the nylon thread. The clothes in their chests of drawers fared better. They reeked of smoke, but held together. Best of all, the family pictures that had been stored in a hall closet not far from Arabella's room were fine, though some were a little browned at the edges. The two albums Caroline had assembled fell apart, but the photos survived. All in all, Caroline felt tremendously grateful their home had not burned to the ground.

On the second day after the fire, when Arabella was in school, Caroline and George were boxing up items they could salvage when Nick dropped by. He told them Violet had gone home, but she had left him a note and explained that she'd been married before and her husband had died in a house fire, and last night had brought it all back to her. She asked him to tell everyone as she herself didn't have the strength to go through it. A cascade of emotions flowed over Caroline: sympathy for Violet, but also fear and relief at the close call her own family had experienced.

Caroline found herself missing Violet, but they were not without support. The other neighbors rallied around, offering what they could. The Red Cross provided them with enough donated clothes to get them through the first few days. A local department store gave them a gift certificate for two hundred dollars, which they used to buy personal items such as undergarments and soap and shampoo. A beauty salon held a fundraiser for them. When Violet returned from the visit with her parents, Turner's T-Bones did the same.

Several days after the fire, Caroline and her family moved into a fully furnished, two-bedroom guest apartment on the base—their home for the next four months. It would be weeks before anyone slept in the second bedroom, as Caroline kept Baby Allen with her and didn't object when Arabella asked to stay with them. The trauma of the fire filled those first few nights. Nightmares jolted Arabella from her slumber, and Caroline would hold her and soothe her back to sleep.

Caroline didn't rest well herself, thinking of how the fire had started in her daughter's room, behind her daughter's bed. Having such a small place to stay for those first few nights was a blessing. She liked knowing they were all together, in case something happened. George tried to reassure her, but she already knew her thoughts were irrational. And she knew, eventually, she would have to ease Arabella back into her own room. For now, though, she needed Arabella with her as much as Arabella needed her.

They celebrated Christmas morning in their borrowed home, feeling out of place and out of time. Caroline could not figure out how to save their tree as each silver filament was dulled by soot. They bought a new one—slightly bigger, a little fuller. Arabella begged to keep many of the ornaments and the manger. They had only a light film of residue, but Caroline left them as they were rather than trying to clean them and possibly damaging their finish. In future years, when they opened the boxes that held those decorations, the odor of smoke rose up, a pungent reminder of the year of the fire. The smell diminished each year, but never went away completely. The second Christmas after the fire, the scent triggered the memory of that night, keen and piercing, taking Caroline's breath away and making her wish she had thrown the ornaments out. But as the years went on, the decorations attached themselves to new memories and the trauma of the night lost its teeth.

Violet hosted a Christmas dinner at her house with all the usual guests, temporarily taking over Caroline's role as neighborhood hostess. They agreed not to exchange gifts and to keep the focus on enjoying each other's company. At the dinner, no one mentioned Violet's husband. They all carried on as they had at Thanksgiving—eating, laughing, talking. The renovations for the Fitzgerald home had begun—and the firemen had been right that most of the home was sound, but Arabella's room had to be rebuilt—and took up a good bit of the conversation. Nick was leaving the next day to see his family, a trip he had postponed a day so he could be there for the neighborhood dinner. Caroline hid her smile when she saw Nick and Violet exchange glances.

Four months after the fire, the Fitzgeralds packed up their belongings—old and new and donated—and moved back into their repaired house. Caroline had kept her promise and let Arabella pick out the colors for her room, but she purposefully kept Arabella away from the house so some of the new things would be a surprise. As George and Caroline stacked their suitcases and boxes in their two cars, Arabella slid her own small carrying case into the car.

"So now we are the ones moving!" she said, her smile still gapped with missing teeth, but the arrangement had changed, some coming in, others going out.

Caroline laughed. "So we are! Too bad there's not another Arabella to welcome us."

"Yep, there's only one me!" Arabella said. Caroline had to agree.

They turned onto their road, and Caroline glanced around with new appreciation. She would never call Magnolia Avenue the prettiest street in the world, but she could call it home. The ruts in the road did not shake the joy that filled her. Spring was tapping winter on the shoulder, and hyacinths and daffodils pushed through the dormant, brown earth, shyly showing their bright colors. A blue sky soared overhead, and the sun warmed the March day. The Taylors had moved out at the end of January, but their yard still looked tidy, and their forsythia and dogwoods were in riotous bloom. Mrs. McCabe's hedges were freshly trimmed and—she blinked a few times—daffodils bobbed their bonneted heads along the front of Mr. Pritchard's trailer. *Had he planted those?* she wondered. Then her eyes fell on her own house, and Caroline spotted something white fluttering in a light breeze in front of their house.

"Well, what is that, I wonder," she said.

48

Violet

March 1970

Violet checked the room one more time to make sure all was ready.

"It's all good, Violet," Nick said.

"Just double-checking."

Tommy, who had been keeping watch outside, popped his head in the door. "They're coming!"

Violet, Nick, Harry, Mrs. McCabe, Mr. Pritchard, and Sadie (she walked out herself), joined him on the Fitzgerald porch, congregating beneath a banner made from an old, white bedsheet that read, "Welcome home, Fitzgeralds!"

Arabella jumped out of the car as soon as George brought it to a stop. She stared at the sign and clapped her hands in glee. The group poured down the steps and gathered around the family as they climbed out of the car. Caroline stood, transfixed, hand over her mouth, her eyes glittering with tears as her friends came to hug them.

Violet put her arm around Caroline. "I hope you don't mind. I took the liberty of letting everyone in. We wanted to make sure the house was ready."

Caroline nodded and gave her a watery smile as her answer.

They sauntered into the house. Caroline stopped as soon as her feet touched the new living room carpet.

"What is that heavenly smell?" she asked.

Violet grinned. "Nick made a lasagna. Figured it would take a while to get settled. And Mrs. McCabe made a cake."

"Oh, Nick! Mrs. McCabe! You didn't have to do that!"

But he waved off her protests. "It was my pleasure."

"What can I say?" Mrs. McCabe said. "I wanted cake."

"And what is all this?" George said. Caroline and Arabella followed his gaze to a pile of presents on the coffee table.

"Oh my goodness!" Caroline said. "You guys shouldn't have. You've done so much already."

Violet waved a hand. "It was nothing."

"Nonsense!" Mrs. McCabe said. "It is something, and we are happy to have done it."

Arabella tugged on her mother's sleeve. Caroline glanced down. "Can I see my room now?" Caroline laughed.

"I guess it's room first, presents after," Nick said.

They went down the narrow hall with the Fitzgeralds in the lead. At Arabella's closed door, Caroline said to the little girl, "Cover your eyes."

Arabella put both hands over her eyes, grinning and quivering in anticipation. Caroline opened the door and led her into the room. The rest of the group tried their best to see from the doorway, ducking and craning around each other.

"OK. Open your eyes!" Caroline said.

Arabella lowered her hands and then widened her eyes, turning in a circle, taking in the pale-blue walls, the crisp, pastel-yellow curtains with sprigs of blue flowers, the matching bedspread, the sapphire carpeting. Her French provincial headboard, dresser, and chest of drawers were painted cream and decorated with scrollwork accents. Arabella's face shone with happiness. She hugged Caroline and George with such fierce enthusiasm, Caroline gasped for breath.

"I love it! It's so pretty!"

"Look over there," Violet said.

A stand-alone chalkboard stood against one wall. Long, pristine sticks of chalk and a black eraser lay in a tray underneath the board. Someone had written a message on its green surface: "Welcome home, Arabella."

"My very own chalkboard! Really? That's mine?"

"Yes, it is. From Mrs. McCabe."

Arabella turned to the elderly woman and threw her arms around her.

"Careful, young lady! You're going to break my poor, ancient bones," Mrs. McCabe grumbled, but Violet noticed her hug was tender and long.

Violet said, "How about we go and check out what else is out there?"

Arabella followed somewhat reluctantly, giving her room one last, longing glance. Once in the living room, Violet ushered the family to the sofa and proffered the first present.

Arabella read the tag. "To George. Something we can all enjoy."

George tore the paper to reveal a set of grilling utensils and a dark-blue apron with deep pockets.

He laughed. "Hey, I retired and passed my spatula over to Nick."

"You're not getting off that easy," Nick said. "Your burgers are quite good."

Caroline opened the next gift—a plush robe and a basket of bath salts and oils.

"We think it's high time you treated yourself to a day off," Violet said.

"Hey, just a minute! She gets a day off, and I have to cook?" George said.

"You can have her day off ... after you take care of Allen all day for a week," Violet said.

"Hamburgers it is!" George said, brandishing the spatula.

Mr. Pritchard prodded Tommy, who ducked his head and blushed. But he stepped to one side to reveal a bulky shape wrapped in brown paper sitting on the floor behind him. He carried it to Arabella, who beamed up at him.

"Here ya go, Bug," he said.

Arabella tore off the wrapping to discover a small bookcase. "Thank you, Tommy," she said.

"It's not a big deal," Tommy mumbled.

Mr. Pritchard cleared his throat, and Violet wondered if he had to rev up his voice because he so seldom used it. "Tommy's being modest," he said. "He made that himself."

Arabella gaped at Tommy. "Did you really, Tommy? It's beautiful!" Tommy ducked his head to hide the blush that stained his cheeks.

Violet handed Arabella another large package. Once Arabella tore the paper off and pried open the box, she pulled out a stuffed dog that bore a strong resemblance to Sadie. She studied it, mouth agape. "I have my very own Sadie!"

"Where in the world did you find a stuffed animal that looks so much like Sadie?" Caroline asked.

"It was a very lucky find for me and Mrs. McCabe," Violet said.

"And one last present," Violet said. She gave Arabella a small cube wrapped in the same paper. When Arabella unwrapped it and peeked inside, her mouth dropped open.

"Miss Violet! This is yours!" She carefully pulled out a beach snow globe from the box that held it.

"It's yours now," Violet said.

"But your grandmother gave this to you."

"She did. And it was a gift of love, and so it is again."

Arabella placed the globe on the coffee table and hugged Violet tightly. Violet clasped her arms around the little girl and had a brief thought that this might have been what her own daughter's hug might have felt like. It left a trace of sadness, a passing cloud over the sun, but then was gone. She caught Nick's eye, and his smile melted her heart. She smiled back, tightened her hold on Arabella before releasing her.

Arabella turned the globe this way and that and showed all the guests how the glitter floated down. Violet scanned the room. There was Mr. Pritchard, the man who everyone thought would sic his vicious dog on them, but who had helped Mrs. McCabe, took in a stray dog, then took in Tommy and was teaching him woodworking. There was Mrs. McCabe, who could still get on her last nerve . . . but who, Violet now realized, had been as wounded as she herself was. And was responsible for getting her and Nick back together. There were the Fitzgeralds, recovering from their loss by surrounding themselves with friends. There was Harry, who could always be counted on for a lighthearted quip but also a hand in need. And Nick. Nick who was proof her heart had not broken forever. Violet thought how incredibly lucky she had been to have landed in this place, right where she needed to be.

She shook herself out of her reverie.

"You all are the best friends a girl could have!" Arabella was saying.

Violet put her hand on Arabella's soft, blonde head. "And so are you, Arabella. So are you."

Nick and Harry went to pick up a pizza. Nick insisted the lasagna he had made was to tide them over for a few days, and that wouldn't happen if they ate it all now.

After they ate the pizza, Harry cut the cake and passed slices to the assembled guests. Just as they were scraping up the last crumbs from their plates, a low rumble from outside made them raise their heads.

"What is that?" Caroline asked.

The sound continued, growing louder. Arabella ran to the front door and peered out.

"Oh, yay! Look! A moving van!"

They spilled out onto the porch and watched as the tractor-trailer lumbered down the street. It stopped almost in front of them, but lurched forward, engine revving. The truck maneuvered into the Taylors' driveway. A man climbed out of the passenger side of the cab and jogged into the yard and began signaling directions to the driver.

"Yay! New neighbors!" Arabella clapped her hands.

Mr. Pritchard groaned.

Caroline put a hand on her daughter's shoulder. "Give them a chance to actually park the truck before you go running over."

"They don't know what they are getting themselves into," said Mrs. McCabe.

Violet felt a warm pressure in her hand. Arabella stood next to her, hand in hers, looking up at her with her freckle-faced, gap-toothed grin. She squeezed Violet's hand.

"We can be the welcome wagon together when they move in," Arabella said.

Violet found her heart lifting at the prospect of helping make someone's chaotic transition easier.

She smiled down at Arabella. "I thought you didn't know what that was."

"I saw it on *Bewitched*."

"Ah. So it's you and me?"

"Anybody can help, but I think you and I are the leaders."

"Well, one of us is for sure," Violet said.

"If y'all can be the welcome wagon, I think Harry and I will be volunteer moving men. Harry, shall we?"

Violet laughed and looked up at Nick. He gave her a puzzled look, and she smiled. "You said 'y'all.'"

"I did?"

"You did."

"Well. Looks like I'm a bona fide Southern gentleman."

"Don't get carried away," Mrs. McCabe said. "You still got some training up to do."

"Yes, ma'am," Nick said, and he saluted her as he and Harry headed over to greet the new neighbors.

George looked at Mr. Pritchard. "Well, I can't let them show me up. How about you?"

"Let's go," Mr. Pritchard said with a heavy sigh. "Come on, Tommy. Arabella, keep an eye on Sadie, will you?"

Arabella did, but she followed her mother and Mrs. McCabe down the steps as her mother said, "You don't think we'd overwhelm them if we all went and said hi, do you?"

"They might as well know what they are in for right off the bat," Mrs. McCabe said.

Violet started to follow, but hesitated on the top step. The

last rays of the day stretched across Magnolia Avenue, striking
the truck's windshield and reflecting back a bright rectangle
of light that moved across Mr. Pritchard's house, then Mrs.
McCabe's, and finally Violet's. Violet surveyed the street.
The dirt-track driveways welcomed visitors with the daffodils
and hyacinths now clustered around the crooked mailboxes.
Azaleas splashed color at the bases of the trailers. Her front
yard was in shadow, the windows darkened, but her heart
swelled at the sight of it. Had she changed or had the street?
she wondered. *Maybe both,* she thought. *Probably both.*

Acknowledgments:

I have wanted to write a novel since I was a child, and, when I pictured that, I had a vision of me at a desk, hammering away at a typewriter and then, later, a computer. But no matter what my writing tools were, I was always alone. Because writers work alone—their only company are their words, their flights of fancy, and maybe a cat or two. Right? Wrong. Apparently, it takes a village to raise a child and birth a book. I am going to attempt to thank those who helped support me along the way, and for anyone I inadvertently forgot, I sincerely apologize.

Because this novel is loosely based on the neighborhood where I grew up, I reached out to childhood friends and picked their memories when mine failed me. So, to Harry Little, Albert Little, and Margaret Edwards, thanks for having better powers of recollection than I do. You guys rock.

I am also thankful to the Princeton Writers Group, who welcomed me to their weekly meetups until the pandemic interrupted us. Sitting alongside people who have a passion for the written word helped convince me to carry on when I might have given up.

I am not sure this book would have made it to publication had it not been for the fantastic and talented hive mind of the Women's Fiction Writers Association, especially the daily write-ins that kept me typing away or sometimes creatively staring into space. These friends offered support of every sort, whether it was character development, query advice, or words of encouragement. That this novel is seeing the light of day owes a lot to their hand-holding.

Thank you to my Early Bird Writers: writing first thing in the morning with you guys was always a great way to start my day.

How many writing groups can one person have? I have at least one more: my fellow Rogue Writers, who have been an abundant source of knowledge, inspiration, and support. Our weekly chats have meant the world to me.

For critiques on my first chapters, I would like to thank the incisive minds of Priya Gill, Stephanie Claypool, Mikaela Huntzinger, Marina DelVecchio, and Marie Parsons. You all know how important those first pages are, and you helped me whip mine into shape!

My beta readers deserve a special thanks: Wanda España, Leena Singh, Beth Sulzberg, and Kim Yue. Thank you so much for reading my early drafts and giving me feedback—kind of a brave thing to do for a friend!

Thanks also to Ten16 Press for their faith in this novel, and to Margo Dill with Editor 911 for taking my rough stone of a manuscript and giving it a little shine.

And an exceptional shout-out to some exceptional friends: my fellow Sep99ers! Mary, Ann T., Ann R., Jan, Sandy, Randi, Susan C., Susan K., Vicki, Ashley, Beth, Roslyn, Brenda, Renay, Pam, Karyn, Teresa, Diana, Helen, Linda, and Angela—these women with whom I share the bond of international adoption have cheered me on from the very beginning. Thanks for always being there for everything, from baby bottles to books!

A huge, loving thanks to my family, who allowed me the time to write, who took me seriously, and who supported my efforts all along the way. To my husband Rich, who read several drafts of this novel, which is not his usual genre at all—thank you for your enthusiasm, love, and support! Thank you to my daughter, Kiana, who was always available for proofreading, website launching, business card design, and so much more. I'd hire you, but I can't afford to pay you! Connor and Kyra, I appreciate your patience and support all through this journey. You are both a source of inspiration to me.

And finally, to my dear readers, I am very glad you are here with me in this book, and I hope to see you in the next one.

Note From the Author:

Dearest Reader,

If you enjoyed *A Boundless Place*, I hope you will take a moment to review it online—anywhere that is convenient to you. It doesn't have to be long—just a sentence or two will do. It's hard for new writers to get traction, so any help you can give to this new writer would be much appreciated!

Thanks,

Pamela Stockwell

A Boundless Place Playlist:

"Aquarius/Let the Sunshine In" by The 5th Dimension
"I Heard It Through the Grapevine" by Marvin Gaye
"Moon River" by Frank Sinatra
"Cupid" by Sam Cooke
"To Know Him Is to Love Him" by The Teddy Bears
"You Send Me" by Sam Cooke
"Only Sixteen" by Sam Cooke
"Will You Still Love Me Tomorrow" by The Shirelles
"Puff, the Magic Dragon" by Peter, Paul, and Mary

Musical Artists mentioned generally:

Joni Mitchell
Simon & Garfunkel
The Beatles
Glen Campbell
Johnny Cash
The Beach Boys
John Coltrane
Bing Crosby (Christmas)
Ella Fitzgerald (Christmas)

PAMELA STOCKWELL was born in Texas and raised in South Carolina. In between, she lived in the Philippines and, along with her big sister, became fluent in Tagalog name-calling. She abandoned her foreign language studies at age five but went on to earn a BA in journalism from the University of South Carolina. She lives with her husband and three children on a small farm in New Jersey. She is a member of the Princeton Writers Group and Women's Fiction Writers Association. Her first novel, *A Boundless Place*, won the 2020 LBW Page 100 Writing Competition, and her poetry has appeared in *Sparked Literary Magazine* and *Hope: An Anthology of Hopeful Stories and Poetry* by TL;DR Press.

CPSIA information can be obtained
at www.ICGtesting.com
Printed in the USA
BVHW082342031021
618014BV00005B/9